THE BEGGARS' SHORE

Zak Mucha was born in Chicago, IL where he now lives and works as a furniture mover and freelance writer. He is currently working on his second novel.

THE BEGGARS' SHORE

by ZAK MUCHA

Portions of this novel have appeared in THE HIGHLAND FLYER and on THE ZERO.

Red 71 Press publications may be purchased for educational or promotional purposes. For information contact Ten Angry Pitbulls, 1701 Broadway, Suite #350, Vancouver, WA 98663-3436 USA. Phone 1.360.737.7548; Fax 1.360.737.7681.

First Red 71 Press edition published 1999

Design and marketing: Harald Graham and Lou Bank, Ten Angry Pitbulls, Vancouver, WA.

• • •

The Library of Congress has catalogued the Red 71 Press edition as follows:

Mucha, Zak, 1971-
    The beggars' shore / Zak Mucha. —1st ed.
    p. cm.
    ISBN 0-9669476-0-6

• • •

ISBN 0-9669476-0-6
Library of Congress Catalog Card Number: 99-70118
Printed in the United States of America
Distributed by Independent Publishers Group, Chicago, IL

10   9   8   7   6   5   4   3   2   1

You'll find the best stories on the
web—*for free!*—at www.Red71.com.

All thanks must go to those people who did not shy away
from a longshot

Lou (Money In The) Bank
Ruby Pasigan
Andrew Vachss

and those who do not bother to read the odds

Don De Grazia
Virginia Johnson

THE BEGGARS' SHORE

The Jesus Hotel

Joseph sat in Preacher Madison's office and listened to the final decision, not questioning or protesting when he was told what would happen. He listened as every detail was explained. No revealing expression crossed his face and he kept his peace. It didn't matter what happened. Joseph had known for a long time what he wanted to do.

His mother and father sat across the big desk from Preacher Madison. Joseph was on the couch against the back wall of the office where he could see only Preacher Madison's face. No one in the room seemed concerned about the lack of emotion in the boy.

Preacher Madison repeatedly said how proud he was of the progress that had been made by the boy's parents. They needed more responsibility. He felt they could handle it. He prescribed a new location as a further cure, a little bit of insurance for the marriage. Joseph would stay with the commune, in the Uptown hotel owned by the church.

"Do you have faith in me?" the Preacher had asked Joseph's parents during the proposal. "Do you want the best for all three of you?" Their answers were the expected affirmative, and the Preacher gave them his decision.

Joseph would remain in Chicago until he turned eighteen; then he could do as he chose. He could stay with the church or venture out into the world that he had never really been a part of. When he turned eighteen.

Joseph wondered if maybe Preacher Madison had not been fooled. Maybe the Preacher had known all along that nothing had really changed in their apartment.

According to Preacher Madison, Joseph and his parents should have been thankful that God was allowing them a second chance.

It had all been agreed upon and planned out without Joseph's consent or involvement. His parents were leaving. Somewhere downstate or somewhere in Iowa. They would visit both places and then a residence would be chosen for them. The minute details would be taken care of later. Joseph's parents were going to be missionaries of the church.

Joseph planned to walk away as soon as his parents left the hotel commune. He would wait until then because he did not want them to know he had left the church. He did not want them to remain in Chicago and possibly search for him. He told himself that he would have left when he was eighteen, anyway. And that was coming soon enough. All he was doing was leaving a month early.

Joseph remembered that, when he was much younger, his parents on some nights tried to console each other. They talked of how they came to Chicago before Joseph was born. The ride from Tennessee had been long and the car kept dying. Joseph now knew that his parents were looking back to a better time. They had come to Chicago for factory work. They came to Uptown because it was cheap and it was where new people seemed to land. Joseph's mother always mentioned the bank billboards she saw: a smiling red-haired man with a handlebar mustache, saying "Come To Uptown".

A few years later, when they were firmly settled, new signs were up and an Oriental man was urging the same. As a boy, Joseph always kept an eye out for the red-headed man and the Oriental who brought his parents to Uptown. He expected to see them side by side, walking happily down the street.

He also used to wonder where Tennessee was, and where his parents' families were. When he asked, his parents never answered him. Joseph remembered the cloud his questions had drawn over his mother and father on the nights they had been trying to make themselves laugh.

When he asked why they lived in the commune, his parents told him only that the church found them at a time in their lives when they needed to be found. Joseph hadn't understood the reason the others in the commune looked at him strangely. An air of pity was reserved for him, and one of disapproval for his parents. The others in the church knew of the screaming. The damage to church property. The admonishments and salvations offered by Preacher Madison. A certain distance was kept between Joseph's parents and the others.

Long before he even knew the words to use, Joseph had tried to defend his parents. He hated reminding himself what a stupid child he had been. A long time had passed since he had asked his parents about anything.

On the day his parents were to leave, Joseph took a long walk up Broadway through Uptown. There was plenty of time before they caught their bus. Joseph had never been far from the hotel by himself. He was embarrassed about it, but the elders' rules were strict. It was one of the rules that the children could not leave without an adult. Joseph felt much younger than he actually was. He felt deprived of some inherent right.

The lights of the LakeBreeze Tavern were off and a CLOSED sign hung in the corner of the window. A short, heavy-set black man was sitting in the doorway. He was staring at Joseph as if he had been waiting solely for him to parade past.

"Almost starting time," the man announced and then shifted his eyes from Joseph's face to his clothes. "What the hell's all over your coat, boy?"

Joseph hesitated as he watched the man struggling to stand. "It's from the Bible," he replied dully.

"I see that, boy. Why you got the Bible all over your coat?"

"I don't know."

Bible scriptures, written in red marker and pale bleach, surrounded two lightning bolts that descended from his shoulders to his hips. Long ago, Joseph had spent an afternoon working over the kitchen sink, painting the verses onto his jean jacket with the idea that it would prove his belief. The lines, which he had chosen only because a word or two had caught his eye, were now fading away. He had never really understood them. And he had ruined his only jacket, which was now almost embarrassingly small.

Joseph drifted away from the question; the black man had to repeat himself.

"You don't know? That ain't much of a Christian answer. Do you take the Book as the word-for-word truth?"

"Yeah." Joseph felt that was the right answer. He didn't want to argue.

"Yeah?" The black man laughed. His eyes lit up and his skin darkened momentarily to the shade of a deep bruise. His white teeth held Joseph's attention. "Well, that's something. There's not many of that kind left, you know; not like you. Now, you believe that the world was built in seven days, and Eve was made from Adam's rib, all that?"

"Well, it's in there," Joseph admitted quietly and unconvincingly. And the black man laughed again, his mouth twisting and dividing his face.

"You see, it's not that I don't believe in God, but I just can't take that whole book seriously. I mean, I can't follow it. There are some great stories and all. It's the best book ever written."

Joseph could see the man was expecting a rebuttal. And the man recognized that Joseph was confused.

"You see," he continued with a wave of his hand, "mostly the book is made of what you call metaphors and fables. Like the old Greek stuff that explains how the sun got in the sky and how day turns to night. That kind of shit. Really, think about it. I'm not trying to argue with you, but I think you're real wrong. Is your old man a preacher or something?"

"No, we live in a commune. The People's Church of Chicago."

"Oh, yeah," the man's face brightened and split again, "I know where that is. Over on Wilson, by the lake."

"Yeah."

Scratching his stomach, the black man thought for a second, "How old are you, kid?"

"Seventeen. My name's Joseph Askew."

"Joseph, I'm Sonny. You want a beer or something?" he offered. "You're too young to drink, maybe you want a Coke instead."

Joseph said okay. What Sonny had said about the Bible supported the possibility that the church and everything that Preacher Madison had ever repeated was built on a lie. And Joseph felt better hearing that. He thought it over quickly and decided that it was too much. Too much to try to figure at once. Everything would become jumbled; he knew from past attempts.

Sonny looked at the closed tavern and stood up, brushing off the seat of his pants. "We can walk to a place where I know they're open. You're young, you can handle the walk."

Joseph agreed that he didn't mind. He was willing to follow Sonny.

They moved at Sonny's pace, down another street Joseph had never seen before. Gaudy colors framed each storefront. The smells were foreign: fish and spices and bread. Raw, halved pigs and barbecued ducks hung in restaurant windows next to racks of glossy pink and blue videocassettes. Photos and ceramic Buddhas bordered the shop displays. Discarded carnival tickets were stuck to the wet sidewalks in clumps; garbage spilled out of the alleys and the whole street gave Joseph the feeling that there had just been a big party and some of the decorations had not been taken down.

The Argyle street El platform divided the block with its weathered pagoda canopy. Beneath the pagoda were billboards for Nike shoes and PrimeCo cellular phones.

All the signs over the shop windows were written in Vietnamese. Sonny pointed at them and gave his own vague explanation. "These people are screwing with us. I want to know what these signs really say in their language. I think that they're insulting us. Now what is LAC VIEN supposed to mean?"

"I don't know."

"Exactly. Like some of the signs are just jokes on our own American. Like some of them say BOW THAI, or TIN LUNG. Now that's just stupid. Who wants to eat there? Come on. I don't like the feeling that I'm being laughed at." Sonny slapped Joseph on the shoulder and turned the corner. "There's an American place down the street."

Behind an alley hidden in the middle of the block, Sonny found a small wooden shack that seemed to be leaning heavily against the neighboring brick building. A neon beer sign was bolted to a tiny window before a checkered curtain. The front door was heavy wood with a painted sign that said the bar was called the BLUE ROOSTER.

The inside was dark and stale; at the bar were four people, three men and a woman, each sitting alone. An afternoon talk show broadcast in pastel pink and orange droned from the television above their heads. Joseph sat down next to Sonny at the bar; the woman, already sitting there, gathered her purse and slid away from them. She settled again at a new spot two seats from Joseph and pulled the ashtray over to her drink. The other three patrons measured the young stranger in the bar. Joseph felt how out of place he and Sonny were. Sonny didn't seem to notice.

"He follow you in here?" The first one asked Sonny without even looking at him. The other two joined in, but it was more like they were talking to each other and not Sonny.

"Sonny, what are you doing with a white boy?"

Joseph didn't catch half of what was said and he wasn't sure who had said it. Someone said something about fuzz on his ass, and another comment mentioned Sonny giving out candy. Joseph looked at his pale face and flat features in the mirror behind the bar. Freckles spotted his cheeks and the bridge of his nose. He tucked his long red hair behind his ears and found in his reflection that that made him look even more like a child.

Sonny's arm draped across Joseph's shoulder protectively. "No one give my man here a hard time, understand? He's a good guy." In the same breath Sonny whispered a suggestion to Joseph, "Ignore them." Then he motioned to the bartender and said, "Keep an eye on him. I gotta piss." The bartender winked and Sonny stepped toward a door in back.

The bartender stood in front of Joseph as soon as Sonny was out of sight. "Why you hanging out with niggers? You always do that?"

The question went unanswered. The bartender didn't move and Joseph didn't know what to do. "Watch out for the niggers," the bartender warned. "They can act nice, but never trust 'em. Like the gooks. You can be friends with them, but only up to a point." Joseph sullenly ignored the bartender. He found no reason to trust the man. Joseph liked Sonny, liked what he had said about the Bible. The bartender paused for a second and looked around as if he were about to tell a secret, but he didn't say anything more.

He stepped back into a shadow as Sonny eased himself over a barstool and sipped his drink. When the glasses were emptied, Sonny paid for two more. The bartender shook his head slightly as he set the fresh drinks down.

When the last drinks were gone, Sonny led Joseph into the blinding afternoon. A moment passed before Joseph could see anything in the sunlight. There were no colors, only a pale white; slowly Sonny's dark figure appeared.

"So, how you like the Jesus hotel?" Sonny asked.

"I don't know." Joseph wasn't sure if he wanted to tell his new friend what had happened between his parents and the church.

"Right, right." Sonny nodded slowly, as if he had decided something important. "Cool, man."

Joseph and Sonny separated at the corner and said that they would see each other later. Sonny winked and slapped Joseph on the back. "Stay loose."

The apartment was on the tenth floor; the west side of Broadway could be seen past the rooftops between the flowered curtains above the kitchen sink. Low three-flats and tree tops dotted the blocks stretching out to the northwest side of Chicago. Far in the distance, two diagonal streets broke the grid of city blocks.

There hadn't been much for Joseph's parents to pack. They each had a suitcase filled with clothes by the door, but the apartment looked like no one was ready to leave. Practically everything in the apartment belonged to the church and the hotel. Pictures still hung on the wall, dishes were still buried in the sink. Two cold cups of coffee sat before empty chairs at the kitchen table.

Joseph's mother hugged him tightly around the neck. Her eyes were red and she looked lost. She told Joseph that he should take care of himself and listen to the Preacher. She told her son that she loved him.

"Yeah." He felt her bony shoulder against his chin as she hugged him once again.

Joseph's father was hidden inside an old navy pea coat. He was dry and brittle. They shook hands and his father advised the boy to be good. "Don't think this is something bad about you. We're not leaving you, boy. The Preacher thinks it'd be better for you to stay here. We probably won't be gone too long."

Joseph believed that his father was glad to be rid of him. He felt the same way about his father. While saying goodbye, Joseph saw he was taller and straighter than his father. His body had grown quickly once his sixteenth year had passed. His gains made him hopeful for something he couldn't actually describe, but he attributed his growth to his desire to run from the hotel.

Joseph's arms and legs were skeleton bones beneath pale, freckled skin. Shadows of ribs could be counted under the paper muscles of his chest. His green eyes were hooded at the outside corners, and his cheeks gave the appearance of having no bones under the puffy skin. His bright red hair was kept long, framing his face, hanging over his eyes and past his collar. In the bathroom mirror Joseph would study himself and see himself as a crude drawing of a stick figure with a round head. He had his mother's body and his father's face. As if the head and body had been sewn together at the neck.

Joseph shut the apartment door behind his parents and their bags. Something sharp and clear settled over the room. As if his surroundings were a still photograph that could not be altered. Joseph leaned back and propped his feet up on the armrest of the couch.

He let his eyes focus on the pattern of the carpet. The frayed edges of each thread became sharp as the rest of the room blurred. He couldn't see the walls around him or the couch he was lying on. He felt suspended in the air as the apartment grew smaller. Joseph saw little details he hadn't noticed in a long time. Cracks running through the plaster from the floor to the ceiling. Cigarette burns in the carpet. A red pillow and a magazine tossed on a chair.

When the boy tried to picture his parents, all he saw was his father's stick frame and blurred eyes. He couldn't find the pieces of his mother's face at all.

His parents had been with the People's Church of Chicago for a long time, years before he was born, and Joseph had lived there all his life. He went to school there, played there, ate his meals there. He knew no other family, no grandparents or aunts or uncles or cousins. They were somewhere, but not with the church. It didn't matter because he had never known them.

Joseph's father and mother had not been born in the commune. The commune hadn't been around then. They had given their hearts to Jesus, unlike Joseph who had it given away when he was a baby. Maybe even before he was born. The Preacher always said all the children were taught right from the beginning how to be good Christians. When Joseph watched his father walking in clumsy slow-motion around the apartment, he had thought it must be harder to give it away than to have it given away by someone else. Now Joseph wondered if there was any difference.

Joseph used to wonder if Jesus liked him more than he liked other people. Then he would stop and correct himself the way he had been corrected before. It wasn't liked, it was loved. Jesus loved him. And Joseph had waited for the burning he was taught that he should feel.

His mother worked in the commune kitchen on the first floor of the hotel. The boy didn't mind when she was gone. As much as Joseph tried, he could never shake the feeling that she was temporary. She always surprised him when he really looked at her. To Joseph, his mother was a sort of faceless person who wandered in and out of the two bedroom apartment. She cleaned and made food. No voice other than a near-whisper accompanied her. When she was out of the room, the boy could not picture her face clearly. He always felt it was possible that she would not return.

Joseph couldn't imagine that these two had really given themselves to Jesus. If they had before, then they must have taken themselves back at some point. All the Preacher's sermons meant nothing to Joseph's parents. He felt that they had lied about their whole lives. If his parents behaved the way they did inside the church, then they would never get along outside of it. He considered how long it would be before one ran from the other. They were only trying to fool each other and get along the best they could. The whole act would collapse sometime. At first Joseph thought it good that he was given to the church when he was a baby, but now he wished he never had been.

"I accept only His word as final authority," Joseph remembered Preacher Madison announcing on a long-ago Saturday morning. He was standing on the corner of Wilson and Broadway, his voice amplified by a portable speaker system. "I believe that if I confess my sins He will forgive and cleanse me. He will be my sufficiency and rest, and I will conduct myself accordingly." Preacher Madison ordered, "You will not make any excuses for your sin and failure."

Preacher Madison had the week's pamphlets to pass out and Brother Samuel was carrying the seven-foot wooden crucifix over his bent shoulder. Joseph had watched the brothers earlier, as they painted the fake blood dripping purple on the cross.

Several others from the commune were already standing on the street corners, passing out flyers. Every Saturday morning they would each take a spot and leave the best position for the Preacher. A cement embankment in front of the chicken restaurant was the Preacher Madison's pulpit.

"Come along, son. You should see this," Preacher had told Joseph that morning, after the crucifix's paint had dried. "It'll be good for you to see what it is like when we are all working outside."

The air was cool and damp and the sun was barely over the buildings on the east side of Broadway. From the sidewalk Joseph could see the top floors of the hotel where he and everyone else he knew lived. He couldn't find his own window. They all looked the same.

Joseph felt the strangers on the street crowding him as the Preacher dragged him across the intersection. The light turned red and the boy flinched when a car horn blared impatiently. Older black boys already occupied the corner; they only shifted a little and laughed to themselves at the men approaching. Thudding music blared from a radio perched on someone's shoulder. Old men leaned against the walls, and a group of chubby Mexican girls circled the pay phones. Joseph tried to stand off to the side, settling behind the newspaper stand as the Preacher set up and took note cards out of the different pockets of his sports coat.

When he was ready, Preacher Madison blew into the microphone and Brother Samuel, leaning forward and reaching high overhead, supported the wooden crucifix hanging over the edge of the curb while traffic sputtered past, inches from his toes. His fingers were wrapped around the painted drops of blood. Words were written across the beam. Retribution. Penance. Love. New words were printed across the beam every week.

The first thing Preacher Madison did was tell everybody on the street to be thankful that they have the morning and the sun to be walking under. He introduced himself as he did every Saturday before starting his morning sermon. His distorted voice and amplified words overtook the cars rushing by and ignored the El trains grinding overhead. Joseph's eardrums were shaking. The Preacher seemed to purposely step in everyone's path and crowd the whole sidewalk with his body.

The Preacher was a big man. His weight fluctuated between two-sixty and three hundred pounds. The collar of his shirt was opened wide over his shoulders and the lapels of his jacket shone in the sunlight. His head was perfectly round and halfway bald and his ears bent under the weight of thick bifocals. There were no eyebrows behind the lenses.

Preacher Madison held the microphone close to his face with a pink-knuckled fist. Sweat rolled down his temples, despite the cool breeze. His deep voice shook through the microphone, rolling from beneath his palm and along the cement until it found a point in Joseph's stomach where it was felt and not heard. To hear the words at all, Joseph had to concentrate; even then, he didn't understand much. The Preacher's words rose high over the traffic, a rumbling boom that momentarily stopped people in their tracks, causing them to either hurry past or wait and listen with half an ear. They only heard as much as they wanted.

The Preacher talked of murder and sins and the Devil. He kept talking about the fires of Hell and Infinity. It was a dot on the horizon, the plains of Nebraska, a spot that could never be reached, no matter how far you walked, rode, or drove constantly toward it.

"The blood of Christ cleanses us from all sins... "

The other men kept handing out the blue and white pamphlets to the crowds wandering past. Most took the papers and tossed them away, without ever glancing at the words or the little line drawing of a desperate face under the title: IS THERE HOPE FOR A MAN LIKE ME? Garbage cans all along Broadway were soon filled with religious pamphlets and the wind pushed the overspill in little dervishes that died in secluded corners. Joseph held a stack of them in his hand but was reluctant to try giving any away. He saw the strangers' reactions to the Preacher and his teachings, and he did not want to approach anyone at all.

A small crowd finally began to gather. Joseph could hear the black kids behind him, talking and joking, laughing at Preacher Madison. Joseph tried to ignore everyone around him; he focused on reading the pamphlet which he knew practically by heart.

The story was about a man who led a very sinful life, stealing and cheating and taking drugs up until the day he broke into a church with the plan of robbing the poor box. He was discovered by a preacher and threatened the preacher with a gun. Eventually they began talking. Years ago, the man told the preacher, he had killed someone in a fight and somehow was never caught. He got married, and right away his wife had a baby girl. The man ran away from them both. The man kept his pistol pointed at the preacher while he confessed these sins. There were a lot of things in the story Joseph didn't understand. But he knew what the man was like, he could even picture the man's face as he explained all of his problems. The unnamed man in the story no longer knew what to do. He said his life had stopped dead still. And the preacher, oblivious to the gun, kept telling the man about the spilt blood of Jesus Christ. In the empty church the preacher talked through the entire night. And before sunrise the man forswore the bad things he had done, tossed his pistol in a garbage can, and returned to his wife and daughter to ask for and receive forgiveness.

Joseph had heard Preacher Madison recite the words all before; he had heard the story many times in the classes at the hotel and during the Friday night services. It had sounded like a simple story, a fairy tale. On the street corner, the tale sounded violent and threatening and Preacher Madison seemed wild, screaming and pointing at strangers as the story poured out of him at full volume. A new person had climbed inside the Preacher's skin.

At the end of the story, the killer gave his heart to Christ. Joseph always remembered the last lines: "Have you got the message? Will you confess and forsake your sins right now and give your life to Jesus Christ? Ask God to forgive you. There is hope for one like you!"

During that morning, two cars crashed at the corner, right in front of the Preacher. The drivers got out and yelled at each other until they started throwing punches. Brother Samuel and his crucifix fell to the ground when the Mexican girls pushed in to see the wreck. More people came to encourage the fight. Preacher Madison couldn't stop any of it.

There was no reason Joseph should stay at the commune. He told himself that he shouldn't have stayed as long as he had in the first place. The only thing that had kept Joseph back was the fear that Preacher Madison and his parents would come after him. Now, Joseph doubted that anyone would. He had the apartment to himself for a couple of days. One of the elders had knocked on the door; he and his wife said that Joseph could come to them if he needed anything.

There was a meeting with Preacher Madison that Joseph was going to miss. There would be a sermon and more rules. He would be reassigned a room on the second floor, near the elders and Preacher Madison. So they could keep a close eye on him.

He put on his scripture jean jacket, grabbed a few extra T-shirts, the thirty dollars his mother had left him, and it was time to go.

Passing through the lobby of the hotel, he heard pieces of a conversation in Preacher Madison's office. It was Sonny's reassuring voice, laughing and joking, entertaining the Preacher. Joseph then remembered what the bartender told him.

For a moment, Joseph thought of the story about the sinful man who forced his way into church and confessed at gunpoint.

Maybe Sonny was confessing something. Maybe he was joining the church. Joseph did not like it. He didn't like the outside world coming into the church. He didn't want Sonny to learn anything. Joseph wanted to start over. He wanted a clean break.

Joseph slipped out the back door of the garage and crawled under a chain-link fence. The sky was dark, and when Joseph was far enough away down a side street he could see the neon sign on the roof of the hotel, standing high over the rest of the block. CHRIST SAVES. The letter V flickered and steadied.

Joseph wondered where Sonny lived. He wondered if Sonny would end up with the apartment his parents had just vacated.

He saw Sonny lying in his old bed, staring up at the picture of Jesus that had looked down upon him for seventeen years. The big, black man would cover himself with the bedspread patterned with wooden soldiers and bury his head beneath Joseph's pillows. In the morning the apartment would be just as it had been left. The dishes would still be in the sink. The cups at the edge of the table would be half-filled with cold decaf and stained with rings near the lip.

A Hundred Miles

Joseph's parents loaded onto the 151 bus that ran down Sheridan and then cut over to Broadway at Montrose. It connected Uptown to Lincoln Park and circled the Loop before heading west to Union Station, Northwestern Station, and finally the Greyhound terminal on Harrison.

They sat down on a concrete ledge facing Harrison Street with their bags between their knees and waited. Fat pigeons pecked at garbage on the sidewalk while smaller birds chirped from their hiding spots in the bushes. Two white clouds raced in slow motion across the sky and Joseph's mother commented on the beautiful weather. When her husband didn't respond, she made herself busy.

She unfolded a laminated map across her thighs and tried to position herself so that her shadow fell somewhere other than directly on the map. Once settled, she held the tip of her finger to the legend at the bottom of the page and estimated the miles that her fingernail would represent.

Air brakes hissed as a bus rolled from the terminal and pulled to the curb. The bus driver jumped off, walked past them, and left the door open with the engine still running.

"Is that ours?" she asked.

"How should I know?"

"What's it say on the side of the door? What's the number?"

"I said, I don't know."

She folded her map and stuffed it into her purse. She thought of patting her husband's arm, but then decided against it.

The driver climbed back inside the bus and the destination was announced. People began slowly working their way toward the open doors. Two workers in gray and blue uniforms were already loading bags into the compartment between the axles.

They got in line and waited again. It was the first time they would leave Chicago since their arrival almost twenty-four years earlier. They had never seen the museums, the world's tallest building, or the Navy Pier Ferris wheel. They had never taken part in the talk show audiences; they had never been to the Gold Coast. Since the day they had come to Chicago they had hardly ever left Uptown.

Squeezing down the aisle among the other riders, they settled into their seats and waited for the others to do the same.

The bus rolled along smoothly once it worked through the congested downtown traffic. Sealed windows kept away the city's noise. The air was the perfect temperature; the seats were like tailored mattresses. Despite all the comforts, the husband and wife felt crowded next to each other. He would recline his seat and she would pull her own forward. Then they would reverse positions and wait impatiently for some relief. They squirmed. They could not get far enough away from each other.

Employment was waiting for them at their new place. A mail order house that sold Bibles and religious tracts. They would be stuffing envelopes addressed from mailing lists of hundreds of thousands of people across the country who subscribed to this or that.

The wife took out the map and began measuring with her fingernail. "One. Two. Half. Turn." She held the laminated graph at an angle. "Half. Four, five. Six. About six hundred and twenty-five miles to go." She turned to her husband for a response. When there was no reply, she went on in a reassuring tone. "It's going to be better. This is right. What we should have done a long time ago. Before. If we knew then what we know now, it would have been real different. Always one step behind in finding things out."

Her husband mumbled something, which she took as encouragement. He patted her hand and squeezed it once. Then he shifted his seat back and shut his eyes. His hands slipped into his lap. He knew that he could be a good father if only he was in a better situation. If he had been given half of a decent chance. He had been told that he was getting in his own way. The Preacher said that he was the one causing all of his problems and maybe the change of scenery would prompt a change in attitude. He didn't believe it.

It was something else pushing him. He had no control at all. The world just kept happening around him as if he had no say in it. There was no way to move anywhere. He came across a mental image of himself holding a fragile baby with red and white splotched skin. They had no plans for another child. He didn't know where it came from. Like the baby was there waiting for him. The thought upset him and he wanted to ask how much longer they had to sit on the bus.

Watching her retrace the expressway over and over suddenly frustrated him. He only wanted to know when he could get off the bus.

The farmland just outside the suburbs of Chicago rolled past her profile as she studied the map. Her lips mouthed the names of each town her finger crossed.

The Darlington Arms

A sign advertised PACKAGE GOODS over the gutters of the Blue Rooster. One fragile-shouldered old man covered in a flannel shirt walked from the door to the alley, taking one bottle of beer outside to drink carefully under the lights before going back for the next. Joseph could faintly see the outline of a bag of clothes and a bedroll beneath the man's feet. He approached and saw that the pock-marked skin was barely hanging onto the man's sharp cheekbones. The man's eyes were slow to focus when Joseph politely asked him to buy another beer and bring it back out to Joseph.

"What? You want to drink with me?" The man was a little suspicious. "You gotta buy me a beer, too."

Joseph didn't really want to drink with the man, but he agreed. He had no idea of what he was supposed to do. "Sure. Yeah, I will."

"Okay. Give me the money and wait over there." The man waved a ragged arm toward the alley where he had been leaving his empties. Joseph handed over three dollars in change.

"Is that enough?"

"Should be," the man made it sound like they might be cutting it close. "Do you got any more? Just in case?"

"No."

The man disappeared inside the shack door. Joseph waited next to a garbage dumpster. A couple of minutes passed and Joseph debated searching for the old man when some commotion erupted inside the bar. A patron came tripping head-first through the front door.

Joseph heard bottles breaking and people yelling. A muffled pop quieted the crowd for a quick moment; then they were louder than before, as if the sound had started a foot race inside the tavern. The country music jukebox stopped with a screech. Joseph heard a woman's voice threatening to kill someone named Vince.

Joseph knew his money and his beer had vanished for good when a squad car pulled over at the mouth of the alley. A police van and another squad quickly joined the first. Three cops shuffled in and began dragging people out by their elbows. Shirts were hanging torn and spilt beer was dripping from almost everyone the cops yanked or shoved to the sidewalk.

They only used handcuffs on one black man singled out from the crowd.

Patrons were limping and cursing as they came out of the door in a disorderly parade. Some were sneaking half-finished beers under their shirts; some were crying and pointing accusations. The silent woman Joseph had seen days before walked out the door with a cigarette hanging from her lip and not a scratch on her.

After the crowd was chased away, there was still one squad car left on the block. The officer was waiting inside for the last stragglers to leave the tavern. A man in an apron kicked broken bottles out to the sidewalk and swept them over the curb.

Joseph had completely missed the old man who took his money and promised a beer in return.

Under the lights of the El viaduct Joseph counted the money in his pockets. He didn't know if he had enough for a room and he didn't know where to get a room or a place to sleep. The night before, he had ridden the El and studied the lights of high-rises and main drags. When the train headed south and dipped into the subway, he got off and crossed the platform to return north, above ground. He studied the city for hours, but didn't learn anything. Fear of getting mugged or somehow stranded on the train car kept him awake. He slept during the day.

After leaving the Blue Rooster, Joseph walked up and down Broadway, looking for a door that would lead to a safe place to sleep. He waited for someone to offer help, but no one did. After a while he decided to eat.

The walls of the restaurant were papered in black with vertical gold stripes. The booths were covered with maroon vinyl. At a back booth, between two wide-hipped women in sequined blouses, sat Sonny. He waved happily and motioned for the long-haired boy to come and join him. The women looked past Joseph as if there were someone else standing over his shoulder.

Joseph approached and noticed that Sonny, dressed in a suit coat and a starched shirt open at the collar, appeared slimmer and well-groomed now. His fingernails shone with a clear polish. The girth and slowness Sonny had had the day they met was gone. Joseph almost didn't recognize him. Last he saw, Sonny looked like a bum. Last he heard, Sonny was laughing with Preacher Madison and maybe checking up on Joseph, or maybe looking for a place to sleep. But Joseph had nowhere to go and didn't know anyone but Sonny, and his suspicions were washed away by a warm greeting.

"My man. What's going on? Why don't you sit down, Red?"

Joseph did and nodded shyly to the two women, who did not respond.

"So, what happened after I left?" Sonny asked. Joseph assumed Sonny was about to start talking about the hotel. Joseph felt he had made a mistake; he should not have come over to the table.

For the benefit of the women, Sonny pointed at Joseph. "This young man," he announced as if the boy should be proud, "was just now outside the same bar where the cracker flipped his shit on my man, McKnuckle."

The women broke into braying laughter as soon as they heard the name McKnuckle. They sounded like horses and Joseph didn't know what was so funny. He didn't know what Sonny was talking about, or who McKnuckle was.

A twenty-dollar bill appeared between the gold rings on Sonny's fingers. One of the women snatched the bill away and walked it over to the cash register like the hand-off had been practiced. They were already done eating.

"Okay. Never mind sitting down," Sonny said as he tugged at Joseph's sleeve. "We're gonna take a walk." Sonny winked at Joseph. "Wanna come along?" The first woman returned from the cash register and slipped her arms into a leopard-skin patterned coat. Joseph let the three of them step ahead and followed them out the door. He wasn't that hungry.

On the other side of Broadway the streets were darker. A row of lampposts had burnt out and the apartment windows were dissolved in shadow. Joseph followed the clicking of Sonny's heels on the sidewalk until they were on the next block and he could see again. Across one side street a yellow spotlight was rigged to hang over a useless neon sign which read: DARLINGTON ARMS.

At the corner of the building the main revolving door was boarded over and nailed shut. Curtains fluttered out of halfway-open windows and two voices could be heard yelling from behind one set. Music came from another window; from somewhere else, a dog was barking frantically.

The women suddenly turned their backs to Joseph and whispered in Sonny's ear.

"Fine, go ahead," he dared them as they started walking away. It looked like they were done for the evening. "Damn," Sonny said, once he was sure they were not going to turn back. "I couldn't have gotten anything with the both of them around, anyways. But I wish one would've hung around."

Sonny shook his head, as if to physically remove the women from his mind. He then asked how long Joseph had been sleeping on the streets. Joseph lied and said that it had been a few nights. He hadn't been gone twenty-four hours yet. He was embarrassed. He should have been out on his own a long time ago. He should have sounded tougher for Sonny.

"Looks like it," Sonny said. "Some guys get it right away, this look. You either get skinny and old, or fat and old. I can tell you gonna get skinny and old, if you stay. Eyes sink back real deep and you get the lines in your face." Joseph checked his own reflection in a car windshield. "Not me," Sonny went on, "I got fat and old. But I still look fine when I want to. See, there are ways to take care of yourself. You don't have to be a damn fool and live on the street, begging all day. I believe that Jesus says that sometimes you have to take care of Number One, because no one else is going to."

"Where'd He say that?"

"I don't remember."

Sonny kicked an empty beer bottle away from his ankle and looked up and down the street. The women were long gone. "Why don't you come inside for a drink?" He saw Joseph's hesitation. "Don't be scared. I ain't gonna do anything. It's just gonna be cold out here and I'm just asking. It ain't yet the middle of summer. Or do you got somewhere else to go?"

A half flight of stairs led from the sidewalk to the basement. Spiderweb cracks had spread across the door's glass. Chicken wire held the shards together. Sonny pushed the door open and walked inside, letting Joseph follow. Two bare light fixtures were burning at the top and bottom landings of the staircase. The middle steps were in darkness. Joseph ascended carefully to the ground floor.

From the size of the deserted lobby and the width of the staircases, Joseph could see that the hotel had once been respectable and finely decorated. Bare wires dangled from ceiling fixtures that had once held chandeliers. Elevators with iron gates had been boarded over and spray-painted with graffiti.

There was no number on Sonny's door. Inside the room, the hardwood floor had been painted white long ago. Water stains made rust-colored circles across the ceiling and the wallpaper fell in strips like wilting flower petals. The only furniture remaining was a television and a bed.

In the open closet were clothes in a variety of colors and styles. It looked as though many people of the same size, maybe brothers, had hung their clothes inside and then forgotten about them.

Sonny sat on the bed and took off his shoes with great relief. Joseph settled to the floor and stayed quiet.

"So you're not at the hotel anymore?"

"No," Joseph said. He wanted to ask what had happened when Sonny met with Preacher Madison. He recalled the two men laughing behind the closed office door. The sound of the voices had made him feel that there was some conspiracy going on.

"How come you left?" Sonny asked as he put his feet up on the bed.

"Wanted to. I can. I'm eighteen."

"You eighteen, now? You look pretty small to be eighteen, but I guess if you say so. That's cool. You won't lie."

"No, I won't." Joseph couldn't remember whether he had already told him he was seventeen.

Sonny stood up again and went to the window. They were on the third floor, looking out over Racine Avenue. With one hand, he took a half-pint of whiskey from the ledge and held the bottle out for Joseph to see. "Keeps it cool out there. And no one can take it except Spider-Man." He did not pass the bottle to Joseph.

"So, you still believe in God, huh?" Sonny continued as if he were discussing the weather. Joseph nodded slightly, hoping that the questioning would soon end. But Sonny continued proudly. "Oh, yeah.

We all gotta trust in the Man. To believe in something that cannot be seen or proved is the highest kind of belief. You can believe in your mama or the president or a baseball team, but that ain't nothing. Your mama could be pretty, and she has to love you. And the president will smile at the cameras, but you won't ever see him on the street. Because if you only say you believe in God, go to church and all that. Go through the motions. Then you just lying to yourself. And then that makes you lying to God, too. Because He's there and He can hear what you say to yourself. But me and the Man, we got a square deal. I'm up front with everything I do. If I'm gonna lie to myself, there's no point. I'll tell God before I do something messed up. He knows it. Because there is a place we go to after this. That's when we gotta pay, we gotta live the righteous way. I always say this. I said it to my brother-in-law; I said it to him a long time ago and always kept telling him, but he never listened. He lives here, too. One floor above me. Him and his cousin."

Joseph listened to the whole story as Sonny talked and sipped from his bottle. McKnuckle was Sonny's brother-in-law.

McKnuckle had his own crew years ago. There used to be kids who ran his errands and women he sold for sex. He had a red Monte Carlo, completely decked out with carpeting, and a party-sound stereo system. There were even little Christmas lights that chased each other around the license plates. McKnuckle had his women that he worked out on the street. His ladies would climb out of the car as he made stops all along Sheridan, like it was a regular bus route. Once in a while, McKnuckle would check on them, sometimes not until late at night or early in the morning. The Monte Carlo would come back around one of the corners, and whichever girl he was looking for would jump in.

The clothes were always new and the car was always clean. There were always more women as the old ones got sick or busted. They got used up quick and disappeared from view. When they reappeared later on a different street or in a less frequented alleyway, burnt out, with saggy skin and sunken eyes, all they were good for was telling stories about McKnuckle. By then their faces had aged into the same sunken features that Sonny had described to Joseph.

McKnuckle finally got busted, not for pimping, but for drugs. They put him in the County for a time, long enough for his string of women to move on without him. When McKnuckle saw daylight again, he was nothing. Everything he had was gone. Everything that could be carried from his apartment had been divided and sold over the open trunk of his Monte Carlo, which had become a makeshift auctioning block.

He reappeared, thin and haggard. The women acted like they didn't notice him, like they didn't even know him anymore. But they stifled their laughter behind his back. There were lines in his face and scars across his nose. Stories circulated that he had had a rough time of it while he was away. Sonny wouldn't even repeat what he heard. McKnuckle's pretty face was hanging and gray. And once people found out that his mind was gone, they laughed at him openly. He was lower than the women he used to sell. No one could gauge if he minded this at all.

McKnuckle now drank from paper sacks and inhaled from rags dipped in toluene as he talked about how it had been for him, years before. His stories, if he was able to speak at all, were all glory and conquest. He told them only to people who had known him back then. No one else would have believed him.

"I still love the guy," Sonny admitted. "But it's one of those riches-to-rags things. He's at the point where he may start to believe in the Lord. But sometimes I doubt it. He's gotten stupider and it's gonna take him longer."

The last time McKnuckle got picked up, Sonny told Joseph, it was for shoplifting. He stole a girlie magazine from a bookstore. In court his sentence was suspended, Sonny believed, because he wasn't even important enough to lock up anymore. At first, McKnuckle was relieved, but later he felt as if he had been slighted. Sonny said that was how far gone McKnuckle's mind had gone.

Now McKnuckle was staying with his cousin, Melvin, at the Darlington Arms.

"That was what happened at the bar. My man just acting up. Every once in a while he does that when he hears what's going on. Like he remembers everything all at once. My man pulled out a gun and began throwing shit around the bar. He threw an ashtray and a chair and then forgot again and threw the gun, too. Threw it away and the party attacked him. I barely escaped with my life, man. It was like a shark tank."

Sonny rolled back on the bed and grimaced at the ceiling. "I tried to show him the right way. And I still try to help the boy, but hell."

"I thought you were a preacher?" Joseph asked.

"I sure am. I do speak the word of God; but you see, it's a racket, just like anything else." Sonny sighed and changed his pace. "Jesus is here, you know, in the room and shit; you don't got to go to church. Did you ever see anyone speak in tongues?"

Joseph had. He had seen it in his church. It went on in the hotel. During services people fell to the floor and had to be carried down the aisle and out the door. Later in the day, Joseph would see the same person behaving as if nothing unusual had happened.

"Anyone can do that. You just got to let go of your inhibitions." Sonny stood up and raised his hands above his shoulders. A couple of seconds passed before Sonny began to move. Quivering grew from his back and neck. His eyes shut and opened again and worked to a flutter before the black irises rolled up into his skull. Clucking noises came from deep in Sonny's throat like his tongue had been cut out. His legs flailed and bent, and Sonny fell to his knees while the rest of his body kept going, shaking violently.

Outside the setting of the white chapel, without the music and the members of the congregation, the act was horrifying.

Joseph moved away and backed toward the window. Sonny moaned and began knocking the back of his head against the floor. His body seemed to swell and fill the room, and Joseph couldn't get past it to the hallway. The moans suddenly snapped, erupted into laughter and Sonny's irises rolled out from under his eyelids again. His body calmed. He straightened his legs out, brushed any possible dust off his clothes, and smiled.

"See, that's how you do it," Sonny said. "No fucking problem. I was just hit by the power of the Lord. It's a scam, boy. I used to do that for a few churches and they would give me a small cut, a flat fee even, but not a percentage of the donations. Not a lot. That would have been too much. They just needed me to be the first one hit with the power. After that, there were others who did the same. Just forgot their inhibitions, their poise and shit." Sonny laughed and wiped off his forehead. "You still believe in your God, don'tcha? What I did don't mean nothing."

"Sure," Joseph said with a determination that didn't sound convincing. "Does everybody fake it?"

"Not that they know. You can start it going in your body, unconsciously. You just think that it's God in you. Understand?"

"Yeah."

"Good. Good. As long as you got the Lord, then you can move on. Now, we gonna show you how to make some money. I like you, boy. You got plans tomorrow?"

"No."

"Good. Beautiful."

Joseph thought about the cash remaining in his pocket and the long night he had spent on the train. He said he would go along with Sonny. It seemed that everything made sense now. It was all a scam. Preacher Madison, all along, had been doing the same as Sonny, but on a scale large enough to keep from having to roll around on the floor himself.

Joseph thought that his first contact outside the church had been a lucky one. He saw Sonny as someone who could change his own image to whatever suited the moment. No one could tell him what he was. Sonny was what Joseph wanted to be. Sonny didn't rely on anyone. In Sonny, Joseph saw none of the restraints or restrictions that he himself had lived with for as long as he could remember. When Joseph was alone, he could feel the words of Preacher Madison binding tightly against him; when he was with Sonny, they were loosened. Joseph believed that Sonny knew the truth.

And his invitation gratified Joseph, as an opportunity to join the other side of the fence. He would be making up for lost time. He would be in control of his own life. Before Joseph could stop himself, he asked uncertainly, "Why you want me?"

"It's the Christian thing to do. By me helping you, you will be helping me. And we need a white boy."

Joseph paused, remembering that Sonny had been in the hotel. "You aren't watching me because the Preacher asked you to?"

"No, I fucking ain't. There ain't enough money for me to baby-sit. I got more pride than that. Anyway, you a grown man and your preacher don't know that I know you."

"He isn't my preacher."

"That's fine. I was over there, boy," Sonny told him, "because I offered my services to the man. I got the idea after you told me you stayed there. That's all." He cracked a polite smile for Joseph. There were no hard feelings. "And to show you I mean what I say, now I gotta ask you to leave. I need my sleep. See? I ain't no baby-sitter."

Sonny walked the boy to the door and repeated that they would catch each other in the morning.

"Are you gonna do that at the hotel?" Joseph asked Sonny.

"Nah. The man told me it wasn't needed. I think it's because they don't got any brothers over there. Do they?"

"No."

"See, I'd stick out too much."

Sonny led Joseph through the hallways and down the stairs. Joseph tried to imagine how the hotel must have looked fifty years ago. He tried to see the heavy gold chandeliers and the hustling bell boys in buttoned coats and little hats, like an old movie he had seen on television. He tried to picture the large front desk and tall potted plants.

Sonny fell back into the dark of the hallway and the service door of the Darlington Arms swung shut behind Joseph.

Someone was already asleep in the sheltered stairwell of the TV repair shop Joseph had planned to occupy for the night; it was a little cubbyhole completely protected from the sidewalk, with an awning overhead to redirect rain. The sleeping figure was so well hidden that Joseph had to climb down a couple of steps before he saw it. The knees were tucked under the chin. The face was covered by an arm bent like a bird's wing. And the sleeper turned slowly to the wall as if trying to hide further, because Joseph was standing there.

Over the prone body Joseph saw the image of Sonny going into spasms and crashing to the floor. Practicing the reception of God. Auditioning in Preacher Madison's office. It made Joseph want to smile.

The high ceiling and the bare walls of the chapel had, in Joseph's mind, defined it as a place that would not change. Events occurring in the outside world barely touched the commune. It was a territory protected by Preacher Madison. Everything seemed to filter through him and his words. The rest of the city was disdainfully observed from afar.

Joseph sat at his mother's side. The men of the commune were segregated on the other side of the chapel. It was a rule that the men must worship together, leaving the women and children across the pews. Heads bowed over the little songbooks as the first hymn began. Soon all the voices clashed in a wavering monotone divided between the men and women. The two sides chased each other across the verses. Joseph studied the rows sitting before him and wondered which women would be brought up to receive God in the healing line. The men worshipped together, but only the women could receive God through the air.

The Lord never came immediately. The congregation watched and waited as they followed the Preacher through the hymns.

At the front of the chapel the women stood completely still and waited for the Lord to enter them. Their figures were dark and thin against the white walls and bright lights. Their bodies appeared crooked and fragile as if they could be toppled by the wind. Their wiry arms hung slack from loose shirt sleeves; each woman began to sway independently.

Joseph knew what was coming. Each woman would act as if she were completely alone. They didn't see the others in the room. They swayed with their feet fixed to the floor. The music swelled rhythmically and circled the room. People would clap and stomp with the beat. The women would begin mumbling after a time, would let the room rise and swirl around them, would talk to God in babbling voices that only Preacher Madison could transcribe. God entered their mouths and their spines, pulling at them as if they were puppets.

The women put the fear of God in Joseph. They would dance and clutch their breasts, fall backwards down the aisle, and stumble again to their knees. The piano sounded like a toy as the Preacher recited from scripture and explained what the women were howling. He sounded far away.

Preacher Madison went down the line and put his oiled palm to the forehead of each woman. They struggled up to the altar, babbling and crying, as the men clapped to the piano's rhythm.

Over the chant and flourishes of the piano, Preacher Madison began to speak. Joseph lost the man's words in his own thoughts.

He wanted to believe that they lost control of themselves. He could feel it in his own body, the swelling in his chest. The sensation that he was about to be taken somewhere. The feeling that something bigger than his father or Preacher Madison existed. It was something Joseph had wanted to touch.

The healing line had scared Joseph the first time he witnessed it. The noise rumbled deep under him like an overloaded truck shaking the street. It felt as if he was about to be lifted from his seat. He could have floated in the air. Joseph believed that something could enter his body and protect him.

He heard that one time a woman had urinated on herself in the middle of the rapture and didn't even notice. She kept dancing.

He was not one of the women. Joseph would never be allowed up to the pulpit to be saved like them. He watched his mother shut her eyes and tilt her head, swaying slightly to the music. He imagined that she could feel it in her chest. He imagined that she felt Jesus' presence.

She appeared to be very far away. She was praying so hard that she was crying. Joseph saw the splotches of bruises on her forearms and wrist. He counted the marks, including the older ones on her jaw and neck. There were so many that he started to lose their number. They could have been stains working their way up to the surface. Joseph imagined the bruises growing larger and darker until they were connected and finally covered her like a new skin.

The Business of Men

That night, sleep came in torn sections. Joseph kicked against the doorway where he hid himself for the night. His dreams kept starting at the same point and playing over again. A woman's slender hand gently moved over his face and another slipped around his waist. At the same time, he had a sensation that did not match the tapered hand; in the dream, Joseph was coughing. His lungs were filled with smoke. Colors shifted from a dark blue to a coarse sandpaper red. He was in a room filled with rows of chairs facing a blank wall. An event was about to take place, but each time, nothing happened. No one entered the room before Joseph woke.

Fits of anxiety moved through him. Several times during the night he woke with an arm or a leg numbed from lack of circulation. Thousands of needles pushed under his skin as the blood began to pump again, away from his heart. His whole body was itching, and scratching only made the matter worse, made the bloodless needles push in deeper. He would wake startled, thinking he saw someone standing over him. Joseph waited for it all to pass. He hoped everything would be fine in the morning.

Shadows hadn't yet lifted from the sidewalks when Joseph felt the toe of a shoe touching his back lightly. Two silhouettes hovered above Joseph as the daylight filtered down to gray details. It was Sonny, standing with another man whose face twisted to one side. The man's eyes and teeth seemed to be climbing out of his skull, pulling away from the rest of his face.

"There you are," Sonny said, as if he had accidentally tripped over Joseph. "We're running late."

Sonny and his companion began walking away, and Joseph hurried to get off the ground. He shook out the jacket that he had used for a pillow and tried to stretch the joints of his knees before he took a step.

The two men continued their hurried pace and climbed into the front seat of a little tan car at the end of the block. Joseph caught up and threw himself into the back seat. The back windows were broken out and covered over with green garbage bags. The handles had been yanked from the inside of the back doors and replaced with wads of newspaper. Sonny, sitting in the passenger seat, pulled an old magazine from behind his back and kicked fast food cartons away from his feet. Then he finally introduced the other man, now behind the wheel, as McKnuckle, his brother-in-law. McKnuckle mumbled a greeting over his shoulder and pulled the car away from the curb in a high idle.

Joseph watched the buildings roll past the windows.

"How much you got?" Sonny asked his brother-in-law.

"Enough for a few months," McKnuckle said as he held a folded rag to his mouth. He inhaled deeply. His eyes smiled at the rear-view mirror, where he saw the red-headed boy. Joseph caught Sonny shaking his head as McKnuckle passed the rag to Joseph. He took it between his thumb and forefinger and wondered what he was supposed to do with McKnuckle's dirty handkerchief.

"Take a whiff, boy," Sonny instructed. "Inhale."

"What is it?"

"It's what we went all the way out to the west side for, what you missed when you was sleeping. It's a get-me-high. Like what I said before, you lose your inhibitions. The city don't let hardware stores sell it no more." Joseph kept the rag at a short distance while Sonny spoke. "You a good kid, you won't do nothing bad; it's not in you," he prodded the boy, grinning widely.

Joseph held the rag before his face and sniffed lightly. It reminded him of paint thinner or varnish; he didn't feel a thing. "It ain't bad for you," Sonny encouraged. "Go on, you gotta take a big one. But not if you don't want to."

Joseph guessed that it must be okay if Sonny said it was.

So he pushed the air from his lungs and tried again. This time he felt something. He clamped down and held the heavy fumes at the bottom of his chest. He began counting. His stomach dropped out from under him and the muscles in his neck slackened. Inside his skull, warm, heavy air made him giggle. There was something funny. He just couldn't find what it was. He wanted to rest his head against the car door, put his cheek in the ashtray filled with Winstons and gum wrappers. Buildings were twirling past the dirty, smeared windows. Joseph wanted to laugh at McKnuckle's crooked teeth or his bug eyes. He leaned back on one elbow and considered the dirty ashtray.

Sonny laughed along with Joseph and interrupted, "Now, how was that?" He had been watching the whole time. Joseph smiled, a little embarrassed but proud of himself for taking the step. He felt that he had gained Sonny's confidence.

Against the blur of the windshield Joseph saw Sonny expanding, growing fatter. He expanded like a balloon filling with water. His arm plopped out of the window and his stomach pressed against the dashboard. Sonny's neck twisted as his head went up to the roof. Joseph heard a whistle blow and Sonny snapped back into shape. Joseph's head reeled.

He held the rag to his face and inhaled again to hide his grin. His mouth became a huge gaping hole, sucking in the fumes. He felt like stuffing the whole cloth in his mouth, but didn't want Sonny or his brother-in-law to see that. He probably wasn't supposed to do that. Joseph was sure that he could feel one half of his brain floating away. He was sure that his head was lop-sided and the thought forced him to giggle. He didn't want to, but he laughed until he was out of breath. Sonny was growing again and Joseph laughed until McKnuckle reached back and snatched the toluene rag away from him. Eventually his snickering subsided.

The boy nodded off as Sonny and McKnuckle drove him in slow circles across the neighborhood. "Virgin," McKnuckle mumbled as he twisted the wheel.

Joseph woke from a good and deep sleep when the engine was cut. There was more to do, the boy was told. Joseph was not sure how long he had been out, but he had had no dreams while he was there. He resented having been woken up.

"Where did you drive to?"

"We just went and had breakfast."

The car was parked right in front of the Darlington Arms.

Gallon cans of toluene were lined up on the floor in Sonny's room. McKnuckle disappeared and then returned from his upstairs room with an armload of boxes filled with ninety-nine cent whiskey bottles. A red plastic funnel balanced like a crown on his head. The bare room was quickly transformed into a one-man assembly line while Joseph was rubbing his eyes.

"I'm sick of the other way," McKnuckle explained. "All them kids asking for a little pour. Arguing over how much. Fuck that." He considered for a moment, then added, "They won't be bothering me. Not like before. And they all smoke their crack rock, anyway. That's what they all like more."

It was now the boy's job to fill the little bottles with the toluene. Sonny and McKnuckle laid out explicit directions, describing the use of a funnel and the best way to bottle toluene.

"Delicate, man. Don't make the glug-glug sound when you pour it," Sonny ordered. Then he mentioned that he had to step out for a couple of minutes. Joseph realized that this was his work to finish alone. McKnuckle had already left. "Be careful, now. It wrecks the bouquet when you pour it quick," Sonny added as he backed out of the doorway. The latch clicked shut.

A dull ache grew in Joseph's head as he absently sloshed the paint thinner into the little bottles. It spilled over his fingertips and soaked through the floor without ever forming a puddle. Little cuts and scrapes on the boy's hands burned incessantly and his skin turned a tender pink.

When Joseph was done with the airplane whiskey bottles, he filled the half-pint whiskey bottles, spilling more with each turn. Time passed unmarked, and eventually every flat surface in the apartment was covered with capped bottles. The floor, the table, the windowsill, and the television were all covered with little bottles, standing like crowds of people waiting for the lights to change at intersections.

The task reminded Joseph of the night he had spent in the apartment writing Bible verses along the sleeves and back of his denim jacket a few years earlier. He had stretched his jacket tightly over the sink. With bleach and red marker he copied scriptures from Revelations and Genesis until the words were like a new pattern across the material. In the morning, when it was almost dry, Joseph was proud of his work. It should have proved his dedication to the church, but no one really said anything about it. His devotion had gone unnoticed. Eventually, the smaller lines written across the denim bled together into pink stripes.

The fumes began hovering like fog in the empty space of Sonny's room. Thick little clouds gathered above him. Joseph couldn't see their colors, but they drifted along the ceiling and gently broke apart when they met the walls. Then they reformed and floated off in another direction. Several times, Joseph ducked under a passing group of clouds. He reached out to grab one, and it slipped from his hand. Exhausted by the day's efforts, he lay down across the bed and slept until the door latch clicked open.

"He's got the tolly," McKnuckle cheered triumphantly as they barged through the door and shook Joseph's eyes open.

Sonny pointed to McKnuckle and then told Joseph, "He's the only nigger I know who does this stuff."

"Are you going to sell it?" Joseph asked with a dry tongue.

"Damn right. Five a bottle and two on a rag." Sonny turned to McKnuckle. "You still gotta cut up the rags."

McKnuckle ducked out of the room and came back a minute later with a crumpled bed sheet. Sonny asked where it was from and McKnuckle answered with something Joseph didn't understand.

Sonny pointed again at McKnuckle, who was already tearing at the sheet with some scissors, and announced, "This asshole just stole his cousin's sheets." McKnuckle opened his crooked mouth and grinned when Sonny asked if his cousin was going to be angry.

"No, he's family," McKnuckle said. He smiled again, like a child caught in some cute mischief he knew would be forgiven.

McKnuckle had left the room. Sonny had everything planned out and he began telling Joseph how the whole operation would work. Joseph was going to help sell the rags on the street.

Only to the kids, Joseph was told. No adults; no one who looked like a cop. He was to tell people to look for McKnuckle if they wanted more than what he had on him. Because he wasn't going to be carrying too much. Joseph was told which streets he would walk down and which playgrounds he would frequent. Sonny remembered where every possible customer would be. He gave their names and what they looked like and what they might be wearing. It sounded like a lot of work to Joseph. The particulars flew past too quickly for him to retain.

Joseph was nodding off, balanced on the edge of the bed. Sonny gently pushed him to the floor. "That's not what we needed you for, Bible boy." Sonny seemed insulted. His attitude had changed since Joseph had last seen him a short while ago. "I just gave you something to do, and there ain't nobody who can think or work while sleeping. Are you saying you done?"

"No. I don't feel good," Joseph whined. He was dizzy and his stomach had folded over on itself. He wished that he could vomit out all he had inhaled.

"Don't worry about that. You're okay. You don't want to help us now? You don't want to, now?" The words rolled out of Sonny before Joseph was able to say anything else. "We'll pay you. Don't worry about it. You make it sound like I ain't trustworthy. Now, I trust you. I been down the hall, working on some other things. Don't worry about what I been doing. Watch, I'm gonna go down the hall and check on my man. Damn, I'll be right back. God-damn."

Something had gone wrong, Joseph felt. He thought that he had been part of some kind of team. He thought that he would learn something besides how to make himself sick and how to burn the skin off of his hands.

As soon as Joseph heard Sonny's steps moving down the hall to find the absent McKnuckle, he picked up two bottles from the table and grabbed McKnuckle's scissors. They wouldn't miss a couple of little things, Joseph decided.

The clouds were gone. Not a sign of them lingered along the ceiling. Sonny's methods were the same as Preacher Madison's. Make nice, and then demand compliance. Sonny was just like everyone else.

Unable to stop after the first two, Joseph continued filling his pockets with the little bottles. There were just so many. He couldn't pinpoint how much time had passed when the door burst open again.

Sonny was standing there, pointing a finger which quivered as he blurted out, "Sonofabitch, I'm gonna bust your head. Give me my shit. You fucking cracker asshole, goddamn worthless. We try and help you, try and give you a chance to make some money. Get your sorry ass a bed. All this and you don't want to do it. Get the fuck out. Before I kick your ass." Then Sonny abruptly stopped, like he had a better idea. "No, don't move, don't fucking move." Spinning around, Sonny yelled up the stairwell, "Man, get me my club. Get it now."

Sonny yelled incoherently for McKnuckle; there was no response. Sonny slammed the door shut on Joseph. Footsteps pounded away from the door, to the far end of the hallway. Joseph didn't want to see what Sonny had gone off to retrieve.

He opened the door and sprinted past a burdened McKnuckle, whose arms were filled with more bottles; a bag of potato chips was hanging from his teeth. McKnuckle reacted slowly to the escape. First, he carefully put the bottles on the floor; then, he hid the chips inside an empty fire extinguisher case against the wall. By the time he turned his head Joseph was gone.

The boy stumbled down the stairs and burst, tripping, through the side entrance. He sprinted down the block, holding tight to the bottles under his coat. Neither Sonny nor McKnuckle had made it to the street by the time Joseph reached the corner at the far end of the block.

The hotel was out of his sight, far behind him. McKnuckle emerged, standing on the sidewalk under the DARLINGTON ARMS sign, tossing away garbled threats meant for the boy.

Joseph was a safe distance from the hotel when he sat down to rest. He put his hands over his head to open his lungs and waited for the dry air to stop burning his throat. Tilting his head back and shutting his eyes, he exhaled and felt the little clouds puffing weakly from his throat. When he realized he had nothing else to do, he dumped a bit from one of the bottles across the sleeve of his jacket and held it to his open mouth.

Daytime Animals

The streetlights slowly turned from a dim orange to a bluish-white as the storefronts snapped off their signs and their accordion gates were pulled across and locked. One shift had ended; another began. Crowds broke apart and were replaced by younger packs. Men with cardboard signs pleading for help deserted the intersections as gangbangers hidden under pastel parkas crossed the streets between waiting cars. Women stood with their toes over the curbs where the sidewalks cornered, watched the cars pass, and yelled out fragments of conversations to each other. All waiting for something. Some quick relief from the monotony of looking at the same scenery every night.

Joseph was able to spend the nights that had passed in an unoccupied doorway. He believed he was safe, hidden in the dark. There was no sign of Sonny or his brother-in-law. That was a small victory that Joseph didn't want to risk by looking for a better spot.

Joseph tried to remain invisible at night; he did not like the change. It was cold and sharp and everyone felt dirty. That was all he could discern about the others. He didn't care much past that.

One thing that he did not mind was that in the half-dark he could not see himself. He didn't want to be reminded of anything he knew. If he sat very still in a quiet corner, he could block out every noise. With the toluene he was able to erase every thought from his head for short pieces of the day. Joseph felt that he could have broken apart like the clouds in Sonny's room. He could have become invisible if only he could be certain that the other people couldn't see him. Unable to sleep, he wandered south of Wilson Avenue. He wanted to look around.

He climbed the fences circling the tennis courts at the city college and straddled the top bar so he could see far down the alleyway. Between the brick walls, a woman was kneeling before a man in a sports coat. She kept her hands on her squat thighs, and the man kept his hands behind his back as if he had been ordered to do so. When the transaction ended, the woman stayed back in the alley while the man strutted out to the street. Joseph watched the woman as she spit several times and wiped her mouth with a handkerchief. Then she adjusted her skirt and walked out in the same direction. Her body was a heavy and cushioned square, balancing cockeyed on two short legs. Her heavy breasts and wide hips floated atop bird ankles.

By the time Joseph lowered himself from the fence, the woman seemed to be waiting patiently for him while pressing more make-up to her face. Joseph walked away without acknowledging her, but he could feel her following closely. She kept her pace until Joseph felt her breath against his shoulder and her footsteps against the sidewalk, almost between his heels. He could feel his face flushing in the dark.

"Hiya, honey. You lost?"

Joseph didn't answer and the woman held his arm as he turned away. She pulled Joseph to her side as if he were escorting her. He noticed then that she was much bigger than he. She was close enough for Joseph to see that he was looking at a man dressed as a woman. Her face had been waxed and whitened with powder, her eyebrows plucked into two definite lines. Her gut hung over a wide, black belt and a sagging chest was hoisted up inside a wire brassiere.

Her voice sounded sincerely harmless. "You looking for something?" she asked. "My name's Bobbi."

"No, I'm okay." He slipped his elbow out of her grasp.

"Ooh, don't be like that, sweetie." Bobbi took a step back and blew Joseph a kiss. Sent it flying with the palm of her hand.

Joseph watched her walk away and found no masculine qualities. He wondered if his judgment had been wrong.

Questions of what to do with the next day easily left him as he drifted to sleep in the same unoccupied doorway.

Bobbi's round face and sharply defined eyes kept coming back to Joseph. In his memory, her voice wavered from a high pitch to a low rasp. There were the distinct voices of two different women. The smoky rasp seemed a little more natural for a woman of Bobbi's size. She slipped out of the voices like she were trying on suits of clothes. Joseph wondered if Bobbi dressed as a man or a woman while she was sitting around her apartment. Maybe she wore a little of both. Boxer shorts and a giant bra. Earrings, necklace, and a pair of trousers. And the more he thought about her, the more he found he could undress her and imagine her as a woman.

He had a dream where he could see her without being seen. Clinging to some windowsill by the tips of his fingers, Joseph watched as she prepared herself for bed. Each article of clothing was stripped off delicately and dropped to the floor until she was naked. Bloodlessly, a top layer of skin, thin and pink, peeled off along with the wavy hair and smooth face. There was another person underneath. When everything was discarded in the corner, Joseph was left with a fat, bald-headed, hairy-backed man to peep at. The man had been under Bobbi's skin the whole time and Joseph was safe only because the distance he kept.

He had another dream where everyone had wolf fangs instead of teeth. They were all laughing and joking because Joseph was the only one without the proper teeth.

The day was better. Sometimes he couldn't wait until the sun came up, even though most of the time he woke and felt like he hadn't rested at all.

The next morning, a clean-looking man with a square head stopped Joseph, who was pulling a discarded newspaper from an overflowing garbage can. The man flashed a badge hooked to a belt hidden under a bright windbreaker jacket.

"What's your name there, Home Team?"

He dropped the newspaper back in the garbage and gave his name. "Joseph Askew."

"You know this guy?" The cop pointed with his thumb to an old man leaning heavily against a shopping cart filled with power tools. Beneath a knit stocking cap and a worn flannel coat the drunk wobbled on his feet as his eyes drooped shut for a moment. The shopping cart rolled a couple of inches, and the drunk woke to catch himself before he fell to the ground. He pulled the cart close and nodded off. The cart began slipping again, and he stumbled angrily to bring the cart to his chest.

Joseph swore that he didn't know the old man.

"He tells me," the cop said, ignoring the burlesque in the background, "that he got the tools from you. That true?"

"No. What tools?" Joseph and the cop both looked over at the little man, who waved a greeting to Joseph. The old man squinted and nodded his head with confidence. Then with one hand shielding Joseph's view, he pointed a knotted finger to the boy, as if that would close the case.

"Okay, two of you," the cop ordered as he grabbed Joseph by the sleeve and directed him to stand next to the old man. Joseph tried to pull his arm away and the cop twisted the material until it tightened around his elbow.

The old man smiled and mumbled something. His lips were heavy and the words were slurred.

"Where'd you get these?" the cop asked the old man.

"I found them." He had an accent of some unrecognizable European sort. The words were all clipped, almost in half.

"I thought you said the kid gave them to you?"

"He did. He found them."

"Where'd he find them?" The cop knew that the old man was lying, but kept going since he had nothing better to do. To Joseph it sounded like part of a daily routine for the cop and the old man to argue about something. The cop laid his questions out slowly like he was talking to a child. And in return the old man let his words out one syllable at a time.

"What?" the old man answered with a question. "Find them?"

"Yeah, where'd he find them?"

"I don't know. Someone threw them out."

"Oh yeah? Where?"

"The garbage."

"Are you sure?"

"Yes."

"I bet you're not."

The old man blinked and a confused expression crossed his face. He knew he had screwed up his alibi, but he wasn't sure how. "In a gar-age. Not gar-bage," the old man tried to rhyme the words.

"Someone threw the tools out in a garage?"

"Yeah. They didn't want them."

The cop's patience was wearing down and he flatly accused the old man of taking the tools from the district station on Halsted. CHICAGO POLICE had been professionally etched into the handle of each piece. The old man denied everything, even when confronted with the engraving on the equipment.

The cop still had Joseph's sleeve twisted under his knuckles, refusing to let him go for some reason.

"Fra-ank. Officer Frank," came a voice from the doorway of the barber shop next door. It was Bobbi, bouncing out into full view, breaking into a jiggling run as she called out.

"Jesus Christ. What?" the officer responded.

"What's wrong over here? Did he do something?" Bobbi was pointing at Joseph like a mother who had just chased down an errant child.

"It's none of your business."

"Well, I was just with him a minute ago. We were talking. He couldn't have done anything."

Joseph hadn't done anything in the first place, but he hadn't been talking to Bobbi, either. Why she was defending him, he didn't know. The dream from the night before came back to him and he wished that Bobbi would just leave.

"Were you two over in your lovers' lane?" the cop asked.

Joseph studied the heavy pancake makeup covering the bluish stubble on Bobbi's upper lip.

"No." She was insulted by this. "We were just talking. He couldn't have done anything."

"Oh, then if she says so," said the cop releasing Joseph's sleeve. "Go ahead, kid, get out of here." Joseph wasn't sure what was going on. It sounded as if they were both joking, so Joseph decided to walk away. He hadn't taken two steps before the cop caught him by the back of his collar and pulled him into line.

"What are you? A fucking smartass?"

"No, sir."

"You look like shit. Where do you live?"

"Around here."

"Where around here, Home Team? Is there a number on your house?"

While this continued, the old man left the cart where it stood and slowly began walking backward down the block, like he didn't want to get caught from behind.

Bobbi reached with one hand and touched Joseph's arm lightly. She looked at the cop. "Honest, Frank, the kid couldn't have done anything. He was with me."

Joseph's face reddened just from the way Bobbi was holding his arm. The cop turned away, disgusted, but still kept a grip on Joseph. They were both pulling at the boy, in a tug-of-war between the collar and the sleeve of his jacket.

"Shit. Fine. Get the hell away from me." He shoved Joseph, who fell forward and brought his right heel down across Bobbi's toes. She squealed and jerked her foot out from under Joseph. Then she shoved him harder than the cop had.

The cop ordered Joseph to stay out of sight. He didn't want to see Joseph on the street again.

"Yes, sir."

The cop took the shopping cart and began pushing it toward the corner. Joseph and Bobbi didn't speak until the cop had lumbered across the intersection. "That was Frank," Bobbi said. "He's good. He's at least fair, but I think it's mostly because he doesn't like to do a lot of paperwork. There aren't a lot of people he feels are real important. Not important enough for the typing. Except maybe for the gang kids. It's not like you killed someone. You know?

"And the other guy, that was Old John. He's a cute little thief. He steals mostly garbage. He's a garbage picker. My friend shares a room with him on Wilson.

"Oh, yeah, and sorry about nailing you like that. Just a reaction."

Joseph wondered what Bobbi wanted. There had to be something, since she jumped so quickly to defend him.

He asked, "Why did the cop call me Home Team?"

"Did he? I didn't hear it." With one meaty arm, she hugged Joseph across the shoulders. "Don't worry, it don't mean anything." Then she changed her voice to a demure squeak and suggested that they would probably see each other later. Maybe they could get a cup of coffee and talk.

"Yeah," Joseph said.

"What was your name again?"

He gave his name again.

"Okay. Don't take this wrong, but you ought to wash your hair. I bet it's beautiful when you wash it and everything."

Joseph didn't know what to say to that.

"Sorry about stepping on your foot," he tried.

"Don't worry about it. Brush your teeth, too. I can smell them. See ya."

Bobbi walked away with the wind pushing at her back. Joseph didn't know what to do next. The street was clear; no one would notice now if he grabbed the newspaper from the garbage as the boredom of the day had previously dictated.

He slowly spun around to see if anyone was approaching and found dozens of cartoon eyes watching him from behind a pane of glass. In a barber shop window rows of little plastic animals stood on a white tablecloth. A small audience of lions and elephants and dogs faced Broadway as if they had witnessed the whole scene between the cop, Joseph, Old John, and Bobbi. The animals stared at the exact spot where they had all been standing. All the little eyes looked back innocently and accusingly at Joseph. They had been expecting more.

They knew about Bobbi. They knew what the boy had dreamt. All their faces were molded specifically to grin silently at Joseph.

At a Burger King he used his last dollar to buy a Coke, solely for the privilege of using the bathroom. Signs all over the restaurant said CUSTOMERS ONLY. He thought he had had more money. He wondered if someone had gone through his pockets when he was asleep.

He finished his pop and threw the cup away in view of the counter girl to make sure that she knew he was a paying customer. Then he asked for a key to the bathroom.

Joseph slipped the thin bolt into the door latch and studied his face in the mirror. Tangles and knots had wound their way into his hair. Dirt was packed in his ears and nose, and his face had broken out in glowing red pimples. Joseph forced a smile and checked his teeth. They were gray, but he couldn't smell them like Bobbi said. It must have been that he was just used to his own smell. The last few nights Joseph had slept in a new place, a little alcove garden behind a playground. Two buildings and a dead alley fenced in the grass, protecting him from the street and the neighboring buildings, one of which was a nursing home. During the nights he could hear distant sirens, dogs barking, peoples' voices always pulling him from sleep and continuing, it seemed, until the sun came out. In the daytime, he would watch the old people wander their fenced and locked back yard, wearing pajamas and slippers. They moved slow, with stiff-legged zombie gaits. They circled along the sidewalk paths or clung to the fences, until the nurse clapped her hands sharply twice and directed them like helium balloons to the open door. Only one thin little woman protested each day when told to return indoors to the lounge or her room. She had to be coaxed backwards through the door in little bird steps, because she didn't want to stop looking at the park and the bit of sky that could be seen over the buildings.

Joseph splashed water on his face and filled his hand with pink soap from the wall dispenser. He stared at his image in the mirror and wondered how much money it would take to protect him for the rest of his life, into his old age. He wanted to know where that dividing line was. He couldn't imagine sleeping in the park for much longer. He wasn't doing it because he had nowhere else to go, Joseph told himself; he was only hiding until the right time. And when the right time arrived, Joseph knew he would recognize it. But what he would do then, he did not have a clue.

He was hiding. Once his eighteenth birthday passed, he would be able to leave the church legally. He would have every right to do whatever he wanted. Even the police would have to let him go. He would no longer be a child to the Preacher or the elders. His parents were no longer a consideration. He knew they were not returning. Even if they did want to see their son, a direct order from the elders was not to be disobeyed. It would be a sign of their weakness and faithlessness as interpreted by Preacher Madison.

But Joseph knew people from the church were looking for him. They must have been. Preacher Madison must have been leading patrols of church people through alleys and narrow dead ends with specially-trained dogs and long, black flashlights. At night they would search the sleeping bags and discarded mattresses along the boundaries of Graceland Cemetery. Their flashlights would wheel over the graffiti-scarred cement walls that kept people out of the graveyard. Spray-paint colors would appear inside the circles of light and then vanish as the beam moved along. The lights would pick up a glimpse of huddled sleeping figures which would never include him. They would walk through garbage and high weeds and broken glass. The search party would lose hope. They would think him long gone and soon give up. He entertained himself with the idea of leaving a clue every once in a while. A piece of clothing or a scrawled message. His name in tiny letters. Something that would always keep them one or two steps behind.

He looked away from his reflection in the bathroom mirror and searched through his pockets. The scissors from Sonny's apartment, the ones McKnuckle had been using to cut his cousin's bedsheets into rags, were still in his jacket along with the little bottles.

He began cutting clumps of his long hair away. Some fell to the floor and some into the sink, in curled bits of red straw. He watched his movements in the mirror and the perspective seemed wrong. His hand kept gliding off, somewhere behind his head. He couldn't judge how close the scissors were to his ear. He closed the blades slowly until he found the hair, pulled tight with his other hand.

Joseph kept cutting until he was almost down to the scalp. When finished, he wore an uneven crew cut with more than a few bare spots and bloody nicks. He reasoned that this would end the itching that had plagued him every morning. Whatever had been living on his scalp now had nowhere to hide. He never thought that it might have been easier to wash his hair in the sink.

He hoped that he was unrecognizable.

"C'mon, motherfucker."

An Oriental kid in a Starter jacket was banging on the bathroom door. He stepped back when Joseph nervously emerged. The kid's friends, standing in the background, were laughing at something, at Joseph or the other boy or the piles of red hair hanging from the bathroom sink.

He checked both sides of the street through the plate glass before he walked out of the Burger King.

In a storefront window, he saw his face, wide and pink and completely hollowed out. A melted wax head. All Joseph could see of himself in the window was a round skull and a thin neck sunken in shadow. The shape of his head seemed to have changed. It was now smaller, like a narrow egg. No one would recognize him, he was certain. He turned his head from side to side, studying his unfamiliar features in the unwavering daylight. He kept admiring the extreme contrasts of his image until another face peered inside his from the other side of the glass.

The shopkeeper behind the window mouthed a few angry curses and waved the boy away.

Joseph's money was gone. He had already spent the small amount he had when he left the commune. A business woman had given him a few dollars the day before; now that was gone, too.

Two hot dogs with fries cost a dollar eighty-nine. Two burgers were two dollars and thirty cents. Tacos were a buck and a half. Beef sandwiches cost too much and doughnuts were forty cents each. The menu was written in red marker on a sheet of white butcher paper hanging in the window to keep idlers from coming inside, reading over the selections for half an hour just to entertain themselves, and then ordering ice water. Joseph stepped inside and found a sign that said Absolutely No Loitering. The customers had to know what they wanted and they had to have enough money up front and ready, before even walking in. No counting of pennies was allowed at the register, there was always tax, and there were no breaks. The guy behind the counter, accustomed to customers who wanted to haggle, had no patience at all. He watched Joseph count his change and search the menu hanging over the counter. "Can you fucking read?" he asked. "This ain't the bus stop."

Joseph went back outside without responding. He drifted in and out of storefronts, knowing he had no money and without really considering what he was doing. He felt as if he was somewhere outside his body, looking over his own shoulder. He kept walking. Acid was gnawing at his stomach. He thought that he could feel the lining slowly dissolve as the empty sensation made its way up the back of his throat.

The bakery on Sheridan had been leaving bags of day-old pastries out in the alley. On one of Joseph's return visits, an old man told him not to bother. They sprayed the garbage with pesticide.

As one woman walked past, Joseph just blurted out, "Ma'am, could you help me get something to eat? Do you have a quarter? A dime?" He scared himself almost as much as he had scared the woman. As she came close, he patted down his pockets as if his own money had been misplaced. She tossed him some ready change and didn't even look at his face. Her reaction eased Joseph and he kept asking passersby. He wasn't disgraced by this. It wasn't something that would last long. All he wanted was lunch. It wasn't like he was trying to buy a car or anything.

"I'm trying to get something to eat, sir."

"Bless you."

"Thank you."

"I'll say a prayer for you, ma'am."

"I'm trying to get a job."

"Thank you. Bless you."

No one said anything to the boy. Most ignored him as much as they could. Joseph felt like laughing.

And when he had collected more than enough change, he went back to the burger joint without loitering anywhere and bought his lunch.

Not one word from the guy behind the counter. He didn't even remember Joseph.

The outside world was packed with broken furniture, foul garbage, hurried pedestrians. Lost shoes and gloves. Junked cars and shopping carts. Joseph was floating from one point to the next like a loose sheet of newspaper. No one saw him and therefore he could hurt no one. There was no one to say he was wrong, so he was not in the wrong. Right and wrong were judgments always made by other people. His father used to disappear for several days at a time to avoid the punishments of the elders and Preacher Madison. He paid every time he came back. Joseph felt his mistake was in coming back at all.

In the middle of the afternoon, the sky darkened. Heavy clouds rolled over the rooftops and the street was shadowed over. There were two thunderclaps and then a sheet of rain fell, growing to a constant downpour. Joseph hid under a Plexiglas bus shelter at the intersection of Montrose, Sheridan, and Broadway. Through the scratched plastic, he watched the doorways slowly fill with girls and women hiding from the rain. Joseph watched for some time as they disappeared, one by one, into cars that pulled to the curb and drove off.

Joseph turned his back to the street and took the last bottle of toluene from his jacket. He held a sweatsock over the top of the bottle and overturned them together until he felt the liquid soak through to his palm. The bottle went back in his pocket and the sock went up to his chin. Fumes coated the roof of his mouth and the back of his throat tingled. The street tilted and the Plexiglas window bumped into his back. He held his breath, exhaling when his lungs were ready to burst. He felt his eyes rolling toward the top of his skull and imagined that his pupils were shrunken to dark pinpoints. Then the pinpoints rolled back after his eyes because they had been left suspended in the air. His grin was growing huge, he imagined, just like Sonny's had.

The women that couldn't be chased away by the rain stepped aside to let Bobbi walk through. She held a Snoopy umbrella perched over her shoulder and waved to Joseph when she noticed his hiding spot.

"Baby, what'd you do to your hair?" she sounded upset as she stepped under the Plexiglas booth. She snapped the umbrella shut. "Oh, it was so nice looking. All you had to do was wash it once in a while." She reached up and raked her fingers through Joseph's stubble. "Don't be insulted or nothing, but you gotta keep yourself clean. That's the way to maintain your self-respect. Shave every day and keep your fingernails clean. You ought to see what I have to do to keep up with myself." Bobbi was speaking in a rapid monologue. Advice poured out of her and the words fell over each other without reaching Joseph. He missed half of what she said and only forced a smile when her eyes caught his. The mothering tone made him feel as if he were growing smaller and smaller.

"Now what's wrong with you?" Bobbi leaned close and sniffed at Joseph's face. "Damn, boy. I ought to light a match in your face. What're you doing drinking paint thinner? You want to get high, drink a beer or something. I'll even get it for you." She looked around to see if the other women were watching. She began mumbling to herself. "Those low-class cunts. I haven't done that in a long time." She patted Joseph's hand. "Wanna go party real quick? I just don't want them to see me."

Before Joseph had a chance to answer, she was leading him away. They crossed the street away from the other women. She led Joseph to an alley they could have all to themselves. They settled between two dumpsters hidden under a loading dock canopy. Joseph placed the toluene bottle in Bobbi's waiting palm. She tucked it in her pocket before unzipping Joseph's pants. He kept the toluene sweatsock to his face while Bobbi knelt down in front of him. He checked both ends of the alley to make sure no one could see what was happening.

He kept himself from thinking what she might look like underneath her clothes. It wasn't hard to do. Toluene was pulling him up out of his skull.

He felt his body being coaxed in the other direction until it finally jumped. It didn't take long at all.

When Bobbi was done she took a few drags from his sweatsock. "I know. I'm cheap."

Joseph couldn't wipe the paint thinner grin from his face as Bobbi patted him on the thigh and walked away. He felt like he had just been declared the victor in some kind of competition.

By the time the rainstorm had ended, Joseph's toluene headache had settled heavily along a wire strung between his temples. He spent what was left of the day searching through alleys for blankets or pillows that he could sleep on. Most mornings, if he had any, they were stolen because Joseph had left them in the garden and didn't want to carry anything.

He had almost perfected a regular schedule. He knew where to get cheap food and where he could sleep undisturbed. In the morning he washed himself in a restaurant bathroom after he bought a fifty-cent cup of weak coffee served in a cracked and stained porcelain cup. Joseph was always able to get enough money for coffee and food. Just enough; nothing more. In the short time that had passed, he had forgotten some things as he learned others.

He ran into Bobbi several more times as the days accumulated. Eventually, he ran out of toluene.

The windows of the nursing home were going dark one by one. Disappearing down the line on each floor as the nurses made their rounds. Joseph stood and watched the darkness slip from one corner of the building to the next. He moved along to his regular spot, only to find it was already occupied. A sleeping body with short legs tucked to a lightly snoring chest was resting in his garden bed.

Joseph recognized the sleeper as Old John, the one with the power tools, and was too tired to evict the thief. There were other places to sleep. As he walked away, he heard Old John arguing in a dream. "No, no. I am on top now. Not you. Is my turn." John kicked a leg in the air several times before settling back down.

The time flashed on a digital bank clock. Then the temperature, then the date. Joseph translated the numbers into months by counting on his fingers, just to make sure it was right. It took him a moment to realize his birthday had passed unceremoniously two days earlier. And no search parties had rooted him out during any of the nights. He did not feel comforted by any of this.

He moved on to the TV repair shop where he had slept before he discovered the park. It was familiar; he promised himself he would wake up early. He drifted to sleep easily.

He was woken by laughter that came rolling closer as he opened his eyes. In that precarious spot half in and half out of a dream Joseph shut his eyes again and hoped to fade back into the quiet warmth he had been pulled from.

White light flooded his eyes when a heavy shoe driven by the weight of a full kick slammed into his back, again and again. The white dimmed to red and then he could see. Sonny and McKnuckle stood over him, their laughter stilled as they kicked at him.

Joseph curled into a ball and screamed. He pleaded to be left alone. A bottle hit the wall over Joseph's head and tiny pieces of glass rained down on his neck. Sonny leaned in close. Cigarette breath forced itself down Joseph's throat and he could see the pink-white of Sonny's teeth.

Sonny whispered that he didn't want the boy on this block, didn't want him near the Darlington Arms. Sonny lived at the corner, so did McKnuckle and his cousin, Melvin. Everything Joseph had forgotten was repeated in his ear.

And then he could breathe.

Joseph lay still until the men were gone. He shook the glass out of his clothes and wiped his neck with his hand. Blood and bits of glass covered his palm; he couldn't tell if the blood was from his hand or his neck. He sat stunned; his chest was swollen tight. It was as if his ribs were cracking under the pressure until something broke open, and he began to cry. Little sobs reminded him of a noise that a kitten would make and he held them back as best as he could. Joseph bundled up his blanket and his scripture jacket and slipped off the block to look for another hiding place.

Freaks

Leaning against a garbage dumpster in a back alley was a gold-framed mirror. The glittering paint was chipped and the wood underneath was peeking through. The silver of the glass was fading away gently at the corners, where there was no reflection. Joseph knelt down to look at his face and then saw how badly he had been beaten. He hadn't felt any physical pain until he woke in the morning.

His lower lip was split like a plum and he had a black eye that was pushing at his eyeball. Small cuts were scattered across one side of his forehead in dark freckles. On the back of his neck the cuts were worse.

He pressed his fingers where scabs had not yet formed and came away with tiny smears of blood.

Joseph ran his tongue along the back of his teeth and nothing felt loose. In the mirror he saw the knees of his pants were black with dirt; everything he wore was covered in mud. He tried to smile at himself in the glass, but he couldn't move the muscles around his mouth. He appeared to be wearing a mask, one that hung loose under the eyeholes.

He thought of going to the lake and washing himself off in the ice-cold water. He would take off his clothes and just jump in until the temperature of the water stopped the swelling. If he didn't, he imagined, his face would keep growing until his eyes were slits and his mouth was too engorged to move at all. And soon his face would keep growing into some horrible deformity. Strangers would avert their eyes from him, then steal glances while crossing the street to avoid him.

He would live on the beach. Little children would run out of the water, across the narrow slope of the sands and hide behind their mothers as Joseph took off all his clothes and slowly stepped into the water. The waves would push lazily against his knees and thighs, then his hips and chest, and he would keep walking until the water was at eye level, then ten feet deep, then a hundred feet over his head. And no one would know where he had gone. His feet would stay anchored to the soft bottom where he could sleep peacefully.

This made Joseph laugh and caused his lips to bleed a little. His thoughts raced ahead of him. During the night he would walk back up from the water. A new person with a face he had not seen before. He would walk the streets at night, completely mute, oblivious of the others who had before forced him into corners. They would step away from him in fear. And before sunrise he would sink back to the water.

Eventually he would begin appearing in the daylight.

People would come to look at him and he would speak and condemn them all for their ignorance. He had no idea how he would say this, how he would talk so influentially that his audience would understand what he meant, but his new identity would enable it all.

He hadn't been swimming at the beach since he was a little kid. The last time he had seen the beach was two years ago at Gerald's eulogy.

Gerald had run away from the hotel, confiding his plans to Joseph, who had sworn to keep the whole thing a secret. Gerald was a misfit slightly older than Joseph. And Joseph only listened to Gerald because no one would speak to either one of them. They had talked casually and uncomfortably during recesses on the concrete playground next to the hotel. Joseph had been proud to be the only one who knew of Gerald's escape. And he never said anything when Gerald was found missing.

Some man had killed Gerald only a few days after he left the church. The body was found in a dumpster somewhere in Rogers Park. Black and white Xeroxed police reports with his picture had been passed around, asking people if they had seen the boy. There was a phone number to call if someone spotted him. The grainy pictures didn't really look like Gerald. The man was later found in Indiana and he was charged with the murders of at least six other people whose bodies were found in fields and ditches between Chicago and the Indiana-Michigan border.

After Gerald's body was found, a harsh silence fell over the hotel. Preacher Madison never spoke of what had happened to the boy.

Joseph wondered why none of this had been done after he himself left the church.

The lake no longer felt like a good idea and Joseph dug into his pockets for change. He had enough for a cup of coffee and he would wash up in the bathroom restaurant like he had every other morning for the past few weeks. The creature would not sink back to his water.

He was determined never to return to the commune. He would succeed without any of them. He knew that was the best way to show them all that they were wrong.

As a squad car slowly passed the intersection, Joseph wondered if the Preacher had even called the police about him or if they had completely given up by now.

Bobbi was hunched over her breakfast at the counter as Joseph walked out of the bathroom, feeling a little cleaner, a little less bloody. "Hey, honey. Over here," Bobbi cheered in his direction. Joseph couldn't think of anywhere else he had to go, so he moved to the stool next to Bobbi. "Where you been keeping yourself?" she asked.

She held out one manicured hand for Joseph and with the other scooped a corner of toast at the last pieces of egg on her plate. There was no more patronizing advice and there was no more toluene and there was no more sense of victory. Just an empty space, as if Joseph had been dropped from Bobbi's list of close acquaintances.

"What happened to your face?" she asked, after mopping up the last of the fried egg. She wasn't as shocked as Joseph expected her to be.

Joseph stuttered, "These two guys..."

"Were they niggers?"

"Yeah, two big niggers."

"Sonsabitches." Bobbi grimaced and shook her head. She clutched his hand in hers. "You gotta watch yourself all the time. You know who they were?"

The answer didn't come and Bobbi released her grip, quickly giving up on the issue. Joseph looked around the room, groping for something to say. He noticed a man sitting in the booth by the front windows, relaxing in the sun. His face was pale pink and the fringe of hair remaining on his head was completely white. Lines crossed his face in deep crevices and his heavy brow shaded his eyes. The man had the appearance of a pale, furless gorilla wearing a button-down shirt. There was no color, no pigment at all under his skin. The man smiled pleasantly at Joseph; Joseph turned away.

"I got a boyfriend," Bobbi whispered conspiratorially. "You ought to see him. He's like a little piston, always moving. Wiry little guy, all defined like some featherweight boxer. He's got one of those bushy, football-coach mustaches and a stiff jaw with a cute, little dimple."

Bobbi held her hands over the counter. "He's got fat, muscular palms with thick fingers, Popeye forearms, and he's tough, too. I seen him in a fight. We were in this old Polack bar. Hank, his name's Hank. He wiped up the floor with this guy just because they bumped into each other and Hank spilled the guy's beer. The other guy was twice Hank's size. No one did anything. All the yashee-mashees were just sitting there, watching. It got to the point where Hank was just kicking the guy whenever he tried to get off the ground. Every time the guy tried to stand up, Hank kicked him in the head." Bobbi threw some feigning jabs over the counter.

"But he's the sweetest guy you'd ever want to meet. He bought me this Mother Goose book because I told him that was what I liked when I was a little girl." She pushed her voice into a high giggle. "He's just wonderful. You have to meet him."

"Sure," Joseph agreed, hoping Hank wasn't about to walk into the restaurant. Joseph didn't really want to meet Bobbi's boyfriend.

"Oh, and I'm not at the Darlington Arms anymore. I'm staying with Hank."

"I didn't know you were there," Joseph admitted.

"For a few months. I been between relationships."

No one ever said where they lived. No one lived anywhere.

"Oh," Bobbi remembered, "and we might be leaving town. I'm so sick of it here, it's the same old grind. Hank's got a friend down in Joliet who we can live with. We're going to go there and play the boats. Hank's gonna play blackjack and I'll just feed the slot machines. Maybe we can get enough money so we can come back here and not work. Hank's real good. He says he can make a few hundred a night when he hits a good week. All he has to do is get together some money for the beginning in case he starts off with a bad streak. He knows how to do it. Says that everyone at the table plays against the dealer. Not every-man-for-himself. I would've never thought that. He can count them. You have to look at the cards everyone else has and then figure what you get next from the deck. Like, the dealer stops at fifteen and everyone goes over. Because the dealer's looking at all the cards. I love Hank. We could go all winter without working."

Bobbi patted Joseph on the arm and Joseph forced a smile in response. He looked again at the albino man sitting in the window booth. The man's eye met Joseph as soon as he turned his head in that direction. As if the man knew the boy was about to look at him.

And the man's colorless irises were unnerving, surrounding the pale pupils was the slightest tint of blood. Like there were cherry Life Savers under his eyelids. Others in the coffee shop turned back to their breakfasts when they came close to making eye contact with the albino.

Bobbi had forgotten all about the two men who jumped Joseph the night before. She wasn't that impressed with Joseph's injuries. Hank had caused worse. Then she was distracted by the albino.

"Ooh," Bobbi squealed. "Let's go say hi." She jumped from the counter and happily led Joseph to the albino's table. She motioned to the waitress to send the check over in that direction.

The albino had his elbows resting on the table, his knotty hands folded before him. "Good morning, Mayor," Bobbi said and the man grinned widely. "This is Joseph."

"Hello, young man." The Mayor stood up for Bobbi as Joseph sat down. The Mayor returned to his seat after Bobbi had seated herself.

Joseph saw that Bobbi and the Mayor were both smiling at him because he had been staring at the Mayor's untouched breakfast. Three eggs over easy, greasy white and shiny liquid yolk. Black pepper sprinkled delicately over hash browns, bacon, and toast. The Mayor slid the plate before Joseph.

"Do you want this? I ordered it and realized that I wasn't hungry at all. The eyes are bigger than the stomach sometimes." The Mayor and Bobbi began giggling as Joseph picked up a fork and napkin. The boy wondered if there was something wrong with the food.

"Your eyes," Bobbi tittered, "are they bigger than anything else?"

"I don't think so."

"Not yet," Bobbi said.

They were leering and snickering while Joseph cleaned the Mayor's plate. And when Joseph finally stopped and looked up from the breakfast, he was reassured by the albino.

"Don't worry, I haven't touched the food." The Mayor broke into laughter, "Maybe later I'll get a little something. Is that right?"

A waitress drifted over and cleared the table and the Mayor asked Joseph how old he was.

"Eighteen."

"Good. You can vote." Bobbi and the Mayor almost fell out of the booth, they were laughing so hard.

The breakfasts were paid for by the Mayor. Bobbi left a fifty-cent tip on the table and Joseph scooped it up as the three made their way to the door. Outside, Bobbi estimated that the rolling storm clouds would give her enough time to run home. "That darn Mr. Rain. I'll see you boys. Wish me luck."

"Where's she going that she needs luck?" The Mayor asked Joseph.

"Joliet. To gamble on a boat."

"Oh."

The pink-faced man smiled and raised his eyebrows as if he were looking at the sky, but his gaze never left Joseph's face. He asked the boy if it didn't look like rain. The boy agreed.

The clouds were so dark it appeared that the sun had already set. Lightning flashed over the lake, far to the east. The wind toppled over two newspaper boxes that were chained to a lamppost.

"Which way are you going?"

Joseph pointed behind the Mayor's back, figuring that the man had just returned from that direction. With cheerful surprise in his voice the Mayor said he was walking that way, also. He took up his plastic grocery bags and pulled his shirt down over his potbelly and walked with Joseph for the next few blocks, making small-talk about the severity of the weather.

Under a stoplight the wind pulled an umbrella from a woman's hand and sent it sailing across the street where a man on crutches caught it with one bounce and swiftly boarded the Broadway southbound bus. Joseph and the Mayor laughed and the woman cursed them and called them faggots.

"Joseph, I have to drop these things off at my apartment, then I'm going to go get something to eat. Are you still hungry?"

"I can eat again. Sorry about eating your breakfast. You should have kept it."

"That's okay. I wasn't hungry just then."

"If you like you can wait down here." Joseph was told when they reached the Mayor's apartment. "I'll only be a second."

The Mayor lived in a three-flat close to the lake. The front yard of the sagging building was filled with garbage and abandoned furniture. Wild grasses growing from the vacant lots looked as if they were trying to knock the three-flat to the ground. The gutters were falling and the front door swung open unattended. Railings were gone from the wooden porch that the weather had beaten to a soft gray. Frames held broken windows on the second floor and mismatched curtains flapped in and out with the wind. Little kids rode their bikes through the front yards and scattered down the block when they saw the man Joseph was with.

They screamed in Vietnamese. The Mayor smiled and waved back. One brave boy tossed a soda can that bounced harmlessly in the street.

"No, I can go inside," Joseph answered.

The Mayor of North Broadway lived in a one bedroom apartment on the third floor. The windows looked over one of the weed-filled lots and the expanse of Lake Michigan was blocked by the kitchen walls which had been painted bright yellow long ago. The color had faded and darkened in uneven patches. A stove pipe gas heater creaked in the corner and the stove was covered with stacks of newspapers. A curtain hung in place of doors to the bathroom and bedroom. A squat couch was shoved against one kitchen wall.

The day passed easily and the Mayor coaxed a little bit of Joseph's recent history away from him. Joseph didn't notice; for once he talked easily. It seemed like the Mayor was out of his mind in a harmless sort of way. Joseph kept his story as clean as he could, feeling guilty about what he omitted when he said that his parents had moved away and he had nowhere to stay.

Joseph was offered the couch for the night. It was soft and warm and he could hear the rain beating against the windows and running down the broken gutters. His body was limp with exhaustion. His muscles had gone to sleep minutes before he had. Joseph could feel his face healing. The cuts and bruises that the Mayor never asked about were going away.

He would never have to go back to Preacher Madison and the commune if he could only sleep like this a few nights a week. Joseph thought that he would easily be able to pass the days humoring a doddering old man, listening to his stories in exchange for a roof over his head. Joseph found nothing threatening in the Mayor.

He had eaten three full meals that day. His stomach was set to burst. During dinner the albino had introduced himself as formally as he ever would. "You can call me the Mayor. A lot of people do."

The Mayor had said nothing else about himself except that he had been so prepared to fall across hard times that it didn't even feel like he fell at all, he only drifted onto another plane. He seemed to have had a full life, like there were many lives under the bleached skin.

It had been quiet in the apartment since the Mayor had said goodnight from the curtained doorway of his bedroom opposite the couch in the kitchen. Joseph fell asleep listening to the rain as it began to fall in sheets against the roof.

It was the first night of a late spring rain that would last for over a month. Every day the sky would become overcast and rain clouds would collect as if on command. Everything was drenched and smelled of standing water. Gutters overflowed and garbage flushed back up into the street. Men would sell umbrellas at the busiest intersections, right after they were stolen from CTA buses and coffee shops.

A Mother's Story

The desperate woman would begin her daily search for a poet after she finished her breakfast. Almost every stranger she came across, she questioned about their writing ability. Only a poet would be sensitive and intelligent enough to help her. And in case she ever found such a person, she kept a pen and a little notebook in her purse. She brought them to the coffee shop, to the bars, and to the grocery store in the hope of finding a poet. Or maybe the mood to write something down would actually strike her.

She doubted it. She didn't consider herself very good at that sort of thing. Not that kind of writing. She did send letters to the Times and the Trib, even to the free papers that only appeared in stacks under the doorways every week. She wrote looking for someone who would write for her. Not one return letter ever came and she worried that maybe one of the neighbors was grabbing the mail before she had a chance to. She knew that they stole her letters whenever a chance arose. So she had to write again and again, asking for any kind of response.

"Will you make a poem for me about my daughter? Not a story or an article. I don't know if you write poems, maybe you know someone who does. It would be nice to see everything written down. You don't even have to publish it if you don't want to. Just write it for me if no one else is interested, or if no one else likes it. My friend told me that everyone is a writer, but it doesn't much seem like it. Please write to say if you will or won't do this. If you will, I can tell you on the phone about my daughter. I don't want to tell you unless you want to do it. I don't think I'm asking for very much. I probably can't pay as much as you are used to. You would be a real saint. Thank you."

Then she included her name and address and waited.

The summer before, her eleven year-old daughter had been killed by a hit-and-run driver. The girl had jumped out from between two parked cars and the bumper of a red sports car caught her hip at forty miles an hour. She spun back between the cars and cracked her skull on the curb, right next to the WPA date molded into the concrete. That was what the woman remembered, the year molded into the cement and the way her daughter spun like a top.

The husband, the girl's father, had disappeared long before the accident. Before autumn ended, the mother painted a little white cross at the curbside. If no one was looking, she would drop some wildflowers pulled from a neighbor's garden between the cars.

In a booth at the coffee shop the woman placed a framed wallet-size photo of her daughter next to the ketchup, mustard, and sugar racks. Before her food came she said a silent prayer for her daughter, then another for herself. Hoping to find someone who could help her write something nice about her daughter. Something she could put in the scrapbook that kept growing heavier with love notes and snapshots.

Passing behind her chair, she heard a man lecturing philosophically as the waitress picked up the check. She saw a much younger man listening intently.

"Excuse me, do either of you..." the woman began as Joseph and the Mayor stepped away from their table.

"Sorry, lady." Joseph cut her off and then went out the door behind the Mayor who refused to acknowledge her at all.

The mother watched the man and the boy sprint across the street, then run from awning to awning, trying to avoid the rain. The boy jogged easily to let the old man catch up. They were laughing about something as they passed a man picking for something in a garbage can.

"Fuck you," she thought.

The Mayor of North Broadway

During the Korean War it had seemed that nothing could go wrong. He was young and bright and had had a strong upbringing, a shiny-faced Naval intelligence officer who had moved up the ranks in an unprecedented series of promotions. The potential held by the young man was unlimited. He accepted every challenge with reserved pride. The first time he saw himself in full uniform he decided that he was someone whom the Eisenhower administration would want doing more than mopping decks. In training they broke him down and then systematically built him back up. He underwent the attempted razing and reconstruction and never fought it.

The new young officer remained cordial and polite, but never gathered a group of friends. He floated on the perimeters of social cliques. Never drank or whored with the men on leave. He was a grown-up Boy Scout. The All-American Pink-Eyed Soldier. He was so enveloped in his duties that the men he had passed in rank questioned his qualifications suspiciously. The men talked and the new officer played mute. Rumors quickly connected him to one of his superiors on board. Both were suspected of the same unspoken acts which the military considered degeneracy. As word eventually moved up the ranks, from one side of the ship to the next, the young intelligence officer was closely watched. More allegations grew from his unit and rumors were filed as official record. No accusations came, the subject was never a matter to be publicly dealt with.

Officer's duties were all secrets and code words, now outdated by years' worth of technology, but at that time written on tablets and kept in locked boxes.

Documents that had never been seen were discreetly noted missing by the top officers. A higher-up used the young officer as a scapegoat on which to place the blame. Better to be a thief and possible traitor than to have what was actually suspected come to light. The young officer accepted a dishonorable discharge and the papers quietly reappeared the next day in the wrong file.

The new civilian went home on a slow ship. He enrolled in college and spent easy years getting his law degree. He passed the bar exam on the first try.

After college there was a wife waiting, and a thirty-year mortgage, purchased and paid off ahead of time in the northern suburbs of Chicago.

As he expected would happen, the wife eventually packed her bags. The occasion was not sad, or even the end of a chapter of a life. It passed like any other day. She filed for divorce when she caught a disease from the only possible transmitter, the All-American husband. Coming home from the downtown office, he cruised the streets of Uptown, buying sex from runaway boys who were as thin and sickly as stray dogs. They would service him while he drove. Or he would park at Montrose Beach in one of the parking spaces that held a clear view of the lake and its harmless tides.

At first he tried to convince himself that he pitied the rough, young boys. Underneath, he said that he couldn't help it. Once he even brought one over to the house while the wife was out of town, visiting family. The boy was given twenty dollars for traveling expenses.

The law practice was eventually forfeited out of boredom and the man bought into a rare coin and paper shop. Through investments, his money doubled and almost tripled while he gracelessly reached middle age. The man knew he was not handsome. In the mirror he found himself quite ugly, knowing it would only grow worse as time passed. His hair had fallen out, and alcohol turned his pale face a darker pink. He brought boys over to the suburban home whenever he could, but that was not often enough.

His savings were divided into stocks and mutual market accounts. He joyfully watched as his money metastasized. After several more years, there was enough cash to live modestly for the rest of his life. He put his house and the lucrative coin shop up for sale. He found an apartment in the city, steps from the Broadway strip. The first year was paid in cash, in advance.

Thirty more years, at least, had been financially prepared and planned for. And there was another good fifteen left out of those thirty. The little bit Joseph was told was even more veiled.

The albino kept his history selective. And anyone who had known his real name was no longer around.

The man considered himself educated in all areas. He could talk endlessly, drawing from a wide range of references, beginning with buffalo nickels and ending the same speech with the reasoning for the pyramid eye on the back of a dollar bill. Egyptian papyrus and rice paper, Krugerrands and pennies minted before nineteen fifty-two. The history of the Ford plant in Detroit. African explorers before Livingston. Moe Berg and Shoeless Joe Jackson. Edna St. Vincent Millay and the Kennedy assassination. All were tucked under the Mayor's umbrella of knowledge. The Haymarket riots, Nazis before the war, and the slave trade in America were all topics he could discuss expertly.

There was a lot about politics in his head. Things that no one he knew could argue or support, so the only possible point of view taken by any acquaintance was his. At first his base of support grew from lectures he had long ago given on the street. Sometimes he preached what he called "Personal Salvation Through Physical Awareness." Sometimes it was, "Historical Awareness." Or "Physical Salvation and Personal Awareness." It depended on how he felt that day. For a short time he considered calling his regular street corner audience, the devoted or unoccupied, his disciples. But the word never passed his lips. He felt that he had been born and reborn too many times to step into those limited shoes.

The Mayor of North Broadway was given his title while he presented what he called his election lecture series. He had run as an independent write-in candidate against Boss Daley during his last reign in the seventies. It was doubtful that the albino petitioned, or even tried to register to vote in the election. He just wanted people to consider him a candidate.

He made speeches from busy corners during afternoon rush hours. Flyers were pasted to bare walls and lampposts.

And the man was awarded the title of Mayor of North Broadway after the polls closed. He had walked up and down the streets as if he had won by a landslide. People congratulated him and it was rumored that he had almost fifty votes counted in the "Other" category. His mock concession speech was an epic given from the corner of Sheridan and Ainslie Street.

By the time Daley died, the Mayor of North Broadway was no longer interested in politics.

That had been almost twenty years earlier and stories about the man had grown with the time. His constituents had long disappeared into the transient community. Some even made it out of town. There was a Broadway bus that ran a fairly direct line to Union Station. Some just went farther west down Lawrence Avenue.

Sitting down to lunch with Joseph, the Mayor of North Broadway cheerfully confessed. "I used to think I was Christ, but somewhere down the path I was demoted to a Mayor. I am not the shepherd." He reverently made the sign of the cross and bowed his head. "Let us give thanks."

Over the table in the dishwater yellow kitchen the Mayor presented the first of several suitcases that were hidden about the apartment. Beaming with pride, the albino was pleased to share one of his little secrets. Joseph watched curiously as he finished the last pieces of a frozen pizza. The boy had been eating constantly since his arrival. The suitcase opened and the Mayor pulled away the thick, clean towels to reveal a Bible that filled the entire case.

The suitcase and the Bible smelled of mold. A miniature mushroom cloud of dust rose under the light bulb as the Mayor lifted the book from its case. A patterned design was carved into the wooden cover and the pages were edged with gold. Sheets of tissue sewn into the thick leather binding protected each color plate. Joseph fingered one of the old pages. It was smooth and the paper was thin, but still heavier than that of most books. Joseph didn't understand how the pages could be so thin and still feel the way they did.

The Mayor explained the whole process of making paper in terms that the boy didn't understand. The Mayor saw his confusion and said, "There's another man I know who can explain these things better than I. But it's still a good way to expand your mind, isn't it?"

Joseph agreed it was. The Mayor was talking slow, like Joseph was some kind of retard. A little kid. He just wasn't very interested and instead was eyeing the empty pizza cardboard, still hungry.

"Do you want more to eat?" the Mayor asked. "You're pretty thin." The voice sounded irritated and tired, the charm disappeared for a moment.

"It's a German Bible," the Mayor switched back to a more hopeful tone after receiving no answer. The book disappeared under the towels, inside the suitcase to close the subject. "Maybe you'd like to sleep a little more," he suggested when Joseph didn't respond again. "We can take a walk later."

"Sure," Joseph said. He didn't know the Bible was German. He didn't want to see any Bible at all. He felt that he had seen enough of them to last a lifetime. After being fed, he felt no need to talk.

Joseph lay down on the couch and wondered what the book was worth. The Mayor had all this money; enough, he said, so that he never had to work again. Joseph noticed that there were other suitcases around the apartment just like the one that held the Bible. He had been told about the rare coin and paper shop. From the closet he caught a quick glimpse of more stacks of sealed boxes. He imagined that those were also filled with Bibles and the apartment held possibly hundreds of the books altogether.

Joseph slept on the kitchen couch without any blankets. His head and his feet hung over the armrests like a baby grown too big for the crib. From his bedroom at the other side of the kitchen, the Mayor yelled to Joseph that maybe he would want to sleep in there. It was warmer and there was more room. Joseph yelled back that he was warm enough. He was fine. "I'm not even sleepy," the Mayor announced. "Maybe I'll go food shopping."

With his head hanging at a backwards angle over the arm of the couch Joseph could see to the windows outside. The afternoon scenery was upside-down. The clouds were a pregnant gray at the bottom windowsill and in place of the sky was the ground, wet and slick from yesterday's rain. Wind rattled the loose window frames until they sounded like someone coughing.

The apartment was darker now, and two small lamps were lit at the opposite sides of the kitchen.

Inside the window panes the sky was pink from the dying edge of a sunset. Joseph let his eyes drift into a stare until his focus blurred and the pink squares were floating in the dark of the room.

It was the unlocking of the door that woke the boy. The Mayor entered with a grocery bag under his arm, greeted the boy warmly and set the bag onto the kitchen table.

Joseph watched the man take off his coat and move around the room, walking like there were small voices floating around his head, swimming past him. Again the Mayor smiled at Joseph, like someone had whispered in his ear. "How does it feel to be completely on your own?" the Mayor asked as he placed a bottle of dark liquor and two glasses on the table.

He mixed the drinks, put Coke in with the whiskey, and handed one to Joseph.

"What is it?" Joseph asked.

"Southern Comfort and Coke. Ever had it before?"

Joseph said he hadn't and the Mayor told him that was all the more reason to try it.

Half the bottle had been emptied in an hour and Joseph was sleepy again. It was just like the toluene, but Joseph didn't have any urge to laugh. His eyes could barely stay open. He had never slept or eaten so much in his life. He was led from the table to the couch when the Mayor decided that he had enough. Joseph saw the Mayor slip through the bedroom curtains before his eyes drifted shut.

Hands grabbed at the boy in his sleep. A heavy body rolled onto his shoulder and pushed him down to the springs of the sofa frame. Joseph reached out in the dark and blindly grabbed a face like soft leather. He kicked and shoved until the weight was on the floor.

In a sitting position Joseph woke. The Mayor was face-down in his lap. A dome of spotted pink scalp encircled by white tufts of hair and two twisted ears. The sensation scared him at first. He saw the Mayor kept his hands behind his back as if he knew Bobbi's procedure. Joseph shut his eyes and guilt flushed his whole body. He didn't know what he was supposed to do. His body was reacting contrary to his wishes.

When it was finished in the next second, the Mayor sighed and stood up. Then went back behind his curtain without saying a word. In his half-sleep Joseph told himself that he hadn't done anything wrong. He was just sitting there.

Restlessly curling up at one end of the couch, he watched headlights drift at a junkboat pace across the window. He tried to wake himself up, but knew that he would not be sober enough until the next day. He was trapped somewhere between wakefulness and sleep.

In the morning, when he found the Mayor standing at the kitchen sink, there was no mention of the incident. A pounding headache was buried behind his eyes, much worse than with the toluene, and he didn't feel like eating. The Mayor laughed and babied Joseph. Made Alka-Seltzers and handed them to his guest, who swore to himself that he wouldn't drink with the man again. Nightmares kept waking him in a panic.

"I have to go out for a while," the Mayor told Joseph. "There's some litigation that I have to take care of. A small issue of slander. You can find something to do for the day, can't you? I'll lock the door behind us."

The Mayor didn't want to leave Joseph alone in the apartment. They were to meet again at four o'clock on the front porch.

From between his fingers the Mayor pulled a ten-dollar bill and laid it on the table like a magician. He told Joseph that the money was for lunch or anything else he had to take care of during the afternoon.

"What do you do," Joseph asked nonchalantly as the Mayor was walking out the door, "to make money?"

"I told you already. I'm independently comfortable."

Rogers Park

While pouring drinks down Joseph's throat the night before, the Mayor had given the boy his scattered version of the state of the world.

"Currency is doled out by the conglomerate corporations after they begin the chain of eating each other and lessening their numbers. And as their numbers dwindle, ours grow. The group we are in. Not that this is a good thing. The group I am talking about is composed of those who are held in debt to the conglomerates. They hold the purse strings. Control where money goes. Control who can follow it. The middle class is being pushed down. Soon there will only be two social groups, the upper and lower classes. I don't have to explain that to you, do I?

"The other group we are in, the one inside the lower and now-conjoined middle class, is that of the completely independent. We do not receive their money. And if we do not follow or receive their money, they cannot control us. Individuals, free thinking individuals, our numbers are shrinking, too. The corporations will subtly hunt us down. We will be sucked in through advertising, and cigarette companies, and taxes, and rock music. We will be controlled eventually. That is how they will eat us also. Notice I do not own a television. I do not have a radio. As individuals, we are a shrinking number. Individuals are being swallowed by allowing themselves to be bought and sold by the larger companies. They are able to make it sound like a good idea. Sell your little computer graphics company for fourteen million. It's small change to Japan. Mergers will kill the American spirit. One board of directors will, or does, control a chain of information outlets, newspapers, radio, television, cable, motion pictures. When one group can hold onto all that, they can control the events of the world. At least the perception of the events. The government allows this. They have great stock in this. The President is only a figurehead. Business tells him what to say. Lobbyists offering campaign contributions decide what the politicians will support.

"The government is allowing us to be driven to poverty by big business, the one half of the ninety-ninth percentile which is eating its way down to zero. Do you know that corporations only pay six percent income tax? And individuals, previously eaten or not, are paying thirty-five percent. The government thinks that the millions of people making twelve thousand a year can cover the taxes for the pinpoint top of the pyramid that makes an average of thirty billion a year.

"So as times passes by and we all slink toward the end, the ones that are not attached to the bottom of the government or corporate conglomerate business, by money, by television, by dependency on employment, will survive. We will survive. The dependent ones will be eaten alive slowly. I am not attached to anything. This place, myself included, is completely independent of anything outside. I have enough, even though it doesn't look like it, I have enough to live the rest of my life.

"My possessions will grow. Valuables that cannot depreciate under government restrictions. My accounts will grow even as the dollar shrinks. I am my own corporation. When the government is broke, they just print more money until there is too much money and its value has to go down temporarily. But then, that is perceived to be fine because then Congress decides that the minimum wage can be raised. And minimum wage means nothing, not a thing.

"The military has a black budget. They can spend what they want, make what they want. Billions and billions of dollars just slipping righteously away. And no one ever sees the books.

"Money is more worthless to us than ever. What does a pack of cigarettes cost? Three bucks? Do you think it costs more to make a pack of cigarettes today than it used to? It does not. It is not that the tobacco is more rare and it is not that the workers are earning better wages. The only cause is that the American dollar is growing closer to what used to be a quarter and eventually will be a nickel. It will probably just altogether pass the dime. It is not inflation. I don't believe there is such a thing as inflation. A fiction of the Treasury Department."

Joseph had listened impatiently. He understood more from the Mayor's tone of voice than he did from the words spoken. Everyone was being cheated, from the minute they were born to the minute the died. Joseph figured that there had to be some truth to what the Mayor was saying, but he assumed that it was not all correct. It couldn't have been. It all sounded so deliberate.

"This country does not care about who or how many live under poverty. They will not care until it is too late and the middle class is completely wiped away. It's not that the government has a motive against the average citizen, it's just that they are in the way of progress and profit. This country's future is on the other side of the ocean. Anyone here can go to hell. Children younger than yourselves can be truly frightening, when they are forced to be. People will sell the last possessions they have before someone else steals them away. And the politicians act surprised when people act like animals. They did it years ago.

"Only now have we won the war in Vietnam. It took thirty years, but they're drinking Pepsi in Cambodia. That's all that matters, selling Pepsi and Calvin Klein to Malaysia and then building a factory on the spot. The workers will be happy to live on ten American cents a day.

"If I were younger, or needed to, I would start my own business. Work right out of my own home. I'd find what people needed and then give it to them. Incense sticks, perhaps. Something like that. Something that can be done with little or no overhead. A lot of people are working right out of their own homes. They don't ever have to leave for the office or deal with incompetent employers. Have you noticed that? A lot of people starting their own businesses?"

Joseph said he hadn't noticed and the Mayor laughed at that. The albino calmed down when his speech was done and it was noticed that Joseph was nodding off.

Through a grayed Plexiglas window Joseph passed his ten-dollar bill to the CTA teller at the Lawrence Avenue stop. The bill itself seemed to irritate the cashier and the change was counted out slowly in return. Joseph fumbled the coins into his pocket and pushed through the turnstile. Two flights of stairs rose on either side of the posted signs for El riders. SOUTHBOUND—TO LOOP. NORTHBOUND—TO EVANSTON.

With the toes of his gym shoes over the ends of the wood planks Joseph stood and measured the distance to the rails below.

An express train came from the other direction and Joseph watched it blur past. He backed away to the middle of the platform and waited. The first train that stopped was heading north to Rogers Park. Joseph had no idea where he was going. He had no plans at all. A new gray sky was hanging low like an enormous canvas tent barely over the roofs of the high rises along the lake.

The block was desolate when Joseph stepped out of the El station. Both sides of the street were lined with small houses and yards with box gardens that hadn't yet hit full bloom. Two liquor stores sat under the viaduct on the opposite corner.

Joseph wandered back and forth along Jarvis, uncertain about where he wanted to go. Finally he decided to venture east, all the way to a park at the lakeshore. An afternoon fog had rolled in and hung itself like a curtain over the edge of the water. The division between water and sky at the horizon was long gone. The line where the sand and rocks met the water became a low cliff and the fog was a great, gray animal nestling under the shelter of the rocks.

Joseph moved on when the rain began to come down lightly. The weather limited his choices.

"Got a cigarette?" a girl sitting at a bus stop bench asked as Joseph approached her. He was trying to guess her age, estimating the freckled, babyfat cheeks and heavily penciled eyebrows. She could have been fourteen or nineteen. A baseball cap was tilted back on her head and a long, heavy Starter jacket was draped over her shoulders. An open bag of cheese popcorn was cradled between her knees; her fingers and teeth were stained orange. Joseph didn't have a cigarette, so the girl kept talking. "Are you waiting for the bus?"

"No, just sorta walking around." The rain had died suddenly.

"Wanna do something?" She raised her eyes and imitated a smile. Joseph saw all the popcorn stuck in her teeth.

"Like what?"

"I dunno." Her voice quieted as if someone else was listening. She didn't look up at Joseph when she finally asked if he wanted a blow job.

Joseph agreed without hesitation. As the girl led him across the street, he realized that it was going to cost him money. He had never really been with a real girl, much less paid for one. He didn't even want to think of his last sexual experience. And the only ones before that had ended as soon as the toluene ran out. If Joseph was keeping track, he didn't want to count any of them.

The girl walked a few steps ahead of Joseph; there was nothing sexy or attractive about her. Not like the women he ever imagined. She didn't move like a woman and with the coat wrapped around her shoulders it was impossible to see anything, even though he was sure about her gender. Cars slowed and braked as she navigated a straight line through oncoming traffic. Not confident, but certain that all would stop for her. She hadn't been run over yet.

Joseph thought of Bobbi and the Mayor and was ashamed of himself. He now had something to prove. This girl would erase those other incidents. This was what he wanted. He knew that this was what he was. He was even willing to pay cash for it.

A door was open before a narrow stairway. Joseph followed the girl up a flight of stairs and down a hall to an empty room with only a couch against the far wall. The window looked out onto the roof across the alley. Joseph felt some sort of excitement pulling at the inside of him. An invisible wire connected to his stomach. The girl was standing, looking around the room when she said she needed twenty dollars.

"Now? Twenty?"

"Yeah."

Joseph didn't try to bargain down the price. He didn't even think of that. He fished around in his pockets, like he knew he had a twenty somewhere. In his back pocket there was about seven dollars. After a long, hesitant search he held the money out to the girl and waited for her to take it from his hand.

"That's all you have?"

Joseph said it was and the girl cursed.

"You don't have no more? Fuck. I'm going to get killed. Let me look." She quickly fished through Joseph's empty pockets and he obediently raised his arms to let her. The girl cursed again, looked around the room, and then toward the door. She offered Joseph a hand job instead. One cost just about seven dollars.

Joseph said that was fine and the girl went to shut the door. She carried herself across the room like she was suddenly very tired.

After Joseph sat on the couch, the girl told him to unzip his pants and take it out. "Are you ready? I hate it when you're not ready." She said this as if she had met Joseph before and it confused him for a moment. He wanted to tell her that she must have meant someone else, but instead said only that he was ready.

She kept her coat on, curled her legs beneath her on the couch, and said, "Okay." She slipped her right arm around Joseph's shoulder as she took him in her left hand. Joseph didn't know where to put his hands until the girl told him not to touch her at all. She kept her head turned away while her hand moved along with the motion of his hips.

Joseph shut his eyes and wondered if her eyes were shut, too. He hoped that her eyes were shut.

The girl wiped her palm on the arm of the couch when it was over. Joseph's legs felt like they were trembling from exhaustion. He wanted to cover them, to hurry and pull his pants back up.

The door bounced opened like it had been torn off the hinges and a muscular little man was standing there, tattooed forearms and neck pulling his body forward, ready to rush into the room. Joseph jumped up and immediately fell forward over the pants tangled around his knees.

"Forget about it. Just let him get out of here," the girl yelled to the door, then whispered to the floor and Joseph's bare legs, "Hurry up. You gotta go."

He struggled to a standing position and twisted his pants up to his waist. In the hallway he didn't even look at the face of the man who was waiting. "Come back when you have some fucking money," Joseph was told.

Under an awning he waited for the rain to die down. It had been on and off all day. Now the ceiling of clouds appeared to be slightly higher than before. Joseph watched the cars pass and wondered what time it was.

He felt that he had proved something, but he wasn't exactly proud of anything. The act had felt good for a moment. But Joseph had no one to tell about his experience.

After a few minutes the same girl crossed the street again and was surprised to see Joseph still around. She asked what he was doing. Joseph told her he was waiting for the rain to stop.

"I just hate it," the girl said. "I gotta stand out here all the time in the rain. At least it's gonna be summer."

Joseph saw numbers written sloppily in permanent marker across the back of the girl's hands. "What's that from?"

"Oh, the last time I got picked up."

"Picked up?"

"By the cops." The girl paused a second. "Where do you live?"

"Wilson Avenue," Joseph said.

"That's not far. If you ever get the money, I can go home with you. You gotta have the money, though. And I don't wanna go all the way down there for nothing." It sounded as if she was explaining a set of rules. She sounded bored and scared and Joseph wasn't really listening to her. He was thinking more of himself. The girl was a nuisance, now that his energy was spent and the tattooed guy was gone. Joseph was a little embarrassed by his earlier clumsiness, but generally felt he was in control. She had approached him. Joseph only agreed to go along with her.

"I'm broke right now." Joseph was hoping the girl would go away.

"No shit," she answered. Someone across the street yelled and the girl waved back.

"You live around here?" Joseph asked, feeling himself growing smaller suddenly, grasping at straws he didn't really want. It felt as if something between them had begun to shift and now it would have been proper for the girl to laugh in his face.

"Yeah, I hate it up here," she admitted, too bored to explain. "There's nothing to do. I used to have a cool place down on Belmont. I used to get into all the clubs and shit. I had a shitload of money. Yeah, now I live up here."

Joseph nodded like he understood and the girl asked him how old he was.

"Eighteen," he said.

"Yeah, right." She smiled, then added, "Maybe I'll see you later." She went away.

Joseph watched her follow some man into a liquor store at the corner. A few minutes went past, the man walked out first, then the girl stepped out and followed in the same direction. At the end of the block she caught up with the man and the two of them turned down an alley.

Joseph had no money left and began the long walk back to the Mayor's apartment. He really was eighteen years old, but the girl could see that Joseph didn't know a thing. He felt like a little kid as he ducked out into the rain. He tried to hold up his pride, but it fell limp. He wanted to ask the girl how old she was. He wanted to question her harshly as to why she thought she could treat him like she did.

Soaked to the bone, Joseph returned to the falling three-flat. The front door was open and water was trickling into the hallway, splashing around under the boy's shoes.

A note written in marker was taped to the front door. The previous three months had been listed and under that was written the word RENT. Payment was demanded by the end of the week. Joseph wondered why the Mayor hadn't paid the rent, if he had all the money he said he had.

Standing alone in the middle of the kitchen, the Mayor shook his head and announced, "I'm in a bit of trouble here, young man." But he said nothing more about the rent. He just left it hanging there to see if the boy would grab for the question of money.

Dinner was boiled eggs and toast. No salt, no butter. The meal seemed like a test of loyalty. The Mayor raved that it was one of his favorites; Joseph didn't believe him.

The Mayor explained that he had spent most of his cash on the litigation he had mentioned.

The rain kept coming all night and leaks formed in the kitchen ceiling. The Mayor asked Joseph if he would like to sleep in a bed. Because the kitchen ceiling sometimes leaked. The Mayor repeated later that it was probably better to sleep in the bedroom.

Joseph said, "No, thank you," and decided that he would not explain what had happened that afternoon. Nothing was left of the ten-dollar bill. Joseph didn't want to be reminded of it.

"Son, if you want to keep living with these comforts, then you'll have to accommodate me, somehow. Tomorrow we'll have to go out and make some money. Do you have any qualms about reappropriating?"

"What's that?"

"Don't worry about it. It's nothing serious. Consider yourself an independent contractor. You'll be working for yourself. Even if the minimum wage is raised again, this will be nothing but a nation of busboys and cocktail waitresses. An economy built on service is no economy at all. There is no honor, no pride in that. Survival is the goal. It is always better to be your own boss. It is a little more work, but that's the American way." The Mayor laughed at his joke in a manner that left no room for anyone else to join him.

"I don't know about that. I'm pretty tired." Joseph wanted a little bit of sympathy.

"You should get some sleep, then," said the Mayor as he stepped away from the table and wiped his mouth with his sleeve. The two bare dinner plates were for Joseph to bring to the sink.

"I thought you said you had enough money," Joseph protested, finally bringing the earlier subject back.

"I do, but I have to be careful. I can't just be throwing it all away. That's my reserve, a proactive measure. So long as I never have to get a real job," the Mayor smiled.

A Wealth of Knowledge

The ceiling of the kitchen had become stained and puddles had collected in the linoleum sinkholes of the floor. Joseph lay on the couch, trying to feign sleep past the early morning. Through slitted eyes he saw the Mayor working across the room with a bucket and a pile of rags. Newspapers were spread in a path from the bedroom to the front door.

"Come now, quit faking. I saw you open you eyes minutes ago," the Mayor happily admonished from his kneeling position under the kitchen table. "We have plenty to do." He crawled out into the open and announced that he had done enough cleaning for the day. With one hand he lifted a stack of newspapers and tossed them across the floor sheet by sheet, like he was dealing giant playing cards to invisible people all around the room. Each folded page spun in the air and landed flatly closed. The black lines of words sank away as water soaked into the newsprint. Joseph decided to put on his shoes and see what the day had for him since he had nothing to offer himself.

Outside the Salvation Army the second shift was waiting for their late breakfasts. The line of people had grown impatient, wriggled out of formation and collected into small groups while each person looked forward and back, checking to make sure no one crept ahead of anyone else. Conversations died down to a mumble between the men when Joseph and the Mayor passed. Joseph kept his head down while the Mayor had his chin tilted upward like a rich man taking his little poodle for a walk. After passing the end of the line Joseph heard one man laugh and scream out, "Gimme some, boy." Then another yelled something else that he did not understand. A crushed pop can whistled through the air and bounced between the boy's feet. It rolled ahead and wobbled to a stop. The whole Salvation Army, it seemed, broke into laughter over Joseph's head.

The Mayor, ignoring the commotion, pulled the umbrella ahead and Joseph stepped up to follow. "Come on, now. You don't have any problems with doing this," he asked, prying Joseph's attention away from the crowd. "Do you?"

"Can we get caught?"

"No chance we get caught."

Joseph noticed that in the rain, the man's skin no longer looked pink. It was gray like the air, like the hide of a lizard that adapted to the light.

"Government-raised niggers," the Mayor grumbled when they were four or five blocks out of the Salvation Army's earshot. "Guinea pigs."

Joseph asked what was inside the box that kept growing heavier in his arms. He didn't know what kind of store he had just stolen from. The Mayor had only pointed to an open, unmarked door in a back alley and ran away before Joseph could follow his directions. Joseph had leaned in without even crossing the threshold, frantically grabbed the first thing his hands met. Then had to run for three blocks with the load before catching up with the Mayor. Joseph had been expecting a plan somewhat more elaborate. He asked again what he had just stolen.

"Comic books," the Mayor told the boy.

A man behind the counter in a used bookstore gave an estimate on the whole package, wrote numbers on a scrap of paper and punched them into a thin calculator before coming to a figure. "I'll give you forty for everything if they're not stolen," he said to the Mayor who raised his eyebrows as if he had been insulted.

Joseph answered that they weren't stolen and he turned to the Mayor for some support. The Mayor kept silent, frowning in mock seriousness.

"How do I know they're not?" the bookseller pressed Joseph.

"I swear." Joseph defended himself.

"You swear on a Bible?"

"Sure," Joseph said.

Without taking his attention from Joseph, the man reached back and grabbed a Bible from a shelf behind his head. The swift motion had been perfected through practice. Joseph was impressed. The bookseller held the book over the front counter. Accordingly, Joseph rested his hand on the gold-pressed letters and raised his other hand.

He swore to God that the comic books were not stolen. His friend had given them away before he ran away and was killed.

"What was your friend's name?"

"Gerald."

"You swear on your sister?"

"I don't got a sister."

"How about your mother?"

"I'll swear on my mother."

"Okay. I didn't want to insult you."

The bookseller began taking money out of his shirt pocket. "Forty bucks."

"How's fifty sound?" the Mayor spoke up.

"I'm giving you a good deal, here."

"Oh, yes," the Mayor agreed. "But a better one would be fifty."

"For you, it would."

"Forty-five?"

"Okay." The bookseller gave in easily, but he sounded upset.

"Certainly," the Mayor said. "You, sir, are a true gentleman."

The bookseller handed the money over Joseph's shoulder to the Mayor, ending the transaction.

"Who was Gerald?" the Mayor asked as they hurried home under the flimsy umbrella.

"He was a friend of mine. Someone killed him."

"Did he run away from home?" the Mayor asked gently.

"Yeah."

The Mayor suddenly seemed to be appraising Joseph's clothes or something less obvious about him. "Why did you run away?"

"I didn't. I'm eighteen, I left when I was eighteen. I didn't do anything wrong."

The Mayor nodded. "Oh."

"My friend was the one who did, years ago."

"Oh," the Mayor smiled. "Years ago?"

Now that the boy, Gerald, was dead, Joseph considered him a friend. It was easier than explaining why they weren't really friends in the first place. Joseph had only thought about the older boy a long time after he left. There was no one who could say that they weren't friends.

"It's very hard to find a good friend, someone who is trustworthy," the Mayor said in grinning confidence.

On his way out of the bookstore Joseph had noticed that the entire shelf behind the front counter was full of Bibles. It hadn't been any big trick.

The two lived like this, day to day, for almost three weeks. The boy stole what the albino told him to and they sold whatever they didn't need to someone else. Some days were much better than others. If there was nowhere to go, Joseph would stand out on the street and grudgingly beg change while the Mayor stood in the background, hiding beneath an awning and supervising the operation. And during lulls in street traffic the boy stood with him and absorbed shoplifting advice.

"Never pass anything twice." That was the rule. "If you see something, grab it the first time around. Keep walking through the store. Smile and nod. Don't act guilty. Act like you have every right to take whatever you want.

"And don't you ever steal from one of the big chain stores. They can really get you. All the big ones, like K-Mart and Woolworth's, they have special procedures for shoplifters. And they got cameras and mirrors in every corner. You can't turn around to scratch yourself if you have to. Only go to the little shit stores. The worst you could get is a beating. Unless there's already a cop in the store, no one will call them. You'd be able to plead your case and you're too old to be given the tough love treatment. Teach you a lesson. I could see it in your face that you wouldn't be worth it. I mean, I wouldn't call the cops on you.

"Even if they did call, the cops wouldn't show up for maybe an hour and they'd be pissed about it. They have more important things to do."

It was like being taught to swim the hard way. The Mayor would shove him through the entrance of a store and then wait across the street. Once in a while he would come inside and start a conversation with the clerk or counterman or whoever was around. Sometimes Joseph felt as if the shoplifting was being done only for the Mayor's entertainment. But Joseph went along with it to ensure his sleeping arrangement, and he had to admit that it was sort of exciting. There was a great sense of accomplishment that filled his chest when he made it safely out of the store.

Proudly, Joseph took a VCR from a repair shop while the Mayor harassed the repair man with irritating questions about the interior mechanisms of video tapes. In a dollar shop, Joseph stuffed several T-shirts under his own while the albino grilled the clerk on the store's return policy. The Mayor's impromptu conversations were rarely any help. Joseph suspected that the Mayor would let him get caught if the chance arose.

Joseph never saw the money that resulted from all his work. He wanted to know what happened to the hidden, untouchable savings and the fancy Bibles that were so expensive they had to be wrapped in new towels and tucked away in suitcases.

The rent was slowly being taken care of. The Mayor was supposedly paying in installments and the landlord was supposedly appeased. And a silent understanding had been built between Joseph and the Mayor. As long as the money kept coming in, Joseph had a place to live. What had happened on Joseph's first night at the apartment never happened again. Joseph wondered if it was because the Mayor knew he would resist a second time. Joseph felt the slight changes in the air. The Mayor's tone was more business-like. Colder and more formal. Joseph didn't mind that.

"I wish I could do more for you right now," he told Joseph, "but we have to wait and see. I'm tied up right now with some other things. But possibly soon I will be able to spend my days in leisure and estimable comfort. And of course you can come along."

Spending money was given to Joseph irregularly, doled out after everything else was taken care of. First, a partial payment of the rent, then food and beer, and sometimes cigarettes were bought instead of food.

Despite their success with the small thefts, the Mayor was no longer talking. No speeches, no advice. Nothing but the bare minimum of communication, just enough to pass through the day. Joseph noticed that he wasn't eating. The Mayor kept in his bed until late in the afternoon every day and Joseph saw how the apartment grew cluttered with wet newspapers and dirty dishes and rotten food. The Mayor didn't seem to notice. It seemed this was something that happened every so often. A cycle that passed through the routine.

Joseph asked the Mayor if he was feeling sick. The Mayor said he wasn't, he was fine. He blamed it on the weather, it always depressed him. Joseph decided that he wasn't going to do anything about the situation. He didn't mind. He could sit in garbage as long as the old man could.

And Joseph didn't mind seeing the Mayor keeping quiet. The albino hadn't asked anything of him in quite a while. Days came frequently when Joseph didn't have to work. The Mayor wasn't pushing him through any doors. Money was now kept openly in a cigar box on the kitchen table as if the Mayor was no longer counting it. Joseph took what he needed.

It had been raining for almost a month straight. A record rainfall, all the news reports said. The streets were constantly soaked and the sky remained a dark gray. Joseph watched the weather reports on an old black and white TV he found in an alley. Some jet stream was pushing rain clouds from the south over the Chicago area in an S-shaped curve that grew wider over Lake Michigan.

The Mayor drank by himself in the apartment's clutter. He tried to coax Joseph into joining him, but the boy refused. The old man chided him, "You're a faggot. I can tell by looking in your eyes. You just don't know it yet. It's in everyone." Joseph ignored the comments only because he didn't know what else to do. He found that an imitation of muteness angered the Mayor more than anything else. Joseph's silence sent him into attacking anything he could think of.

"It's better that they are addicted to their religion and their God. Most of those people are weak spirits. If they did not have their God, they would be hooked on something much worse. Let them preach. They think there is safety in numbers." The Mayor was drunk; Joseph felt the words biting slightly at his skin.

Some nights Joseph heard the Mayor's bare footsteps stalking to the couch. The man stood there doing nothing, while Joseph watched through half-shut eyes.

The menace fell away from the Mayor's body one night as he straightened himself and said contemptuously, "You can't dislike what you don't know. Didn't your parents ever tell you that?"

Joseph could feel the apartment growing smaller. One morning he found the television's cord severed. "I thought I would let you slide for a while," the Mayor explained, "but I got tired of it. Don't you know that the screen is an instrument of control? You don't want these people controlling you, do you?"

The lights were off behind the Mayor's curtained bedroom and Joseph couldn't sleep. Joseph had saved and stolen fifty-two dollars from the Mayor. It was the most he had ever had. With the money he felt some kind of freedom from the old man. He would be able to leave soon, maybe in a few more days if he could come across a little more. The cigar box was empty.

He swung his legs off the couch and eased himself to a standing position, waiting for the floorboards to creak. Joseph took small steps toward the red curtains before the Mayor's bedroom. He could feel the wad of bills in his pocket.

And found the man lying on his back, naked and unmoving. The light sneaked in over Joseph's shoulder and he could see the Mayor's skin splotched pink and white. His flesh was wrinkled and ruddy like a half-deflated balloon. His stomach was a beach ball, the flesh stretched tight over the fat. In sleep the albino face was contorted in a silent growl. One eye twitched several times, close to opening.

Cigarettes were stubbed out on the linoleum and a bottle of vodka was half-empty on the floor. The Mayor was completely unconscious; Joseph couldn't even hear the man's breathing. He backed away from the curtain and the light closed over the old man's body. Joseph felt sick to his stomach. The Mayor didn't even look human. Some kind of hairless animal was sleeping across the mattress. Joseph had an urge to place a kick in his ear.

He knew what the Mayor wanted from him. And he knew that he couldn't stay much longer. He tried to laugh about it, feeling for that moment as if he was in charge.

He grabbed what was left of the vodka and brought the bottle out to the couch in the kitchen, certain that the Mayor would not wake until the late morning. The cushions settled under his hips with a soft squeak. He took the cap from the vodka and rolled it slowly between his fingers. He sniffed at the bottle, then at the air. The vodka didn't smell like anything. It was the room that stank of something sweetly decaying. Joseph imagined the whole flat rotting from the inside out. He thought of all the others who had been there before him and had left something of themselves behind. Joseph imagined that they all left in a rush in the middle of the night, taking nothing but the clothes they wore. They should have scratched their names somewhere, along the wall or underneath the table, to mark the time spent or lost.

With the first few swallows of vodka Joseph felt his throat burn and his muscles relax. His uneasiness shrank as the alcohol built his courage. He stepped lightly to the closet and pulled the door carefully. He wanted to look at one of the Bibles, try to find what made it so valuable.

At the back of the closet Joseph found several heavy shoeboxes. One, he could barely lift. He shoved it along the floor until it sat under the light falling in from the windows. The box held coins wrapped inside handkerchiefs and sweatsocks. Joseph didn't recognize any of them. Some had English words, some were printed in another language. Silver and copper like American money, but there were women instead of men on each coin. Some coins had animals on one side and a flag on the other.

Joseph couldn't find any American money. What was in the closet was useless to Joseph. He opened every box, every wrapping. He piled the coins up in stacks like a child collecting his mother's trinkets. Making an inventory of junk jewelry. Joseph drifted away. He sat there with the boxes and the coins spread out around him on the floor.

The red curtains parted and the Mayor appeared in the doorway, covered by a bathrobe tied tightly under his gut. "Did I give you permission to go through my belongings?" His voice was calm and steady as if he were teaching a child an important lesson. "Now put everything back in the boxes and put the boxes back in the closet like a good boy and then go back to sleep."

The Mayor supervised while Joseph put the closet back in order. Joseph felt that there was some kind of competition between himself and the Mayor and he knew that he would lose. It was a game that the old man had played before. He knew all the rules; he had made them up.

Joseph went back to the couch and watched the rain fall under the street lights. Somewhere down the block a car was circling, music blasting out of the windows, louder than the engine. The music grew clearer each time the car came around.

The Bicycle Thief

It was a perfect morning out on the lakeshore. The sky had cleared and its rich blue was dotted by only a few clouds out over the lake. The water was a dirty gray that blurred with the smog out at the horizon. The night's rain had ended and the puddles were crawling into the cracks of the cement ledge that held back the lake.

The morning had gone badly for Joseph; he had failed twice at stealing something for breakfast. All eyes were on him and the Mayor's shoplifting instructions did not help. So he wandered away from the dingy shops toward the water.

Perched on the ledge of the cement wall was a man holding a fishing line steady in the water. A Walkman covered his ears and there was a new mountain bike lying unevenly a few feet behind the man's back. A coolness lightened the air. It was early and the sun was still low.

Joseph waited for some joggers to lope past. Their feet slapped the pavement and their elbows swung in half-circles as they moved away down the path. He watched until they were tiny, silent figures out in the distance. The water pushed rhythmically against the metal and cement breakwall.

He heard nothing else as he moved close behind the fisherman. When the faint music coming from the headphones became distinct and the fisherman hadn't turned, Joseph figured he was safe.

He took a deep breath before quickly placing his hands between the man's frail shoulders. Then shoved as hard as he could. There was a slight yelp as the fisherman tossed his pole to the side and grabbed at the air. Joseph watched the lake's calm surface as the man's chest cracked the water open. The Walkman floated over the choppy waves for a second. The tape player went under first and then pulled down the padded earphones.

Joseph wished that he could have caught the Walkman in mid-air.

When the man's head came up through the dark water Joseph paid no attention to the look of panic or the flailing arms. He only yelled, "I'm gonna borrow your bike. Okay?"

The fisherman splashed and spit and his screams were cut short by an intake of water. It looked like he was going under again.

Joseph straddled the bike and began pedaling. The handlebars stopped swerving once he picked up speed. He was moving in a steady, straight, fast line. It felt good. The wind caressed his head and flapped the sleeves of his shirt while he tried to guess how fast he was moving along the cement strip. He imagined that it had to be near forty miles an hour. He wanted to ride like that for the rest of the day. He wanted to glide, taking miles at a stretch in a casual line across an imagined map of the city and the lake with each strong stroke of the pedals.

He raised his arms in victory and screamed at the top of his lungs. With both his hands off the foam grip, the bike jerked awkwardly toward the water. Joseph caught the handlebars, balanced himself again and decided to get away from the lake before he got hurt doing something stupid.

Joseph rode against the morning traffic, feeling as if this was the beginning of something good. He had won and was only waiting for the decision to become official.

The apartment was covered in mold and garbage and the Mayor stirred around in a foul mood. Rain had soaked the ceiling and the back of the couch where Joseph slept. In the middle of the kitchen the Mayor was pushing a ragged mop through a puddle of water. A bottle of Pine Sol stood on the counter.

Joseph rolled the bike a few feet into the kitchen. Two gray lines of tire treads had followed the bicycle across the freshly mopped section of the floor.

"Do you see I just washed that?" The Mayor pointed to the floor with his mop handle.

"No, I didn't see that." Joseph couldn't have cared less about the floor. He had figured that the bike was worth at least a hundred bucks. Maybe a hundred and fifty. "Sorry about your floor."

"No, you're not. You didn't even bother to look," the Mayor corrected the boy; his tone sharpened. "I'm not your mother and I'm not going to treat you like it. Act like the man you want to be so badly."

It was the Mayor's newest trick. The old man was trying to be cruel, trying to hurt him. He wanted the final word over everything Joseph did. Joseph figured that the old man didn't like to wake up alone in the crumbling apartment.

Joseph ignored him. He estimated that the bike balancing under his hands would be his ticket away from the albino. Not that he was going to ride it anywhere. He planned to sell it.

They were both silent as the Mayor finished cleaning the apartment. He sloshed water across the floor and poured the Pine Sol over it. Nothing was any cleaner. There was only the smell of kitchen cleanser on top of the filth. Joseph sat down on the only dry portion of the couch without offering to help with the housework. He crossed his arms and watched the clouds moving across the sky in the window.

From the closet the Mayor took a shoebox full of the odd-looking coins. He put a half dozen into his coat pocket and then announced that he had to go out. "I have to take care of some business. Can I use your bicycle?" the Mayor asked casually, as if the bike had been in the apartment all along.

Out of spite Joseph wanted to tell the man that he couldn't touch the bicycle, he couldn't do what he wanted anymore. But eventually he said yes. "Hurry up with it, though."

The Mayor answered that he would be back soon. He explained that he was planning a big dinner and that he wanted to get to the grocery store before the rain started again. Joseph didn't say anything else, didn't even raise his eyes as the Mayor carried the bike out the front door.

"Don't go anywhere," the boy was told as the door shut weakly.

An hour later the Mayor returned with one bag of groceries. There were two thin cube steaks, a loaf of Wonder Bread, and a six-pack. The Mayor walked in without the bicycle.

"What'd you do?" Joseph asked.

"I went to the store."

"No. Where's the bike?"

The Mayor set the groceries down and sighed sadly, preparing to tell a story. "I went into the store, and you know there was no lock for the bike and I couldn't bring it inside, so I left it on the rack and just tried to hurry. I took longer than I thought. When I came back, the bike was gone. I'm sorry," the Mayor smiled. "I started talking to someone and I lost track of the time, I guess."

Joseph knew there was nothing he could do. The albino had lost the bike on purpose. He probably gave it to some kid on the street. Joseph jumped from the couch and punched the grocery bag off of the kitchen table. One beer bottle broke as the bag hit the ground and the Mayor didn't even flinch.

"Goddammit, boy." He squatted down and took the bag from the floor, pulling the food away from the foaming beer and broken glass. "I apologized. What else do you want me to do? Go buy you a new bike?"

They didn't speak during dinner except for the Mayor telling Joseph that he could leave anytime that he wanted. Joseph knew the old man didn't mean it. He liked that, because he knew that he was going to leave and it was the only way he could hurt the old man, aside from not letting him on the couch during the night. Which the Mayor hadn't tried since the first night.

The dinner plates were left out on the table, uncleared because of the wordless opposition between Joseph and the Mayor. Silently they went to their separate beds. Joseph lay down on the wet couch in the kitchen.

He listened as the old albino drank his whiskey, washing it down with the remaining beers. Joseph could hear the man lecturing himself in a low mumble.

During the night Joseph went through the pockets of the Mayor's windbreaker jacket. The coins were still in there.

Joseph found a book of matches between the sofa cushions. He lit the first one and let it burn down to his fingertips. An orange halo glowed in the dark after the match was gone. He lit the rest, one after another, flicking them in twirling arcs at a tiny puddle on the linoleum. They hissed and died when they hit the floor, leaving a trail of red points in the air.

He wondered how long it had taken the fisherman to climb out of the water. The cement walls would have been slick with algae. Joseph remembered the expression on the man's face and wondered if the guy knew how to swim. It hadn't looked like it.

For the first time in a few years Joseph said a prayer. He knelt down on the floor and clasped his hands over his chest and shut his eyes, the same way he had seen his mother praying in the kitchen of their apartment. He recited the words from memory and repeated them several times. Praying first that the man knew how to swim. Then that the man could climb out of the lake. Joseph prayed for himself mostly, hoping that the cops never caught him.

Pain circled Joseph's kneecaps where they pressed the hard floor; he remained in that position briefly, feeling that he deserved it.

Joseph didn't hear the Mayor creep out of the bedroom and walk up behind him. He stood there silently. Rested one hand on Joseph's shoulder and confided, "Boy, sometimes I think you've gone crazy."

Then the old man staggered back into his curtained bedroom.

The only noise was then the hiss of the rain against the building. Joseph dressed, put on his jacket and shoes, and went out to the front porch. Water splashed through the rotten awnings; in the dark he couldn't see any light except for the rings along the surfaces of the puddles that were again quickly forming.

The feeling Joseph had that morning of finally winning, of moving one step ahead, had slipped away from him.

Joseph stepped off the porch; the rain fell across his face and chest. He stood out there on the dark walkway until his clothes were soaking wet.

Deinstitutionalization

At the intersection where Broadway changes its course like a river, veering from the lake at a sharp angle, sits a building of rose-painted bricks fifteen stories higher than the neighboring liquor stores and auto repair shops. Its deep green lawn is surrounded by a high iron fence while the security gate remains open and unguarded twenty-four hours a day.

Patients in bathrobes and orderlies in green scrubs walk the yard during the good weather. There are picnic benches under shady trees and a birdbath sometimes filled with rainwater.

Ambulances and police wagons drive around to the rear entrance to drop off new patients who stay as long as their circumstances allow and walk out the front door when they are as cured as possible.

Final prescriptions are written and passed through the receptionist's window. The patients drift out with their papers and whatever they had brought into the hospital, past the back gates and across the lawns.

The street was crowding in on Joseph. He had been following the Mayor's tactics, but without the Mayor's support. There were too many people. They were all in the same spot, fighting for the good corners for bumming change and intimidating pedestrians. Fights sometimes started over a quarter or a dime and Joseph knew when to move on. He moved carefully, tried to keep a distance between himself and the others.

There was one man who barked like a dog at the grade school girls as they walked home every afternoon.

There was another man who wore no shoes and swore that he had no feet. He would curl his toes up to prove that half of his foot was gone. The cause, he cried, was athlete's foot and he was accepting donations toward a cure.

The gangbangers were out, walking in packs and whistling calls to each other. Carrying golf clubs and signaling to passing cars.

"Fuck you looking at?"

"Nothing," Joseph answered and moved on.

He saw the crippled men with missing limbs and useless eyes and resentfully understood when passers-by told him to get a fucking job.

Cat Eyes was a small black man who wore the same pair of overalls every day with nothing underneath. He was a prominent mugger and purse-snatcher who saw people as no more animate than parking meters. Cat Eyes would knock someone down from behind and search for a wallet before stabbing them as a final measure. He saw no difference between that and flashing a knife before taking their money. It seemed that everyone on the street knew that he had knifed at least a dozen people. The police had yet to bother him; if he were ever arrested, he would be returned to the hospital. He had been deinstitutionalized twice so far.

Joseph saw the overalls and the muscular shoulders moving past and couldn't bring himself to raise his eyes any higher.

As the El trains move past the Berwyn stop, the rose-colored building becomes visible, with the American flag waving high above the rooftop horizon.

"Jesus the Lord loves you. Believe in him," a woman muttered as she limped past Joseph. Her spine was bent at such a curve that her profile resembled a question mark. Heavy make-up was applied to her face. Two spots of blush smeared her jowls and light-blue eye shadow covered her eyelids. Black eyebrows were accented low across her forehead. As a whole, it looked like ghoulish clown make-up.

On some days she wore a plastic tiara knotted into her hair or white leather roller skates slung over her shoulder. She passed out flyers for a church far west on Belmont Avenue called the Chapel of the Precious Blood.

Rumors said that she had been a Catholic nun in her youth and had left the convent of her own accord when the call of Jesus was not as strong as the call of some young man. The rest of her life had supposedly been lived in a kind of self-imposed penance after her husband had her arrested for some crime, for which she was found mentally unfit to stand trial. People said that she had suffocated her first-born child, but no one knew for sure. Joseph heard that the baby's body was stuffed in a garbage can and found by the neighborhood children playing in the alley. That was what the Mayor told him. To Joseph, it sounded like children were always being stuffed into garbage cans.

"God bless you, young man," she said as she turned around and began hobbling in the opposite direction. Joseph said nothing and the ex-nun kept at her work. In her plastic tiara she repeatedly blessed every passing stranger. Joseph couldn't believe that she had done something like what he had been told.

One Saturday morning, in a parking lot filled with shoppers, Joseph ran across the ex-nun passing out her flyers. Approaching from the opposite side of the street was a red-headed woman Joseph knew only by sight. She had a penchant for sneaking up behind people and screaming obscenities in their ears. Joseph had seen her frisbee-tossing storefront welcome mats across the lanes of Broadway traffic and laughing at the cars that swerved.

She believed she was being discreetly stalked every minute of the day. Without warning she would break into a jagged run and scream about the phone company. The wires were everywhere. Above her head, under the ground, and criss-crossing at every intersection in the city. She believed the wires carried more than conversations. The red-head saw herself as the only one who knew the truth and because of this, someone was out to get her. She carried out sneak attacks. If she found an Ameritech truck on the street, she did her best to obstruct the work. She stole the tools, spit at the men, and kicked the truck. She hurled welcome mats and obscenities before being forced to retreat. When the coast was clear again, she would go looking for someone else who hadn't yet received a warning about Ameritech.

Joseph watched the red-head and the ex-nun working their way toward each other. He saw the two women as trains locked onto the same track, grinding along in slow motion.

The red-head halted her march two steps before the ex-nun, blocking her path and daring her to pass. She lifted one hand to her hip in an outdated pose, brought a cigarette up to her lips and puffed and laughed through the smoke that seemed to hang from her face.

The ex-nun blindly blessed the red-head and offered one of her religious pamphlets. "God loves you very much," she whispered from her hunched position. The red-head was silent, building herself up for something. Street vendors and pedestrians stopped to watch. They had seen the confrontation approaching as clearly as Joseph had. The red-head grinned with the left half of her mouth and with her right arm slapped the other woman's hand down. Sky blue papers fluttered to the ground all around them as they burst into a screaming match. Both were screeching like parrots, hearing only their own voices.

"Apologize and Jesus will forgive you."

"I'll call them. I'll call them on your phone and then they'll be after you."

"Jesus will love you..."

"I know where you live and they know who you are. I have a friend, a friend who can get you. He'll know your phone number. Your phone is hooked up wrong. You better go home and turn it around."

"Jesus loves you."

"The phone company will get you, you little whore."

Grinning and pointing, an audience gathered around the women. Grown men cheered, rooted for one woman or the other. A majority supported the red-head because she had taken the first shot and possessed a much longer reach. The ex-nun was the longshot and it seemed that no one wanted to take the chance of rooting for the underdog.

After the initial burst between the women a lull spread through the crowd before a second effort was made by the ex-nun. Through smeared lipstick she smiled at the red-head and held out a different pamphlet, this one in Spanish. The red-head grinned back and slapped the pamphlet away from her face. She tossed a second punch against the side of the ex-nun's head. Shopping bags fell to the ground and the smaller woman did a half-somersault into the side of a parked car. All movement on the street halted until she opened her eyes. She searched the parking lot, looking for someone who could help her.

Now it was obvious that the ex-nun wouldn't even fight back. People began to step further away, to distance themselves from the responsibility of stopping the one-sided brawl. Someone even bravely cheered for the little woman. "Go, get her, girl!"

Sonny and McKnuckle sat against a car hood, drinking beers with a third man Joseph didn't recognize. Sonny watching intently and McKnuckle smiling blindly. When the ex-nun was upright again, Sonny set his beer down and slipped off the car like he was lowering himself into water. He held his hands in the air, trying to gather the women's attention while pushing through the crowd.

"Ladies, ladies. There is no reason for this," Sonny broke through the front ranks of the audience, deep into his preaching voice. "We are all here together, we are children of God, all of us. Show no animosity to others. Act unto others as you want others to act unto yourself." Sonny's voice was rolling, more fluid than Preacher Madison's had ever been. The audience waited.

Immediately the ex-nun bowed her head. She was ashamed, even though she had been the one knocked to the ground. The red-head kept muttering curses, less convinced of her own wrongs, while Sonny continued in a deep baritone, coaxing the two to a truce. The women eventually shook hands and the distraught little ex-nun walked away. She told Sonny that she was going to the lake to watch the birds.

The red-head was left standing on the sidewalk, looking for some reason to be hostile.

Joseph tried to sneak away at this point. He knew that Sonny and McKnuckle had already spotted him. The space between them cleared as the crowd split apart, disappointed at the lack of violence and embarrassed once the anonymity of being hidden in a group fell away. And Joseph couldn't slip away fast enough.

Sonny wrapped an arm around Joseph's shoulder and led him in a direction he was not heading. "What's up, brother?" He breathed in Joseph's ear. "Where you been?" Sonny grabbed roughly as if he was readjusting Joseph's shoulders, pinning his arms down at his sides. McKnuckle was smiling, showing his broken teeth to the other man Joseph hadn't seen before.

"Hey, boys, you remember our friend?"

"Yeah, what's his name?"

"I can think of it, sorta. Like it's on the tip of my brain."

Sonny encouraged them to continue. "Now think, you niggers."

"Was it Red?"

McKnuckle and the other man began making up a list of names, boys' names, pet names, girls' names. Yelling them out one by one to see if any would fit the boy. Sonny just kept shaking his head and telling them they were cold. They were way off. Joseph said nothing. His stomach was crawling, twisting itself into knots. He felt his face flush. If the street was too crowded before, now it was pulling the air from Joseph's lungs. Fear rushed the blood away from his unsteady legs. He was waiting for another beating to begin.

McKnuckle jumped off the car, pointing his finger at Joseph. "I know what it is." Sonny and the stranger opened their eyes wide, expectant. "I know," McKnuckle said, pausing to build anticipation, "His name is Faggot."

The three of them began to howl and fall over each other. Sonny pushed Joseph out from under his arm and announced, "Yeah, you used to only be a little cracker coward. Now you a faggot. We heard about you. We seen you with the old man. The big-ass Mayor." Sonny began to laugh again and then McKnuckle joined in. Joseph took a stance like he was ready to fight, fists held at his sides. They all saw him and they began laughing harder. The third man flipped open a gravity knife and unsteadily pointed the tip at Joseph's face, giggling while Sonny explained.

"Boy, we were gonna help you. You could have been fine now. But I'm glad we didn't fucking bother. If I knew you were such a no-count, weak-assed motherfucker, I wouldn't have even stopped you on the street back then. Fuck you. Fuck a whole bunch of you.

"I wouldn't be in your shit now if I knew you were anything. You fucked up and now you gotta suck a dick. Now go 'way, boy," Sonny finished, "before you get cut." None of them were laughing.

Joseph saw the red-headed woman watching him from a safe distance.

The apartment smelled of alcohol, whiskey, and burnt plastic. A hint of smoke was still in the air. A fire had grown and died while Joseph was gone. Nothing much was destroyed, but the oven was covered in black soot and the yellow paint was burnt up the wall to the ceiling. The Mayor's right hand was bandaged with a dirty undershirt. He exploded when he saw Joseph step through the unlocked front door.

"Where the fuck were you? I could've used you here. You can't just go and do whatever the hell you want." The Mayor was stumbling drunk, slurring his words. "I know where you've been. You went around and saw all the people I know. All of my friends." Joseph knew that when the man was sober he would sometimes acknowledge that he had no friends at all. "And I know they all talked to you and asked you about me. You said ... I know what you said, you shit, you said you didn't know me. That you were just using me. I'll tell them all different. They'll take it for the truth. Everyone knows me. I have told them all different.

"I know you denied me. I know what happens. I don't have to be out there to know what is going on. You little shit."

Blood rushed away from Joseph's face. He could feel his skin turning white. The names Sonny called flooded back to him. The albino's accusations were far off the mark, but that didn't comfort Joseph.

The Mayor grabbed a pan from the sink with his one good hand and threw it at the wall. It missed and crashed easily through the window. Triangular shards flew apart and jumped out after the pan. The glass barely made a noise.

"You're just a little beggar. All that religion they pushed into your soft head doesn't mean a thing. Yeah, I know that's where you lived. And I know what they did, how those people work. Like I said before, they're as bad as junkies. Same addiction. And you have no morals. None. Don't think you're any better than me." The broken window hadn't satisfied the Mayor. "There's nothing wrong or sinful about me, you'll see. There are others that make me look like a god-damned saint. You'll leave and be no more of a man than you were before. You're a scared little boy."

Joseph leapt forward, aiming weakly for the man's throat. The Mayor caught Joseph's left hand in his own, while the boy's right grabbed the hanging fat of his neck. They both stumbled to the ground, rolling until they were on their sides under the kitchen sink. Joseph's punches felt weak, like those thrown in a dream. His knuckles glanced off of the side of the albino's head. Slow-motion, he was pushing his fist into a pillow. The Mayor began laughing and twisted over and forced Joseph onto his back. Joseph panicked and thrashed and accomplished nothing. The Mayor kneeled on the boy's thighs, pinned his hands to the floor over his head until their faces were inches apart.

Everything that had been said he feared was true. The false accusations, he knew, would follow him forever. The farther along he moved, the more he had to hide from. What others said was truer than what had actually happened. He couldn't understand what he had done wrong.

He felt the roles between himself and everything outside his body had been reversed. The accusations now came from another direction. Joseph's fear of living as the sinner in the family, the cause of all their problems, had filled him entirely in the hotel. He took every chance he could to prove that he was as receptive to the Lord as all the others. He, too, had been righteous. Prayers were said aloud before bed. Hymns were sung so that his voice was the only one he could distinguish in the chapel. He studied, copied the scripture by hand. Carried a Bible with him at all times. Did all this before his father ever did. And none of these acts were caused by Joseph's deep faith or fear that he would be eternally damned. That meant nothing to him now.

The fear that had been inside him, that had been placed there by them, had grown like a piece of meat. It was blood and soft tissue. Another organ, new to his body, which had grown apace with those he was born with. Planted by someone else, it grew unnoticed, despite Joseph's wishes. And now it belonged to others. He was marked.

The boy felt tears rolling down to his cheekbones. One strayed and trickled into his ear. The struggle died and Joseph and the Mayor held completely still, each waiting for the other to make the next move.

"Go," the Mayor ordered. "Get the hell out of here. I don't want to see you in the morning, little boy. Remember what I can do."

The Mayor shifted his weight to pinch Joseph one more time, stood upright, and disappeared behind the red curtain to the bedroom. Joseph heard the familiar sound of the mattress catching his body and sagging under the weight.

The Mayor's muffled voice called Joseph an ingrate, a lousy beggar, a child.

Joseph left the door open behind him. He didn't want to make a noise, didn't want the Mayor to even hear him leaving.

From the downstairs porch he watched the rest of the block prepare itself for the night. A car drifted past with its headlights off. A figure inside signaled and another yelled something. The horn blasted and the car turned the corner. The gleam from the hood and darkened windows flashed in the boy's eyes, as if the car drove down the block only for Joseph to see. There were others outside, sitting on their porches or playing in the yards, but none had noticed the car slicing the street in half.

Joseph had once seen a man standing in an empty doorway, dead asleep. His shoulders were braced by the wall and his chin was resting against his chest. The sleeper held that position until the sound of a CTA whistle toppled him over. He came off the ground with fists ready, thinking someone had rudely pushed him. He saw no one within fighting distance and sat down again to shut his eyes. Now Joseph wondered how someone could learn to sleep standing up.

He walked aimlessly, seeing only the image of the man falling to the sidewalk. And kept seeing that over and over until he found it funny.

He finally laughed out loud. Barely consoled by the thought that at least it was not him.

The park across from Montrose Beach was lit by police lights. Flashing red with a streak of blue light jumping over the grass and the expressway. Several cops crowded the walkway passing over the lanes of Lake Shore Drive. The beams of their flashlights bounced in the dark and the far-away crack of their radios faded out over the water.

Joseph thought immediately of the man he had pushed into the lake. He wondered if they had found a body that had somehow drifted to shore. He wondered how the man had ever gotten out of the water. The wall looked so high over his head.

Joseph crossed the park to the shoulder of Lake Shore Drive and sneaked up on Old John the tool thief who was quietly watching the scene. A week's worth of alcohol was soaked into John's clothes, plastic bags holding all of his belongings were spread out in the grass at his feet.

Sheets of light-blue paper were floating across the expressway and blowing around the park. Once they hit the wet ground they were dead and stuck.

"What happened, John?"

"Oh," John jumped at the surprise visitor and then shook his head. "It was the nun. On the bridge." John pointed at the walkway over the six lanes of snaking headlights and made a whimpering noise.

"Who's the nun?"

John groaned, "You seen her. She's the one with the yellow hair. She wears a lot, a lot. A lot of make-up." John tapped his fingertips against his face. "And she passes out the little things, the papers all about God."

"Oh, the ex-nun."

Those were her papers floating through the traffic.

"What'd she do?"

"Nothing. She was just walking up there and some guys mugged her. They killed her because she wouldn't let go of her purse. Her bag flew off the bridge and went through the front window of a car. The driver crashed and died and the muggers got away."

Joseph now noticed that the whole scene was bigger than he first thought. Six police cars and three ambulances.

A car was wrapped around a lamppost and another with a crushed bumper had been spun in the wrong direction at the side of the lane. The windshield before the driver's seat of the first car was cracked in a spiderweb pattern. An ambulance and a fire truck blocked two lanes of traffic.

"How did a purse go through the windshield of a car?"

"It broke it."

Joseph asked again how a purse could break a windshield.

"Oh, the nun, she carried a brick in her purse so she could protect herself. She did. I used to talk to her all the time. She didn't want to get hurt." John made a noise in his throat like he was holding back a cry. "She used to be a nun at St. Sabina's. She said she was a good nun."

Joseph stood with John for a few minutes as the police wandered around, back and forth between their own cars, the ambulance, and the victims' cars. No one was in a hurry. Another ambulance appeared with its sirens off and parked on the shoulder of the road. The paramedics climbed out and joined the policemen's conversation.

Joseph asked, "John, how do you know what happened?"

"I heard."

"Were you here?"

"No."

"Did you see it?"

"No."

"Then how do you know?"

John was guilty. "I was here. I saw."

Joseph asked if John knew who the men were.

"I seen them before. You know who they are. There were three or four black guys. I don't know."

Joseph asked Old John if he told the police anything.

"No. No. The police don't like me."

"What about the nun?"

"Yes. She liked me." If John didn't completely refuse to answer a question, it seemed he was responding to one that hadn't been asked.

"Are the cops here for anything else?" Joseph imagined the bicyclist he knocked into the lake.

"No. What for?"

"There was nothing else?"

"No. What else did you want? Jesus."

Joseph walked away from John's useless answers and crossed through the park that separated Uptown from the lake. His shoes were becoming wet, he could feel rain and mud soaking through his socks. The police lights flashed against his back and over his shoulders. Some stray religious pamphlets tumbled past his ankles.

A notice was posted to a tree and Joseph struggled to read in the dark. There was going to be a D-Day reenactment at Montrose Beach next month. The poster said there would be carriers, fighting planes, jets, explosives, and four hundred soldiers repeating the invasion of Normandy. Assurances were made that viewing from the beach would be totally safe. No one would be hurt in the celebration of the greatest day of the Second World War.

Joseph didn't know if it was a joke or not. He had never seen anything like that before.

Free Money

That night Joseph slept against a wooden fence at the edge of a parking lot. No one bothered him. He dreamed that a woman bit his chest and tore it open. Silver coins, nickels and dimes, spilled out and the woman dove to the ground, grabbing for the money. Joseph did the same, but could use only one hand because with the other he was holding his chest together. His heart was racing when he woke.

In the morning Joseph found Old John again and they stood together on the corner, begging change and sipping from forty-ounce beers they had bought as soon as enough change was collected.

Old John was a refreshing change for Joseph. He had no memory at all. Didn't know a thing about Joseph. The little drunk was amiable and didn't talk, except to point out other drunks he knew on the street. None of the other drunks talked to John.

Joseph didn't mind sharing everything fifty-fifty, even though he suspected that John was always hedging his half of the money, keeping a little out of each collection. That was okay. Joseph felt like he had a partner who had to be babied once in a while. The day passed easily and the more they drank, the more disjointed the conversation grew.

Joseph asked if John had seen Bobbi lately, but John didn't know who the boy was talking about. Instead, he told a story about taking his cat to see a doctor.

"I had to go down to the hospital. I had to go and wait."

Joseph asked which hospital. He knew there was an animal shelter farther north on Broadway, but John pointed in the other direction to correct the boy.

"Not the clinic. The hospital. Right there, Thorak. I had to wait forever. I had to take my cat. Meow, meow. I took the cat, took him and waited. All the other people were going ahead of me. It was forever. Finally I saw someone who saw me. I took the cat, held him in my hand. And the doctor was nice, he was. He looked like you. He asked what was wrong and I showed him the cat. Put it right in his face. I said, 'I think he has a cold.' The doctor was very nice. Very nice. He looked at the cat. Looked in his mouth and ears. Put the thing, the ear thing, to his chest and listened.

"The doctor told me I was right. The cat had a little bit of a cold. There was no medicine he could have. No cure for a cold. But he told me to give him a lot of food and a lot to drink. No alcohol. Water. So I took the leftovers for the cat from the Salvation Army. I didn't even eat the meat. I put it in my pocket and brought it home. He liked it. Ate it all."

"Well, that's good," Joseph judged, not knowing what else to say.

John studied Joseph's face and his clothes and thought for a moment before asking, "How come you got no money?"

"'Cause. I don't."

"You should apply for something. I get my checks and then I go find things. Did you sign for unemployment? There's another one you can get besides that if you act crazy. Or drunk." John measured the boy again. "Try the unemployment."

"I haven't had a job."

"Never?"

"No."

"Oh. Then you can't."

John dug into the pocket of his coat and brought up a crumpled envelope. "Look at this. My check. I almost forgot I got it this morning. Free money. I don't always get them like this. Wanna go with me to cash it?"

Government aid and disability made up most of John's income. Every month his government money was sent to the Salvation Army where John ate his meals and received two small checks a week. The rest of the money was sent from the Salvation Army to John's landlord. The bills, rent and food, were all taken care of without John handling more money than he needed for a few days at a time. Otherwise, it was feared, John would drink himself to death. Twice a week all he had to do was arrive at the office sober and receive his money. The Salvation Army would not give John anything if he was exhaling alcohol and John found this extremely unfair. There were some days when he woke up feeling more drunk than when he went to sleep. He couldn't explain how that happened.

He told Joseph how unfair the world could be.

The liquor store smelled of beer mixed with heavy roach killer and ammonia. Joseph immediately noticed the gun holstered to the bald-headed man watching television behind the counter and saw an aggravated look grow from the armed cashier's face as soon as Old John came staggering in his direction. He knew John, as did most of the liquor store owners in the neighborhood. The cashier anticipated what was coming.

John tried to pout and gather some sympathy as he pulled the folded envelope out of his pocket and passed it over the counter.

"Would you cash my check for me? Please?"

The man took a while to read the front of the envelope. There were only a couple of words on the Salvation Army stationery, but he read them over and over.

"This isn't your name here, John." The counterman jabbed his index finger at the envelope.

"Right here." John pointed to the upper left corner. "It is."

"This one, I mean." Another name was written much larger in the center of the envelope. "This is your landlord's name. Did you steal this from the box, John?"

There was no answer.

"Did you steal your rent check, John?"

"Yes."

The counterman let out a groan and shoved the check back at Old John. "Take this back and put it in the fucking mailbox. You're gonna get thrown out of your place. Your building could call the cops on you. This is a federal offense. You stole someone's mail. Go, now."

John took the envelope and held it in his hands as if it were something fragile, now capable of crumbling between his fingers. He cautiously turned the paper over and over, looking for the faulty name that had given him away. He was heartbroken. He had been betrayed and didn't know how.

"It's a good check. It's in my name," he tried to reason. "Open it. I swear my name is on the check. I allow you to cash it."

"It's supposed to be for your rent. You spend this, then you have no rent money. Then you have to sleep on the streets. You want to sleep on the street with all the bums?"

The counterman spoke as if he were standing before a child and Joseph felt a pang of embarrassment for John. It looked like the words were beginning to sink into the old man's head. "Okay," John said. "I'll be back later."

Once out the door, John began looking for somewhere else he could take his check, squinting harshly at the signs over the storefront windows to see if they could tell him something he didn't already know. Joseph saw this and wondered if John could even read.

"This thing," John waved the check in the air, "is like gold and no one wants it. It's like one of those nuts that you can't open without the cracker. What are those? I don't know. I would even trade this with someone for a little money. A little bit. Something. I want to get rid of it before it goes bad."

Joseph walked along with Old John and tried to think of somewhere they could take the check and exchange it for real money. He had no idea. Joseph didn't want to stray too far from the rent check which the old man was ready to trade away for a couple of beers. He didn't seem to understand the value of the paper he held.

When the afternoon had almost passed, John decided that he would try one more liquor store. The day had been a sustained failure. John received the same treatment everywhere he went. Joseph silently followed, angry at himself for wasting the whole day with an old man who kept himself just drunk enough to forget everything a minute after he heard it. Joseph was tired of repeating himself and John wasn't as entertaining as he had been five hours before.

"What are you doing?" John asked.

"What?"

"Why are you following me?"

"I'm not. We were hanging out today, remember? Drinking."

"Are you going to steal my check?"

"No." Joseph acted as if he was insulted, even though the thought did cross his mind.

They kept going late into the afternoon like John had received a second wind.

John promised himself that he would return the check to his landlord if he couldn't cash it soon. Throughout the whole day he kept asking Joseph, "Rent is important, isn't it?"

The last liquor store was connected to a bar tucked away behind a beaded curtain. Country music played from an unseen jukebox and people were laughing and hollering for something on the news. The mustached Indian behind the counter was trying to catch what was going on in the next room, attempting to listen to the television, the music, and the patrons all at once. The Indian looked old and slow and thoroughly distracted. John went up to the counter, holding the check aloft like he was delivering the mail. He stepped close, moved right up into the Indian's face and began explaining his problems while Joseph quickly stuffed three pints of Kiwi Mad Dog under his shirt. John pleaded his case with no success. The Indian wasn't even listening and just kept waving his hand back and forth. Joseph headed for the door as John was being berated and shooed away.

Someone else entered as Joseph was trying to get out. The metal frame of the door caught Joseph square in the chest and an audible clink came from under his clothes as he stumbled back on his heels.

The old Indian hurdled like an Olympic athlete when he heard the bottles. Joseph was certain the man gave out some kind of battle cry as he leaped over the counter.

An arm went around Joseph's neck and his body twisted. He felt one hand claw for his throat. The first bottle fell out and shattered to bits of green glass and Joseph, for some reason, tried to save the other two from breaking.

The Indian yelled for help as he punched Joseph in the face. Joseph didn't feel a thing as he fell on top of the broken bottle. Customers plowed out of the adjoining bar to watch and join the action. All Joseph saw were feet stomping dangerously close to his face. He thought there was a crowd swarming him. Someone jumped on his back with both feet and someone else kicked him in the ribs and a sharp fist landed above his eye. He forced himself to stand upright and a pair of hands tried to grab him by the hair. He was knocked down again and for a few seconds all he could see were hands and feet and shelves of bottles coming down. A second time he made it to the door, but someone had locked it during the fight. He shut his eyes and accepted his beating until he was lifted from the ground. Someone locked Joseph in a full nelson and carried him easily into the back room. He now saw that it was only two people who had kept him from escaping. It had felt like a dozen more were trying to twist his limbs into unnatural positions.

People along the bar were laughing and making jokes as Joseph's heels dragged along the floor.

The last thing Joseph saw before the back door swung shut was Old John standing alone at the end of the bar, waving his check lazily through the air, hoping to catch someone's attention.

Dusty cases of beer lined the walls and one caged light bulb was centered in the ceiling. The boy was released, dropped to the floor in the middle of the room. A bit of blood dripped from his nose and his tongue absently licked it away.

Another man walked in and shut the door. Joseph noticed it was the same cop who had caught Old John with the shopping cart of power tools. Frank the Cop. The boy could hear Bobbi repeating his name in a sing-song voice. He waited for the cop to recognize him and then drag him to a cell because Joseph had been warned. He expected he and John would both be arrested for stealing the tools John once had and the liquor Joseph almost got away with.

"What do you got here?" The cop's voice sounded only halfway interested. Joseph rubbed his hand over his head and figured that the cop didn't recognize him without the long hair.

The cop asked the Indian if he wanted to press charges. The answer was no and Joseph was relieved. At least he wasn't going to sleep in a jail cell. All the Indian wanted was money to pay for the three bottles of Mad Dog.

"Only one broke," Joseph protested.

Frank the cop told Joseph to shut up. The Indian wrinkled his forehead as he figured out what the total would be. The final amount was eight seventy-five.

Joseph groaned and thought about telling the men he was broke. They had already beat him and there was a cop sitting right there. It would have been no problem to turn out his pockets and take the money and Joseph decided against the lie.

He dumped his money out onto the table and watched the Indian expertly sift through it, leaving only three dollars and twenty-five cents in change. His face grew warm and he tried to blink back the redness in his eyes.

"See, we're honest here," the cop said. "We could have taken it all."

And the Indian added, "You have all this money and you steal from me?" He folded the bills and tucked them away. "What is wrong with you?"

Joseph put what was left of his money back in his pockets and refused to let tears collect in his eyes. He had been robbed. And he swore to himself that he would not cry. The men stood him up and shuffled him back through the bar where everyone got one more look at him. The front door was held open and Joseph was shoved from behind, jarring the tears loose and finally sending them rolling down his cheeks. The Indian yelled, warning the boy to never set foot in the store again. The door shut and the men stepped away from the dark glass and beer advertisements.

Old John was standing against the wall, next to a life-size poster of a model selling beer in a bathing suit. For just half a second it looked like the model was alive and her arm was reaching across Old John's shoulders, holding the little man tight to her side. His landlord's rent check still dangled from his fingers. The envelope that had before been so delicate was now wet and dirty from the day's travels.

"What happened?" John asked as the model flattened herself to the wall and became a piece of cardboard again.

"Nothing." Joseph paused a second and asked, "did you get anything?"

"No, I couldn't cash my check."

"You didn't take anything?"

"No." John shook his head. "There were too many people."

A throbbing ache persisted in Joseph's head. When he coughed the pain was sharp and he could taste vomit creeping up past the bottom of his throat. He thought that maybe he had a concussion. Maybe he had a fractured skull. A doctor should look at an X-ray or something. Maybe his brain had somehow changed shape, shifted around in his head. Tenderly, Joseph moved his fingers across the nerves on the crown of his skull, feeling around for a telling sign.

Joseph leaned back and rested in the doorway of the Rainbow Roller Rink. Boards covered the broken windows at his back. The walls, which had been painted in wide vertical stripes, were now washed down to mint pastels. Graffiti ran waist-high all around the building. The colors of the walls made him sick.

He stirred around for a position where his head did not hurt. Any quick movement rushed blood through his brain. First there were a few seconds of blackness; then, after the little blue and white points of light shifted through the dark, the daylight appeared again. Joseph had received a solid kick to the head when he was on the floor of the liquor store. The lightheadedness almost felt good, like when he had inhaled from McKnuckle's toluene rag. The high disappeared after a few heartbeats and was replaced with an incredible hangover.

He wished that John, who had gone back to his room, had helped him in the liquor store. Joseph vowed to stay out of liquor stores.

His money was almost gone again. And earlier Old John had chosen to return the rent check to his landlord's mailbox. "No good," he had decided. "This isn't real money. Some days I can find nothing any good."

The Open Sky

The temperature grew warmer and Joseph worked back into his regular routine of sleeping in the Racine Gardens under the watch of the nursing home and hastily washing up at the coffee shop in the early morning. Leaving the rest of the day open. On a Monday the idea struck him that he should make himself as presentable as possible. The narrow path he had been walking seemed to open wider. He had not seen Sonny or the Mayor or anyone who knew him. If he saw no one who knew what he was or thought they knew what he was, then the definition of himself was safely up to him.

Joseph didn't know what he was, but he knew what he didn't want to be. That was a great help. And he felt that the days coming might hold something new.

Joseph didn't know what would make a difference, so he wanted to be ready for anything. He took his time in the bathroom that day, eventually emptying the paper towel rack while ignoring the impatient pounding outside the door. He slipped inside a pair of clean pants and pulled a new Salvation Army t-shirt over his head. With a bundle of dirty clothes under his arm, he stepped out of the toilet, past the curses of a squirming man, and headed toward the El.

"Gonna rain like a motherfucker," Joseph had heard someone in the restaurant predict.

The dull gray buildings and fire escapes flew along beneath the scratched window at Joseph's side. His bony profile sometimes appeared thinly and then flashed away. He looked better than he had before. And when his image did not return in the glass, he watched the scenery. Car lots with colored banners, abandoned billboards, spray-paint murals, all rolled by as if they were waving to the boy. He felt good. A sign for a Chinese restaurant, a tavern, a grocery store. Joseph watched the little neighborhoods change under the wheels of the train. For no reason at all, he felt like cheering.

As the train started moving away from the Addison platform, an odd motion at the other end of the car caught everyone's attention. Some were stealing glances and others were staring outright at a man whose body spilled over itself in tremendous folds. He was working his way across the car in an incredibly slow process of twisting between the seats, stepping sideways with one leg, inhaling, bringing the other leg after, and exhaling. Between each row he had to pause and take a full breath. People were ducking and leaning out of the path as the man's midsection, almost of its own accord, disrupted hats and bumped shoulders and pulled purses to the floor. Joseph heard a woman at his side tell someone else, "It's what's called morbidly obese. That's the medical term." And the man kept coming like a natural force until finally he reached the seat Joseph had been previously sharing with no one at all. The fat man rotated and grunted and lowered himself down before Joseph had a chance to move. The boy's good spirits were crushed as if they had been sat upon.

He could hear people across the train car, snickering in safety; as much as he tried to shift or twist himself, leaning forward or back, there was still no room for him anywhere near the man. Somehow he was expanding, pouring slowly over onto Joseph's lap. Joseph scanned the aisles and found no other available seats. Joseph immediately decided that the day had been lost.

Across the aisle was a girl watching Joseph squirm. She halfway smiled and Joseph didn't know if it was a sign of sympathy, or if she was just entertained. The seat beside her emptied at the following El stop.

Joseph took in her features as the fat man groaned under his breath. He studied her angular face and sharp cheekbones every time he felt her turn away. She had dark eyes surrounded by porcelain skin smeared with charcoal powder. Her nose was bent slightly to one side and her hair was cut like a boy's, brushed back in soft spikes on top of her head and grown down to her collar at the back of her neck. Her lips were as pale as her eyes were dark and it was a beautifully crooked face.

Joseph tried to find something that he could casually mention to the girl and found his chances slipping away as his mind went blank. He glanced at her, caught her eyes leveled at his own. She had been watching him and Joseph shrugged his shoulders in response to being caught. She looked Joseph over and then turned away to study everyone else on the train.

She caught strangers checking her out, challenged them to turn their eyes away. But here eyes switched back to Joseph, and now her expression seemed open, as if she was waiting for him to speak. Joseph squirmed in his seat and she smiled without parting her lips. She nodded her head to the side, discreetly telling Joseph that he could sit next to her.

A long minute passed and Joseph could feel the body heat pouring from the fat man. "Why don't you sit over here?" the girl finally asked, posing the first question as more of a rude comment. "What? Are you pinned in there?" Now she was grinning at Joseph, who was scared to respond. "Can you feel your legs? Blink if you can hear me."

He squeezed out of the seat, out from under the weight of the overlapping thigh and back, and dropped himself next to the girl. Smiling because he felt, for once, that he was in on the joke and not on the receiving end.

"That's disgusting," she said. "How do you let yourself get like that?"

For a moment, Joseph thought the girl was talking about him and the state of his own clothes. He began to apologize and the girl laughed. "Not you, him." She nodded across the aisle to the fat man who was sweating through his shirt.

"Mudslide," Joseph whispered, wanting to add his bit into the conversation. It felt good to gang up on someone else.

The girl laughed and said aloud, "Fucking mudslide. He probably has an oral fixation from his mother breastfeeding him for too long."

"Probably." Joseph agreed without knowing what she was talking about.

The girl laughed and Joseph felt as if he had an invitation to enter a room that had previously been locked. The day had been resuscitated.

"What happened to your face?"

"I got into a fight."

"Did you win?"

"Not really."

"That's okay. I like black eyes. You look fine with one."

She was as bony and thin as Joseph. She was older by maybe a few years. Joseph tried to guess her age, but he couldn't find any numbers that seemed to fit. And the girl was left drifting for the moment, somewhere between numbers.

"Where you going?" she asked.

"Nowhere really. Just riding around."

"Nothing to do, huh?"

"No, nothing."

She nodded. The sides had been drawn and the morbidly obese man was ignoring everything. Joseph hoped the girl didn't get off the train soon; he wanted this to last for a while. He felt that he had been taken as an ally for the duration of the train ride.

A man wearing a knee brace appeared at the far end of the car and began asking passengers for spare change while explaining his problem. Any donations were to help pay for an operation, it was an injury that had ruined his life, he lost his job and his home and his wife. It was a curse that the man hoped no one else would ever have to suffer. Also, his sister was sick and his mother had to take care of her. Afflictions piled up as the man moved across the car. Behind the Lawrence Avenue El station Joseph had watched the same man pull the brace from a paper bag, wrap it around his leg, and test it with several limping steps before jumping the turnstile. That was when he began holding his cane as if he really needed it.

Both Joseph and the girl had no change, and when the man was within earshot she said to Joseph, "He ain't hurt. Look at him. He's got the cast on wrong and he's got the cane in the wrong fucking hand." She raised her voice. "Why don't you give it up? No one believes you."

The man stopped and turned on his cane. "If I wasn't so busted up, I'd kick your ass, girl." He began hobbling toward the next car.

"If he was busted up at all, he would kick my ass," the girl informed Joseph.

The injured man spun back. "I ought to shoot your ass, bitch."

"Fuck you. You couldn't shoot your own ass."

In disgust, the man waved his hand and moved on. Joseph decided that he liked this girl.

He tried to think of a way to continue the conversation as he followed her down the red metal stairs of the El station, through the turnstile, and out into the street.

Before he had a chance to say anything, she turned and anticipated his first question. "I gotta go to work," and then the obvious ones following. "Around the corner. Used clothing store. A lot of combat boots and stuff."

Joseph casually mentioned that he could use some boots and maybe a new shirt and he might come into the store sometime.

His confidence drifted when he saw the girl checking out his shoes. He had become used to standing in puddles and washing his feet in sinks and sleeping with his shoes on. They were falling apart. The cloth had rotted, one sole flapped loosely and some of the stitching was unraveling.

"That fat dude really crushed you, didn't he?" She changed the subject after an awkward pause.

"I'm okay." Joseph was relieved when he saw her smile. It was inviting, the first smile Joseph had seen in a while that wasn't making him the object of its amusement. He thought that maybe the girl hadn't noticed his shoes.

"Yeah, you ought to come in. I could buy something for you, I get a good discount. You just pay me first."

"I don't want you to buy anything for me."

"I wasn't gonna. I said you'd have to pay me first and then I buy whatever."

Joseph couldn't be sure how that would work out, but he agreed that he would come back later in the day.

"My name's Amanda," the girl said before stepping into a easy jog. The store was right across the street, inside a heavy-looking stone building with tiny windows and a glass door covered from the inside with a confederate flag. She disappeared behind the glass door and Joseph made a mental note of the address.

Joseph wasted time walking in circles through the unfamiliar neighborhood. Clouds had darkened and slowly crept over the street. Wind kicked up as soon as the last bit of sunlight had dimmed. "It looks like it could rain just like a motherfucker," Joseph repeated the prediction he heard before to a couple cracking their umbrellas open over the sidewalk.

In front of a doughnut shop Joseph found kids his own age begging change while wandering the parking lot. Some were squatting along the curbs and others were standing around a bank of pay phones. The counter of the doughnut shop was crowded with the same people. Joseph watched as the groups mingled and rotated from one spot to the next. They drifted along the sidewalk like garishly decorated pigeons. Black leather jackets painted over in band names, slogans, death-head symbols. Cut-off jeans and torn fishnet stockings. Shaved heads with dyed mohawks, white-face powder and black raccoon eyes. Piercings and tattoos. Joseph couldn't imagine anyone walking around like that all day. He wondered how they got the money for these things if all they did was bum change.

Joseph crossed the street and tried his weather report on a few of them. A girl who looked about twelve years old replied, "Fuck off, poser."

It was apparently a closed group. They had made their own community and separated themselves from the outside world. Joseph went back across the street with his mood undamaged.

For a while he watched these kids as if he were a seasoned veteran of begging. He told himself that they were doing it all wrong. They were too young to act threatening and they didn't look crazy enough to scare money out of anyone. Joseph wanted to laugh when he saw the same little girl who had called him a poser spit at the feet of a woman who had no change to throw away.

The block was crowded with signs, new shops, brightly-painted brick walls, professional graffiti, sex stores with mannequins in bondage, expensive restaurants, candy stores, coffee shops with foreign names. Signs for runaway shelters were pasted on every other lamppost.

Joseph wasn't sure if he felt a few raindrops land on his neck. In a window he checked his slightly bruised face, which Amanda had said she liked.

He walked up Clark Street to Wrigley Field and was surprised at how big it was. He had never seen it before except on television. The surrounding parking lots were filled to capacity and people were rushing into the gates. Obvious tourists wearing Cubs t-shirts and carrying little stick banners were hoping to catch a few innings before the next rainstorm. Souvenir vendors carried racks of peanuts and cotton candy above the crowds. Raindrops had already marked dirty windshields throughout the parking lots.

After he asked two families for some spare change and received a dollar from each, three cops walked up behind Joseph and told him to move on. If they saw him again near the park, Joseph was told, they would take him in.

He left and the rain broke while the national anthem played. He spent the two dollars on a cup of coffee and a place to sit and rest. He checked himself again in a bathroom mirror and found that he didn't look bad at all.

Before dark, all of the seats were removed from the counter of the doughnut shop. The booths were sectioned off with rope and no one was allowed to sit inside the shop. At night, it was carry-out only. The punk kids didn't leave the parking lot. They appeared safe in such a large crowd and Joseph admired them for that. He wished he were part of a group.

The store where Amanda worked was filled with a drifting mixture of flowery incense and leather oil. One wall was completely covered with shelves of shiny boots and another had nothing but black leather jackets. There was a mannequin wearing silver-studded cowboy chaps and a gas mask. Racks of lingerie hung in the middle of the room. Joseph looked at a few of the prices and knew it wouldn't be possible to buy anything in the store. It was a thrift store only in name.

Joseph waved to Amanda and tried to smile. He hoped she didn't see his face when he finally found a price tag.

"You gonna buy some boots?" Amanda stepped out from behind the counter and slid closer to Joseph. He wondered if she was being kind, or if she really couldn't see that he had no money.

"Nah, not today," he answered as if he had decided right there. Then they stood uncomfortably. Joseph shifted his weight from one foot to the other. He could hear rainwater squeaking inside his left shoe.

Amanda lowered her voice and asked Joseph what his name was. She was embarrassed that she hadn't asked earlier.

He gave his name and Amanda said she would get off work in a few minutes. She asked Joseph, making sure to use his name, if he wanted to go get a beer.

"I don't know," Joseph said, imagining that she would want to go to some nice place, where his age would be noticed and he would be immediately bounced out the door. "I don't have much money on me. A little short." Joseph hated to admit it.

Amanda said that it was no problem. She would buy.

Joseph looked at the clock on the wall like he had somewhere to go, then he said okay. He didn't even see what time it was.

Floating in the dark of the tavern was a cigarette machine, video poker, a jukebox, and a Love Meter that looked like a neon doctor's scale. The walls were gray and sparsely decorated with worn beer posters. Joseph and Amanda sat at an unsteady table in the corner of the room. A heavy blonde woman was working behind the bar. The television in the corner broadcast a lackluster baseball game. Two men sat at the bar. They were not speaking and did not seem to notice anything around them.

"I wasn't really gonna buy shoes for you," Amanda admitted. "I was only gonna take them from the shelf and take your money."

"You still want to do that?" Joseph didn't get the point.

"No, that's all right. If you need them, I could charge you something. But not full price."

"Maybe later."

"You know what you're like?" Amanda asked Joseph after they each had finished three beers and were bobbing slightly at the table. "You're like, like, you are one of these people that really has their shit together. I can tell. I mean it's not like the way other people, them, how they got their shit together. With money and health insurance, you know. There's something very solid about you. Don't take this wrong."

"I won't," Joseph interrupted.

"But you know what you want, I think. You don't care much about your looks, you stay pretty quiet. Yeah, there's something very concrete. You look like you can act like an old man, and that's not a bad thing. Do you know a lot of old guys?"

"Nah."

Amanda's earlier cockiness had somehow dissolved into a stuttering hesitance. "You look like you've done a lot, I mean."

Joseph felt like he hadn't done anything at all in his life and he thanked Amanda for what he took as a compliment. She smiled at him and began talking about people Joseph understood were famous but didn't otherwise recognize. Amanda quoted books and movies and went on and on and the bartender kept bringing beers to the table while Amanda skipped from one subject to another.

Joseph felt himself grinning. It was genuine and strong and his whole body felt lighter. He wanted to wrap his arms around Amanda. He was close to laughing, but fought it down so as not to offend her. He couldn't remember what she had been talking about, and maybe it was nothing to laugh at.

The street tilted and swerved drunkenly. Joseph didn't remember walking outside. Amanda was still there with him, and he felt her arm bracing his back. She kissed his neck sloppily. Joseph laughed, wiping the saliva away. Cars blurred through yellow lights. Joseph saw the punk kids watching him. The sign changed, told them to walk. Joseph could feel Amanda's fingertips pressing at the small of his back, leading him somewhere.

For Joseph everything had changed. He had forgotten all that had passed. He didn't consider the possibility of his memory ever returning.

Amanda walked Joseph through the alleyway beneath the elevated train tracks. They kept going until they were far under the metal I-beams where weeds grew from gravel and the brick walls leaned closer. No windows faced them and no light reached them. The trains running overhead sent blue sparks down from the tracks. Joseph saw them falling far behind Amanda's shoulders.

He waited for Amanda to lead him, to tell him what to do, since he was not at all comfortable or experienced. This didn't feel like the other times. They fumbled and tripped and gracelessly fell into each other. He waited for her to unbutton her pants and she unexpectedly laughed about something. He couldn't see her in the dark. He kissed her teeth. There were voices yelling from the lit street and Joseph didn't know if the voices were for him and Amanda.

She whispered to ignore the people out there. She leaned Joseph against the wall and slid down his body until her knees touched the gravel lightly. She tugged his zipper down. A minute later she placed Joseph's hands on her throat and let him guide her.

Then came back up and kissed Joseph, slipping her tongue in his mouth. He groped at her until she said it was time to go. He didn't understand why he couldn't touch her, but he never asked anything. He was elated.

They walked the long alley back to the street. Joseph and Amanda made plans to see each other again, neither giving out a phone number or an address. He knew where to find her. He was certain that she would be there the next time he appeared.

Back on the train he counted what was left of his money. Almost two dollars. Now he was drunk and hungry. At a liquor store on Argyle Street he bought a fifty-cent loaf of pasty white bread and took it back to the garden.

The skies began to clear and Joseph laid back and watched the pale clouds drift apart, revealing the sharp black sky as a wide and liquid dome rolling over the rooftops. He could tell that the clouds were moving away, even with his eyes shut. A clear sky smelled different from a cloudy sky. Especially at night. The smell of the wet grass made Joseph feel that he was in a bigger place than he actually was. He could keep his eyes shut and imagine an open field, a farm, with nothing in his sight but the horizon.

He chewed on the soft bread and thought about Amanda. He thought of the girl in Rogers Park. He couldn't figure out what was so different. Joseph had felt young when he was talking to that girl, separated from something inside himself. With the girl in Rogers Park Joseph found quickly that he had been used, more so than he had used the girl.

It didn't feel so bad anymore. Now he had been with Amanda and no one had been used. It was as if they had made room for each other. That was how it felt to Joseph. He wondered if that was how it felt for Amanda.

Joseph thought of the punk kids at the doughnut shop. They had no room for others. They had divided the world as if all were in neat uniforms that declared undying loyalty. It was them against everyone else. Joseph didn't like being considered a part of the everyone else, even if he didn't want to be a part of the group that was excluding the others. He wanted to be hidden inside a group of people. Even if it was just a group made of two. The world was divided a hundred different ways.

Lines that criss-crossed the whole map designated who belonged in what place and who would have the ability to cross the lines. Joseph felt that everyone kept their lives inside the boundaries and passed the days with their eyes closed to everything but their own interests. Nothing else from the outside world mattered. It wasn't even real.

Joseph had the vague feeling that the distinctions had to do with money. Not actual currency, but some kind of denomination that seemed to be ingrained in people, that worked to separate them.

A stroke of luck and grace had carried him over one of the lines for a couple of hours. Something good had happened during the night. His world had parted open like the sky. He knew where he belonged only because he knew where he did not belong and his concerns had stretched the tiniest bit. He felt bigger because of the change.

Joseph shut his eyes again when he finished eating and he tried to picture the wide field of wet grass. And then he tried to picture Amanda's face. Slowly each feature and blemish came back to him, sharp and clear. He saw the squint of her eyes right before he kissed her teeth.

Initiate

It couldn't hurt to try, Joseph told himself as he watched a man unloading an air-brushed van in front of a tiny liquor store. A small, hand-painted sign that only said LIQUORS hung over a dark picture window protected by an accordion gate. Joseph had walked past a hundred times before without ever noticing the storefront wedged between a taco stand and a barber shop.

The man circling from the van to the front door had an egg-shaped body, fat grown without any discernible gut or hips. Just an expanding waist circled by a long leather belt. A square jaw protruded from a turkey neck and a pair of thick glasses covered dark, little eyes. The man didn't appear capable of lifting one case of beer, much less the three he grabbed in one stack and carried effortlessly to the door. As he headed toward the door he saw the skinny, red-headed boy walking in his direction.

"Excuse me, sir, but do you have any work you might possibly need done, maybe?" Joseph's voice was quiet and pleading. He tried to make it sound strong at the same time. He wasn't sure how it came out.

The man squinted one eye and aimed the other at Joseph, like a carnival psychic trying to guess someone's weight and age. "Maybe." Then he nodded toward his van filled with cardboard boxes and cases of beer and said, "Grab a box and follow me. We'll talk about some work. Some things I might need done in the store. I own the place in case you don't know."

The man kept silent until the van was empty. Joseph caught glimpses of the liquor store as he shuttled back and forth. The shelves were filled with junk food, toilet paper, canned goods, and liquor. Mostly liquor. Bottles of Mad Dog, forty-ouncers, and wine were kept in dusty glass refrigerators. All the little bottles were behind the counter. The larger bottles, the ones that wouldn't easily fit under a shirt, were left out on the open shelves. Everything but the alcohol looked like it was covered with a thin layer of dust practically unmolested by fingerprints.

Neither Joseph or the owner spoke until the van was emptied. "C'mon in," the man finally said.

From behind the front counter the owner pulled a strip of lottery tickets from a roll hanging over his head and began scratching at the silver coating with the grooved edge of a dime. Joseph waited for a decision.

"Shit, nothing." The owner threw the tickets to the ground. "Okay, kid. This was just a tryout. I got nothing else for you today. We'll see how you do. Come back tomorrow and if it works out, who knows.

"One thing, no fucking thievery. I catch you stealing anything, that's it. Not even a pack of gum. Understand?"

"Yes, sir." Joseph didn't know what else to say. He didn't think the man knew what had happened at the last liquor store; he was just being careful.

The idea of working for a straight pay instead of shoplifting and begging for spare change was a relief that hadn't yet settled in Joseph's mind. He had never really made any kind of plans. He knew that eventually he would have to get a job. But he hadn't thought about what kind or when. Now he felt a wave of pride swirling in his chest. What Joseph wanted most was to look like what he considered a regular person. Only for Amanda. He wanted to be able to tell her that he did have a job. Maybe later he would be able to tell her that he actually stayed somewhere and had a bed.

"My name is Bates." The owner held his hand over the counter. Joseph shook it, felt his own knuckles crushed inside the grip. "What's yours?"

"Joseph."

"Joseph what?"

"Joseph Askew."

"How old are you?"

"Twenty-one."

"Bullshit."

"Eighteen."

"Okay, kid. Don't lie to me, and don't worry about it. Show up here at nine, tomorrow. Can you do that?"

Joseph said that he could. It would be no problem.

"Good, go set your little alarm clock." Bates took a ten from a roll of bills in his pocket. "This is for today."

"Thanks. Do I have to wear a uniform or anything?"

"Uniform? Fuck no. And don't thank me. I'm not handing out money. You're working."

Bates took another strip of lottery tickets from the roll over the cigarette rack. And Joseph heard another losing curse as the glass door swung shut.

Walking down Broadway he wondered about the last thing Bates said. He wondered if the fat man had seen Joseph before on the street. He didn't know if it would make a difference. He tried to convince himself that he didn't care if Bates had seen him begging once or twice before.

Old John was sitting in the garden where Joseph slept, watching the cars trail along Wilson Avenue. He straightened his back when he saw Joseph hook a leg over the fence and drop down to the grass.

"They took it," John began muttering over and over. "They took it."

"Who took what, John?"

"They took my check. My rent check. My rent is important, right?"

Joseph nodded and agreed that the rent check was important, but he still didn't know who took it.

John whispered, "The niggers. They took my check." Then John pointed to a lumped bruise above one ear. "They gave me this." Tears were in John's eyes and his jaw was quivering. The old man shook his head, telling himself that he should have known better. "They said they would cash it for me. We were in the alley, over there, and I told them no. No. I told them again and then they just grabbed it. There were three of them. Nothing I could do."

John was ashamed of himself for being taken again. He couldn't understand why this always happened to him. He had lived on the streets for a long time. Longer than anyone else he knew. He cried that he had never hurt anyone. It wasn't fair because he was old and small and all he had was his cat and the two girls who sometimes lived with him. John wiped his face and blew his nose into a dirty handkerchief. He sat at the edge of the garden for what felt like a long time. Finally Joseph broke the sniffling silence and told John his good news.

"I got a job." He was going to wait for the congratulations and then tell John about Amanda.

John squinted as the words and their meaning sunk in. Then he shook his head sadly again. "Uh-uh. Not me. Never get another job. Now what are you going to do all day? Work?" He clucked his tongue three times, telling how ashamed he was of his new friend.

Soberly, the old man stood up and walked away with an irate dignity that Joseph didn't understand.

It was only dumb luck and an early morning rain that woke Joseph in time for his first day of work. At the coffee shop he locked himself in the bathroom and dressed down to his underwear. He scrubbed himself clean as possible with cold water, got back inside the same clothes, and then stepped outside for a cup of watery coffee.

Joseph followed Bates around the store as he turned on the fluorescent bar lights and quickly checked the stock. Beneath the cigarette rack and the lottery ticket dispenser Bates counted the day's starting cash close to his chest. He kept the bundle from Joseph's sight and then hid it away in the register. Two lottery tickets were taken and scratched away.

And when the first chores of opening for business were finished, Joseph stood next to the front counter and began his lessons.

The end of each week and the beginning of every month was always the best business. That was when everybody had their money, welfare, aid, food stamps, WIC, and pay checks. And at the register nothing was accepted but cash. Joseph was told to not let anyone cheat him, but not how he was supposed to know if anyone was cheating him.

Bates described the people Joseph had to keep an eye out for. "Niggers, spics, and Indians. Eastern and American. And the thieves and beggars are always trying to con something out me. Either a few pennies or a case of beer. It's a point of pride with them. They can't leave until they get something for free." Bates added, "Yeah, and the street crazies. Watch for them. Some you can't even tell by looking at first. But I get the lunatics coming in here like there's a neon sign flashing over the door, saying 'C'mon in, psycho.'"

The little bells over the door rang tunelessly to announce the entrance of every customer. Some only wanted to talk, inform Bates of all their problems and complaints. Conspiracy theories and marital difficulties were shared freely. Some were just desperate drinkers who wanted to bargain down the prices. "Ain't a flea market," was the standard answer for them.

Joseph studied several who came in early for a pack of cigarettes, a bag of chips, or a pint of something. He saw nothing suspicious.

Bates talked and joked with most of the customers. He knew a lot of their names, he knew about their jobs, wives, friends. Loyal and frequent patrons didn't earn any special treatment. Bates insulted most with imitations of their ethnic backgrounds or plain racial slurs. They either ignored him or didn't care. Bates' liquor store was the last resort for most of them. It was the cheapest and the crappiest of all the liquor stores along Broadway.

"My wife, the bitch, is in the hospital again," one man confided to Joseph early in the day. "It used to be that it wasn't too bad. Maybe once or twice a year, but now it's every month. The doctor said she's a manic depressive. I'm gonna bring her some smokes and her vodka. I hope she's not fucking all the other nuts in there." The man shook his head and began telling the same story to Bates without waiting for a response from Joseph. Bates later introduced the boy to Mitch Koe, one of the regulars. Mrs. Koe was the one in the hospital. Mitch was a good customer, not a nut, Bates had to explain.

Customers came and went. Bates watched talk shows on television and sent Joseph out to pick up burritos for lunch. "You fly, I buy."

The Greek, who Joseph quickly realized was another frequent visitor, informed Bates of the city's plan, led by Mayor Daley's suggestion, to take away the Greek's cats. "They're gonna tax 'em. The city wants a cat tax. If Daley wants thirteen bucks for every cat I got, he could bring his fucking ass up to my place and look for them. Let's see him do that. Like I'm gonna really tell him the truth. Fucking Daley. If his name wasn't Daley, he'd be a bartender. Not even that. He'd be selling beer at Cominsky Park. I think the cat tax is supposed to help pay for the schools. Good luck."

The day went by, Bates complained about niggers and spics and Indians continuously, but treated them respectfully if they bought something and didn't cause any problems. Bates warned Joseph repeatedly that he had to watch everybody who walked through the door. Joseph said he would do exactly that. He was waiting to see someone who was obviously out of their mind. In the liquor store, Joseph assumed that no one like that could threaten him. Under the counter he saw a thirty-eight sitting in its holster next to a baseball bat and a can of mace, but Bates never left the gun unattended.

"I been to Mars," one potential customer finally assured Joseph in a calm whisper after Bates had momentarily slipped into the storeroom. "I went with my mother. It's just like this planet. Looks exactly the same." He gave Joseph an affirmative wink, shot a free throw over the cigarette rack with an imaginary basketball and then left. The little bells barely rang.

Joseph told Bates about the one he missed. "Him? He's a fucking nut," Bates knew. "I ought to kick his ass."

Stock rotated from the shelves to the storeroom and the storeroom to the shelves. Other than alcohol, nothing new came into the store. Expiration dates on cartons of juice and cases of Pop-Tarts had long been passed. Several cans of spinach looked slightly beaten. Joseph brought them to the back room along with some cans that had no labels at all.

Bates said to put them in the surprise box where the other unlabeled cans were stored. He considered someday making them sale items.

Bates stuck the day's pay into Joseph's palm after the street darkened. Joseph compared the light inside and outside the picture window. It was warm and comfortable in the store and Joseph didn't want to leave. "Why don't you get some dinner," Bates suggested. "You gotta be hungry. Go home."

Joseph said goodnight and pocketed the money. He debated asking for permission to sleep in the back room. But after hearing Bates rant all day about every kind of person in the neighborhood, he decided that he didn't want his boss knowing that he had no place to sleep. The homeless, no matter how temporary their situation, seemed to be a point of great frustration to Bates. Joseph liked the fat man, didn't want to change anything between them by sounding like he needed more than the day's pay. His wages might be cut down to nothing in return for the use of the storeroom. It wouldn't be that bad outside, Joseph thought. Not if he fell asleep quick enough.

Over the remainder of the week Joseph grew more and more comfortable with the liquor store. Regulars drifted in and out constantly. Joseph was introduced to the ones he hadn't met and was allowed to stand behind the counter as if he were almost part of the conversation.

There was Mitch Koe, Terry and Owen, the Greek, Blake, and the Printer. All half-drunk with an afternoon buzz. All at once forcing their voices over each other. They were planning their Saturday night card game. Joseph was invited. They said he could hang out and watch, have a beer with the men, if he had nothing else to do. He just couldn't play cards with them. It was a serious, ongoing contest that was not open to newcomers or children. Joseph was honored and the men rushed ahead with their conversation in which each man interrupted the others with a story that had nothing to do with the previous one.

"I once worked in this bar. It was a stage upstairs and the bar was in the basement. I was the bouncer down there. There was one fight, these two guys were just smashing bottles on the ground. Just pulling them from the garbage and smashing them. Now, I'm a nice guy. First, I asked them to stop. They started cursing me, so I took one by the arm and started leading him out when his buddy took a swing at me. I punched the guy I was holding onto and ended up fighting them both. I dragged them out of the place. I had them each in a headlock. I tore their shirts right off their bodies."

"Nothing. I know a guy who hit someone so hard, he tore their ear right off."

Joseph enjoyed being at the liquor store, being included. Having somewhere to be, at least for a couple of hours a day. He was proud of himself. He thought of Amanda and planned their next meeting. He wanted to tell the men about Amanda.

As they all talked about themselves Joseph watched the tallest one, the one the others referred to as Printer. He never spoke, just watched and listened to his friends. It seemed like he wasn't really part of their group. He was floating somewhere outside their circle. His body was even different. The other men were coarse and heavy while the Printer was pale and thin, his body swaying like a cornstalk. Maybe, Joseph thought, the man was waiting for his chance to speak. Several times he opened his mouth, but no words ever came. No one really noticed this. The Printer just kept his hands in the pockets of his thin overcoat and kept the collar pulled close to his throat as if he was hiding himself. Holding something inside. He would only slip a hand out of his pocket to fix his collar or rub his knuckles into his eyes. And Joseph watched the blue-veined hand shake violently when it rose from its hiding spot to pull at the buttons of his overcoat.

Joseph nodded to the Printer. He was trying to say that there was a connection, trying to let him know that they were both outsiders compared to the other men who were determined to prove their value with pointless bits of knowledge and self-appraising anecdotes. The Printer blinked uncontrollably in response.

At closing time the party broke up. Bates kicked everyone out and paid Joseph for the day. Joseph noticed that his money was adding up.

Inside the Army Surplus elaborate selections of belt buckles, Zippo lighters, rings, and watches were displayed beneath the gleaming glass counters. Ashtrays and cigarette cases were next to brass knuckles and butterfly knives. Everything under the glass looked dangerous and impressive. Police badges and weighted blackjacks and Chinese stars were lined up side by side. Joseph thought of arming himself. More importantly, he wanted people to know he was armed. He imagined that the indescribable, expensive stuff, spy things with secret compartments, were hidden somewhere else in the store. Kept out of the sight of regular customers. Like a watch that had a camera inside. A walking cane equipped with poison darts. Hand grenades.

Joseph spent some time admiring the store. Slick leather jackets were held to racks by large metal hoops to prevent shoplifting. There were cowboy boots and work boots and all kinds of different hats. An armed security guard stood by the front door to keep little kids from running like herds of animals through the store.

Joseph couldn't decide what he wanted to buy. He wanted to look like the people he imagined Amanda saw every day. He didn't want her to know of his real life. Joseph had never said anything about himself, but he could tell that Amanda thought he had a life just like hers. Joseph would let her believe the lie until his life caught up with it. Joseph searched the store over and over, determined to find just the right thing.

He purchased a pair of green army pants with pockets over the thighs, and a vest that the clerk said was for fishing. He explained why, but Joseph wasn't listening.

It felt good to have an armful of new clothes. Joseph decided that he would buy his weapons another time.

Saturday morning the sun was out and the sidewalks were drying. Pasteboard concert posters had peeled down in melted layers. Shadows hung in checkered patterns from the El tracks that angled over Broadway. Dealers hovered over the hoods of their custom cars. Women drank from juice bottles with Mexican labels in the warm sun. Children ran circles around their mothers toting grocery bags. Under the Argyle Street viaduct an old man was arrested for fighting drunkenly with his wife who protested the police action by throwing herself across the hood of the squad car. A day of bright weather had brought everyone outside.

At the doors of a dollar shop Joseph stood and watched a hunched woman in a plaid housecoat mopping the white tile floor diligently. Slowly she worked her way down one aisle and up the next. In her he saw his mother cleaning every inch of the apartment after a long winter that had kept them locked inside. Winters were the worst. They were cooped up. The sunlight and the breeze and the floor cleaner brought back an afternoon from the hotel. He saw his mother working a slightly damp mop across the floor, marking an even trail, into the corners and up the wall to the windowsill. As if she could not differentiate between floor and wall. Joseph could see the motion of her body and her indecision. Even with her husband out of the apartment she was flustered and scared. All the windows were left open and the apartment would slowly air itself out as the boy's mother scrubbed.

All the furniture was moved and the rugs were scoured and the walls were wiped clean and bedsheets were changed. And after every spring cleaning the boy would feel that he was in a new place for a short while. Whatever had happened while the rooms grew musty and dirty through the winter before would be gone and forgotten until the same events repeated themselves.

His parents always described their troubles as Joseph's doing. If it weren't for him, tensions wouldn't keep building to such levels, causing such explosions. All would have been peaceful and no one from the congregation would have to turn away when they saw Joseph or his mother or father.

Joseph tried to make sure he did nothing to upset the precarious balance. Even when he sat like a shadow in the apartment and there were no violent outbursts, the rooms felt the same. Like something was always just about to happen and he could change nothing.

Joseph went through the days, experimenting by not saying one single word, or by staying in his bedroom, or by hiding in another part of the hotel. But it didn't calm his father or his mother or anything that surrounded him.

Then after a long time had passed, Joseph's father became a new person. He went away for a while and came back different. It wasn't like the times he had disappeared on his own; he had been sent somewhere. No one would tell Joseph where his father went and he didn't ask. Preacher Madison came and talked to Joseph, told him that everything would be fine from that point on.

The boy's father had given up his drinking. He worked in the soup kitchen with his wife. He prayed diligently over the Bible at home and appeared at the Sunday morning services, singing monotonously and louder than anyone. Joseph still saw a flash of rage appear in his eyes at times when no one else was watching. Some uncontrollable incident could set it off and the man would have to fight his reaction down before he acted. Joseph saw that, inwardly, nothing had changed his father. It seemed as though he could only change so much and he had changed so that only other people could see. It was the same as before between Joseph's mother and father. His father learned to scream in a whisper; using his eyes. His mother hid the gripping bruises on her arms. Preacher Madison had tried to smooth everything over the best he could.

Joseph's father had realized that life outside the church would not be as easy. No safety net would be there to catch him when he fell. And it was determined, Joseph felt everyone knew, that he would fall.

Everything was now okay, Preacher Madison had said, without convincing Joseph.

No one had noticed Joseph at all. He believed that he had been separated from the rest of them. They were all healed now because Joseph's father had recited prayers as falsely as Joseph had before.

The reasons behind his zealous obedience had been killed, but he followed the same pattern of behavior because he found nothing to replace it with. He did not want to become his father, or what his father tried now to hide. Joseph wanted to have no resemblance to him or anyone else. So he kept on as the shadow in the apartment.

All along, Joseph had hoped that the apartment would change after each spring cleaning. Each season, this period of grace, of imagined pleasant conditions, became thinner. Winter months grew longer every year.

Time passed and Joseph waited, having no other choice. When he finally left, it was for himself and no one else.

Joseph was glad to be back at the liquor store when morning came. He left his new clothes in the storeroom and waited for the day's instructions.

Bates refused to close the store until every bit of the working day was past. It was possible that a customer could wander in at the last minute. "Sometime, I might show you how to work the register. I know you're not old enough, but it should be okay. I know a few of the cops around here, I'll talk to them if they ask about you. Some of these guys got little kids working the register. Five years old and shit. But that's family. That's how some of those people are." Bates paused and looked at Joseph, estimating something. "You look like you're working out, here. This should be okay."

"Yeah," Joseph agreed. He wasn't sure if he should compliment the store or maybe Bates. He wasn't sure if Bates noticed all the missing candy bars and bags of peanuts Joseph was responsible for. So he said nothing else.

"You coming to the game on Saturday night? Hang out and have some food. Saturday we're gonna play some cards," Bates reminded Joseph.

"Oh, yeah. Actually, I can't make it." Joseph was mumbling and his eyes moved around the rack of candy against the wall. "Saturday I got a date."

Bates cocked his head back to show how surprised he was with the boy. He seemed proud. Encouraged Joseph to go on.

And Joseph began talking about Amanda because he wanted to prove that he had a life, too. Just like everyone else. He kept going, as if bragging were contagious in the liquor store. He wanted to talk the same way he heard the older men talking. But all he could provide were descriptions of Amanda's face and body.

"She's hot," Joseph blurted out when he saw his audience drifting. "She sucked my dick the first night we went out."

"Good. That's fucking great. I figured you a little shy with women." Bates at first sounded genuinely happy, then went on to ask a series of more intimate questions about the girl. Asking about all sorts of positions and acts Joseph couldn't imagine. Bates wanted to know all of the kinds of things Joseph didn't know how to answer. Joseph lied through Bates' grinning interrogation. He stammered his way through until his boss was pleased. Bates slapped Joseph on the back patronizingly and went to the storeroom to turn off the lights.

Joseph was left at the counter, angry at himself and embarrassed because of everything he shouldn't have said. He felt like he had betrayed Amanda somehow. He shouldn't have told Bates anything. There was a hollow spot hanging in his chest.

The man who had gone to Mars was tapping his fingernails at the door as Bates shut off the lights. So Joseph went to the door to receive his excited message. "The CTA is building an expansion line to Mars. It's real nice, like a deluxe ride. leather seats, a bar car, a dining car." The messenger sighed, knowing there was one drawback. "Of course, you know this means the fares are going up." The he brightened again, noticing the store was dark. "I can't wait. I'm not buying anything, so I won't stay. I gotta save my money."

Joseph locked the door. He went across the room and quickly shoved a handful of candy bars down the front of his pants. Maybe there was a place the spaceman considered as another planet. Maybe the planet grew a little smaller each time the spaceman told someone about it. Maybe afterward he regretted telling people. Joseph couldn't imagine what the man thought. He turned the sign over in the window. The candy was getting crushed in his pants. Bates appeared again, went outside and locked the accordion gate before touching the day's money.

The register was old. There were no paper receipts, only the end count at closing time. Joseph watched Bates write every sale down on a scrap of paper and later write them again in a notebook.

Joseph watched the numbers as they added up. Saw the total figured under a dark black line at the bottom of the list. Bates hid the big number from Joseph, shielding the evening's profits with his fat hand.

In the garden Joseph unlaced his shoes and slipped them off of his feet. He then peeled back his socks which had hardened under his soles and stuck to his heels. Where the skin hadn't been rubbed raw, his feet were blacker than his socks and he wondered how that had happened. The toenails had turned orange and grown long and ragged.

Joseph stuffed his socks inside his shoes and slipped his shoes under his head for a pillow. Beneath the waistband of his jeans the candy bars had splintered and turned soft. Crumbs of chocolate spilled from the wrappers. Joseph ate three in a row, let the wrappers drift away, and saved the last one for the morning. The weather was crisp and dry and the breeze felt good.

Joseph barely knew Amanda. He had spent more time with Bates during the last week. It was possible that he would not see Amanda again. And if he never saw her again, what he told Bates would then be okay. Still, Joseph felt he had done something horribly wrong, and he wanted to see Amanda again.

He promised himself that he would repair the damage he had caused by telling Bates about her. He would make sure that they never met. He would treat Amanda better than she had ever been treated. That would lessen the mistake somewhat. But it would still be there. Joseph knew that these things could not be completely erased.

In the morning Joseph found that his shoes had been stolen and he hadn't stirred.

He walked barefoot to the nearest thrift store and found a pair of gym shoes that fit decently for only three dollars.

The Master Race

The back stairway was dimly lit by one light bulb hanging from the ceiling three floors above. People shoved and pushed each other as they tried to reach the alley first. Angry play. Someone screamed, fell, and forced their way back up through the descending crowd. Shadows distorted features and obscured the spaces between bodies. A plastic cup filled with beer sailed overhead and emptied against the wall. Three more cups went up into the air like graduation caps and sprayed their contents. A neighbor's bag of garbage was kicked over and spilled. Split cantaloupes were crushed to pulp and the rank smell of the rinds filled the stairwell. The party cheered and continued to tramp out into the alley.

Two boys with crew cuts were standing by the back gate of a pick-up truck. A third kept throwing rocks at a streetlight, missing each time and searching for another in the dark. All three boys wore high black boots and torn jeans held together with safety pins.

Everyone pouring out of the doorway looked basically like the first pair. They varied slightly in their combinations of blue jeans, boots, and shaved heads. The two who were already at the truck were the leaders of the group. It was known that their group was not really part of any larger, more unified organization. They were too small and too weak. They were seen as wannabes by the real orders, just a bunch of kids who liked to break windows. But they consoled themselves by saying that at least they were in charge of their own group instead of being little men who got ordered around. And they were the leaders partly because they were the loudest, partly because they were always the first to act. People automatically approached them and competed for their attention. They had that kind of leadership quality.

They planned to tell a few people what had happened and then let the story exaggerate their achievements through each retelling. Each rendition would become more dramatic. That was what made leaders. Stories that kept growing.

One voice was shushing all conversation as the crowd gathered around the truck. Several individuals made approving remarks. Most stayed silent when it was initially seen that there was a black man laid out in the bed of the pick-up.

"He was raping Tracy practically," the first said as he slapped the side of the truck. "They were hiding in the alley behind the club. We come out there and find the two of them. We were real calm at first, walked up and said what's up, but then like exploded on him. Three kicks and he didn't get up. Me and Tom got him." He patted his partner on the shoulder and told someone else to go get a blanket.

People were laughing. A few pushed closer to get a better look. One girl climbed up to a standing position on the hood of the truck. "Get your shoes off the truck. You're gonna wreck it." The girl jumped back down reluctantly.

Someone asked if Tracy really got raped. "No, but even if she wasn't, she shouldn't have been with him. They were probably gonna screw in my truck."

The story was relayed through other voices to the back of the crowd like streams of water being poured over rocks. "He was fucking begging, crying for us to stop."

"Where's Tracy?" new voices asked.

"We dropped her off. She was pissed. Said the nigger didn't grab her. Fucked up bitch didn't even know what happened until someone told her. I sent her home and told her she can hang out when she acts right."

A girl with a blanket forced her way through the crowd. Reaching the bed of the truck she squinted at the figure, trying to discern injuries, and was told not to bother. "They don't give off light like we do. They suck it up. You can't see nothing."

The girl laid the folded blanket over the young black man so that only his feet were left sticking out. "Damn," someone said and placed a tool box over the protruding ankles, but it didn't hide anything.

More details were given of their night. The crowd was laughing; momentarily they ignored the keg of beer and the tank of nitrous upstairs. Everybody watched the black man and waited for him to wake up. They wanted to see the fear of God in his eyes. They watched both ends of the alley. No one was coming. It was explained by the two in charge that the black man couldn't have been left behind when he was jumped because people knew who was out behind the club and they knew whose truck it was.

The crowd had easily worked past the possibility that something other than a rape had been prevented. Congratulations were passed forth. Someone ran upstairs to get a couple of beers.

The initial excitement had passed and the story was retold with a different emphasis. Tracy, the absent girl, was to blame.

"Is he alive?" someone asked as if they knew it was a ridiculous question but was just making conversation.

"Yeah, he's alive. If I killed him, you think I'd bring the body over for you all to see? And I didn't do nothing to him anyway. Tom did."

"The fuck you saying? You were right there with me."

The embellishments and the bragging died down to a frustrated justification. The encouragement of the previous minutes slowly withdrew and it was obvious that the responsibility wasn't going to be shared equally. No one was talking. Someone poked the black body with a fist and there was no response. "We need some music," someone else suggested before slipping upstairs.

"Is anyone upstairs?"

"Where's Amanda?"

"Fuck her."

"Yeah, fuck her."

"What are you gonna do?" A finger was pointed to the truck bed.

"Dump him somewhere."

"Shit." Someone announced their boredom.

After that made the rounds a couple of times, the conversation slowed and drifted away. Everybody avoided looking into the back of the truck. They wouldn't have admitted it, but the partygoers had become unsettled by the situation. A few had stepped away and the others had gone back upstairs. The guy hadn't moved once.

A pair of headlights swept across the alley as a car turned in from the street. In the glare of light all froze and the figures in the alley flattened momentarily to black cardboard cut-outs.

A moveable spotlight snapped on over the driver's side window as the tires cautiously rolled over gravel. Then everybody ran. Blue bar lights splashed the hanging wooden porches. The truck drove off and the others ran after, hopping fences and cutting through yards all along the block.

The cops grabbed two girls, half-drunk stragglers, who screamed and kicked as they were tucked head down into the back seat. The truck was gone. The party broke, disappeared down the side streets.

The girls told the police they didn't know whose party it was. Swore they didn't know anybody there. After an hour at the station the girls cried and hated themselves for it. A couple of names were given. Amanda's name was given even though she was only staying at the place for a short while. The girls knew who Amanda was only because everybody had been talking about her before the truck came with the black guy in the back. The girls never said anything about the pick-up truck and the police never asked about it.

The last clink of the register rang and Amanda handed a zippered moneybag to the store manager. She stepped around the counter and kissed Joseph lightly on the cheek.

The guys Amanda was temporarily living with were having a big party. She asked if Joseph wouldn't mind going.

"Sure." Joseph wondered why she was living with guys and he wondered how many guys she lived with. He never asked and Amanda made small talk along the way to the party. She was able to pry a little information away from Joseph as they walked. She now knew that he worked in a liquor store.

"That's it there," she said, pointing to a row of brightly-lit third floor windows. "These guys are decent. I'm just staying there until I find a place. I left my boyfriend a while ago. I can't tell if anyone's up there. It should be a big bash."

Inside the apartment there was no music; there were no people. The white walls were dingy and the carpet was spotted with stains. Half-empty beer cups were left all around the room. Amanda spun in a circle, checked everything out before she said, "Excuse me for a minute." She crossed the room to another door. "Make yourself at home," she called out as it swung closed behind her.

There was a keg of beer sitting in the kitchen. Joseph found a clean plastic cup and filled it. Behind the kitchen was another bare room. Television light flashed against the walls. One guy whom Joseph guessed was a little older than himself sat immobile on the couch, staring at the flickering TV screen. Three girls seemed to be circling the room, chattering and staring at the guy watching the television.

"Who let you in?" one girl with a severe lisp asked when she saw Joseph in the doorway.

"Amanda." And Joseph felt immediately that this was not the right answer. The girls had shaved heads with little bangs that hung just to their eyebrows. Joseph thought they looked silly. He was surprised that Amanda knew them. They seemed so young.

"You know anyone else here?"

Joseph shook his head.

"How long have you known her?"

"We just met a week ago."

"Don't worry," the girl told Joseph. "She didn't run out on you. She'll be right back. She's in the bedroom."

It felt like the girls were laughing at Joseph.

And he drank steadily through the next hour. No one spoke to him and no one looked at him. Invisible to the four strangers, he sat at the far end of the couch and watched sit-coms. The actors spoke strangely, in a language that sounded like a parody of normal English. The programs were senseless farces to Joseph, but he noticed that no one else in the room had any reaction to what they were watching. He sat with them and didn't take his eyes from the screen.

Preacher Madison considered television a sinful waste, a promoter of the wrong values. As a commercial started Joseph stood to go get another beer.

Later, his head was swimming and he had to concentrate to keep from throwing up. Two of the girls lay down on the floor before the television. Sounds of gunfire poured from the television. Joseph noticed a bumper sticker was pasted to the TV, right above the screen. A circle with a sloppy A inside it.

The channel was switched and a talk show returned from a commercial. Three skinheads were the guests, under their picture on the screen was the word, SKINHEADS, along with the boys' first names. They were adamantly telling the audience that blacks were lower than whites on the evolutionary scale. They said you could tell because blacks looked more like monkeys than white men. The audience groaned and complained and hissed. The skinheads didn't seem to mind, they acted as if they liked the booing.

All the evidence anyone needed was in the Bible, they asserted. It was all there, proof in black and white. Pages you could turn with your own fingers. The Bible says that blacks are less than human. Scripture says that Jesus was white and Christianity was a white religion. Everything had been justified thousands of years before and they were only spreading Christian teaching. They made a point of stating that they did not hate blacks, they only loved the white race.

The people on the TV show said that they had all been attacked and harassed by blacks and that was why they joined their group. Some of the women said they had been raped, others said they had only been mugged. The last group said they had never been bothered but they wanted to make sure that they never were. To do this, they felt they had to keep the white race pure and strong. Joseph found these people as unconvincing as the ones from the sit-com.

Later in the show a fight started and a black man from the audience knocked one of the skinny white kids to the floor. Somehow the host also got punched in the face and then the show ended.

Joseph wondered if Amanda had crawled out the window. She would have left him if she had found out what he had told Bates. He imagined her squatting on the ledge outside the window of another room, leaping to the roof of a building next door. From there she ran level with the tops of the streetlights until she climbed down the fire escape and slipped through the alley to the other end of the block. He pictured her bony legs running in shadow through the streetlights.

Joseph stood up when he saw Amanda standing in the doorway behind the television. No one else acknowledged her. They focused harder on the television screen as if they refused to see her walking into the room.

"I'm sorry. I wasn't feeling good. I'm okay, now," she said, her mouth close to his ear.

Amanda took Joseph by the wrist and led him into the kitchen. She poured herself a beer and then refilled Joseph's cup.

"Are you feeling all right?" Joseph asked, a little annoyed that he had been left alone for so long. Amanda kissed Joseph and repeated that she was fine. They drank their beers in silence and then Amanda dug through a cabinet until she found a large pitcher. She filled it under the keg's tap and led Joseph into the bedroom.

He sat on the bed and Amanda stood in front of him. He reached out for her hands, but she drew them away. She stepped back and unhooked the buckle of her belt. Twisting at the buttons of her blue jean cut-offs, she let them slide to the floor. She pulled her T-shirt over her head, snaked it away from her arms and climbed into Joseph's lap, gently pushing him back on the bed.

Joseph untangled himself from his clothes. Amanda moved slow, different from the last time. She kissed his chest, tested her teeth against his ribs, biting and tickling.

She sat upright and pressed into Joseph's hips.

She whispered for him to not do anything. "Lay there." And Joseph held his eyes shut and did what she said.

The slow-motion in which Joseph imagined he was moving ended frantically. It had barely started when he felt his spine quiver. He tried to apologize and Amanda told him to be quiet. She drew him toward her again, cradling his head against her chest. And after that she was asleep, laying on her side.

Joseph stayed awake. He ran his hand gently over Amanda's thigh, trying hard not to wake her. Her skin, pale and almost glowing in the dark, felt like it was covered with the barest traces of powder. Rolling over to one elbow, Joseph looked at Amanda. Her shoulders were delicate and thin, like they would shatter easily. Amanda leaned back into the pillows and shut her eyes.

Joseph saw dark veins spiderwebbed from the patch of black pubic hair like they were filled with ink. Joseph found the same ink inside the veins of her forearms and thought they could not be dark like that all through her body. It looked like the darkness went deep into her body, far beneath the muscles.

He imagined holding Amanda up before some kind of mirror that would allow him to see past her skin. He wondered if this was some kind of disease that could grow all the way to the end of the line and reach her heart.

The flaw didn't yet ruin the perfection Joseph thought he found. He had forgotten about waiting in the living room. He had forgotten about the unexplained roommates and the missing hour. He told himself the inked veins were a trick of the light.

The flesh of her hips and backside was marked with tiny hollows. Clustered marks pulled at her skin like a knotted thread stitched in a soft pillow. Joseph ran his hand along Amanda's back, down to the scars. The skin was smooth, Joseph couldn't feel the marks that appeared in the half-light of the bedroom.

Amanda slowly woke up and turned over like she had been asleep for days. She rubbed her face and asked Joseph what he was doing.

"Nothing."

She rolled onto her back and fell asleep again and then Joseph followed.

He jumped up to a sitting position to find Amanda sitting on the edge of the bed. She was wearing all of her clothes and the room was still dark. Amanda was whispering Joseph's name. He couldn't think of where he was.

"It's okay," Amanda said. "Relax."

Joseph looked at the posters on the walls and the dresser in the corner and remembered the evening.

Amanda told Joseph that he had to get going. She had to work early in the morning and they had to get out of the bedroom.

"Come on," Amanda was pulling him off of the bed as he grabbed for his clothes.

"How come I have to go now?"

"Because this isn't even my room. The guys are gonna kill me. We shouldn't have even been in here. They just came home."

Joseph said okay and hurried to put his clothes on.

Walking out, he saw that the apartment was now filled with people. Shaved heads and black boots. One of them was holding a sweating can of beer over his swollen eye.

"About fucking time," someone yelled as Amanda pushed Joseph out of the bedroom, through the group and into the hall.

"Ignore them," Amanda told Joseph. "I can't wait to move out of here."

"Where you gonna move?" he asked.

"I don't know." Amanda let her answer hang there.

Joseph nodded and said nothing. The waning buzz of the crowd was coming through the front door. He heard someone calling Amanda's name. Joseph waited for her to say something but she only led him down the hall. He wanted to make plans to see her again, but neither one spoke until they were far from the apartment door.

Amanda suggested that she and Joseph get together again, maybe later in the week.

"I got nothing going," he said.

"Sorry I had to kick you out like that. That's how these guys are. You'll be okay getting home, won't you?"

"Yeah, I'll be cool." Joseph didn't want to leave. He was wearing his good clothes and was still drunk.

Amanda asked Joseph if it was okay if she called him before they went out. Joseph said that would be fine, too, even though he didn't know where she could reach him. He didn't know the phone number of the liquor store.

"Listen," she leaned in to confide, "these guys are gonna give me shit tonight. Things haven't been so fucking great here. I could feel it. I have to get out soon. I don't mean to be pushy or nothing, but can I come with you?"

Joseph's mind flashed to the Racine Garden. He couldn't see Amanda lying next to him. He didn't want her to see that. Or even know about it. "I don't know," he hesitated.

"If you don't want me to come over, that's fine. Just tell me."

"No, it's not like that."

"You got a girlfriend you live with?"

Joseph swore that he didn't and he wasn't sure that Amanda believed him. She leaned against the stair railing and looked at Joseph, deciding whether he was telling the truth or not.

"Don't be embarrassed. You live with your folks or something?"

Joseph said he didn't. "I don't know where they are."

Amanda ignored the quick confession Joseph had made in order to change the subject. "Where do you live?"

"It's not that great a place. I wouldn't want you to see it, yet."

"I hope you're not saying that because you're done with me for the night. I don't want to be a sperm receptacle just for whenever you feel like it."

"No. I want to see you again. I just can't now."

"Okay then, I'll just see you later." Now Amanda sounded irritated. She kissed Joseph on the cheek, which confused him. He didn't know if she was angry or not. There wasn't any experience that he could refer to. But he suspected that she was upset.

Joseph took the stairs down two at a time. His feet landed softly on the carpet. Two floors above, he could hear Amanda knocking on the apartment door. They had locked her out. Before Joseph reached the front door she was screaming and pounding on the door. Joseph could hear laughter from the upstairs apartment.

A bank clock on Belmont flashed the time. It was four-thirty in the morning. Most of the businesses were still closed against the night, leaving a twenty-four hour doughnut shop alone to defend itself. There were people standing at the counter and Joseph could see the tired cashier trying to appease the belligerent customers and control the rowdy ones.

Standing under the lights of the train platform, Joseph still didn't understand much of what had happened that night. He wanted to ask

Amanda why she had locked herself in the bedroom for so long. He wanted to ask if her roommates were skinheads.

He fell asleep on the train and panicked when the conductor woke him up at the far north end of the line. The trees and the buildings he saw from the platform were unfamiliar. It took some time for his head to clear before he realized that all he had to do was wait for the next southbound train. Sleepy-eyed and hung over, he walked to the opposite side of the platform and waited to be taken back to Lawrence Avenue.

A faint line of rose sunlight peeked over the buildings east of Broadway. The sun was coming up from the lake and Joseph decided that sometime soon he should see what that looked like. He promised himself that he would wait for the sunrise another day. He would bring Amanda to the beach.

The Ruin of a Man

Joseph drank the lukewarm coffee down quickly and left a dollar on the counter as he stepped away, wiping his mouth with his sleeve.

"Big shot, now," the waitress sneered weakly. She was tired of the kid using the restroom as his own. She watched him walk toward the front door, unable to decide if he was strutting slightly.

Joseph did feel a little larger than usual. He decided to find Amanda when he got off work. Joseph wasn't sure what she had meant by her parting comments in the hallway. He wanted to make up for anything he might have done wrong the night before.

Joseph turned his face up to the afternoon sunlight, shut his eyes and felt the red spots growing and burning under his eyelids. After a moment of focusing on the sidewalk as his sight returned, he found Old John standing at his side, staring up at the sun with his eyes wide open.

"What'd you see? A UFO?" John asked as tears poured down his face. He smiled dizzily and blinked.

"Hey, John. Where have you been?"

John looked at Joseph and blinked half a dozen more times. He announced that he was now blind. Blind for life. "I cannot see you." The whites of John's eyes had dulled long before to a yellow tint lined with broken blood vessels, the result of too much alcohol and too little rest. John wiped at his eyes with the back of his hand. "Whoo. My eyes are crying."

Specks of tobacco stuck to John's chin. His smile revealed the rotten lower teeth which had turned black from the cigarette tobacco he chewed like sticks of gum. It appeared that John had no teeth at all on the days he could enjoy a whole pack all to himself.

"Why don't you smoke your cigarettes?"

"No. That's too bad for you." John searched the street to see if he had missed anything and then looked up at the sun to see if it had changed in the past minute. He asked Joseph, "Are you still working?"

Joseph said he was.

"Where did you get a job?" John was checking facts. Like he was working up to a running start.

"A liquor store. Up Broadway."

John's eyes lit up. "Which one?"

"John, you seen me there before. The one right next door to the barber shop. The one across from the gangbangers' park and the hotel. You go there all the time."

Old John nodded, trying to picture the liquor store in his head. It seemed to take some time for the picture to materialize. Then John turned back to Joseph and studied him. "Do you got new clothes?"

"Yeah." Joseph did. They were the clothes he bought before his date with Amanda.

"You look nice," John nodded approvingly. "You look like you go to college. You could go to the prom." He smiled and exposed his dirty teeth before he changed the subject to more serious matters. "Can you give me something if I come in to the store? I have no money. I had to take my cat to the hospital. I need some beer."

"I can't give anything away, John."

"No one will know. They won't notice."

Joseph repeated that he wasn't going to steal a bottle of beer. Sometimes it took a while to make John understand, but this time the little man immediately stopped pleading. "Then the hell with you. You're no good. I don't like you. Not anymore. What's the good of having a job, then?"

Old John stood his ground and pouted in silence. Apparently, the two of them had some pact Joseph didn't know about. Neither one of them was ever to get a job and if one did, he had to help out the other in whatever way possible, to make up for having gotten it.

Bates was drinking an imported beer behind the counter. The other five bottles were still in the six-pack. "I ain't driving today," he explained. "I don't have my car. It's okay to start with a beer."

His car was an auction-bought converted yellow cab. Rust crawled up from the wheel wells like ivy on a wall. There was no back bumper and the license plate sat safely inside the rear window. The van Joseph had first seen had already been sold for scrap.

"I let Mitch borrow the car. He had to pick up his wife from the hospital. Kid, you ever hear about his wife? He says she's a manic depressive. Once the guy called the cops on her. They came to the apartment and she went after one of them with a kitchen knife. She threw the thing and it hit one guy in the chest, handle first. The cop picked up the knife, handed it to his partner, and slugged Mitch's wife in the face. She lost two teeth. It was self-defense for the cop and resisting arrest is what she ended up with, along with assaulting a cop.

"Even though she regularly beat the hell out of him, Mitch never pressed charges against her, but the cops did. In court the judge decided she was mentally insane and put her away for a while. Mitch is getting her this afternoon. I want to hear how it goes." Bates smiled and shook his head at the episode. "What'd you do this weekend, kid?"

"Nothing much. Went to a party."

"Oh, yeah? You get laid?"

"What?"

"Get laid, have sex. Intercourse."

"Yeah. Yeah, I did." It didn't feel like an occasion to brag about. He cursed under his breath as soon as the answer left his mouth. Bates was another old man who thought he knew better what others should do with their lives.

It was a slow day in the store.

Bates related his dating history to Joseph. He was a confirmed bachelor and his reasoning was carefully thought out.

"It was a blind date or something someone set up, the bitch, she was from Winnetka or Hinsdale. I don't remember. But yeah, she was one of these suburban liberals. You know, you can't say nigger, can't say spic, can't say this or that. Defending every-fucking-body's rights. One of those weepy liberals who never saw anything in her life and still had a thousand different causes she'd support.

"I had a for-shit day when we were supposed to get together. I was working on boilers back then and I woke up that morning with a bad one, so I thought I'd make a drink, you know, hair of the dog. First thing I did was make a Bloody Mary and I think I had three before I went off to the first job. I was feeling good, no pain, I was jacked up and bouncing around. After two jobs, it was already lunchtime so we went out for a beer. Actually, I had a six-pack and didn't even eat. It was one of those days when you could tell it wasn't going to stay down. And I kept drinking so the hangover didn't hit me.

"I was swerving around after lunch. Holding onto furniture and trying to keep a straight face and shit. I was plastered. My partner was covering for me. I don't even remember the next job, I don't remember what happened. But something happened wrong with the one after that, the boiler, it blew right in my face. Whoosh. I thought my god-damned body was on fire.

"Back then I had pretty long hair, down to my shoulders. It was the style then, not like now with the shaved heads and pierced faces. And screwing was pretty nice too, no rubbers or nothing. Anyway, it was all fucking gone, my hair. Burnt off, parts were falling out in clumps. So I was done for the day and had to go get a haircut. My eyebrows and fucking eyelashes were gone. My face was burnt red like I been in the sun all day. I called the girl and tried to cancel. I never even met her before. I told her I had an accident at work, but she said that was okay because she didn't mind. Real big of her. I couldn't even drive because I was still fucking drunk. I had to one-eye it down the yellow line out to Schaumburg or wherever.

"I picked her up, told her she looked nice, all that. She told me I didn't look too bad. And we ain't even back in the city yet and she tells me that next week she's going to see 'The Wiz'. That's how long ago this was.

"She said this and I told her, 'Oh yeah.' I knew what it was. 'The shine play.'

"She looks at me like she can't believe her ears, like I admitted to some perversion. She goes apocalyptically ape-shit. Starts calling me a racist and a pig. She was screaming, demanding I let her out of the car. So I did. I dropped her off right where we were. Let her walk her ass back to Schaumburg."

Joseph nodded. He didn't really know what to say, didn't know if he should laugh along with the story or feel bad for his employer because he lost his date.

"I mean, she didn't grow up with the niggers." Bates started again. His smile disappeared and his voice sounded tight. "Me and you did. You know what it's like. She, she had all these safe little theories from her safe little suburb. You know? She never had to actually deal with the people."

"Yeah," Joseph said, hoping that the story would end soon.

Bates puffed out his chest and took a drink from his beer. "Yeah, boy. I remember when." He launched into a long line of stories about past sexual conquests. Joseph doubted most of them and wanted only to take a nap in the back room.

"But, every time," Bates drifted off to another point. "Every time I think of it, there's a bunch of guys who got their lives wrecked by a chick. They can do it, the chicks, cause they got the control. If you think about it, all guys want is to fuck. Boil it down and there's only sex. Everything else is icing on the cake.

"Any one of them, from the genius broads on down the line, have the control. The stupid ones, too. Especially the ones who act stupid but really aren't. Jesus, they can ruin a man. Because the man thinks that he's in control and he's the boss, but there'll be the day when he finds out; when he realizes that everything he has done has been for her. See, he quits his job, gets a different one, drops his friends and gets new ones, no more drugs or nothing, no weekend vacations, no ball games. He's done all that already and agrees that he can take a break for a while and then he figures it out later. Figures out that it was all for a piece of ass. And by then it's too late. Your typical set of testicles is whipped quietly and slowly."

There was an incomplete silence when Bates had finished with his lecture. It was a practiced monologue, one he had given many times before. He asked Joseph a question and Joseph didn't hear it because he was no longer listening.

"I said, so what are you planning to do?"

"When?"

"When. In your life, is when. I mean, what are you gonna do? You gonna try school? College? Vocational classes? What?"

"I don't know."

"Well, you ought to think about it. You gotta have some kind of idea for the future. You can't just cruise around all your life bouncing around from one bullshit thing to the next. Look at all the guys who come in here. They got nothing. Live from check to check, that's all."

"Sure," Joseph agreed, not wanting to talk about it.

"Well, what do you like to do besides fuck?"

"I don't know. Never thought about it."

"What did your old man do?"

"Little bits of stuff. Not much work. Some here and there." Joseph pictured his father sitting in his chair, drinking, waiting to get angry at something. Waiting to erupt, waiting for his wife to get home from work. He was angry about his life, angry that his wife had a job and some friends and he had neither. He had nothing that couldn't be taken away. And over time there was nothing he saw that he could control unless extreme behavior was exerted.

Self-perpetuating explosions seemed to fuel the man. The trigger was on the inside. Nothing his wife did ever caused this. She screamed and cried but to no effect. Bates' theory didn't fit Joseph's parents. It didn't seem like there was ever anyone in control of the apartment. The boy's parents moved through the place like tornadoes, picking up random objects and tossing them across the room. They were like dogs chasing each other's tails. There was a night when the apartment caught fire. It was only seconds before the room was blackened and burnt and then everything was soaked. The rest of the church hotel escaped the flames. Their apartment was the only one damaged. They were marked, Joseph and his mother and father. Blackened like bits of the apartment. Joseph knew that was how all the others saw them.

Joseph didn't think that his mother was the ruin of his father. There was something wrong with his father ever since the beginning, ever since Joseph could remember.

Bates told Joseph, "Well, stick with me, kid. I'll make something out of you. Get some ambition into you."

The words slowly worked their way into Joseph's head. He saw his boss' smile and didn't know if the man was trying to be friendly or not. There was some kind of insult disguised in his words. As if Bates could also see the mark that had been left on Joseph.

"What did you want to do?" Joseph asked in sudden defense. "What were your big plans when you were young?"

"I wanted to play football. I could've, too. I was picked up by a college downstate. But, you know, got a bad knee." Bates ran his palm lightly over his kneecap as if that would prove his point.

"I gotta piss," Joseph said and pointed to the back room.

"Hurry up. I got a lot for you today. Maybe I'll show you how to work the register today. Maybe."

Joseph spent the day sweeping and mopping the floors, dusting the shelves of canned foods, cleaning the fingerprints from the glass of the front counter. He rotated the stacks of beer and cases of wine and liquor, taking them down and building them again on the opposite side of the room.

Bates was working on his second six-pack when Joseph finished in the back room. "Good job, kid," he said without checking the results. Then paused thoughtfully before he asked the next question. "I don't mean to be nosy, but how do you know the Mayor? I sorta remember seeing you with him a few months ago. Something like that. I mean I just now thought of it. The picture stuck in my mind."

Joseph felt like had been punched in the stomach. He steadied himself and mumbled that he didn't know. He said that he didn't remember how he met the Mayor. A hot pin prick slowly prodded somewhere behind the muscles of his stomach. He felt it expand and hollow, drift toward his spine. Joseph knew what Bates wanted to ask. If the rumors about the Mayor were true. Even though, to Joseph, it didn't matter one way or the other. If he told the truth, it would be doubted. Bates had known all along. After a six-pack, he was able to ask.

Joseph wanted to tell Bates that he never touched the old man. He wanted to say he had never even met him. Joseph was marked just like the Mayor said he would be.

"You aren't friends with him, still?" Bates wanted to make sure. "Are you? It's okay if you are. I just didn't know."

"No, I'm not," Joseph said.

"Good." Bates cracked his knuckles one at a time. "He's a sick old dog. See, he's another one of them who never planned for his future. Just some old guy who has to live day-to-day, steal little shit when he has to. He's a con. I seen him conning these young guys out of their money. He has them stealing for him so he don't even have to do it. I guess he's got some line of bullshit going, says he's a millionaire or something."

Bates told Joseph to watch the store for a minute and wandered into the back room.

Joseph thought he knew the truth about the Mayor, but he didn't want to tell Bates about it. The Mayor was well-off, had enough to hide comfortably for the rest of his life. A voluntary exile from what he used to have. When he first appeared on Broadway he was slumming and eventually he allowed it to evolve into a permanent situation. The filth became an everyday comfortable grind. And Joseph hated the man more for having that choice. The rare coins and books that he sold off one or two at a time was just as good as a bank account, a cash machine. Joseph remembered seeing how quickly and easily the Mayor would grab a handful of coins from the kitchen closet and run out the door. There had to be much more hidden there. It was all so casual. The man never had to work, didn't have to have the boys stealing for him. He liked it. For him, it was some kind of power to have other people do his work. Degrade themselves in return for a place to sleep. Bates said it was all bullshit, but Joseph found it easier to believe the Mayor rather than Bates.

Joseph thought of the things people knew. He wanted his life to be something else. He wanted the past erased. There had to be a point where it was no longer painful. Where he could live day by day, forgetting what the previous day had built. A point where the things he had done before would be too far past him for there to be any connection.

The Printer entered the store alone, his overcoat dragging from his shoulders. Without the others from the poker game, the man seemed confident and relaxed. He had grown comfortable being alone.

Under the folds of tanned skin the Printer's eyes were a pale blue that appeared out of place among the other worn pieces that built his face. Graying cataracts would have better fit his wrinkled stance. Joseph imagined that when the Printer was younger, the delicately bright eyes had been perfect and inconspicuous.

"How are you, kid?" the Printer asked as he steadied himself at the counter. He had started drinking early in the day.

"Fine."

"Good."

The Printer and Joseph looked at each other.

"You don't talk much. You know that?" the Printer said.

"Neither do you," Joseph replied.

"That's true, I don't." It was a slow and proud admission. "The two of us will have to get together sometime and not talk."

Joseph nodded and then the Printer began to describe in detail an article he had seen in the newspaper about old coins and how the prices had shot up recently. The Printer told him that the article said there were probably a lot of people who were sitting on gold mines and didn't even know it. "Very interesting." The Printer tilted his head to one side like a dog. "We'll have to talk about it again some time." He shoved a shaky hand under Joseph's face and grinned. "Can you spare some rare change?"

The Printer's abrupt laugh spilled over into a violent cough. After it subsided to an occasional hiccup, he said he would see Joseph later. The Printer walked backwards across the room, saluted Joseph, and spun through the front door.

"Do you need anything else for the day?" Joseph asked when Bates finally emerged from the storeroom. "What about showing me the cash register?"

Bates considered it. "How about tomorrow?"

"Okay." Joseph held his hand out and waited for the day's pay.

Beery and slow, Bates took fifteen dollars out of the register.

Across the train's aisle, a black man hidden behind mirrored sunglasses unfolded a newspaper in his lap. He took three whiskey caps out of his shirt pocket and announced to the El riders that he was giving money away today. To win, all someone had to do was find the red ball. The man warmed up and moved the whiskey caps in a blur across the headlines as if he might try to trick himself.

A woman with a haggard face walked over from the other side of the car. She wanted to try. Joseph watched the red ball go under the cap. He watched the cap move around in circles and half circles, and then backtrack. It was on the left side. The woman also knew it was under the left side. The cap was lifted and the man smiled, took a new twenty from his pocket and gave it to the woman. She sat down a few seats away and watched.

A clean-cut Oriental boy wearing a gray college sweatshirt and baseball cap announced that he would play. His friends, who were dressed the same as him, stood back and cheered as the whiskey caps were casually walked in his direction. It looked like an easy way to make some cash. The red ball disappeared and the Oriental boy tried but couldn't find it again. "You were close, though," the dealer consoled.

Joseph got off at his stop as the dealer and another man were explaining to the Oriental boy that he owed them twenty bucks. Before the doors shut Joseph heard, "You don't think I'm gonna sit here and just give money away, do you?"

Joseph walked to Amanda's store. She wasn't there and the manager behind the register told Joseph that he didn't know when she would be working next. The manager said that it was against store policy to give out any employee's phone number or schedule.

Joseph had made the trip for nothing. He didn't have her phone number and didn't want to go back to the apartment where she was staying. But he felt he had to find her right that minute. Maybe she was still pissed off. She and all her friends might be sitting in the apartment, laughing at Joseph. Bates was laughing at him and the Mayor of North Broadway was laughing at him. Joseph walked out into the street thinking that he was the punchline of some elaborate joke.

At a pay phone on the corner of Grace and Broadway, Glenda the Good Witch was on the pay phone, arguing with her mother. Glenda wasn't the woman's real name, but it was what Bates called her. She was a tiny bleached blond with freckles sprayed across her face and sagging chest. Her hair was uncombed and the dark roots pushed through unevenly. Her gums were receding, leaving her teeth hanging few and far between.

She wore summer shorts and a tank top under a ratty fake fur coat. She knew that you could never be sure of the Chicago weather; besides it was her only coat. No one was certain how old she was. She looked somewhere between thirty and fifty.

At home Glenda would sing her original compositions into a portable tape recorder. She sent the tapes off to Publishers Clearinghouse every time she received one of their letters. She was despondent that the letters never mentioned her voice.

Every time she went grocery shopping she claimed that someone else's cart had hit her and threatened the sue the store. Once she even lay down in an aisle until the manager forced some brown-aproned store worker to drag her outside. In the parking lot Glenda asked the young man if he would help her move some things out of her mother's apartment. It was her most reliable pick-up line.

Some men went along with Glenda, knowing that, although the apartment was filled with two lifetimes of boxes, they wouldn't have to lift a thing. Maybe they would have to dig through a couple of boxes for some random piece of personal memorabilia before Glenda began stripping away her coat and shorts and shirt at the foot of her mattress. The boxes hadn't moved in years.

There was a group of Mexican men who took turns helping Glenda move. They laughed about it outside the liquor store. When she passed by with her shopping cart, they threatened to all come over and move her belongings. All at once. The men laughed and she threatened to cast a spell, cursing their lives. She spit at the ground at their feet and dragged along.

"Hey, cutie," she yelled to Joseph and then returned to her phone call, "One fucking minute, mother. Gawd. You know I got my own life to tend to. I can't be running around at your every command. Hold on." Glenda dropped the phone, let it swing and dangle from its cord. "Where you going? You wanna help me?"

Joseph said he couldn't help today.

"You can never help me. Do I scare you?" She smiled and tried to act demure. Joseph could faintly hear her mother screaming from the earpiece. He told her that he would see her later. He didn't call her Glenda to her face. He didn't call her anything.

"Fine. Be like that," she hissed. "Get over it." And went back to screaming at her mother.

Glenda offered Joseph a moving job every time she saw him, even when she was already walking with another man. Bates always suggested that the kid should take the opportunity. "I bet she used to really be something. She's still sorta got a cute little face. Couple of miles on it." Bates had flicked his tongue like a lizard and faked a couple of slow-motion jabs at Joseph's stomach. "Really, I'd throw her one. Maybe I'd need a few beers first." Joseph saw that Bates would have seriously considered it.

Murmur

In another liquor store the Printer was laughing with the dark-haired counter girl, both of them speaking in another language. Something the Printer said before bowing formally made the girl blush and giggle. Turning around to depart he found Joseph standing there, waiting to be seen. Both Joseph and the Printer looked out of place in the much more affluent neighborhood of Lincoln Park, with its coffee shops and clothing boutiques and bookstores and clean sidewalks, but only Joseph felt it.

"Good afternoon, kid. How are you?" The man grinned widely and his pale eyes brightened comfortingly, much more sober than the last time he had seen Joseph. Two women in neon bathing suits roller skated past the open door.

Joseph and the Printer bought a couple of beers and sat down at a park bench across the street from a block of shining high rises. More girls in pastel leotards ran along a curved path cut through the grass and some little kids were flying a kite at the far end of the park. The lake was out past the children and the red kite jerked back and forth across a clear blue sky. The runners kept a steady pace until they disappeared behind a low wall of bushes.

The Printer and Joseph talked about the liquor store and Bates and money. Joseph told the Printer that he has been sleeping in the park, in the garden on Racine.

"Oh, yes. I know of that park. It's nice."

They spoke at length of Joseph's routine before the Printer had a suggestion. In the building where the poker games took place there were abandoned apartments scattered throughout each floor. The landlord didn't keep track of vacancies; he was never there. The Printer didn't know if the building had been condemned yet, but official notices were always being posted and torn down. The Printer proposed that Joseph sneak into one of the empty apartments and claim himself a space. The plumbing might even work.

"All you have to do is slip the lock, try not to break it, and turn the knob. Very easy," the Printer said. "Why don't you come by tomorrow night? Watch the game and then later you could find a room to sleep in."

Joseph thanked the Printer and they drifted onto other subjects. For almost an hour straight the Printer lectured on Richard Nixon and how he had caused the most embarrassing moment in the country's history. The Printer supported his opinions with precise dates and minute facts. Joseph couldn't even pay attention. The words became a hum in Joseph's ear. He felt the afternoon slipping by; it was another half hour before the Printer was done. Then they shook hands and agreed to see each other in a day or so. They would find Joseph a place.

Joseph wondered why the Printer had not mentioned anything about the rare coins this time. He figured that maybe the Printer had just been drunk the day before and had brought up the subject at random. He tried not to get excited about the prospect of finding a room. He didn't know if he could believe the Printer, but he wanted to go to the building immediately and knock on doors until he found an empty apartment. He wanted to have a place to show Amanda before he went to find her.

Joseph wandered to another park, away from the lake and the crowds, and went to sleep in the shade.

Later, he found Amanda at work. He had to wait while two men in line ahead of him bought billy clubs and fake police badges. After the couple and their purchases were gone, Joseph and Amanda both apologized for their behavior at the party. Neither one was sure what the other was sorry about, but they each accepted the apologies and made plans for that night.

"We didn't do anything wrong," Amanda had said. "It was just a bad night. We shouldn't even be saying we're sorry."

Joseph was dying to say something about looking for his new place. He couldn't even stand still.

The Greek and Mitch Koe were crowding the interior of the liquor store. Bates was holding court behind the counter while Old John bounced along the outer edge of the conversation. He seemed like a mascot, tiny and shriveled compared to Bates' friends. John was wearing his new clothes. A yellow sweatshirt with a big, pink Q on the chest and a matching pair of pink pants. It looked like an outfit for an enormous four-year old.

Old John had a full pint of Irish Rose and was sharing generous sips with the Greek. The men were holding a political discussion and John couldn't keep up with the topic. He didn't care about local politics.

"You see Cardinal?" Mitch Koe asked. "She had a parade the other night. Right down Broadway. They had strings of them Chinese party lights running around each car. Then two convertibles with banners and then a bunch of pick-up trucks full of people. Cardinal was standing in the back of one of the convertibles, doing the grind to some blues shit. She was dancing because of all the money she's gonna make reelected."

"Do you call her an alderman still if she's a chick?"

"You can't call her a chick," the Greek said and took a drink from John. "That's sexist. She's penis deficient."

Bates cut in. "You see her signs all over the place for her realty group. It's nice to see the shithouses being torn down, but that's just putting people out. That's when the neighborhood gets really ugly for a while. Because then all the piss bums are out on the sidewalk. She buys up the cheap stuff and sells at double the price to fucking rich people. Young urban professionals."

"She's not doing it that much, I mean, there are whole blocks she could torch and put up shopping malls. She says she wants to make sure there are places for everybody to live. Because not everybody can afford to live like white men."

"But the thing, her parade, looked just like a party," Mitch swore. "Looked just like a wedding."

Old John was circling the conversation, trying for some kind of entry. The wine was flowing easily and he wasn't going to be kept from joining in much longer. With one finger poking at the cigarette smoke in the air, he challenged, "What was Artie Shaw's theme song? On 8th and 42nd? What was it?"

Bates acted as if he was thinking of the answer, as if it had suddenly come to him. "Was it called 'Get The Fuck Out Of My Store?'"

John laughed at this. "I like you. You're Santa Claus. You're King Kong. I don't know why I like you, but I do."

Old John had been there all day; he was beginning to irritate the men. They noticed Joseph edging his way to the counter. Bates checked his watch. "Mickey says you're early." Then he focused his attention back to Old John. "I like your shirt," Bates grinned and reached out to test the canary material between his fingers. "What's that? From your spring collection?"

"I got ten more just like this," John lied just so no one would ask why he was wearing the same clothes as the day before. "Exactly like this."

And the Greek slid back to the previous topic. "You know she owns a whole lot of stuff around here. Cardinal does, not for sure. Her name isn't on anything, but there's a murmur."

"A rumor. Not a murmur," Mitch Koe corrected the error.

"Whatever. But wouldn't you think an alderman couldn't own a realty company in her own ward? Isn't that something like a conflict of interests?"

"Just wait until all the scumbags are out on the street all night," Bates said. "We ought to rent a bus, get them all drunk, and drop them off at her place."

"You like that, John?"

John said he would enjoy that.

"Yeah," the Greek offered. "Ring the bell and run."

Amanda told Joseph that it had to be the quietest street in the city. It was a dead end where the porch lights of the three flats around the block burned dimly. Traffic bypassed the lane completely. A grade school built of pale brick was surrounded by a cement playground and rusted basketball hoops. Lights hung like a canopy over the cement playground while Joseph and Amanda hid in the dark of the steps leading to the front doors of the public school. Joseph held a forty-ounce beer in a paper bag. Amanda had a small purse over her shoulder.

They could barely see each other in the dark. Joseph drank while Amanda talked. She didn't want any of his beer, she was digging for something in her purse.

She told Joseph all about her parents and how she had successfully left home when she was sixteen. She had tried every year since she was twelve. "Except for when I was fifteen, I did it twice that year. Every time, I always chickened out and came back after a couple days or a week." Her father used to own a video store on the northwest side, over on Pulaski. He had owned a bunch of different stores, each one going out of business faster than the last.

Everything was strip malls now, she told Joseph; she had even seen a church squeezed between a hair salon and a Seven-Eleven. "It looked like a dry cleaners. It was all that kind of cheap shit that kept chasing him out of business." She spoke extensively of her father but said he really had nothing to do with her departure. She still talked to her mother every few months.

"How old are you? Can I ask?" Joseph said.

"Twenty-three."

Joseph felt that he also had to give something, so he told Amanda that he was only eighteen years old. He waited for the shock to show on Amanda's face. He waited for her to get up and walk away, but it apparently didn't matter much to Amanda.

"You sure you don't want any beer before I finish it?" Joseph moved ahead.

"No, that's cool. I got something." Amanda found what she had been looking for in her purse. "You get high?"

"Once in a while, pot or something." Joseph had only inhaled toluene and drank beer, but he didn't want to admit it. It seemed low-class, it seemed childish. "What do you got?"

"If this, if it will freak you out, I won't do it in front of you."

"What is it?" He wanted to tell Amanda that he didn't have to be sheltered.

Amanda held something up to the edge of the light. Joseph couldn't see what it was, but he said it wouldn't bother him. He knew she had something that he hadn't seen before.

Amanda turned her back to the street. A sliver of light crossed over her shoulder and Joseph saw the orange flash of a match strike. There was a tin beer cap and a needle flickering in the dark like a blimp over a klieg light. The flame went out and a needle poked deep through a ball of cotton sitting in the cap. Amanda held the needle upright as she placed the other things carefully on the pavement and unzipped her shorts with one hand.

Light fell away from her as she stepped back and wriggled her cut-off jeans down past her thighs. Rolling to one hip and looking over her shoulder, she aimed the needle at the flesh of her butt, right where Joseph had seen the scars in the bedroom light.

There was no resistance. It didn't even look like it hurt Amanda. The plunger pumped away once then went back down and the needle hung between her back and her fingertips for what seemed like a long time. Joseph watched everything. The needle balanced there, the plunger held lightly between two fingers. The syringe bridging the space with the hand and body independent of each other. Amanda's eyes could have been shut, but Joseph wasn't certain.

He searched the street for headlights or figures moving across the lawns. Still certain of the fact that no one was out there, Joseph kept looking around only because he couldn't look at Amanda. A porch light flickered and died far down the block. And when he turned back to Amanda, everything was returned to her purse and she was sitting just like before except her head was resting against the top step. A long time passed before she said anything. Joseph thought that she forgot he was sitting there.

"You don't do that, do you?"

"Never have."

"It's okay once in a while. I feel like I can do this in front of you. I get a good feeling from you. This'll work. I think we're okay tonight."

Joseph didn't know what to say. They sat leaning against each other until Amanda became a little more animated.

She told Joseph that her roommates were throwing her out. Actually they already did throw her out. Something happened the night of the party and police returned in the morning, looking for Amanda.

"What did you do?"

"Nothing. Just some bitch gave my name. Said I did something. Accused me for some shit they pulled. I always get blamed. I'm done with these people." Amanda could return to get her belongings, but she wasn't going to sleep there one more night. She didn't trust anyone in the apartment. She didn't tell Joseph what she had been accused of.

"I think I have a place we can use," Joseph offered quietly after he decided to not ask any more questions. "I'm sorta without a place, too, right now."

Amanda told Joseph that she barely had any money.

"Neither do I. I don't think this will cost anything. The building is in my neighborhood." He hesitantly told her about the Printer's suggestion and she knew exactly where the building was. Joseph tried to make the empty apartments sound as inviting as possible without even wondering why she knew of the building.

"There's a guy I know lives in there," Amanda offered. "He's the guy I get my stuff from. I don't know, it might not be a real good idea, living right there."

She seemed embarrassed about something Joseph didn't understand. He wasn't exactly sure what she was talking about. Maybe he wasn't paying attention. He figured she got the syringe from the guys she lived with. He assumed that it belonged to them. Maybe she stole it.

"I need the place," he said.

Amanda hesitated and then finally said okay. The two decided they would live together in the apartment the Printer had described. Joseph only had to find it and break in.

They spent the night on the school steps. The sky was clear and warm and the pale concrete looked rich and deep like a carpet under the streetlights.

"When did those guys let you back in that night?" Joseph felt that he could now ask.

"Pretty quick. I screamed until they did."

"Good. Then when did the cops show up?"

"The next morning."

"What'd you do?"

"I climbed out the window."

"How did you know they were looking for you?"

"I didn't, I was just a little paranoid. This shit's illegal, you know."

"Yeah." His mind had drifted to other subjects during a long silence. "Hey, what would it take to own a whole building?" he asked.

"Like a house or a skyscraper? Those are both buildings."

"Medium-size."

"I don't know. Couple hundred thousand."

"It'd be cool to own a place. Live on the top floor, rent out the rest."

"It's probably not that great. It's possible. I think it would basically pretty much suck. I think the rich suck."

Joseph took Amanda's judgment as slightly more reliable than his own. She dug her fingernails into the flesh of his hand and he knew that she didn't want to be taken so seriously.

He picked out a spot behind the school where no one would see them until the morning. They curled around each other and slept peacefully until the sound of children running through the playground woke them.

The Printer

In an apartment on the third floor the men sat around their card table. A dozen centerfolds torn out of girlie magazines had been taped to the walls. A single mattress was covered with crumpled clothes and a plastic ashtray balanced in the deep center of a pillow. The air was musty, the windows hadn't been opened in a long time.

Terry and Owen were the youngest at the table, but each was older than Joseph by at least ten years. They were partners in some kind of business, a 1-800 phone line. Terry dealt. Owen only folded through a few hands before he sneaked off to a corner, begging broke. He was the only one who appeared at the games with no money. The Greek was always there. He lived on a cop's disability pay that started coming in after he took a bullet in the neck. Bates was present every week. Sometimes there was Mitch Koe, who lived on a monthly check from his remaining one-seventeenth of an ore mine in Montana. It was the last of his family inheritance, which supported him and his wife. The Printer had been there for the last five weeks in a row. He played cautiously, making sure that he would never win or lose too much.

The Printer had told Joseph everything on the afternoon they sat together in the park.

The Printer had retired because of bad eyes. His hands shook all the time now. The only things he needed to survive were both nearly gone. Useless. Now he had his pensions and his savings and his Social Security. Long ago he had worked steadily. He had been one of the best intaglio printers there was. Employers had requested him personally. There had been a waiting list of future employers. The Printer had worked in Canada, in Toronto, in Texas and Montana. He spent years, the bulk of his career, in downstate Virginia where he printed money and stocks for a private firm that supplied currency to countries all over the world. Only the artists with the most skill and patience ever got as far as he did. They printed foreign money that most people wouldn't even recognize.

He remembered the vaults and the security guards and how all employees were physically searched before they left the buildings. He remembered that there were only seven or eight countries that printed their own money. America was one of them. American money was the easiest to copy. They, the printers, all joked about it. America was cheap.

The green ink used for U.S. currency was made by one hundred and eight different companies in the world, and everybody made the black ink. Black ink was black ink. Etching the plate was the toughest part. It had to be done by hand. Cross-hatches had to be barely visible in the collar of Franklin's coat. It took time back then, the Printer had explained. He wasn't sure if he knew how it was done today.

A million dollars in twenty-dollar bills weighed ninety-three and four tenths of a pound. The Printer remembered that.

Friends he once had were still printing. They were much younger and they didn't have to squint for the thinnest lines and soak their hands in warm water before they began working. They still had information and connections. They were printing stocks for the Toronto Exchange. Months in advance they had to be told how much stock to print, how many prints to run off of the plates. They had to be given time enough to prepare plates and numbers. Some months an order doubled. Which meant a stock was about to split and the other printers invested beforehand. It was a side project that would double a year's salary. The Printer had never invested.

Terry and Owen and their game was unimportant. The Printer knew they cheated. They didn't know anything about the Printer. He was an old man they had humored for the past few months by letting him sit in on the game. He had been passing the time with the poker games. Now he was preparing to invest.

The first few hands of the game passed in silence. Mitch began talking about tuna. He itemized the benefits of the canned lubricant which he believed was fish oil. And between Mitch Koe and the Greek began a heated discussion that flared up and died away before anyone else could join in. The Greek was certain that the oil was only vegetable oil. Fish oil was castor, or cod liver oil. The Greek concluded by asking what Mitch did with the oil from the tuna fish cans, anyway.

"I drink it when there's no tuna left," Mitch explained. "Do you think that's bad?"

"I dunno, How do you feel?"

"Pretty good."

"Then I wouldn't worry about it."

"Yeah, I mean, I like it."

Mitch then began a plotless story about his distant cousin who used to be a professor at Harvard.

A thin, layered cloud of smoke hung against the ceiling as the men all drank their beers and smoked little Walgreens cigars. They all began talking at once, as if some signal had been given.

"Last summer," the Greek announced, "I went to the Vicksburg Mansion in Virginia. It's on seventy-three hundred acres. When the commodore first bought it, it was. I think that was in the eighteen-hundreds, maybe early in the century."

"How old are you?" Mitch abruptly asked the Greek. "You couldn't have been there. You're not old enough. The thing's been a landmark for the past forty years."

"I know. I told you I was there last summer."

"Oh. They're letting people in? I didn't think people were allowed into landmarks."

"Sure, they do all the time. Like Graceland."

Mitch took a book about Nostradamus out of his jacket and read the table of contents aloud while he waited for Bates to shuffle. The ashes from his cigarette spilled down the inside of the book. The Greek asked Mitch what he was reading.

"Nostradamus."

"I saw that movie about the little kid who went to school to play football. He finally got to play a few minutes at the end of the year and I think he died. I don't remember what the name of the kid was. It was the same as the name of the movie. If I were that kid, I wouldn't admit getting beat up for four years only to play for thirty seconds at the end of the season." The Greek took a breath and looked over to the Printer. "You ever play football? Was that when they had leather helmets?"

Printer said that he never played football. And for the next few minutes, football was the topic. And at the outside of the conversation the Printer moved himself, waiting for someone to tell him to go home. Everyone went on around him.

No one listened to the other voices, only waited for a silence they could take and fill with things they had done a hundred years ago. Personal things no one else could disprove.

"When I was a kid," Mitch swore, "I used to train Arabian horses in Mexico. They were about fifteen hands."

"Small ones, huh?" Bates asked.

Empty bottles piled up and the cards stayed unshuffled. The Greek leaned on Joseph's shoulder and drunkenly explained, "When I was a kid. When I was your age I could have made it big. I was seventeen years old and I could have been set for life. IBM wanted me. And instead of signing a contract with them, I told them I had to graduate high school first. I was going to be the first one to graduate in my family. But they wanted me. They wanted me bad. They wanted me because when I was your age, around seventeen, I invented back then what is now known as the cellular telephone."

There wasn't a hint of a smile on The Greek's face. He was serious. All at the table nodded at an unchallenged story of bypassed fame and wealth. None of the stories anyone told could ever be verified. Most went unacknowledged in this sort of competition. The Printer and Joseph listened. The Printer watched how Joseph listened.

"So he goes in," Terry continued some story from weeks ago, "and beats the foreman near to death with the tire iron from his truck. The union don't know what to do."

The others kept on, hearing only their own voices.

"I told the bitch right there and then that she made her first and last impression."

"Nostradamus predicted that Franco wouldn't let Hitler into Spain. And he predicted the bombing in New York. It takes some artistic license to see it, but it's there."

"In the army, I saw one guy eat his wife's afterbirth. He put it between two slices of Wonder Bread. Seriously."

The barely remembered half-truths and complete falsehoods kept going. No stories came from the Printer's mouth. There was nothing he wanted to announce before this audience, just hints and asides to Joseph when they were alone. The others were good to drink and play cards with, but the Printer would never share anything of his own with them.

Joseph believed that the Printer's stories were true, there had been no bragging of the past. He had never won the fight. He had never drunk anyone under the table. And the boy understood bits and pieces of what the Printer had planned for the immediate future.

The Printer read the business section everyday and waited for a phone call from a friend who lived somewhere else like Toronto or Virginia. The one phone call that would be his big break. The Printer had never made the call during the years he was working. Now, he wanted to relax in his retirement. He wanted to put the money away like he was preparing to live forever. It was something he never relied on when his hands were smooth and his eyes were sharp enough to see the fine lines. But he depended on the phone call to come with the information.

There was a framed etching of a sunset over a shoreline hanging on the Printer's bedroom wall. A friend of his had done it a long time ago. That guy was the only one Printer knew who tried something different with his etching tools. His friend had carefully scratched out etchings of sunsets and horses and beautiful girls and sailboats. After a while he stopped. He couldn't sell many of them and there were easier ways to make money. The Printer liked the one of the sunset and had asked to keep it for himself.

On a scrap of paper before Joseph the Printer had scribbled figures, subtracted and added, and estimated that he had almost five thousand for the investment. It was everything he had and he was holding off on paying his rent.

It would be a long process until his money grew. Someone would tell the Printer what stock was about to split and that was what he had to buy on margin. Then when it doubled and the investors couldn't pay it off, the Printer would be a nice guy and ask for only the margin and the profit, not the whole stock. He could do this several times. There were some other steps in between. The Printer had to check on this, sometimes the procedure became blurry. He knew he was getting old. There was another part about banks in England that didn't make foreigners pay taxes if the money wasn't going to be spent in the country or used for business purposes. That was what the Printer remembered. Maybe, he thought, maybe he should check with someone on that.

The Printer hoped that the phone call would come soon. He was not making any money while spending time at the card games or the liquor store.

He told Joseph how beautiful the etched sunset was. It took a real talent. The Printer liked having something like that to look at. Something more detailed than a photograph because there were lines in the etching that were not in nature but the Printer knew they should have been.

So the Printer kept returning to the card game.

And after the conversation break, the game resumed and again Owen quickly folded and slid his chair behind the Printer's shoulder. The Printer edged his chair closer to the table. Hunched his shoulder over his cards to block Owen's view. Joseph was in a chair against the far wall, out of the game's range. He saw how badly the man's hands were shaking and saw how stiff he kept his wrists to hide the shaking. Joseph didn't know anything about poker.

After five hands, the Printer became irritated because he had already lost fifteen dollars. Over his shoulder he told Owen to get in the game or get out of the room.

Owen didn't move. Terry kept dealing and no one said a thing. They acted like they didn't even hear him. The Printer never told any of them what to do. He pushed his cards over and said he was done. He took his coat and moved toward the door. His hands fluttered as he tried to slip the buttons into their holes. The table mumbled something after he was gone and from the hallway the Printer heard the Greek laughing.

Joseph followed the Printer out the door, wanting to tell the man that he hadn't yet found an apartment to occupy. Now it was urgent. He and Amanda had been waiting to see if any good news would be presented.

Joseph and the Printer walked through the dark hallways of the apartment building, listening at doors, trying to hear the shuffle of feet and the quiet voices of squatting tenants. The Printer leaned his ear close to the door and barely touched his fingertips to the wood. It was the position of a safecracker or a thief. Someone who had to work with the tiniest silences.

They gave up. The Printer said he was too flustered, but told Joseph not to worry.

They left the building and walked together in silence until they reached a tavern on the corner. Joseph waited outside as the Printer bought two cans of beer. It was the same place where Joseph had been caught shoplifting the Kiwi Mad Dog with Old John.

The Printer again told Joseph about the stocks, Toronto, Virginia, the security guards, and all that foreign money. He spoke in the same desperate rush as if he couldn't stop himself.

Joseph forced a smile and nodded at the repetition. The Printer noted Joseph's disappointment and promised, "I swear to you I'll find a room before I go. That will be my going-away present to you. Be patient."

The Printer went back to the topic that had consumed him, explained how much a million dollars in twenty-dollar bills weighed;

told Joseph about the people he knew who were still working. Joseph kept nodding and agreeing.

The Printer fell silent after a while. Joseph saw the man drift away and then snap back. He looked at Joseph and said, "I think the two of us can work together, kid. Maybe I'll get back to you if this other stuff does not work out. If it does, none of you will see me again."

Joseph didn't know if anyone ever called the Printer about the investment. After they finished their beers, the Printer said goodbye and Joseph told the old man good luck. If the fortune didn't come, Joseph didn't know what the Printer was going to do. He would be completely broke. He would lose his five thousand dollars which alone sounded like a fortune. Joseph wondered if the Printer would come back with the work he had mentioned. But in talking to Joseph, the Printer had already given him all he had to offer.

Tyrone the Avatar

"You don't know who I am. You cannot begin to imagine all the scenes I been in. I threw out opportunities that you, or anyone like yourself, would kill for. I didn't need them then, and I don't need them now." Tyrone shut his eyes and his fingers fluttered along the edge of the counter, absently searching for remembered piano keys.

Joseph stood at his post and said nothing. He had seen Tyrone in the liquor store often, but this was the first time the man had spoken. Tyrone was fairly conspicuous, a frail little man under ropes of dreadlocked hair that over time had collected bits and pieces of foreign matter, enough that his girlfriend eventually convinced him to do something about it. So he wore a fishing hat balanced atop his dreadlocks. It became an essential part of his appearance, just like the buck teeth that constantly bit into his lower lip and the black-framed glasses that were always sliding down the bridge of his nose.

The regulars at the liquor store told Joseph that Tyrone was a burn-out case from the sixties. Supposedly, he had traveled with a bunch of different bands whose names no one could rightly remember. Tyrone still played a couple of weekends each month at a transvestite bar, The Manhattan.

The information Tyrone related to Joseph was that his unnamed band was going to begin taking itself seriously, but Tyrone's girlfriend had given him an ultimatum. She was tired of waiting on tables for sixty hours a week to support Tyrone while he sat around the apartment, drinking Colts and playing his Casio keyboard, and he had to go find a real job. "What can you do?" he had asked, drifting away without ever leaving the counter.

Tyrone's eyes opened again as Joseph sneaked a pack of cigarettes from the overhead rack. The crinkling of the cellophane had woken him up to immediately defend his position. "Now you can't be accusing me of this kind of thing. I'm not bullshitting you. I'm the artist and you ain't. Artists have to do their art or they die. You don't know what it's like. I been doing this since before you were born."

"I didn't say nothing," Joseph protested.

"Yeah." Tyrone leveled out to a more casual manner. "I know, I was thinking about something else. But you know what I mean, don't you?"

"Yeah." Joseph was still unwrapping the cigarettes hidden beneath the counter.

"Can I get a square from you?"

"Sure." Joseph thought it would be rude not to share cigarettes that hadn't cost him anything in the first place.

Tyrone pointed to a beaten and torn Xerox taped to the cash register. It was a police bulletin asking for information regarding an armed robbery that had occurred in the store two years earlier. In the center of the paper was a line drawing of a black man with a pointed mustache and a baseball cap. His physical description was given at the bottom of the page. Six-foot-two and one hundred seventy pounds.

"They ever catch the dude?"

"No, I guess not. I don't think so," Joseph said. "If they did, I don't know why the picture would be up."

"That shit scares me. Don't it bother you someone robbed the place?"

"I haven't really thought about it. Bates never said anything about it." Joseph had seen the bulletin, looked at it every day and read the same words over and over, but had never taken in the information.

They smoked their cigarettes and Tyrone told stories from the old days. "I opened for Sly a couple times, and man, the parties were better than the concerts. He was heavy. Always pissed at the band, and they were family. But he liked me. I don't know, we were kindred spirits or something. I know there was one night," Tyrone paused to straighten the events in his head. "Yeah, one night where I think Sly wasn't in the mood and I already had a chick. So he gave me two of his which he didn't want. His chicks were pissing him off because of something I don't remember. I had three then. Three chicks. And we made it that night all in one big pile." Tyrone smiled and shut his eyes again. "It was a beautiful thing."

Bates led Mitch Koe and the Greek through the front door, all laughing with an afternoon buzz. The Greek held a forty ounce beer, shaking it with his thumb over the neck of the bottle, watching the foam build and then descend just before spilling over. The three men stood still, shushing each other and stifling their laughter, waiting to hear the conclusion of Tyrone's next likely tale.

A wall of white men had assembled behind the diminutive Tyrone, who hadn't noticed them. And he went on proudly until the Greek bellowed and slapped a heavy arm across Tyrone's shoulders, leaning down to give him a sideways hug. "My ma-an. What's up, blood?"

"Nothing," Tyrone seemed to shrink further under the surprise.

Bates went around behind the counter and said hello to Joseph. Mitch Koe and the Greek crowded Tyrone and asked questions in such a swift succession that the little black man couldn't answer them. Tyrone stuttered and shook his head.

"I saw your man, Santana, on a bus," the Greek said.

"Where?" Tyrone looked vaguely out at the traffic passing the window.

"No. Not now. I saw it the other day."

"The man, Santana, was on the bus?"

"No, no. His picture was on the side of the bus. An advertisement for ice cream or something."

"Well, I can't see him doing that."

"Saw it myself."

"Don't tell me," Mitch Koe challenged, stepping in and pointing to the Greek. "Don't say you're calling him a liar."

"I ain't calling no one a liar."

"That's what it sounded like," Mitch assured Tyrone.

The Greek defused the situation. "Okay. Don't worry about it, no one. All you forget it. No one here ever lied in their life. Awright?"

"Okay," Tyrone said. He raised his hand slightly to Joseph. "See you later, man." Then to the rest of them, sullenly, "Later."

Bates wasn't paying attention to Tyrone; he saw Joseph's cigarettes under the counter. "Those yours?"

"No," Joseph said. "Tyrone's. Tyrone, you forgot your cigarettes." And Joseph held them up in the air.

"You keep them, baby," he mumbled. "I'll come back."

As soon as Tyrone was gone, the men felt they could talk freely. It was now their clubhouse, Tyrone was an outsider and so was Joseph, due to his recent association with the Printer and Tyrone. They kept the young man at bay with the promise of eventually allowing him to enter their group. The next card game was coming up.

The men all snickered. Some secret had emerged and Joseph didn't understand.

"Fucking Tyrone."

"The musician."

"Was he a singer or an instrument player?"

"He couldn't have been a singer. He can barely speak two words in a row. How could he sing?"

The Greek pointed at Joseph. "Kid, never listen to that nigger's stories. They are complete bullshit. That dude fried up his brains so long ago, he ain't sure what happened to him and what hasn't happened to him. He just aims for the middle and hopes he hits something."

The men continued laughing. Mitch was imitating Tyrone's strut which looked more like the step of an old woman crossing an iced parking lot. He walked slow around the room with tiny steps, holding his elbows bent with his hands up at his chest.

Mitch and the Greek were falling over each other they were laughing so hard.

And eventually the topic of Tyrone lost its energy and the men became tired. Drank their beers like they had just run a marathon.

Mitch grabbed three more from the refrigerator. "On the tab?" he asked Bates.

"Fuck no. Pay me."

The little bells over the door startled Joseph. Tyrone was loping into the store.

"Check this out, you get a chance." He held out a shrink-wrapped record album and spun it around so Joseph could see the cover. "Is anyone else here?" Tyrone asked abruptly, ready to take the record back.

"No, just me."

"You don't got a record player here, do you?"

"I don't think so." Joseph, thinking that Tyrone wanted only to hear some music, handed the record back without glancing at it.

"No, baby, keep that. Listen to it when you can. Expand your mind. If you don't want to keep it for yourself, then sell it here. Sell it for ten bucks. We'll split it seventy-thirty. Okay? I gotta go."

Tyrone left before Joseph could tell him that he didn't want the record. From the sidewalk Tyrone flashed the peace sign and Joseph inspected the record album.

Tyrone's name was across the top in letters built of little drawings of stars and moons. TYRONE LESTER. -Transcendental Moon Carnival-. And on the cover was a picture of Tyrone standing barefoot on the craggy slope of a hill. His hands on his hips, one knee leaning on a sharp rock. He looked about thirty years younger, but the date in the lower corner of the record was 1983. Tyrone was wearing a rainbow-colored shirt with black and white striped pants. His clothes looked tight as a wet suit. Tyrone had a wide grin behind his glasses and there was no fishing cap covering his slick dreadlocks.

Liner notes were centered inside an astrological chart on the back side.

"This trip is the notification of a True Arrival of a Musical Avatar. The Deity of Consciousness. Once upon hearing this album you will know in your heart and soul that The Prophet Speaks.

"As Tyrone once said to Sly Stone—Man, you're heavy.

"Sly replied—Yourself also."

Beneath that was a list of the musicians who worked on the album. It looked like Tyrone had played almost every instrument.

Joseph didn't know who Sly Stone was, and he didn't really want to hear the music. He propped the record up in plain view, right in front of the cash register. Just to see what Bates and the others would say.

The photo of a grinning Tyrone, standing proud on a mountain side, caught Bates' attention as soon as he entered the store. He waited a little, checked the receipts, the stock, and had a cigarette before he asked, "What the fuck is that?"

Joseph replied that it was Tyrone's record. Tyrone was selling it for ten dollars and Joseph would be able to keep seven.

"Tell your pal that this ain't a swap meet. He better get that out of here before I throw it out. I don't need this shit in here." Bates added, "Didn't anyone tell you to never go into business with a shine? You cannot trust them. They'll be nice to your face and everything. But you walk away and they say to their friends how bad they gonna rip off the Man.

"Besides, anything gets sold in here, I'll get the seventy percent. Jesus kid, you got a lot to learn about running things. I'm a little worried about leaving you here alone. Sometimes you don't show you got the brains of a white man."

Bates picked up the record and twirled it around so that it rested across his forearm and he was reading the back cover.

"Okay," he laughed. "Tyrone the fucking Avatar. And you want to do business with some bake-brain. Okay, I'll put him in the hall of fame."

Then Bates dropped the record back to its display, right over the yellowing police bulletin taped to the cash register.

With Muscles of Straw

There was no dead bolt on the door of apartment 402. The only lock was stripped and loose inside the doorknob. The Printer had told the boy in parting that he had located an empty room and whispered the number of the room in Joseph's ear. The Printer made a special trip to the liquor store just to pass the word to Joseph. He disappeared right after, didn't show again at the store, didn't come to the card games. He never said anything to anyone. To Bates and the others it was a mystery.

Joseph slipped the lock with a fake driver's license that Bates had confiscated from some kid trying to buy alcohol on a Friday night. A stale odor swept into the hallway as the door swung open. Joseph held his breath until he was able to force open a window that had been painted shut.

It was a vacant one-room apartment with a basin sink hanging from one wall above a curling piece of linoleum. Threadbare carpet, marked by stains and cigarette burns, covered the rest of the floor. Two windows hung like square cartoon-eyes in the opposite wall and between the windows was a door that held eight more little windows. The door led to no porch, only a straight drop into the alley four floors below. The door had a handle, but no doorknob or lock and Joseph figured that it was safe enough. The apartment was on the fourth floor. Across the gangway a windowless brick wall assured privacy.

The yellow tiled bathroom was littered with black spots of mold. Joseph touched his finger to a spot the size of a dime and smeared it away from the sink. The bathtub was stained with the rings of a rust-colored rainbow. Joseph hesitantly flushed the toilet and waited for the pipes to erupt on his shoes. In an echoing swirl the stagnant water finally went down and came back up clean.

Joseph wanted Amanda to see a normal apartment, new, or at least one that had not gone neglected for so long. What little money he had he would spend on some cleaner for the walls and bathroom. Later he could buy some curtains and fix a few things. For the time being, Joseph decided that he and Amanda would save and gather their money until they would be able to move on to a real place. This apartment would be a step down in status for Amanda. It was actually more of a room than an apartment. Joseph hopefully thought that soon they would be able to resume a life that was normal to her.

From a pay phone Joseph called Amanda at work. After being put on hold, he was informed that she had already left for the night. He left the address and the room number and hoped that whoever was on the other end of the line was writing all of this down. He dreaded that his words were being lost as soon as they crossed the phone lines. Joseph imagined the person at the other end of the line was doodling on scrap paper, or the phone had been abandoned and left hanging from its cord.

Sounds from the street filtered into the room as the night passed. He was able to hear everything with both windows open. On the floor below, someone was lazily dribbling a basketball. Repetitive music weighted by a heavy bass line worked its way up through the alley. The tiny rumblings of airplanes grew and faded overhead. The slow chopping of a helicopter circled the block twice.

Pigeons nested in the gutters above Joseph's windows. He watched them fly from one ledge to the next. They stepped away from the roof with a jump and caught themselves after they began falling.

Trains roared past on the other side of Broadway. There was the metal clatter that always sounded like something necessary had come loose. Like bolts had fallen from the underside of a car or a wheel was off the track.

Joseph finished his carry-out dinner of a burger and fries and tossed the crumpled wrappers out the window. Then he began scrubbing the bathroom floor with a rag and cold water.

Thunderclaps came ashore from the lake. The sky flashed blue several times before the rain started. Joseph sat in front of the windows with his legs crossed over each other. He watched the rain pour down and darken the brick walls across the alley. He wondered where Amanda was. He couldn't imagine she was sleeping behind the school. Not in the rain. He tried to fight off the possibility that she had found a better offer in the last couple of days.

The room darkened with the rainstorm and Joseph slept well for the first time in a long while, despite his concern.

Joseph left the apartment only once during the next day, to buy a loaf of bread and a couple of beers. He didn't have to work at the liquor store. Bates had given him the day off for no reason in particular. Joseph didn't want to miss Amanda if she appeared at the door. Time passed, achingly slow. He cleaned the bathroom and the linoleum section of the floor again, just to give himself something to do.

Three short raps repeated against the frame like some bird's pecking hours after Joseph had already watched the sky turn pink and then darken against the alley wall. He was not certain if he had heard anything. He remained sitting in the middle of the floor until Amanda called his name a second time and then tiptoed to the door.

She had a bedroll over her shoulder and a bag of clothes hanging from a cord around her wrist. Amanda looked around the apartment and Joseph couldn't tell if she was disappointed or not. Rain had pressed her shirt to her shoulders and chest. Her hair was wet and flattened against her forehead. It changed her face radically and Joseph almost didn't recognize her. She looked like a little girl.

The first thing Amanda did was lay out the sleeping bag and pull Joseph to the floor. Her wet clothes were peeled away, thrown with a slap to the linoleum floor. Goosebumps jumped from her cold skin to Joseph's legs.

Amanda leading, pulling Joseph by the elbows, directed him here or there through the hurried and frantic motions. The hard floor dug into Joseph's knees and elbows as he finally cradled himself into her; by then, the chill was gone from her body.

Everything went well after that. Joseph showed Amanda around the apartment, clowning as if it were a mansion. They ate junk food for dinner and drank beer. They listened to people yelling outside. Sirens raced the corners of the block. Pigeons cooed and jumped from the gutters. Joseph and Amanda both skipped work the next day and sat happily in the park. They ran around like little kids and wrestled playfully until they were both out of breath and covered with grass stains.

Joseph bought Amanda a blue cloud of cotton candy on a stick. She lay down in the shade and Joseph pulled the cloud apart, feeding it to her strand by strand. She held her mouth open so Joseph could watch the candy melt.

Two days passed lazily.

Amanda woke on the third morning with dark half-circles under her eyes, her whole body aching and covered in sweat.

Joseph found her sitting naked on the toilet. The skin was pulled tight across her face. Instead of muscles, her body was stuffed with straw. She looked as if a post driven into the linoleum of the bathroom floor held her upright with wires crossed tight through her ribs. Joseph thought of the opaque lines beneath her skin. The soft wires bowing through her muscles and up to the surface. Joseph imagined them now diseased, growing in both directions along her bloodline from random points in Amanda's body. He didn't know what to say to her.

"Can you go down and see if he's there?" Amanda asked Joseph once she saw him standing in the doorway. Joseph didn't know who Amanda was talking about, couldn't get over how her body had changed during the night. "Campbell. Downstairs. You know, the guy who sells me stuff." She stopped herself as if the explanation would be wasted. "I'm just not feeling good."

"Are you supposed to go down there now? Why don't you do it later?" Joseph wanted to comfort her somehow.

"It's not like he has a schedule," Amanda snapped and then turned sarcastic. "Yeah, I'll be back in five minutes. Maybe he should leave a little note on the door. Come back in half an hour. Or, the key is under the mat." She took a deep breath and her body sagged. "You shouldn't try to help so much when you don't know what's going on."

"I'm sorry," Joseph said. "Can I get you anything?"

"Can you check to see if he's there? Just go down two floors, he's in the corner apartment."

"What do I say to him?"

"Nothing. Don't knock on the door. Do not. Just go listen to see if he's there. You'll hear him. He's a big, fat, dirty motherfucker. If you could go check, that'd be enough."

"Okay," Joseph said. "You don't need nothing else?"

"No."

"Do you have to see him because you're sick?"

"No, honey. I think I got the flu. I'm sorry I snapped at you. I don't know, if it's not the flu, then it's something I ate. They got like the same symptoms."

"You need anything else?"

Amanda curled over until her head was almost touching her knees. "No. I'm okay."

Joseph shut the door and pushed it softly until the latch clicked. Amanda was moaning from the bathroom, moaning she was going to be late for work, how she might have to skip work.

The hallway lights were all burnt out. The window at the end of the hall was broken and the slivers of glass were carefully pushed into a corner. Another sheet of glass was spilt across the floor next to the stairs.

Amanda only said that it was the corner door and Joseph didn't look forward to the prospect of listening to every corner door. He wanted to run back upstairs and tell Amanda that whoever she was looking for wasn't home.

A doorway on the second floor opened as Joseph walked past. First he saw a flabby bare arm and an outstretched palm. Stepping out into the light of the hallway, behind the reaching hand, was an old woman in a housedress. Her ankles were thick, lumpy and veined. Her collarbones and shoulders pressed against thin skin as if gravity had spent years pulling the flesh down her body. She stood in front of Joseph and cried softly, "Help me, son, they're killing me in there." He peeked over the woman's shoulder and saw no one else in the apartment cluttered with stacks of boxes and garbage bags and unlit lamps. The woman stood her ground at the threshold of the open door. A radio was playing big band music from somewhere inside the room. "Sorry, ma'am," Joseph said.

There was no apartment in the first or second corners of the hallway. A door in the third corner had no numbers. Joseph stood outside the door, listened, and begged that the door wouldn't open on him.

Other random noises in the building covered up whatever he was supposed to be listening for. Joseph stepped closer until his head was inches from the door, the fine hair on his ear barely touching the painted wood. Then the sounds came. There was a woman inside, and children, and one set of heavy footsteps that could have possibly been a fat man behind the door.

Joseph stepped carefully away. He passed the old woman's door. She was standing there in a slip, now, singing along with the old-time music that was meant for dancing in ballrooms. Sometime in the past minute the woman had thrown her housedress to the floor.

"Does this dude have a wife and a lot of kids?" Joseph asked Amanda when he returned. She said he did.

"Yeah, then he's down there."

"Thanks, I didn't want to make an extra trip if I didn't have to." Amanda was prone across the floor of the bathroom. "This is nice. I feel better already. The floor's real cold," she said without lifting the side of her face from the tile.

Joseph gave Amanda ten dollars. He had two bucks left in his pocket. She said that when she was done, she would come back upstairs. She said that she would go to work. She would pay Joseph back.

"No big deal," Joseph said.

Joseph spent two hours checking the wristwatch Amanda had left on the floor. The morning was taking forever to end.

Amanda came back with color in her eyes even though her skin was still pale and cold-looking. She was wearing someone else's deep red lipstick. "I'm sorry I got pissed off before. It wasn't you I was mad at." Amanda kissed Joseph and deliberately smeared the lipstick down to his chin. She was three hours late for work and after she had gathered herself and left for the day, Joseph fell asleep on the floor. When he woke up she was still gone.

Joseph didn't want to leave the room when Amanda was gone. Someone else could walk in just as easily as he had. Getting into the building was no problem. The back door at the end of the alley was always open. There was no lock. Someone had stolen it or broken it and all that was left was a round hole in the door. Windows were broken throughout the building. The lock of the front door was packed with mud and made completely useless.

There were people sleeping in every hallway of the first floor. Stick figures hidden under piles of clothing. Bodies resting in a shallow sleep, practiced and learned from summers and months and years of living in places with no real privacy. They sneaked in the back door. They hung out in the alley. Joseph could step over their legs and their pint bottles and no one would stir even though it seemed they always knew he was there.

Amanda

With two candles in a paper bag, Joseph returned to the room. The candles were in orange glass bowls covered by wax nets. Joseph thought they were the kind that the good restaurants would have on every table. He tapped along the walls like a blind man until he was in the center of the dark room. This was what he had to do every night.

Joseph wasn't sure if there was electricity. He sat on the floor and waited for Amanda. A week had passed in the room since Joseph first took it. Amanda usually didn't return until after dark, no matter where she was. One morning Joseph told her to be careful, like any concerned lover would, and Amanda all but laughed in his face. Joseph only left the room when he had to.

He lit the candles. An orange light flew up to the ceiling and then poured down the walls and the room shrank, resembling the inside of a pumpkin skull. Joseph almost liked the room better when it was dark.

"I'm gonna go downstairs for a little," Amanda said, right after she walked in and kissed Joseph. She spun her body in a circle, checking out the new light.

"You gotta go now?"

"I might as well, while I know I can catch him. He hasn't eaten his dinner, yet."

"Why don't you stick around here for a minute? Have a drink with me?" Joseph held out the bottle of vodka he had taken from Bates' store, along with a few bags of candy. Half of the candy was already gone and Joseph was picking some of it out of his teeth.

"How about I have one with you when I get back?"

Joseph said that was fine. He hadn't opened the bottle.

"Do you have something to mix it with?"

"Like what?"

"Anything."

"I'll get something while you're gone."

"Okay." Amanda looked around the room and nodded. "I like the candles. Looks like the whole room's on fire."

Amanda hurried out the door and Joseph could hear her footsteps light down the hallway until she hit the stairs.

Joseph blew out the candles and went to the corner store to find something that mixed well with vodka.

They talked late into the night after they had sex. Flames contained in the little glass bowls flickered against the floor and threw shapes across the room. Joseph held one arm up in the air just to watch his shadow touch the ceiling.

They played with the shadows and the distorted images of themselves. Reluctantly Amanda let Joseph see her scars in the candlelight. Three pock marks inside the crook of her left arm. Spots that she could reach. Patches of grayed veins that Joseph traced with his fingers. Amanda told Joseph that she didn't use her arm anymore. She wanted to stop before the whole thing went bad. She thought that sometimes she could feel things collapsing in her like little pup tents being pushed over by the wind. She didn't show Joseph anything other than the veins in her arm. He knew there were more and wondered if she was ashamed of them.

Joseph rested with his head on Amanda's stomach. He could feel her frail ribs against his temple. He tucked his hands beneath her shoulders and listened to her muted heartbeat as he fought off sleep. At that moment Joseph decided that Amanda was perfect and he was going to make a life for the both of them.

"I think I first got turned on with Santa Claus," Amanda informed Joseph in the middle of the night. "An aunt of mine took me downtown before Christmas to look at the lights and displays. First time I saw all the windows on State Street. We were shopping, getting my gifts for ma and dad. I was real little, I didn't know what was going on, ultimately. I think my ma gave me twenty bucks because for my dad I was supposed to get underwear. The size was something like 38, to me this inhumanly huge number. Like I thought my pop was the biggest man on the planet. I used to see his underwear in the laundry. These big dirty, gray things. Pillowcases almost. They were so old they were worn thin and I don't know why, but I felt bad that he wore these ratty-looking things. We weren't broke or nothing. In the laundry room I would hold the shorts up in the air, put my hand in the crotch and see through like I had X-ray vision. Ma would get angry at me like I was doing something perverted. I was just looking at my dad's shorts. I wasn't doing anything rotten.

"But anyway, I was glad to be getting my dad some new underwear. And I guess I was sorta glad to see Santa. Santa Claus was this guy, this stranger. This guy who was real, but who I never met, someone who was supposed to sneak into my house to bring me what I wanted. There was something mysterious about it and it was sort of a let-down when I saw him in the store. I expected him to be floating in the air. Flying up and down chimneys. All cute winks and sparkle dust. Instead, he was surrounded by a bunch of bratty kids and parents and racks of discount purses and belts in front of the cosmetic counter. I don't think I believed in him, but I know I was let down by the whole thing. One of those things I felt I had to go through.

"The line kept moving forward like we were in a little maze. We had to follow the red ropes around like we were at the bank. After about half an hour I could see the Santa up close. He wasn't even real fat. I could tell his stomach was all padding and his beard was fake. He had these flat-looking, sleepy eyes, like yours. He sorta pissed me off. Not that you do, though. I like your eyes, they just didn't fit Santa.

"I got up there and he pushed the last little boy off his lap. The kid didn't look at me, just sorta ran past to his mother, crying. The Santa waved me up and an elf, some teenage girl dressed in red felt, came to lift me up the step and right into his lap. I jumped around, I think I kicked him real polite. Like when you're a kid you can do that. I knew his stomach was padded, I could feel it was too soft. You could tell there was no blood there. I wiggled around until I got comfortable. I had my head right under his armpit and I could see the beard where it was strung behind his ears. Real cheap shit for Marshall Field's. His costume didn't even feel like cloth. It made noises, crinkled, when he moved. And his whole body smelled like bitter sweat and his breath was like salami, that one smell that turns your stomach. You know?

"And maybe I imagined it, but I thought I could smell all the other kids who sat on his lap. That feeling of when there's someone near you, some skanky bum, and you can feel the germs floating in the air. It would look like dust in sunlight and it was all over the Santa. The germs.

"My aunt was off somewhere, like at the perfume counter. I gotta say now that I was sort of a weird kid. I had some strange ideas in my head which I couldn't have put there. I wasn't real sure what a blow job was, I mean I knew what the physical act was, but it didn't make much sense to me. But I told Santa that was what I wanted.

"I mean, I learned stuff from my cousin. She showed me things when I was way too little. She did things, showed me what to do. Later she turned into a freak and took off, but I guess she never really did me any harm. I mean, I was the littlest one out of all the cousins. At family parties she would take me upstairs and say what we did was our girl play-stuff. I don't know.

"It was just a funny idea to me. I saw Santa's face behind the beard, he looked real frightened when I said that. He didn't know what to do. That made me feel good, I was a cocky shit. All I knew was that my cousin was always talking about that stuff, so I learned a lot backwards. But Santa was bugged and I smiled right in his face. No one heard what I said, so I wiggled my butt in his lap like I had an itch. I don't know why I did that. Just my reaction.

"But the Santa, I know now that he had a boner and that should have scared me. Maybe it was an accident on his part. I don't know. I didn't know, I just thought I was being cool. I didn't want to get off his lap. Santa picked me up under the arms and dropped me to the ground. He didn't say 'Merry Christmas' or 'Ho-Ho' or nothing. Two elves came and got me off the ground. Other parents were sorta looking funny at this kid who got shoved off of Santa's lap.

"The elf-girl took me by the hand to the edge of the stage. She asked where my mommy was and then we found my aunt. I saw the next kid was sitting on the edge of Santa's knee, as far away as possible. Like Santa didn't want no more kids touching him."

Joseph didn't really know what to say. He kissed Amanda on the ear and pulled his head back so he could see that she was smiling.

"And once, years later," Amanda added, "I was followed home by these two cops in a patrol car. I was like thirteen, riding my bike home, and this cop car pulls up. They ask if I want a ride. I can sit up front, they say they'll throw the bike in the trunk. I said no, thanks. And they kept following me, real close. They scared me. I thought they were going to rape me. Just that creepy feeling that some people give off. Just like with the Santa's germs. It wasn't because they were cops, I just didn't feel good looking at them. They were going to cause something bad. Something weird had gone off when they saw me. Like the lights in the street had changed color. I mean, I knew what was going on. As a kid I knew about sexuality in some kind of way. They say that kids do have sexual feelings, and they do. But they shouldn't know about them until they are able to handle the stuff. Some say that kids can be sexual, but that's bullshit. It's like letting a four-year old drive the family car."

Joseph wanted to change the subject. He saw Amanda growing dour and the topic made him feel left out.

"So, did you ever live with a guy before?" he asked after a respectful pause. "Besides the guys at the last place?"

Amanda thought about it for a second. "I guess. Yeah, I have, but that was a long time ago."

"When?"

"Let's see," Amanda said and began counting on her fingers.

Joseph pointed to her hand and asked what she was doing.

"I'm trying to figure this out. I lived with seven. Seven guys before. Not counting the last place."

"They were all boyfriends?"

"Yeah, but there were only two I was serious about. And one of them wasn't that serious. It lasted only three weeks," Amanda laughed, "and we were married."

"We didn't drink this stuff," Joseph said, changing the subject again and reaching for the vodka. He didn't want to hear anymore. Something had just squeezed tightly in his chest.

Amanda knew nothing about Joseph's life and didn't seem worried about it. He felt that his position in her life was temporary. He didn't like it. There were gigantic gaps in Amanda's life that Joseph wanted either to fill or forget about.

"Oh, yeah," Amanda remembered. "Did you get something to mix in it?"

"What?"

"Your vodka."

Joseph pointed to the liter of 7-Up he had forgotten about.

They were both laughing, bouncing off the walls, drunk and clowning in the dark hallways. Joseph ran backwards so he could watch Amanda coming down the stairs behind him. She laughed when she realized what Joseph was doing and grabbed him lovingly when they reached the landing.

Amanda was taking Joseph downstairs to meet the dealer. He had repeatedly asked, almost begged, to see what Amanda was doing.

"Who is the guy downstairs?"

"Why?"

"I was just wondering. Does he sell you stuff?"

"Yeah, he does." Amanda was grinning at Joseph's inexperience.

"Do you know him good?"

"I know him as much as I have to." Joseph knew Amanda saw him as a child. He said he just wanted to go along, not to check on her.

"Is he like a dealer, or what?"

"Sorta. Not a big shot or anything."

She finally relented and said, "I guess it won't kill either of us."

Joseph was reassured once Amanda invited him along.

From behind the corner door there was a woman's voice chasing children's footsteps. The sound of a television talk show blared behind a man's laughter.

"Get the god-damned door," the man's voice snapped after Amanda knocked a second time. The door stayed shut and there was another yell. The children and the woman quieted as the door opened. The dealer smiled when he saw Amanda.

The man's features were buried under layers of fat. Even his forehead looked soft and his eyes were two dull yellow marbles under a heavily padded forehead. A wispy mustache covered the dealer's upper lip and thick glasses shielded his eyes. An expanse of white belly hung out under a Stones concert T-shirt. The date on the shirt was summer of '81. At the shoulders the fabric was worn thin.

"Who's he?" the dealer pointed a fat finger at Joseph's chest.

"He's cool. We're together," Amanda said.

"Oh, if you say so," the dealer backed away sarcastically. "Then come on in."

The walls of the apartment were the same dirty gray as Joseph and Amanda's place. A doorway led off to one side, to a bedroom and the bathroom. Two bunk beds were in the living room, surrounded by piles of discarded clothes. Dishes pasted with food were piled in the sink and stacked on top of the stove as if someone else was about to come in and take everything away to be washed.

In the corner of the room was a reclining chair that had over time been slowly crushed. It would eventually drop to the floor and fall apart into stuffing and splintered wood. The chair creaked helplessly and settled to an embrace as the dealer lowered himself into his seat.

The rug had been trampled upon by hundreds of footsteps day after day to the point where bald patches formed a trail from one end of the room to the other.

A tin-foil antenna crowned the television, the VCR was new and a disconnected cable box sat on the floor. One end of the couch was crushed down just like the chair in the corner. The apartment was cluttered with furniture and clothes and appliances, all secondhand and mismatched. Put together piece by piece. Joseph couldn't imagine how the fat man could get around the room, but it looked like he had been there all his life.

There was a shotgun on the floor, only inches away from the dealer's chair. The gun was shiny, like it was paid great attention or was factory-new. Joseph could hear the children laughing from the other room.

"You just saying hello, honey?" the dealer asked Amanda as the room swirled around Joseph.

"I just wanted to pick up something."

"Yeah. You owe me money, too."

"I know."

"But I won't embarrass you in front of your guest."

Joseph listened to Amanda and the fat dealer talk vaguely about money until she stood up and placed a folded bill in the palm of the man's hand.

Two little dark-skinned kids ran racing through the room, interrupting Amanda and the dealer. One child had no shirt, the other wore diapers. Both looked like little girls, but Joseph wasn't certain. They touched the refrigerator as a halfway point of their sprint and then ran back into a bedroom.

Joseph pointed. "Hey, whose kids?"

"Whadda you mean 'whose kids?'"

"Oh, are they yours?" Joseph realized that he had made a big mistake. The dealer leaned forward and shifted his weight.

"Yeah, they are my fucking kids. You think I just went out and stole me a few nigger kids? Maybe I'm gonna sell them."

The woman who must have been the dealer's wife or girlfriend yelled from the next room. She told the dealer not to use that word.

"What word, darling?" The fat man bared a grin and aimed it at Amanda.

"Nigger. Don't say nigger. You know what word I mean. I won't have my kids hearing that."

The dealer whispered in confidence to Amanda that the kids were only half-niggers. His wife came out of the bedroom and shut the door on the little children who were now screaming the bad word over and over again.

The wife was dark and thin. The lines in her face were darker than the rest of her complexion, charcoal rubbed into razor scratches. The woman shot Amanda a dirty look and then she turned her head to check out Joseph. After a quick assessment she made a grunting noise and announced that she was going out. The dealer didn't ask where and she didn't bother to tell him. Joseph assumed that they both knew where she was going, or neither one cared where she was going.

The children kept happily chanting the bad word after the wife was gone. The dealer lifted himself slowly from his lounge chair and went into the enclosed bedroom. "Shut up, shut the fuck up," the man barked. "Jesus Christ. There's something wrong with you people."

The naked children stopped chanting.

The dealer came back and dropped two crumpled pieces of tin foil onto the couch next to Amanda, then went back to the television as if she and Joseph weren't there at all. Joseph wanted to leave, but Amanda motioned for him to wait a second.

A commercial rudely interrupted a television program and the dealer turned to Joseph.

"What's your name, kid?"

"Joseph."

"Yeah? Nice. Good name, kid."

Joseph waited for the next question but the dealer only scratched at his stomach with fat claws and watched the commercials on television.

A woman on the TV screen proudly confessed that she felt guilty calling a dating service, but through it she eventually found her perfect mate. She gave the phone number and the address of the service three times. Then she dove into a pool of clear blue water and swam to her future husband.

The dealer slid down in his chair and his shirt rose up across his stomach. The skin was pure white, no hair, no birthmarks. It looked like bread dough or some kind of plastic filled with water, rolling with every breath.

"Wanna go?" Amanda asked Joseph.

"See ya," the dealer answered before Joseph had a chance.

Amanda locked herself in the bathroom and Joseph sat on the windowsill. He could hear her getting sick. Could hear her vomiting as if there was an endless supply and an incredible hurry to retch it all out of her body. Joseph listened until there was only a dry cough dying slowly. He knew she would be fine once she came out of the bathroom.

There were people in the apartment next to them. More voices ran along with the clatter of plates and silverware. Joseph had never heard anyone over there before, not on that side. He wondered when they moved in, or if they had been gone for a while. Their voices were coming right in the window. Their laughter was loud and harsh. Once in a while the pigeons jumped at the outburst and then came back to their gutter after crossing the alley. Joseph wondered who in the building would have enough silverware and dishes and room to serve all those people.

In the cabinet under the sink Joseph found a paperback Bible while he was waiting for Amanda. The spine was broken and curved. The pages were turning yellow at the outside edge. Joseph immediately thought of the Bibles he had blindly paged through in the chapel and in the apartment and he wanted to confess. He wanted to tell Amanda all about his parents, his father who would continually hurt himself to spite others. Who thought he was winning even when he was proving that he was the loser they all said he was. Joseph wanted to tell Amanda all about the fights and the black and blue face that his mother would have in the mornings. He wanted to tell Amanda about the Preacher Madison and the whippings and the little office and the street sermons. Joseph wanted to give Amanda everything.

Joseph couldn't imagine what Amanda would think if he told her about everything. He hoped that magically she would become bonded to his side.

He didn't want to chase her away. He wanted to show her that the situation, the apartment and the fat man, were all temporary, but he wasn't. They would both move ahead. Joseph wanted to tell her everything and bring her closer.

Some things he would leave out. Joseph would not mention Bobbi or the Mayor or Sonny. They were best not known. Joseph wanted to forget them.

But if he told her everything else and nothing changed, then Joseph wouldn't know what to do. If he told her everything about himself and she let it drop to the floor, then Joseph would have nothing left. He would be hanging on by his fingertips. If she didn't respond correctly Joseph felt that he would be crushed, ashamed and furious at himself. Surely, then Amanda would disappear as quickly as she had appeared.

For some reason Joseph felt protective toward Amanda and wanted Amanda to feel the same way toward him. He felt that it was his responsibility to watch over her.

Nothing she had told Joseph seemed to have hurt her. She was made of stone, had laughed away each incident told as the weirdness of other people. She was fine. She wasn't ashamed of anything.

"Where'd you find that?" Amanda asked when she saw the Bible in Joseph's hand.

"It was already in here," he jumped, immediately feeling like he had been caught in a lie. "It was under the sink. I looked under there because I thought I heard a dripping."

Joseph backed away. He wasn't ready to tell Amanda anything. If he told her something, he would have to tell her everything. And there would be nothing left. He would rather let her be, at that distance, instead of completely losing her.

"Oh. Sorta like a hotel," she laughed. "Every room gets a Bible."

That was the end of that topic and Amanda looked around the room as if it was now her turn to find something. "We really need a radio in here. Or a TV. We need something to do," she concluded.

"Yeah," Joseph agreed. "There's nothing to do."

Joseph promised that he would look for a television the next chance he had. He took her suggestion as a promise of some kind of permanence between himself and Amanda.

"Honey," Amanda asked, "do we even have electricity?"

A Cabin in the Woods

Amanda confided to Joseph that she was worried about the marks that were digging into her flesh. She thought the scars were growing worse, getting deeper. A friend from work told her that there was a vitamin of some kind that she could massage into the skin that would erase the scars somehow, but the worst part was Amanda thought she could see the veins darkening. That was why she had stopped using her arm. The points where the needle had entered were becoming hard, scarring over.

Joseph kept himself from saying that he had noticed the same thing.

She had tried to shoot into the veins above her crotch, the dim spiderweb between her hips, but she didn't like it. It was too harsh of a reminder of what she was doing to herself.

The rush wasn't as strong now, she told Joseph, because it wasn't going into a vein. It wasn't even a rush. Warm gauze just slowly moved over her, barely touched her skin. She used to feel it enter her brain like a roller coaster hitting the first drop. Her body became weightless and immovable.

What she was taking had never been explained to Joseph. Maybe Amanda figured that he knew. She had warned him not to try it, that was all. Amanda said she was quitting soon.

The needles were always clean. Amanda even tried not to use the same one twice. And no one else ever used them. She wouldn't let anyone touch them. The needles were kept in a flower-patterned Kleenex box under the bathroom sink.

And every time Joseph saw the box, he thought of how conspicuous it was. There was nothing else in the apartment, no furniture, no food, no decorations, nothing in the bathroom except for toilet paper and the Kleenex box. Not even a shower curtain. Joseph stared at the box whenever he was in the bathroom. The pink and orange patterned cardboard just didn't seem to belong in the bare apartment.

A light brown crust had dried inside the rigs of the used needles that Amanda didn't yet throw away. Joseph couldn't forget about them as Amanda had asked him to do. He wondered how she considered them clean. The afternoon Joseph met Amanda on the train, the both of them unzipped and unbuttoned under the El tracks, and the night surrounded by Amanda's old roommates had all been left behind. They were spots of light disappearing behind a fog that moved in over a body of water. Joseph knew the lights were still there, but they were severely dimmed, or it was he who had drifted. He could no longer think of her in any other way but connected to their one-room apartment and the fat man downstairs.

The flowered Kleenex box sat at Joseph's feet. A cockroach crawled past and found nothing of interest in the daylight.

Once, Joseph had stage-whispered through the closed bathroom door to ask Amanda if she was okay.

"Yeah," she whispered back. "I think I'm lost. Send a search party."

Joseph wondered if she was laughing at him. He heard her vomiting into the toilet. Her dry heaves sounded like a dog barking at the splash of the water.

Amanda was gone during most of the day; once Joseph realized that she would not return for several hours, he went to the liquor store to see if there was any work for him. Bates was curt. Said he didn't need any help right then. Joseph felt that Bates suspected theft or was offended by the days Joseph had not shown up for work. The imaginary accusation angered Joseph.

Joseph bought a rubber ball from a vending machine for a quarter. Alone in the apartment he bounced it off the walls. Off one wall and back to his hand. Off two walls and back. Two walls and the floor. The ceiling, the wall, and the floor. That went on until boredom forced Joseph to throw it out the window.

He went through Amanda's backpack, the only thing she brought to the empty apartment besides the sleeping bag. There were no needles in it; they had their own place below the toilet.

A notebook was buried beneath the underwear and T-shirts. Joseph knew that Amanda wrote things once in a while. She talked a lot about poetry and music, but Joseph never knew what it was she was speaking about.

He stopped flipping pages when he found some legible handwriting. It was a note to Amanda's parents. The paper was stained with overlapping rings of coffee like it had been written a long time ago and pondered over several times. Joseph estimated that it must have been written sometime between boyfriends.

"How are you? Everything is fine. I'll let you know my new address as soon as I can.

"I hope that things are fine with you and I want to thank you for what you sent. I still don't have a job. No one is hiring. I hate to sound like this, but could you send some more when you get a chance? Thank you, Ma. It is not going as good as I thought. You didn't have to come to the hospital. I didn't want you there in the first place like I told you. I guess I should thank you for coming anyway. It was not as serious as the doctor said."

Joseph wanted to know how much and how regularly money was being sent to Amanda. Then he realized that nothing was sent because Amanda hadn't mailed the letter. Joseph wanted to ask Amanda why she hadn't sent the letter. Maybe she had sent a different letter, a more polished version. Joseph wished he could see what the response was.

He wondered what Amanda was not saying about herself.

Vague references to college were made in the letter. Amanda wrote that she might return to school and Joseph took the tone as doubtful. She was saying what her mother wanted to hear.

Amanda wrote about her cousin, he was a lumberjack or something. That was what Joseph thought it sounded like. Maybe he was a forest ranger. He was somewhere in Oregon and Amanda wrote about possibly going to school out west. She could live with her cousin, the lumberjack.

Joseph tried to build a picture of that in his head. A cabin in the woods. A log cabin lit with candles in every corner. It would be quiet, the air would be cool and dry, crisp like autumn all year long. The trees would grow straight to the sky with no branches near the ground. Outside their cabin would be shade and cool darkness. Joseph and Amanda would walk under the shelter of tree branches woven together to form heavy shadows. The grass would be a sharp green spotted with orange leaves. He was sure that he had seen trees like that somewhere before. He liked that and wanted to believe in it.

Out in the wilderness there would be only Joseph and Amanda. Maybe her cousin would live within walking distance. He would be a big, quiet man who drank straight whiskey without ever getting drunk. The lumberjack cousin would be an older man, helpful and knowing in the ways of the wilderness. He would be able to catch little birds in his bare hand. Joseph tried to picture the lumberjack's face. Found the features, took them from billboards advertising cigarettes.

The solitude of Oregon or wherever Joseph and Amanda settled would separate her from the things she did, the people she knew, and the needles she kept hidden. Joseph imagined she would probably bring as much as she could out there with her, but soon would run out. She would get sick and Joseph would take care of her. There would be sicknesses for a few days, sweating and vomiting. That would all go away. Joseph would suffer alongside her until they left her body clean.

Joseph would be away from anyone he ever knew. A clean start for him. Amanda would thank him for this. She would be forever grateful. And he decided that they would not have to tell each other their secrets. Joseph didn't want to tell Amanda anything which she may not approve. It would all be best forgotten. Only Joseph and Amanda would be left. The two of them would grow closer until they could read each other's minds, finish each other's sentences, until they were inseparable. He wanted her to feel as attached to him as he wanted to be to her. Joseph knew it hadn't happened yet. Joseph wanted the both of them to be together, on equal ground. It would be the two of them separated from everything and everyone else. The two of them would leave the city. Go out and live somewhere in the country, some small town with only one grocery store and one church that they would never attend. They didn't even have to go that far, not to Oregon. They could go downstate, to Joliet or something. Like Bobbi had done.

Sometimes it seemed that there were two distinct voices inside his head. The one he liked and the one he believed was telling the truth. One floating on the surface of the water, easy to read and easy to reach out for, was the voice that Joseph wanted to hear. The true voices were buried further down. In water so deep it became rare that light touched them.

Joseph kept building scenarios as he paged through the rest of the notebook. A new scenario built upon the last until Joseph noticed he hadn't read a word on any of the pages he had passed.

They were drifting on Magnolia Street, Joseph and Amanda. Days had crawled past with the minimum of money or energy being used. Amanda slipped out every morning. Joseph took short walks and sometimes talked to Old John near the park benches outside Truman City College. John mentioned that some celebrity had died. Joseph didn't know who it was. "He was old. I mean old, old." John said that the movie star died a vegetable in his living room, sitting on the couch while reading a magazine and watching westerns on TV. He didn't want to be interviewed, he didn't want to be on TV, didn't want any funeral at all, John said. "I want to know what he said when he died," the little man complained.

Joseph slept off and on throughout the days. He felt his body growing soft. He could no longer see the ribs in his chest or the bones of his face. Joseph slept because there was nothing he wanted to do without Amanda. The shadows were leaning in different positions against the walls every time he woke. And by the time the shadows had faded away into the blank walls, Amanda was home.

The doorknob clicked and the tumblers shifted backwards as Amanda jimmied the latch. She entered the small room, her shoulders and hips moved fluidly like she was under a flickering light. A slow motion film skipping frames. She kissed Joseph and reached down to the bag of black licorice he was eating from. She ate two pieces and dropped the rest into Joseph's lap.

Joseph braced himself for the usual routine. He saw Amanda growing fidgety, refusing to sit on the floor with him. He tried to picture the cabin in the woods as the eventual solution to their problems because he knew what would happen sometime before it got too late.

Amanda would head down to the dealer's apartment for an hour, come back to the room and then disappear for half an hour with her Kleenex box in the bathroom. The door was kept shut until she was done and everything was put back in its proper place. Joseph was no longer allowed to watch Amanda stick herself. She said he was making her self-conscious. Joseph wondered if that was a good sign. He couldn't tell. Sometimes she didn't even notice him.

Joseph couldn't stop thinking about the notebook and the lumberjack cousin. "Do you talk to your folks at all?" he tried.

"Sure, I had coffee with my mother the other day, Tuesday." Amanda smiled. "I told her that the guys didn't pay the phone bill, so now we got no phone and I can't call her except from a pay phone. I didn't want to tell her I moved again. She thinks I'm unstable."

"Hey, you ever been in the hospital?" Joseph asked as if he had just thought of it.

"Yeah, for my tonsils."

"That's it?"

"Yep."

Joseph replied that he had never been to the hospital. He said that he had never been sick in his life.

"That's something," Amanda admitted.

Joseph felt certain that Amanda was toying with him. He believed she knew that he had found the note to her mother. She knew why Joseph was asking all the questions. She knew that Joseph had gone through her things and she would not acknowledge it. Amanda would only allow Joseph to get so close. After going a certain distance, she would turn her back to him.

"You ever think about moving out of the city?" Joseph tried another route. Amanda said she considered it once in a while, but the tone of her voice told Joseph that the chances were a million to one. It was too far away and too serious of a decision. If she were someone else she said, had another life, maybe she would be able to move.

Something hadn't been explained. Joseph no longer understood the letter he had found, he didn't understand why she hadn't sent it and he wondered if the whole thing was just a fantasy of hers. Maybe she had lied, or considered lying, to her mother about being in the hospital. Maybe her family knew what she was doing and she had been disowned. Maybe everything she had told Joseph was a lie.

"You know anyone out of town?" Joseph asked.

"Why? You thinking of leaving?"

"No, not for real." Now he knew that she had noticed the subtle questioning. "Just thinking about it."

Amanda shut her eyes and folded her fingers behind her head. A few minutes later she was asleep and Joseph was left to listen to her breathing. Under her shirt her chest rose and sank, deeper and slower with each turn, as if her lungs had grown bigger inside her ribs. When she woke up hours later, she asked Joseph what time it was. There was no clock in the room and Amanda said she lost her watch.

Rain fell steadily all the next day. The gutters across the alley were rusted away in two spots and the water poured down in streams past the windows. Amanda was at work. After growing bored with the view Joseph went into the bathroom and sat down on the toilet. He reached under the sink for Amanda's tissue box.

With the tissue box balanced on his knees, Joseph mimicked poking an imaginary syringe slowly into his arm just to feel what the motion was like. A shiver ran across his spine like little bird claws, more quick than sharp, and he wondered what the needle actually felt like dipping into his skin. He wanted to know if it slipped right in or if there was a moment of resistance. He couldn't remember ever getting a shot of medicine. He must have at some time in his life. All babies, Joseph mused, had to get some kind of shots.

Under the stack of Kleenex was one more needle. Joseph held the syringe to the light and turned it in a slow circle, rolling the plastic cylinder between his fingers. A tiny reflection of light floated along the surface like a bubble trapped. Joseph pulled the plastic cap away from the tip and brought the needle to his arm in the same motion he had practiced.

There was nothing inside the syringe. It was clean.

Amanda never really talked about what she was doing. She wanted Joseph to regard it as something unimportant, like taking cold medicine. She didn't want to be examined anymore.

She used the needles every day, or every other day. Joseph sometimes wasn't sure. He couldn't tell unless she was sick. What she did when she was out of the apartment Joseph couldn't imagine. Now they were living together and Joseph could only watch, even though he felt he was a part of it. He let her do it and he had given her money whenever he could. He didn't like it, and wasn't sure if he liked her when she did it. But if he tried to stop her, Joseph feared that she would leave him.

He felt that his time was limited. He could barely hold on to Amanda. Joseph already felt the wedge between them because it was something Amanda was holding in place.

Joseph brought the syringe down to his arm. He watched the tip of the needle slip under his skin and felt the sharp pinpoint a second later beneath his biceps. There was barely any resistance at the surface. It didn't go far, it didn't go near a vein. He pushed it a little farther, at a shallow angle sliding between the muscle and the skin. He couldn't see how deep he had gone. Joseph was scared to touch the plunger. He had heard about air bubbles that went right straight to the heart.

Slowly and carefully Joseph pulled the needle away in the straightest line possible. His hand was shaking. He had gone dizzy at the sight.

A drop of blood grew thin and slow, coming up from his skin.

A Sermon

Preacher Madison paused and let his fingers creep to the edge of his podium. The microphone was not operating correctly, so he switched it off and let his voice carry quietly through the white chapel. Two pictures hung from the walls behind the Preacher's shoulders. At the left was a picture of a tanned, wide-eyed Jesus. A tongue of flames over his head. At the right was an unframed mirror with Jesus' face painted in delicate white lines over the surface. Directly behind Preacher Madison was a plain wooden cross suspended against the wall.

The room was quiet except for the humming lights. It was time for his sermon, his chance to step down and informally speak to the congregation. Introduce the intimate into what should already be a very personal experience. But it had to be done because sometimes the Preacher thought he could feel people drifting away from the word.

"For this day and every day, Lord, we need your mercy and discipline. They go hand in hand, mercy and discipline, as partners in definition. Because without one the other does not exist.

"Without the left hand there is no right hand. There is only a hand. And every grasp, a left hand and a right hand, is stronger than two of the same hand. One without the other teaches nothing. The left hand and the right hand are the Family and the Lord. Each alone has great strength, but together they are protectors for life. Guides for life. Gifts for the blessed.

"A child once possessed these gifts, though never concurrently, never at the same time. They were too little and too far apart. When the gospel is not brought upon right, it does no good. It is a doctor's diagnosis when the doctor is informed of only half the symptoms. Do not get me wrong. The Lord knows. The Lord is strong beyond all comprehension. The man knows this. The child does not.

"In a piece of glass the child saw his own face. White light flashed once brightly and he retreated. He saw his skull in an X-ray. He saw the blood coursing beneath his skin.

"He saw faces he knew and turned away. He knew half of what a child should know. The Family without the Lord. The Lord without the Family. He saw what he thought to be his dreams at the bottom of a deep watering hole. His dreams and nightmares mixed together, floated up and shone inches beneath the surface. In this mixture he lived his life. What he needed was too far out of his reach. The only ones who could fill the hole and bring the necessities of a good, strong life was within reach. The child ran instead, scared of what he could not touch, scared of what he knew but could not decipher.

"His shadow floating on the surface of the water scared him. Everything was backwards. What was to be love was not. Words were hollow and actions were false. He woke at night with smoke inside his lungs. Fire took him wrongly. It did not take him completely, but it took him away from the first thing which he saw, the first thing which he knew could be right."

Preacher Madison went on in a tone he hoped was worthy of his Lord. He could see it in the congregation that the meanings were floating past, rising unheard to the ceiling. He wondered if there was a problem. Certain people whose reactions he used as weathervanes for each sermon stared blankly ahead or kept their eyes down. There was something else holding their thoughts. Some distracting gossip that he hadn't yet heard. Some miserable, petty thing that he would later have to straighten out.

The Preacher plowed ahead and waited for that certain click and the inaudible buzz he felt inside his head when he spoke. The signs that told him he was on the right course. The markers never came and his voice was dying out in the air. His thoughts began to wander farther and farther away from the sermon laid out at his hands.

That night Preacher Madison was brought dully from his sleep, the harsh electronic ring of his bedside phone went unanswered three times before he fumbled for the receiver. It was the Chicago Police calling from the front door of the hotel. Reverend E. Madison was requested by a voice that broke the sentences apart into separate, block-like words. The voice said that there was a body on the sidewalk in front of his building. The Preacher was asked to come outside.

Only then he noticed the lights flashing red and blue in a corner of his window. Voices out on the street, not those of the police, were talking and laughing, ignorant of the obvious problem somewhere outside. These people never go home, Preacher Madison thought as he made himself presentable.

A crowd had gathered. The body was already covered with a dark plastic sheet. Cars slowed as they drove past, passengers peered over the squad cars blocking the view. A uniformed officer who Preacher Madison had known for years walked out of the crowd with a clipboard in his hand.

Preacher Madison saw nothing he hadn't seen before. There had been a lot of accidents and deaths in front of the hotel throughout the years. Hit and run. Drive-by shootings. Overdoses. Stabbings. He figured that he would be asked a few questions and then be allowed to go back to bed. He knew the police innocently figured that he knew most people passing under his windows. Politely he would answer their questions.

Preacher Madison was told that Brother Samuel had somehow fallen out of his fourth floor window. The voice was almost a whisper. The Preacher was taken aside, away from the prying crowd, and told that the fall was most likely an accident. A curtain rod and half a set of new drapes were clutched in the old man's hands when he hit the ground. Two officers asked permission to go up and take a look at the room. Preacher Madison said that was fine. He understood what he had been told, but it felt like he was numbly floating up from the sidewalk.

Windows opened overhead. News had already made its way up the hallways. The lights of the squad cars and the ambulance were seen. Men and women stumbled out the front doors of the hotel. Panicked questions broke into tears. One woman tried to wrestle the drapes from a police officer who had pulled them out of Brother Samuel's hands. Another woman began the grieving process by throwing herself against the fence that had recently been installed across the tight boundaries of the hotel lot. People surrounded the Preacher with unanswerable demands and his heels drifted to the ground again.

Sobbing, loud and hysterical, filled the Preacher's ears and he did not think he could comfort any of them right now. The distractions that had previously occupied him were nothing. He was certain of this. It was his own boredom. His own selfish concerns. All this now, he felt, was the result. More people, hurriedly dressed, filed out the doors of the hotel lobby as Brother Samuel was carried away. Preacher Madison stood there feeling very helpless.

The familiar officer appeared from the crowd and whispered to Preacher Madison. He said that he was certain the death was an accident. A chair had toppled over in front of the open window. One set of new drapes was already hanging from the rod. "I'm very sorry for your loss."

Preacher Madison saw two children in their pajamas, taking in all the lights and the commotion without any of the understanding of what had happened. They only knew that something out of the ordinary had taken place and it was a welcome diversion. The Preacher wondered where their parents were. He couldn't think of the children's names.

Two Tribes

Joseph remembered a sermon. He was sitting next to his mother in the white chapel. Preacher Madison was having a good time in the pulpit and the scene may have stuck in the boy's mind because of the Preacher's holiday mood that night. He was joking and laughing, imitating dialects and winking lewdly, possibly at the women in the front row. Joseph didn't know what was so funny, it made him nervous. And he saw that his mother had no reaction at all as to what was going on around her. Joseph remembered his mother's posture, stiff and unchanging. Sitting at full attention while the rest of the congregation broke apart into peals of laughter at Preacher Madison's definitely unique gospel.

Joseph wasn't sure if he remembered the story right because he still couldn't find what was so funny. It wasn't that he had such compassion or concern for the peoples in the story, he just didn't get it.

Once there were two African villages separated by a desert plain, able to only grow enough mangoes to collectively feed one tribe at a time.

This was a long time ago, so long ago that the tribes were separated from the rest of the world to such an extent that they didn't know it existed. They only knew of each other and their mangoes.

No matter what kind of barter system was worked out between the two peoples, there was never enough food. This led to tension between the tribes and eventually a war began before the approaching harvest. To the victor went all the mangoes and the other tribe would starve through the next season. Nothing was settled during the remainder of the year and the harvest came again like a surprise. There were nighttime ambushes and spears flying and knives spilling blood. There were traps in the jungle and fires in the villages. One man was gutted like an animal and left hanging from a tree. Another had his head cut off and delivered to his mother by a young girl who would not be harmed crossing over to the opposing village. Amid the bloodshed and cruelty the good fathers, the leaders, would sacrifice their food to care for their mothers and wives and children. It was the pride of both tribes that no children died during the harvest battles.

Victory alternated yearly. If the tribe to the east won the first year, then they lost the next. This pattern went on for generations while the same amount of mangoes were grown every year. The men grew weaker and lessened in numbers as time passed. And each generation was smaller than the last until the two tribes, after years of warring, were barely populated and left with more than enough food for all.

Not even enough survivors were left to pick the mangoes and many rotted sourly on the vine. But the ritual war continued feebly during each harvest.

That was all Joseph could remember. He checked to see if the story was in the Bible, but he couldn't find it. There was a moral to the story, he knew, but he could not think of it.

For some time Joseph debated using one of Amanda's needles when it was not empty. He thought that maybe they would become closer if he did the same things she did. Joseph once asked Amanda why she did it and all she said was, "Feels good."

Amanda lost her job. For four days in a row she hadn't shown up at work. The assistant manager covered for her on the first day. He said he couldn't warn her because he couldn't find her. He couldn't imagine where she had been. Joseph was only working a couple of days a week, making fifteen dollars a day and giving Amanda twenty-five a week, which was not enough for either of them to live. It was enough for one person, but definitely not enough to feed two plus one habit. On the days Joseph didn't work, it felt like the job was slipping away from him. He waited for the day when he would walk in the liquor store and be told that he didn't work there anymore.

Amanda repeatedly told Joseph that she was going to get another job. She assured him that it would not be too tough.

Joseph waited impatiently for the whole of her life to snap into focus. He felt like he had entered too late.

Amanda and Joseph lay naked on the floor. It was so quiet Joseph was scared to speak. He ran the flat of his hand across Amanda's scars and she rolled away when she could feel what he was doing.

"Don't. I told you I was stopping." Half-asleep, her voice was different, like a child's.

"I wasn't doing anything."

"You were reminding me of it."

"I wasn't trying to."

"Yeah. I know, it's my problem."

Joseph still wanted to brush his hand across her backside to feel the marks. Evidence of what she had done before he came along. Joseph harbored the thought that somehow he would save her. On good days Joseph believed that she wanted to be saved. On the others he consoled himself with the reassurance that he at least didn't start her on the stuff.

In the afternoons Joseph had begun taking walks that led him to the park by the lake. Behind him, the Lake Shore Drive traffic sounded like dragonflies. Avoiding the people on the street had chased him out there, had crowded him to the lake. He tried to tell himself that no one saw him. They didn't see him and they weren't laughing at him. But deep down, in the part of his mind where the true thoughts rested and waited, the part he tried not to use, he imagined that behind his back they were laughing like hyenas. Joseph kept walking until he was at the lakeshore.

He sat on the rock ledge and watched the workers putting up tents along the beach. Some of the tents were olive green canvas, others were white plastic with PEPSI printed in red, white, and blue along the sides. More men sat in a row along the flat rocks and made comments about the women passing by.

That evening, Amanda was not in the apartment when Joseph returned. The walk had tired him out and he fell asleep in the middle of the floor. It was sometime in the afternoon, Joseph couldn't be sure what time it was. Humidity was choking him. There had been a sudden jump in temperature. Joseph had seen the bank clock flashing ninety-five degrees. The whole building felt empty. That was how every day felt. Sleeping on and off until Amanda walked in.

A knock at the door woke Joseph and through the fish-eye peephole he saw the dealer's wife with one of the little mulatto children twirling from the end of her arm.

Joseph yelled out, trying to sound tough, "What do you want?"

"Let me in, asshole."

"What do you want?"

"Send that skinny bitch out here."

"She ain't here." After he opened his mouth, Joseph knew that he should have instead informed the woman that there was no skinny bitch living in the apartment. He shouldn't have said anything at all.

"Then I'll wait for her." Came the decision from the hallway.

Joseph went and sat back down on the floor. He didn't know how long the dealer's wife would wait for Amanda. It was completely silent in the hallway and Joseph checked through the peephole, but he couldn't see the woman. He wondered if she was standing with her back to the wall, waiting to jump him when he stepped outside.

Joseph stretched out on the floor and shut his eyes again.

Apparently the dealer's wife was gone since Amanda was not molested coming through the building. She kissed Joseph and dropped herself to the pile of collected blankets on the floor next to him.

Amanda looked around the room, checking if anything had changed. Nothing had while she was gone and she reminded Joseph, "Honey, we need a TV. I made sure, we do got electricity."

"Yeah. When I get some money, I'll look for a cheap one."

"Cool."

Joseph kissed the side of Amanda's neck. She reached back and scratched his ear. "You know," he said as a warning, "that woman, the fat guy's wife?"

"Yeah."

"She's looking for you."

"What's she want?" Amanda was unconcerned.

"I don't know. I didn't let her in. She stayed out in the hall, waiting for you for a while."

"Probably good that you didn't let her in."

"Yeah, I guess." They were both quiet for a second. Lying side by side, holding hands and looking at the ceiling. Then Joseph asked, "You ever hear from those guys you were staying with?"

"Nah, they were glad I left. Those pricks told me I wasn't worth it. There wasn't anything to be worth, all they did was let me sleep on the couch."

"And use the bed," Joseph added, smiling at Amanda. His attempt at an inside joke was ignored.

"Yeah." Amanda patted his thigh. "We need a TV."

The week kept crawling past. Joseph worked three days at the liquor store. Amanda went somewhere, disappeared during the afternoons and reappeared before what would have been dinner time. Finally, she awkwardly admitted that she had been staying at the library across the street because of the air conditioning. "I like reading," she admitted.

Joseph had fifty dollars saved up at the end of the week. There were two men he had seen working out of the back of a van always parked at a dead end street near the lake. The van sat with its nose end pointing toward the guardrail that punctuated the block, past the guardrail was the expressway and the heavy gray of the lake. The two men sold mostly furniture and clothes from the back doors of the van.

In lawn chairs they sat in the street, drinking beers as if they were in their own back yard. One man wore a cowboy hat with fake animal teeth around the brim, the other wore cowboy boots and gym shorts. Neither man wore a shirt and their tanned guts hung over their waistlines.

Joseph stood impatiently between the men and hoped that they would speak English when they were done laughing. Joseph described what he wanted the best he could and after a minute the men's laughter broke down to wide grins. One man translated for his brother and then relayed the information back to Joseph. It was possible that they would have a television the next day.

"How much?"

"Tomorrow," the brother translated again, "we'll see what kind of television it is. Then we'll know."

Joseph was proud of himself. The next day he was able to talk the two brothers down to forty bucks for the television set. He had kept the plan a secret from Amanda, since there was always the chance that things would not work out.

But now Joseph had his TV. It was still in the box, sealed and shrink-wrapped. That was as valid as a receipt, the English-speaking brother promised. Joseph handed over two twenties and hoisted the television up to a precarious balancing point on his shoulder. It was a ten block walk back to Magnolia Avenue and four flights of stairs after that.

Satisfied with his accomplishment, he left the television out in the hall to heighten the surprise. He felt like a normal, married man bringing home something nice for his wife.

"Where have you been?" Amanda wanted to know. The apartment had been sweltering since the morning. In her underwear she sat in a lotus position, reading an old newspaper in the middle of the room. Drops of sweat dangled from her chin and dropped to the newspaper, soaking dark little circles into the text of several pages.

"I went shopping."

Amanda couldn't see what Joseph had bought. There was nothing in his hands, he smiled and motioned for her to wait one second. He ducked out into the hall and came back with the heavy box pulling him forward. ZENITH was written in blue letters across every side.

"Jesus Christ," Amanda cheered up suddenly. "How much did that cost you?"

"Not much. These guys," and the story was interrupted by a knock at the door. Joseph and Amanda both fell silent and waited for whoever it was to go away.

"I hear you, goddammit." The dealer's wife was in the hallway. "I hear you in 402. I hear you." She kept screaming until she finally left, stomping her skinny legs down the hall.

"Okay, let's see this thing," Joseph said when he was certain that the woman was gone. He tore at the plastic and crumpled it into a ball. Aiming for the window, the ball of shrink-wrap caught a weak breeze and floated short to the floor. He pulled at the cardboard until the heavy staples tore away with little popping noises. Amanda watched as Joseph yanked the tissue and styrofoam from the box.

Inside the television box there were only faded red bricks. Amanda saw the disappointment on Joseph's face. "What's wrong, honey?"

"Shit. Fuck."

She knelt down on the floor next to Joseph and saw what was in the box.

"Oh, you're fucking kidding me." Amanda rested her head on Joseph's shoulder and said nothing else.

A car horn honked out on the street and somewhere down the street people were yelling at each other from the windows. The voices were cursing and laughing. Joseph thought of the hyenas that were watching him. He thought of the voice that knew people were laughing at him and knew that Amanda was much farther away than she appeared.

The weak lock gave way with a dull crack. The door banged against the adjacent wall and jammed there. The dealer's wife blocked the path between the apartment and the hallway. One hand rested on her hip, the other held the heavy wrench that had broken the doorknob. Her mouth opened. Words were about to flood the young couple when she saw the wrapping plastic and the tissue all over the floor. She saw the bricks inside the box. She saw Amanda sitting half-naked.

"Son-of-a-bitch." The dealer's wife began laughing. "Oh Lord. Lookit this. The stupidest little whore and pimp in the world." Barks of laughter curled from her mouth. How much had Joseph paid for a box of bricks, she demanded to know while gasping for air. "You just a couple of kids playing grown up." The dealer's wife worked to control her joy. Joseph stood up and moved toward her as if he was going to throw her out. Amanda grabbed Joseph's arm as the woman lifted her wrench and waited for the appropriate moment to swing at Joseph's skull. The wrench looked like it weighed more than the woman.

Before she went back out the crippled door, the woman warned Amanda to stay away from her husband. She said she would have more than a wrench next time she came to the apartment. "Split your spoiled white-girl skull." The woman's eyes never left Amanda's pale chest. "I should have."

The door swung on its hinges and hung halfway open like a toothless mouth. It couldn't catch onto anything. Air just went in and out.

Eventually, Joseph imagined, nobody was left in either African tribe. It had to be the mango plants that won. Vines and weeds overran the abandoned villages. They curled across dirt roads and poked through the open doors and windows of the abandoned huts. Over time there would be nothing to be seen of either village. Slowly obscured in a carpet of flowered vines and wild grasses until no evidence was left of either tribe.

Joseph wondered then how Preacher Madison knew about the tribe. He didn't question the integrity of the story, only the teller. Joseph wanted to know who saw these tribes kill themselves. He wanted to know who else was there to record their mistakes.

Joseph had barely heard what the dealer's wife had threatened from the front door. She only made it worse, she was there to laugh at him, accuse him of being a child. After he bought a box of bricks.

In the middle of the night Joseph said that he was going to go back to that van and kill the two brothers. With the quietest voice possible Amanda told Joseph not to. She said everything was going to be all right. She was careful about what she said. She told Joseph to calmly think about what he wanted.

Amanda wanted to tell him it was a stupid idea without sounding patronizing. She could tell that Joseph wasn't a killer. It didn't even sound right coming from his mouth. He couldn't hurt anyone. She knew that he never could, but didn't want him to know that she knew.

"It's no big deal. You should forget about it."

Joseph looked at the ceiling and thought about it for a while. He watched the cracks in the ceiling pulsate, from dark black to a thin gray thread.

The room was sweltering. Joseph and Amanda could feel the drops of perspiration rolling down their ribs to the blanket. Their pale bodies in the dark room looked as if they were floating underwater. They were the only objects in the room reflecting any light.

"What did the old lady mean? For you to stay away from her husband?" Joseph asked.

"I don't know what she was talking about. She's a bad junkie. That's why her husband sells."

Street noises, girls' voices, roaming dogs and car alarms came in on a weak breeze through the uncovered windows. Next door there was another meal going. A clatter of plates and the scatter of another language.

Joseph and Amanda had tried to fix their front door the best they could. It remained delicately shut as long as no one touched it.

"Honey, please don't go after those guys." Amanda squeezed his hand.

"I love you," Joseph said. He meant it as much as he could. It did not sound right to him. Uncomfortable seconds passed and Amanda didn't say a thing. The words had died out somewhere in the air.

Joseph's Dreams

Joseph kept jumping up from his sleep in the middle of the night. He thought he saw people breaking in, a succession of thieves and beggars. Each dream took place in the apartment. The door that went to the hallway, the one the dealer's wife tore down, was the one Joseph kept seeing the people clumsily and violently breaking through. During his dreams, there was a second door which opened out over the alley and faced a featureless brick wall. There was no fire escape or porch. It was a narrow drop to the ground four floors below.

The people in his dreams had all passed him on the street. They had all taken parts of his life. McKnuckle, the Mayor, the Printer, Sonny. There was the red-headed woman who fought with the ex-nun and a skinny white drunk who never wore a shirt, only to defiantly expose the black sores growing on his chest and throat. There was Glenda doing a strip tease. Bates and the Greek and Mitch Koe. Joseph saw Old John falling drunk through the door, clutching his bottle every night.

The front door would fall with a crash of wood and an echo of footsteps. Bodies would tremble and hit the floor, toppling over each other. Some nights the faces appeared silently and suddenly over him. Living ghosts watching him. They told him that they knew where he was, they knew what he really was.

And while all this was going on, Amanda never stirred once.

If Amanda was feeling well, she liked to talk. "Hey, Joseph?"
"Yeah?"
"Isn't that weird?" She listened to her own voice. "Joseph. Joseph. We never really use each other's names. I mean you never say my name and I never say yours."

It was true. For some reason Joseph never called Amanda by her first name. He tried not to say her name if he could help it. The hesitance, the fear in Joseph, was irrational and he could not help but feel childish. Something in his chest would tighten whenever he had to say the girl's name. He was scared to say her name incorrectly even though some days Amanda was the only person Joseph ever saw or spoke to. Saying her name aloud made Joseph cringe. As if she might realize that she was with Joseph and would leave that much sooner.

It was more uncomfortable than the moment after Joseph told Amanda that he loved her. Even though, at the time, he was certain that she loved him too. Now Joseph knew that they both resented the words. The words were nothing. He had believed it until they were said aloud. A boundary had been marked and Joseph felt that he could not move.

Amanda asked more questions. "Why don't you ever say my name? Hey, what's my last name?" She saw a flash of panic cross Joseph's face. She saw that he didn't know her name. "I mean, it's okay if you don't know. We haven't really been together for that long and I think I only told you once or twice."

Joseph apologized to Amanda and silently cursed himself.

"It's no big deal. I'm not mad."

"Okay," Joseph said. But Amanda still didn't give away her surname. As if it were already too late for that.

Shadow patterns crossed the ceiling as Joseph and Amanda listened to their neighbors. A Hispanic radio station was tuned in next door and a song played over an excited conversation. When the song ended Amanda asked Joseph a new question.

"Anyone ever call you Joe?"

"Nah." It had never occurred to Joseph that he might be a Joe.

"Why not?"

"I don't know. Everyone just used my birth name. No one ever shortened it or anything like that."

"Not even Joey?"

"No, never." Joseph wanted to say that it was probably because those names didn't sound biblical. His father's name was Francis and his mother's was Josephine. He dreamed of them sometimes, too.

He wasn't going to tell Amanda anything about his dreams, not if she wasn't going to tell him her last name. He decided to keep that to himself. Maybe she could hear Joseph yelling at them, the ones coming in. If she asked about the dreams, Joseph decided that he would refuse to tell her.

Amanda broke through Joseph's thoughts as she traced her fingers along his jawline. She pulled Joseph's face close, her eyes traced paths across his cheeks and chin, then up the bridge of his nose to his eyes.

"No, you're not a Joe," she decided.

"I'm not?"

"No. It just don't sound right." Amanda tried the name a few times out loud and Joseph waited for a further decision. "Really, no. You're not even a Joey. I just don't see it." She laughed about something. "It's supposed to be a sign of unreasonable self-importance when a person can't think of someone else's name."

"But you never told me."

"I know I did."

"You didn't."

"Don't get mad at me. I'm not mad about it. But, really, we've been sleeping together for how long? I don't want an answer. I'm just asking."

Joseph didn't want to quiz Amanda about his own name because she probably knew it.

They both settled back to the floor. Joseph was glad that he didn't have a new name to get accustomed to.

Amanda laughed to herself and then whispered in his ear. "Joey."

He cringed. The spot in his chest tightened just like it did when he had to say her name. It didn't sound right. Just like when Joseph said that he loved her.

"Joey. Joey Joe. Joey Joe Joe."

Amanda laughed again and it sounded dry and harsh. Like there was nothing else she could do but force a laugh before they slept.

In his dreams, Joseph would look at the window and see himself reflected in the glass. Outside the window another face floated upward and close. The transvestite, Bobbi from Montrose, peered inside as if also trying to see past her own reflection.

She was just as Joseph remembered last seeing her in the coffee shop with the Mayor. He had seen her since then, but they never spoke. Sometimes she had a five o'clock shadow. One week she had even grown a full mustache.

In Joseph's window she had a fresh shave. Fingers tapped at the glass and a gray bathrobe floated out behind her. Her feet could have been pressed against the wall across the narrow alley.

The dream ended as Joseph was pretending to not see Bobbi.

Joseph would always wake and check the alley from the window. He couldn't see anything out in the dark.

Amanda didn't move. She slept through everything.

Joseph felt weak compared to Amanda. As weak as Amanda had looked curled up in the bathroom. The straw that he once saw filling her body had been stuffed inside his own while he was asleep. A fist could reach into his stomach and pull out the stiff, dry grass. Wind could pull the rest from the gaping hole, pull the strands from between his ribs.

Everything had been fine before. Joseph was with Amanda and his future looked good. He didn't know what had happened to make him so unsure.

On the street during the day, when Bobbi was with her boyfriend and they walked past, Joseph checked her eyes for some flash of recognition. Sometimes she would notice Joseph and her eyes would dart away, smiling. And other days she walked blindly past.

Bobbi never told Joseph how she made out at the gambling tables in Joliet. They had returned long before. Either that, or they had never left. She and Hank were supposed to make enough money to coast through the coming autumn and winter without ever having to return to Chicago.

A Fortune

Near the liquor store, young Vietnamese boys pitched quarters at a crack in the sidewalk, their smiles just a pinching of skin and muscle. While the older ones stood against the wall and watched silently, dragon and sparrow tattoos gliding like shadows across their shoulders, the peewees raced to the coins and judged the distance between lines with a shoestring's length. Arguments and demanding laughter chose the winner before the boys all went back to the line where they started.

Joseph saw several of the younger boys grinning and stealing glances at him. One side-armed a penny in his general direction amid the foreign gossip. It bounced high off the sidewalk and rolled out of sight as if it, too, was laughing at him.

They could have been good customers for Joseph, but he blew it as soon as he started working again at the liquor store. Thirteen year-old Vietnamese gangbangers had decent money to pay for their alcohol. The older ones gave Joseph no attention, but the littler kids approached Joseph one night after he was allowed to close up the store by himself. The Vietnamese Pee-Wees offered to buy their alcohol directly from Joseph. Only one spoke in English, the others stood casually organized in the background. They were very polite when they asked for a very heavy discount. Joseph said that he would get them something, but they would have to pay him. They all smiled and the one who spoke English said yes. Joseph knew that they all understood him, but he wondered why only one spoke.

They didn't pay Joseph when he brought the first bottle of Peach Schnapps. The next time, the spokesman told Joseph, they would have the money for two bottles. And Joseph said nothing when they asked for a third bottle without paying for the first two. He just stood there with one hand out, innocently expecting to be paid. He was outnumbered by the thirteen year-olds. Several hands slid into the pockets of baggy coats. One of them said something Joseph couldn't understand. They were laughing when Joseph decided to walk away and he couldn't understand a thing any of them had said to his back.

Joseph and Amanda sat on the cement ledge before the library window. Across the street was the building in which they stayed. And at the corner the Vietnamese Pee-Wees were pitching quarters. Amanda didn't know about Joseph's recent sales attempts. She pointed to the boys and asked Joseph, "Should I go ask if I could play?"

"No."

"Why not?"

"I don't think they'd let you."

"Shit. They'd get a kick out of it." Amanda didn't want to pitch quarters, she just wanted Joseph's reaction. And now that she had it, she was bored.

"Are you gonna?" Joseph asked.

"Nah. I'm tired."

But she was able to find a reserve of energy when the dealer waddled out of the alley that ran behind the building. Amanda took off, running from him. Joseph followed until he found that it was a dead end. Amanda stopped when she hit the chain-link fence and Joseph waited to see if she would try to climb over the three strings of barbed wire crowning the lot.

"I just don't want to see him right now."

A bubble filled in Joseph's throat, ready to burst. It was the first time he had seen Amanda scared.

"How much do you owe him?"

"Not much, don't worry."

Joseph began to ask another question and Amanda answered it before the words left his mouth.

"I know you got no money. I wasn't going to ask you. I gotta fill out some applications for a job today. I'll get some money soon." Amanda peeked out to the far end of the alley and didn't find the dealer. She didn't notice that Joseph was ready to lose his composure.

Joseph couldn't think of anything to say. He was not making enough money to feed both of them and had been stealing food from the liquor store whenever a chance arose. He wanted to scold Amanda for blowing their money, but he knew it wasn't really her fault. She got sick all the time. Then she took a shot like a miracle cure, slept for a while and was like new again. Joseph knew the pattern. Sometimes he even knew which mornings he would find her hiding in the bathroom or when she was already downstairs. Maybe it was good that he knew these things. Everything was under control, he consoled himself.

In the shaded corner of the alley Amanda leaned up against Joseph and gently pushed him until his back was against the brick wall. She pressed up against Joseph and he could feel the heel of her leg wrapped around his calf and her hand sliding over the crotch of his pants. She whispered in his ear and told him that he shouldn't worry about anything. Then she kissed him and stepped back.

"I gotta get going," Amanda apologized and kissed Joseph again. Before crossing the sidewalk she craned her neck to the left and the right, checking for the dealer again, and then moved on.

Joseph's idea of a cabin in the wilderness drifted in and out of focus depending on Amanda's behavior and how he thought she would react to the possibility. Joseph didn't want to be left alone. Sometimes it was unimaginable, what he could be doing years ahead. He couldn't reasonably consider anything that was past his reach.

He had all kinds of goals that he wanted to believe he could reach through nothing more than the passing of time. He knew better, but he pushed the worry from his head. He walked through the weeks, safely thinking of only the day he occupied.

Under the mismatched colors of the New Chinatown banners the Printer was shuffling along. He kept his head down at the same angle as the brown paper bag that hung from his fist, swinging limply with each step. Joseph could see that the man had been drinking and he wondered if it was in celebration of some financial windfall. The stock from Toronto or wherever could have made him a millionaire.

As Joseph approached him it became obvious that the Printer wasn't celebrating anything. His eyes were circled in pink and the man was wearing the clothes he had slept in, in the same clothes Joseph had seen the last time they had spoken. Joseph knew that the man owned other clothes and wondered if it was possible to lose one's pants in the stock exchange.

"Oh, kid," the Printer moaned and staggered and Joseph didn't know how to respond. He didn't even know the old man's name. It was only the Printer. Joseph didn't know any full proper names, just nicknames and titles left over from lives concluded a long time ago. As if their names didn't matter at all anymore. "Oh, kid. I lost it all. Every dollar I poured in has vanished."

Joseph wished that he knew of another name to call the man. His name seemed cruel now.

The Printer broke into a long explanation. The stock, or whatever it was, had never split. Something, some abstract value Joseph didn't catch, just kept dropping, like the prices had only held at one level and waited for the Printer to invest some money. And then it kept sinking invisibly because some business contract somewhere had been canceled. All the man had left was the money in his pockets. He had been caught between someone else's deals. "A success story gone backwards in double-speed," the Printer said, forcing a chalky laugh. All of the confidence and the conspiracy that had been in the man's eyes before was now gone.

The Printer thought it would be a good thing to do, a fitting thing, if he bought Joseph a beer. They would sit in the park and have a nice talk.

Joseph agreed and went along since he had nothing else to do.

Off in the distance Puerto Rican boys were letting their dogs run through the outfield of a baseball diamond. One dog had something dark held between its jaws and the others were chasing as it zigzagged through the field and along the gravel warning track. The boys were cheering for the dogs, and it was impossible to tell what the cheers were for since there seemed to be no finish line.

"I need money. I need it right away," the Printer said to Joseph. "If I could get one score, one thing, it doesn't matter. Anything." The Printer was spiraling from a good drunk and Joseph wondered how long the man would be able to stay awake.

The Printer listed all the commodities he could use for profit if he only owned them. All kinds of stocks and bonds and mutual markets that Joseph didn't understand. Joseph listened carefully when the Printer began speaking of rare coins.

The Printer knew the Mayor. They passed each other on the street once in a while and they had talked several times long ago in Bates' liquor store. The Printer never asked how Joseph knew the albino.

Sunlight poured in through the windows of the Mayor's apartment in solid, dusty squares. The rooms had been temporarily abandoned and the lock on the door gave under the pressure of a butter knife and Joseph's shoulder.

The Mayor had announced that the coins were his pension, his security. The old man lived like a bum, but was proud that he received no checks from the government. He would accept no handouts. Joseph knew all the worn maxims from the time he spent sleeping on the Mayor's couch. Welfare and food stamps were all dehumanizing and degrading. People had to take care of themselves and then if they could, then they helped other people. The government could not be relied on by any citizen. Systems were built brick by brick to keep people where they were in the unspoken caste system. Once a paycheck was taken, the recipient was told how much space, money, and possessions were allowed. The Mayor said that freedom must be attained on all levels. Thievery was more respectful than conformity. Joseph knew all the stories about the Mayor. He heard them all after the fact.

The Mayor's advice crossed Joseph's resentful mind, interrupting and gracefully scolding, the same way the Preacher's words once did. "People have to take care of themselves first."

A garbage bucket and a large pan both holding rainwater sat on the kitchen table. Plaster had fallen from the ceiling and the water had warped and curled sections of the linoleum floor. Stains spread down the sunflower-faded walls in shapes that resembled fingers poking down from closed fists. Dirty clothes were strategically placed across the floor, left there to soak up the overspill of water. Empty cartons of take-out food were piled under the table and the stink of sour liquor was drifting from the bedroom.

Joseph dug quietly through the closets and boxes as he listened for heavy footsteps at the stairs. His heart was pounding against his chest and his hands were covered in sweat. Joseph could barely control his stomach. He had to run to the toilet.

Crossing the room, he slipped in a puddle and the back of his head hit the ground after his feet went into the air. It sounded as loud as a gunshot inside his ears and pain rushed around his skull. Like everything, blood and brains, was expanding and trying to burst out.

Joseph rolled to his stomach and didn't even notice he was sitting in a puddle of water that covered most of the kitchen floor, didn't notice that he hadn't yet made it to the bathroom.

Joseph wondered if there was something wrong with his head. He remembered that it was the second time in past months he felt like he cracked his skull wide open.

When no longer dizzy, he got up again and found that he had plenty of time to relieve himself.

In the back of the kitchen closet Joseph reached back until he pulled out the jean jacket he had left behind. He snapped it in the air like a beach towel to shake off the dust and dirt. The cobwebs were scraped away from each sleeve and then Joseph put the jacket on. He kept digging through boxes of old books and newspapers, shoes and clothes, umbrellas and broken walking sticks until there was a box he recognized. One side ripped open as Joseph pulled. Coins, each wrapped in a patterned handkerchief, rolled to the floor. Joseph unwrapped the first coin and weighed it in his palm like he knew what he was doing. For a moment he saw himself as some kind of master thief. But all he discerned was that the coin was silver and polished and heavy in his hand and it definitely looked old. Joseph sniffed at the coin, as if that would settle any last questions.

He kept all the coins wrapped in their handkerchiefs as he shoved them into the pockets of his jacket. It was bulkier and weighed him down, but the coins didn't jingle against each other. Joseph pushed the box into the closet and shut the door. He dug his hands into his pockets and pulled his jacket tight over his body. Then he ran down the stairs and through the yard behind the building. A group of black girls saw Joseph running through the alley and they yelled as his heels kicked at the gravel, but Joseph didn't think they would bother telling anyone that they saw a white kid running from something.

As he ran he dreamed of the amounts of money he was going to make. Joseph guessed the number would be somewhere in the thousands.

"No, I said you can't come with." The Printer shook his head at Joseph. "This guy doesn't like to meet new people. He's very private. It's because of his business, he's a little paranoid about his place getting broken into. I guess he should be."

Joseph swore and promised that he wouldn't tell anyone where or who this guy is. The Printer said that didn't matter. "We're splitting the money fifty-fifty. You shouldn't worry."

"I did all the work," Joseph pouted.

"But I'm the one who has to try and sell them."

"I thought you said you could sell them easy."

"I can, but they're stolen. I have to be careful."

"How about I sell them?" Joseph offered, even though the coins were already in the Printer's hands.

"If you sell them," the Printer explained gently, "you won't get one tenth of what I can get. Who do you know that will buy these for what they're worth? Nobody."

The Printer remained calm through the whole exchange. His voice was flat and soothing. The drunken panic from the day before when the plans had been made seemed to have evaporated. The prospect of some easy money centered the Printer. Joseph's suspicions fell away slowly. There was no reason to doubt someone who spoke in such control. Besides, the Printer was right. Joseph didn't know how to sell the coins, he couldn't even sell alcohol to little kids. Joseph would have to trust the Printer and he began to enjoy the idea of having a partner, a business partner.

"Okay. Let's shake," the Printer concluded.

Joseph relented. He held out his hand and the old man grabbed it roughly, pulling his knuckles up and down as if he wanted to take the boy's arm out of the socket.

Pieces of Advice

"Oh. You're here now." Old John noticed Bates behind the counter after the wind chimes over the door stopped ringing. Bates didn't answer, so John reached up and touched his finger to each little bell hanging over his head.

"Leave the bells alone, John, will you?"

Mitch Koe and the Greek were at the counter with Bates. They had been watching Court TV, but turned away long enough to smile at the old man.

John looked around unsteadily, took a glance down each aisle, inspected Bates and the other men and asked, "Is the boy here today?" Old John seemed worried, Bates was the only one he recognized. "Is the kid in back? Where is he?"

Bates fired rapid questions at the little drunk as a form of interrogation. "Why? What do you want? Is he supposed to be here? Did he tell you that? Or does he got something for you? You got something for him? You trying to sell him something? I ain't gonna buy your crap. Are you gonna waste my time?"

Old John staggered after the barrage went past like a rumbling train. He only caught a few words and the men laughed. "He won't be here at all today?" John wanted to be certain.

"No."

"Then can I ask you a favor?" The old man's nasal whine came with the favors. "A big, big favor."

"I ain't giving money away."

"Lookit this."

In slow pulls he turned out the pockets of his coat. Each fist came up spilling little tarnished coins. Bates slapped them flat to the counter before they rolled to the floor. On top of the coins John then laid a box of staples, a staple gun, paperclips, a Mercedes-Benz hood ornament already fastened to a chain necklace, and a heavy plumber's wrench. After searching all his pockets a second time John dropped two more coins, useless just like the others, to the counter.

"How much for everything?"

"What makes you think I want any of it?" Bates wanted to know. Mitch and the Greek were watching from the side and added nothing since Bates seemed to be in charge.

"Please?"

"I don't want everything."

"But lookit this." John hefted the wrench unsteadily from the counter and stumbled backwards. "Ooh. It's heavy," he chuckled, "that means it's good. They don't make them heavy anymore."

"I don't need a wrench."

"What do you need? I got a lot."

Ignoring the old man, Bates began picking the coins off of the smooth countertop. Old John tried to help, he was able to get one between his fingers by the time Bates had the counter cleared. As if he was doing the old man a favor, Bates finally offered to pay John for the coins.

"Lookit these. These are old. I don't know where they're from."

"Canada."

"But they got the queen on them. Old, old, old. God save the queen." John saluted the cigarette rack and Bates offered three dollars for three handfuls of the Canadian coins.

"But look how old they are. I bet they're expensive."

"They're just Canadian coins. Go to Canada they're all over the place. Three dollars. They aren't worth shit."

Old John thought about it for a second and then finally agreed. Bates unfolded three singles from his pocket and handed them over.

"I'm not done yet." John took a beer from the refrigerator and brought it to the counter.

"Two bucks." The price was rounded up to the next dollar. John handed over two dollars and put the last one deep in his pants pocket. Now everything was settled. He stood there and searched the room, expecting Joseph to appear from behind one of the large men. No such thing happened, so John stared at Bates until he was told that he could drink in the store as long as he didn't bother anyone.

John liked being accepted into any drinking group. Quickly he twisted the cap off the neck and listened to the beer hiss. He tilted his head back and shut his eyes while his Adam's apple struggled to keep up with gravity.

When the old man stopped for a breath, the Greek pointed out a long scratch running from the corner of John's eye to the edge of his lip. "What happened to you?"

"I got into a fight with one of the girls." John shrugged.

"You got into a fight with a girl?" Mitch Koe asked.

The Greek added, "You didn't pull her hair, did you? That's not fair."

"They ain't girls," Bates cut in to explain. "They're his girls."

"What are you, a pimp?"

"No." John shook his head. "No." He was not a pimp.

John lived in a Wilson Avenue flophouse where there was always someone watching the television at the front desk and someone always asleep in one of the two chairs that sat in the lobby.

John's rent was paid every month in one lump sum, unlike the young men who surrounded the front door, who had to try and pay every night. They never had enough all at once, so they would beg and intimidate people in an attempt to pay for that night's room. John knew that if he didn't give them something, they wouldn't go away. They would follow him wherever he went. They had taken John's money before. It seemed they didn't beat him as bad when he was able to give them something. The front door was a gauntlet for the old man who felt that the building was specifically designed to make a person feel locked in, but never very safe because he was always locked in with other people. He wouldn't have minded being locked in by himself.

Chicken wire and accordion gates covered the upstairs windows and the fire escapes were hanging dangerously outside the windows on every other floor by one or two rusted supports. Each floor had a bathroom at the end of the hall. John had been there for two short years. Time had flown past. He liked it better than the last place, which was nowhere at all.

So he kept his complaints to himself and caused no problems when two transvestites followed him home, coaxed their way in, and never left. Big white girls who looked good when they had all their make-up on. John had been tempted with whiskey and promises of blow jobs. Upstairs, he was given the whiskey, but nothing else that first night. He was proud when his guests immediately dropped to the floor and played with his little kitten at three in the morning. And days had passed with John nearly unconscious in a free drunk before it was noticed that his guests were not really women at all. In the dark he never had to notice.

Old John couldn't really understand the two young men who dressed like women. Sometimes they were nice and sometimes they weren't. John called them "the girls." Sometimes, if one of them felt generous, John would get a blow job. He would never ask for one, because he knew that the girls could also gang up on him and throw him out for the night. They were strong. He never complained, just went to sleep in the hallway.

Every once in a while John called the cops to throw the girls out. They got loud and they played music, which was against the rules. He didn't like them using the drugs, he was scared that they would get him in trouble and he would lose the room that the Salvation Army had worked so hard to find. John liked the ladies in uniform, the ones who did all the paperwork that seemed to eventually solve things. The Salvation Army would harass John and be very angry if he lost his place and it would be a long time before they found him a new one, so he tried not to complain much. After the police visited, the girls came back as if nothing had happened. They had only gone out for a stroll.

There would be no blow jobs for a long time after that. John didn't mind, he wouldn't want anyone to know about that. He sometimes worried what people would think of him if they knew. He was married a long time ago. Had a wife and a house.

"The faggots," Bates asked with a grin, "they giving you trouble?"

"No."

"No?"

"A little." John seemed to always collapse under repeated questioning.

He stood there with Bates and the two other men until a solution was offered. "You got a frying pan at home?" Bates inquired. John took a mental inventory of his room and found that he did. He nodded and Bates continued. "You get your frying pan at night when the faggots are asleep. When they're asleep. Make sure, now. And you hit them both in the head. Knock them out cold, then call the cops. Can you do that?"

John thought about it and nodded, grinned easily, and repeated everything that had been planned out. The other men all agreed that this was a good idea. They believed John could do it. He would wait until late at night and hit the girls in the head with a frying pan.

When the beer was finished, John stuck the empty in a torn pocket of his coat, then went to the refrigerator and this time brought a can of beer back to the counter. Cans cost a few pennies under a dollar and John was proud that he knew how to watch his money. The Salvation Army gave him enough money, just a little at a time, to buy his daily amount of beer. It was just enough to barely get by and he had to work hard to make any extra money he needed. He hid the can inside a paper bag, gathered his wrench and staple gun, and steadied himself for the walk home.

"So you gonna do what we said?" Bates asked.

John was confused. "What?"

"The frying pan."

The little man wrinkled his forehead and chewed on his lip as he worked the operation out again in his mind. Then he said okay. On his way out the door he couldn't help but lightly palm the bells hanging in the air. When he stuck his finger inside one and held the knocker, the bell only made tiny clicks.

Right after the store opened for business the next day, Old John carried himself through the door and presented his face up to Bates for inspection. His lip was split in two places. He had a black eye that was halfway shut and four more deep scratches curved from the top of his forehead to his upper lip.

Bates was alone in the store, scratching at lottery tickets. He put down the silver tab and addressed Old John.

"You do what we said?"

"Yes."

"How'd it go?"

"No good."

"Sorry to hear that."

"Me too."

With the conversation ended, yesterday's humor gone, Bates went back to his lottery tickets and waited for Old John to leave. When it was realized that the little man wasn't moving, Bates suggested, "John, why don't you try that again. Get them while they're awake, though."

Old John said nothing. Bates scratched three more tickets away and tossed them in the garbage.

"You win?" John asked with teeth clenched.

"Nah."

"Good," he snapped back. "You should lose." And pointed an accusing finger across the counter. "You should never win. I don't like you. I am not coming back here again."

And then he flung the door open and pulled the little bells down from their fixture. The tuneless crash died as soon as the bells and their thin knockers hit the ground. The sound dropped away as if Bates had suddenly gone deaf.

Confession Box

In the bedroom he grew up in Joseph had nightly studied a reproduction of a painting of the young, golden-faced Christ. The skin appeared smooth as porcelain and the wispy beard looked as if it had never been touched by a razor.

The eyes came down across the room to meet Joseph's.

It was a Jesus that Joseph knew would always be listening and always be watching. One that provided for those who needed the most; one who would answer the smallest of prayers.

In a voice the boy could not find, he wanted to ask the Jesus a question as to what he was supposed to do. Some nights Joseph believed that his voice had been taken away.

In the dark of the bedroom he listened to the crystalline sound of glass shattering beneath his father's screaming. His father was certain that the church was wrecking his life. The boy's father would deny any assistance, he would ignore any helpful suggestions or authoritative interventions. He would contradict the Preacher until no choices were left for him. Joseph knew that his father had considered leaving on several occasions. His bag was packed and his shoes were on. But only Joseph and his mother were there to see the man's protest.

Joseph had seen the other men, the elders of the church, make his father do what they wished. He boarded the Ready-Man buses in the morning. He sullenly worked in the soup kitchen, shoveled snow in the winter, and pulled weeds from the sidewalks in spring.

Joseph had heard the other kids say that there was something wrong with his father's head. They never said this to Joseph. Joseph was left alone.

One night he heard the silverware drawer empty to the linoleum. Dishes were pulled from the sink. The apartment fell into silence and then one howl of protest came from his mother. A flash of light slid under the frame of the bedroom door and then there was more screaming. She sounded like a siren. A scream thin as wire. The crack of light under the door grew steady and pulsed into a bright orange. Joseph could see the shadows in his bedroom. He could see that patterns of the regimented wooden soldiers on his bedspread and he could see the vinyl-bound Bible on his night table, flickering in the light.

Joseph was locked in. The room shrank and the air grew heavy across the thin sheets. He repeated a short prayer over and over. There had been fires in the apartment before. Obvious evidence had been found in the morning, blackened sofa cushions doused in water and deep smoke marks scarred into the ceiling.

Pulling the covers up over his head, Joseph waited for the exhausted silence that always followed his father's rages and announced everything was settled until morning.

A still moment passed before he heard people running through the apartment. While smoke crept into the room, blossoming thinly to the ceiling.

The bedroom door burst open and Joseph saw the living room cut and divided by shafts of yellow light retreating through thick smoke. Arms scooped him from his bed, the sheets holding his arms tight to his sides. A hard shoulder knocked the wind from Joseph. He shut his eyes.

Sparks of ashes burned his face and smoke closed his throat as he was passed through the apartment. Down four flights of stairs he was taken over someone' back. In the lobby firemen were dragging a hose up the stairs toward the smoke.

Joseph opened his eyes and saw stars popping. Puddles of water splashed across the tiled lobby floor as people ducked out under the hallway emergency lights.

Wearing only nightgowns and bathrobes, residents from the hotel covered themselves with winter coats and ran into the street. Joseph saw Brother Samuel beneath him, holding him high in the air.

The snow was falling peacefully outside. It fell on the inhabitants of the hotel as they hopped around to keep their slippered and stockinged feet dry. More police and firemen conferred around the front doors of the building. Some were directing the residents out into the street.

Where the crowd had parted, Joseph could see his father beneath a pair of twirling cherry lights, wrestling his body around a set of handcuffs. A policeman tucked his head down into the back seat of a white police car with one blue stripe. The rest of the block seemed to be pitch black.

"It was an accident," Joseph heard his mother pleading to Preacher Madison. "It was an accident. I knocked over a candle. Really, I'm so sorry. My God. I don't know what he was going to do with that stuff. But it was my fault."

Other kids were out on the sidewalk. Joseph knew they were talking about him. He heard an adult's voice in the crowd tell someone that the man was seen carrying two buckets of gasoline, sloshing them around on the sidewalk as he carried them into the hotel.

A few days later Joseph and his mother had a new apartment on a new floor. Some time after that Joseph's father joined them.

"I don't regret anything," Amanda admitted to Joseph. "What would the point of that be? I can't fix anything. And feeling guilty isn't a natural reaction. Animals don't feel guilt. That's the difference and I don't know if it's good or bad. It shouldn't be normal, even though society says it is. But that's what religion does. That's what it's meant for. To make you feel shameful. I mean, I was raised Catholic and the whole drive behind it is guilt. That's how you control people. Not you yourself, but that's how other people can control people. You know what I mean? That's the Catholic Way. I had one friend, this one girl, her mom was an ex-nun. She left the nunnery when she found a dude she wanted to marry. I guess it was this big thing a long time ago. Now it's a lot easier to leave the church, but back then, I think my friend's mom was excommunicated, maybe. At least I know she wasn't married in the Catholic Church."

Joseph listened. He hadn't said anything to prompt the conversation. Sometimes Amanda started talking as soon as she opened her eyes in the morning.

"They went to the county judge and got married and eventually my friend's mom, this woman, finished college and got her teaching degree. Her husband had some kind of job that don't matter. Sat in an office all day. He was gone in the morning and came back home around five. But mom was teaching junior high science in the school district they lived in. And when my friend was old enough, she had to go to the same school after her mother had already been there for fifteen years or whatever. Bad enough, you know, seeing your mother every day in junior high, but to have her be a teacher and to know that she used to be a nun. One of God's chicks. My friend never said anything, but somehow people know these things. Kids hear from their parents or older brothers or whatever. So the word was always floating around and my friend always acted like she never heard it. Life was supposed to go on like normal.

"And her parents were so hard on the kid. The slightest thing and they went around the bend. You know how you actually start talking to boys in school around those years and when my friend did, her mom went nuts. She found notes from boys in her daughter's pants when she was doing the laundry. Boys were calling the house. Her mom one day caught her in school holding hands with a boy and she ran up to them and pulled their hands apart and led her daughter off into an empty classroom to fucking scream at her. That was not how girls were supposed to act. Said they would discuss it when they got home. They, mom and dad, sat her down for a family talk, but that was the only time that happened. Her folks told her that they were at the end of their rope. They just didn't know what to do. Holding hands. Said the kid was the same as a whore and a prostitute. They said that passing notes to boys and that sort of physical contact was the same as a girl advertising herself, saying she was up for grabs. But that was all the girl ever did, hold hands. It was the only time.

"She was scared to death to do anything else. From then on, her parents forbid her to talk to boys or go out at all. Television was bad, music was bad. The girl couldn't do nothing but sit at home and study her geography and algebra. By the time we got to high school, I didn't know her at all. You know, you just drift away. We all just sorta forgot about her, never saw her much after that. It was her parents that were perverted, because they saw something horrible in something that wasn't even there. You know?

"But that's how it always is. The ones who are the most guilty are the first to condemn, instead of being the last. Which they really should be. They put their own guilt on someone beneath them and they know they're doing a good job as long as everyone beneath them is miserable. Notice the Catholic Church ain't really the cleanest organization, but they got the strictest rules. Guilt is always someone else's invention.

"Tell me, why can the Pope tell American citizens how to vote?"

"I don't know," Joseph admitted. He didn't know. He didn't know what the Pope was telling people.

"The Pope said not to vote for Clinton because Clinton supports abortion rights and the Catholic Church doesn't. Why should the Pope be telling anyone how to vote? He's not even a U.S. citizen. Makes me wonder what he's hiding. He's so righteous about everything. It'd be a little more lax if the Pope was a woman. Or if the Pope ever had a normal relationship with a woman. Then maybe he'd have some room to move. The holiest thing is to never have sex. That's the closest they can get to God. That's the big sacrifice. And the prize for making that sacrifice is that they can tell women what to do."

Amanda was pleased with her position on the subject which she had brought up out of nowhere. Joseph hadn't asked her anything about the Pope or guilt. It was obvious that she felt no guilt. Or it was obvious that she wanted Joseph to know that she felt no guilt.

As Amanda got up to leave for the day, she asked Joseph to throw out the television box. All it was doing was taking up space.

Joseph promised he would. "Where you going?" he asked before Amanda placed a goodbye peck on his forehead.

"Just out to see a friend. I won't be long."

The television box full of bricks was still sitting there in the corner. Whenever Joseph saw the cardboard and bricks, he suddenly lacked the energy to drag the mess away. He had carried the sealed box ten blocks the night he bought it. But now he could barely look at it without feeling exhausted.

In the high windows of Truman College Joseph could see his reflection, thin and wavering across the sidewalk. The building was a mirror, all black metal and slick glass.

His figure in the glass looked small and dark. Light shone on the top of his crew cut and touched his shoulders, knees, and hands. That was all Joseph could see of himself. He raised his hand and moved it across his face. Catching the daylight in his palm, he brought the white skin across the image of his face and dropped his hand back down to his side. His figure was dark again, like a silhouette inside the sun's reflection.

A fumbling crash came from the bushes behind Joseph. The delicately flowered branches parted and Old John stumbled to the sidewalk. Blood had dried under his nose and one eye was a murky yellow surrounded by tender leather skin. His bottle of beer was empty, but he still held it tight. As soon as John righted himself and brushed the dirt off his knees, he began a sob story as if he had known Joseph would be waiting for him at that exact spot. "They did it. They did it again. It was the same as before, just the same."

John was crying. He spit tobacco from his brown teeth and wiped his nose with his sleeve.

Joseph asked what had happened this time. He was in no mood to hear John's problems. He was waiting for his money. His big payoff. The Printer was supposed to drop off Joseph's half of the return from the Mayor's coins.

"They took my money. They knew when I cashed my checks. I knew they were following me. All the way, all the way to the currency exchange they followed me."

"Who did, John?"

"The niggers."

"Which ones? There's a lot of them."

"The same ones. They did it to me before. The ones who hurt the nun by the beach."

Joseph didn't have much advice for the old man. "Stay away from them, John."

"Can I help it if they follow me all over the place? I'm old, I can't run from anyone. I try to fight, but I'm no good." John then added something else. "The faggots, the girls, they beat me up, too." John showed Joseph some scratches that were beginning to heal along one side of his face.

Old John forced his expression into a pleading pout. "Can I ask a favor? A big, big favor?"

"What is it?"

"A big favor."

"What?" Joseph tried to sound irritated, but he didn't think he was very convincing. He liked the little drunk.

"Can I borrow a dollar fifty? I don't got any money." His yellow eye began to water.

"Neither do I, John. I can't fucking do anything. I can't."

John put away his begging face, gathered his pride and walked away without saying another word.

Once the Wilson Avenue traffic cleared, the old man inched himself away from the curb and began across the street to the garden where Joseph had been sleeping a month ago. A car turning the corner screeched to a stop instead of plowing into John. Undeterred, the old man kept moving and ignored the curses of the driver.

No spare change was going to solve anything. Old John was too far gone to be walking the streets, Joseph decided. The old man could barely take care of himself. A pang of guilt flushed Joseph's face. Only a couple of weeks ago he had debated stealing Old John's Salvation Army check and he wanted to apologize to the little drunk for even thinking about it.

Joseph watched his reflection. He watched the vague figures of other people move across the window. It felt like a long time had passed.

Joseph wanted to announce that he was quitting. He wanted to give it all up, even though he couldn't find what it was that he could give up. He wanted to forfeit something, but there was nowhere to go from the point he was at.

"Afternoon, kid."

The Printer suddenly stepped between Joseph and the sun, erasing the boy's image in the window. Joseph immediately wanted to ask about his money. There had to be hundreds, he imagined, maybe a thousand from the rare coins.

"I have some bad news."

"What?"

Joseph had not considered the possible complications. The Printer had assured Joseph that the coin dealer was honest, he wouldn't call the cops or try to cheat them. The Mayor used to be a coin dealer, Joseph thought, and maybe the Printer's friend remembered him. Maybe he recognized the coins. Joseph imagined that the Printer was dealing with some man with thick eyeglasses who could spot a dime on the ground a hundred feet away and read what year it was minted. Some man who kept a jeweler's loupe scrunched against the bridge of his nose and sat at a table with a little white light hanging over his shoulder for closer detail inspections.

Or, Joseph feared, the Mayor knew what happened already. He was coming after Joseph. The cops would be called and some freakish coin-dealer circle would begin to close.

"We didn't make much money," the Printer told him, knocking aside other worries. Joseph's panic began to drop down to an aching disappointment.

"How much?"

"Your half is seventeen dollars."

"Bullshit."

"No." The Printer took the folded bills out of his shirt pocket. He counted out seventeen and handed them over to Joseph as if that were proof enough.

"I don't believe you. This is total bullshit. Those coins were good, they were old." Joseph held the seventeen dollars in his hand as if each bill was contaminated. He didn't want to put the cash in his pocket. He wanted to hold out for more.

"Kid, I feel real bad about that, but the guy told me the coins were no good. They weren't rare. A lot of them he bought for only a dollar a piece. Although there was one that he bought for a couple bucks."

"But the coins had to be good," Joseph reasoned. "The Mayor used to be a coin dealer. He had his own store."

"That was all I got. I gave you an even half."

"I deserve more than half. I was the one who went into the apartment."

"But I was the one who sold them."

"You're full of shit." Joseph didn't believe his own voice; he knew the Printer was the only one trying to help him. "Old fucking liar." Joseph stood up and the Printer backed away. Joseph couldn't hit the man, but he felt that something should be done. He couldn't tell if the old man was lying. He told himself that the Printer would not cheat him, but his voice, independent of his thoughts, kept attacking only because the Printer backed away.

"Maybe we can try again," the Printer suggested. "Were there any more coins? Maybe the good ones were hidden better."

"I don't know."

"There has to be more. Remember, that one was okay. We should try again."

"If you only got seventeen bucks, why you wanna try again?"

"Because I think we missed the jackpot, but we were close. I can feel it."

"If we do, I'm coming with to your coin dealer."

"I'll get back to you on that. I'll stop by the liquor store. You still work there, don't you?"

"Yeah, Maybe, I don't know when next."

"I'll come in this week sometime. I really feel bad about this. I was expecting much more money, also. I say we try again. Why shouldn't we? What is it that we are saving for?"

The gaunt man in the overcoat and the pale-faced boy settled down to the bench. Joseph studied the mirrored window across the walk and the Printer's image appeared much worse than his own.

"Yeah, come into the store this week. I'll try again."

The Printer said he would do that. He nodded his head, and Joseph watched his own image do the same across the sidewalk.

"Does this guy know the Mayor?" Joseph asked. "Does he know where the coins are coming from?"

"He doesn't care, it doesn't matter."

"If you say so."

Amanda was on the floor of the apartment, studying the ceiling. Joseph kneeled down gently and kissed her on the lips, then on the forehead, then on the lips again. Her skin was damp and her lips felt brittle.

"Are you okay?" Joseph asked.

Amanda nodded that she was fine. Except she needed ten dollars to run downstairs.

"You gotta do that?"

"You don't know anything," her voice was quiet and gentle, not angry, but barely pleading. "You don't know it, but I'm trying to quit. I went out and looked for a job today. Filled out a bunch of applications. There's no number, you know, where they can call me back. So I gotta go back there to all the places I applied for in a week or something. But right now I don't feel good. Can I get ten from you? I'll pay you back when I get the money. Soon as I get a job it'll all be like before. Don't worry."

"It's not the money," Joseph began to explain. There was nothing he could say, Amanda would do what she wanted. Without uttering a word she was able to make him feel like a child. Joseph felt that it was a good thing that she at least noticed that the situation had changed; she really needed him. He took out a ten dollar bill, the one the Printer gave him, and handed it over to Amanda. "Can I come down there with you?" Joseph thought that he would protect Amanda from the dealer's wife if she happened to be around. He didn't give any consideration to the dealer.

"Yeah, if you want to." Her eyes brightened under the lids and she now had some energy with the hope of visiting the fat dealer. She sat up and began lacing her boots. Joseph thought that ten dollars wasn't really that much. Amanda must have some of her own money. Or maybe she was receiving some kind of a discount.

The drapes of the dealer's apartment were open, tied in a knot and hung over the curtain rod. Out the window was the low roof of the library and beyond that were the rows of houses sleeping peacefully along the block. The trees between the houses were thick with wet green leaves and against a perfectly fake blue sky they appeared plastic and clean.

The dealer's apartment was filthy. Worse than the last time Joseph had seen the place. Styrofoam food cartons and greasy paper bags spotted the floor and the kitchen table. Big, dirty clothes like collapsed tents lay strewn about the apartment. And the kids were still screaming at each other in the bedroom as if they hadn't stopped since Joseph left. The dealer was in his chair, wearing red shorts and a sleeveless T-shirt that exposed pale stretch marks running in ripples down his biceps. A stack of VCRs balanced in front of his chair and two televisions were huddled in the corner. They were not in any boxes.

"C'mon kids," the dealer said to Joseph and Amanda, "I'm in a little bit of a fucking hurry. I got things to do."

"What happened to your place?" Amanda asked.

"What the fuck's wrong with it?"

"A little messy."

"Oh. That's cause the bitch left. You can't trust no one anymore. She split the other day and left the kids here, thank God. I wouldn't want them with her."

Something heavy toppled over in the bedroom. The kids howled and laughed. The dealer ignored the noise and Joseph wondered how many children were locked up in the next room. He wondered if they ever got out of the apartment.

Amanda must've been thinking the same thing because she asked the dealer what grades all the kids were in and Joseph figured that she asked just to double-check the original story about the kids.

"They're not in any grades. We were teaching them at home."

"That's good," Amanda said. "Kids should be taught by their parents. Schools are shit, anyway."

For some reason Amanda displayed a quick grin for Joseph and hid it away. Joseph noticed that there were no schoolbooks, or books of any kind, in the apartment.

"Yeah," the dealer agreed with Amanda. "So what do you need today? The same shit?"

"Yeah, sure. Yeah."

Amanda gave him the money and he slapped a little package into Amanda's palm. Joseph didn't see it.

The two huge televisions in the corner were almost twice the size of the box of bricks Joseph had carried down Broadway. He wondered how much those televisions would cost, but he didn't want to ask the dealer about them. Joseph remembered that he hadn't moved the box of bricks.

"What you gonna do with the TVs?" Amanda asked the dealer as she led Joseph to the door.

Looking up from his TV Guide, the dealer told Amanda to not worry about it. "I'm taking them in for repairs."

"What's wrong with them?"

"I don't know. The fucking fan belt, maybe."

The young couple trudged back up the stairs to their bare room. "We should try to buy one of those TVs," Amanda suggested, oblivious to the fact that they had no money. It was not a real problem to her. What little bit of cash Joseph had was to go for food, cigarettes, and maybe some beer if he couldn't sneak any out of the store. He tried to figure out how to stretch the eight dollars he had and still have something left over until he worked at the liquor store next. The amounts and meals and subtractions multiplied by days soon became blurred and distorted.

Joseph stopped and questioned Amanda. "What do you think happened to the dealer's wife?"

"I don't know. She probably wants to call the cops on him, especially if he has the kids. She'll probably end up with the kids. I don't know. The wife seems to always get the kids. The men should get stuck once in a while."

Amanda told Joseph that she hoped the wife didn't call the cops on the dealer. Then she arched her hips away from the ground to slide her pants off of her hips. "Come here," she said to Joseph who was swaying in the middle of the room, thinking of something far away.

He hesitated for a half second. He wanted to ask Amanda about the needles. But she apparently didn't need to do that right now.

The shadows moved around the room like clock hands and finally faded when the sun dropped behind the rows and rows of three-flats stretching past Ashland Avenue.

Before Joseph and Amanda drifted to sleep there was someone knocking on the door. A whisper came after the knock.

"Kid. Are you in there?"

Joseph got dressed after he recognized the Printer's voice. Amanda followed Joseph's lead and slipped inside a shirt that didn't reach to cover everything that should have been covered. Joseph didn't notice. He was already at the door.

The Printer spoke in a hushed tone and Joseph imitated his whisper. The Printer wanted to get back to the Mayor's apartment immediately. Joseph argued that they should watch the Mayor and his apartment. And when they were sure he would be gone for a while, Joseph would go in again.

The Printer was determined to go the next day. As soon as possible. Joseph thought it was a bad plan, but finally he agreed.

The Printer stood under the frame of the door. "It's set then," he said. "We go see your friend's place tomorrow." The Printer smiled about something. "I'm not much for this kind of thing, but I don't mind stealing from the Mayor." The Printer laughed and Joseph realized that the old man didn't know Amanda was in the room. "Yeah, the big sting. I'll meet you on the Truman benches tomorrow morning."

Joseph shut the door before the Printer stepped away.

"How do you know the Mayor?" Amanda asked as Joseph turned to her.

Joseph blushed in the darkened room. His environment seemed to keep shrinking. Every time he turned around, something was taken away from him. He had no idea Amanda knew of the Mayor. It wasn't fair. Again Amanda asked how Joseph knew the Mayor.

"I just seen him around. People told me who he was," the boy explained quickly while silently begging that Amanda wouldn't know about Joseph and the albino.

"Oh yeah? When I'd be downstairs, before I knew you, he'd come over to see the dealer. He always had some young kid with him and he'd be buying the kid some pot or pills, whatever was around. That old fucker would be drunk, getting the kid drunk. Then I guess he would take him home and screw him.

"The guy just made me sick," she continued. "Thinking about him gives me chills. He'd always be grabbing the kid he was with, winking, running his hand across the kid's back. Always touching. I don't know why the guy is called the Mayor, though."

"Nah, me neither," Joseph answered weakly. He felt very small. Somehow, the skinny girl who was only a few years older, had lived with seven or eight boyfriends, was married once and had lived a lifetime more, knew about this, too. Everything Joseph had ever done must have become public knowledge. He wanted to crawl away and just sleep until the people who surrounded him were long gone.

Joseph had the idea that he and Amanda would have an equal relationship. But everything he knew, it seemed, Amanda knew before him. He would never catch up. He was a little thief, a lousy thief stealing bits and pieces from whomever was closest while chunks were being taken from his own life. And Amanda was buried deep inside herself. The outside world didn't seem to matter all that much for Amanda.

Joseph wished to bury all of his life except for Amanda deep somewhere in the earth. He had always heard what the other children said about his father. He could feel what the adults thought of the man. Joseph took all the recriminations as his own.

When he was still living in the hotel, Joseph always walked lightly. He was always hiding. On one of the days Joseph needed a break from his parents, he expected to see Preacher Madison writing at his desk as he always was when Joseph slipped by. Instead, Joseph's father was standing there, his back to the open door. The Preacher's voice was hushed and stern, telling Joseph's father that he had been given his last warnings.

"You cannot go on and behave however you feel. You have a family. The church. God can see you even when we can't. You are responsible for your actions. You have fallen somewhere, somewhere far back. You betray and lie to the ones who love you. And that's all of us, Francis Askew."

Joseph's father held his chin to his chest, exposing the bald crown of his head to the Preacher. "You know there are ways I can help but the first step must be made by you. You must show me that you want the assistance. Believe me, that is all I can do, assist. What is it that you want? Your wife is and has been willing to do anything for you. She does what she can. Everybody does. But you must do something. What do you want to do?"

Joseph's father mumbled his answer.

"I can send you to a doctor. I am usually against doctors of any kind. I believe the Lord can heal better than man, but this may be different. I don't know. Is it this place? The city? There are other places. A so-called geographic cure. There are other places that the church is connected to. There are groups you can join."

Preacher Madison began talking of the temptations of the city, the sins of other people. In times of weakness they permeated an individual. Joseph listened outside the door as Preacher Madison tried to coax some kind of response from his father. It sounded as if the Preacher was speaking to an empty room. Joseph held every word he heard. Then slipped away down the hall when the private sermon ended. He didn't want to know what his father's punishment was going to be; he knew his own would be worse.

There was nothing Joseph could do to erase what had already been done. He adamantly told himself that he didn't want anyone's forgiveness. Joseph wished to separate his life from the first memory that had tied itself to him; to draw a line between what he was and what he wanted to be. So that no trace of his old self remained.

"Don't Catholics have something?" he asked Amanda during the night. "Where you tell the reverend what you did wrong and it all goes away?"

"The priest, yeah," Amanda nodded. "Confession. It's bullshit. We had to go every week. I never felt better afterward."

Joseph felt nothing would change. He knew he was being taken again. The coins were probably all rare and expensive. The Printer was probably making a ton of money off his work and all he received in return was seventeen dollars.

Joseph decided that he would grab everything he could carry from the Mayor's apartment and he would carefully watch the Printer. He woke up during the night and thought about it. He wanted to wake Amanda and tell her of his plans.

The next day he waited at the Truman benches and the Printer never appeared. An hour passed before Joseph went home, stopping at the liquor store along the way. Bates hadn't seen the Printer. He said that he hadn't seen the Printer in a long time. "I thought the fucker left town."

At the apartment Joseph again waited. There was no note, no message of any kind from the Printer. Amanda was gone for the day and for the first time Joseph didn't feel like looking for her.

He thought of all the different ways he was being cheated, and didn't know if it was he who had screwed up somehow. There was nothing else he could do at this point except go along. He thought that maybe he deserved what he got. Maybe everything would turn out okay after this passed.

Announcement

There was finally a television set in the apartment. Joseph had bought it from Old John. A five-inch black and white set, the antennae was bent and the metal tip was broken off in a sharp curl. It had cost Joseph only three dollars after a couple of minutes of haggling. Old John was happy, since any money was good money, and Joseph was pleased with the transaction.

He brought the set home along with a pint of vodka that he had stolen from the liquor store. Amanda didn't even say anything. Not one word of praise. She just made a face like she was very tired of Joseph. Then she said she was going out with some friends.

Joseph kept the television set on all night when Amanda didn't come home. He lay on his side with his head resting on his arm so the little television was at eye level. Joseph thought of turning the television also on its side so that the picture would be right-way around.

The ten o'clock news was on and the bottom of the screen said that it was a re-broadcast.

So Joseph tried to watch the little blue screen. He knew that Amanda would not be home until the sun was up.

The anchorman smiled from the grainy picture and said good evening. A little square appeared over his left shoulder and inside the square was a blurry image of men running. Joseph turned up the sound.

"Today's top local story: On Saturday, the City of Chicago will celebrate a powerful moment in our history, the day the tide turned in World War Two. Allied troops led by the Americans raided the beach of Normandy fifty years ago Monday.

"Saturday afternoon at Montrose Beach on the far north side there will be a re-creation of the military maneuver that began the Nazi defeat. Five hundred soldiers, not the real soldiers, actors, will represent the Allied and Axis troops. At noon sharp they will charge the German shore of Lake Michigan."

Old clips of soldiers running through explosions and climbing ropes down cliffs appeared on the screen while a new voice narrated, giving the same information with more of a dramatic tone.

"In celebration of the anniversary of a war that was won fifty years ago there will be a reenactment on the beach of Montrose Harbor. German camps have been built along the sands usually reserved for more peaceful types of recreation. But this Saturday it will be war. The drone of airplanes will cross the sky. Gun turrets are already set behind heavy-looking walls set down in the sand, built to stop the fake Allied forces from bringing tanks up onto the German occupied lakeshore."

The news reporter was shown walking along the beach as he narrated out of the corner of his mouth. From the beach to the parking lot he talked all the while of the excitement that was already building. Except for one big tent, a sandwich cart on the beach, and several pick-up trucks where workers were eating their lunches, the parking lot and the beach were empty just like Joseph had seen before.

The anchorman's voice again. "The mayor held a press conference specifically for the event." The Mayor of Chicago appeared before a podium of microphones, his face slightly lopsided like the left side of his nose was pressed against a sheet of glass.

"This is a proud moment in the country's history. In the city's history. Chicago took a proud part in the war and we thank the veterans who served. Not the whole world, but those who served for the Allied armies. The city is taking every precaution that this will be a celebration. Something we should be proud of." He chuckled about something said off-screen and added, "The Chicago Police. They are. This is not the time to talk about that. This is so I can recommend the anniversary show to Chicagoans and visitors of the city. I'm very proud of this event what will be taking place tomorrow."

The tape ended, catching the anchorman by surprise. He gathered himself and started abruptly, "On Saturday all are welcome to the beach. Bus lines will be re-routed to Wilson Avenue and there will be no fee for the ceremony or for the transportation.

"The park district is asking that no alcohol be brought to the park. It will be confiscated. Vendors will be selling beer and food at the ceremony. You will be allowed to bring your own food.

"Also, just a reminder, real ammunition and explosives will not be used during the anniversary invasion." Then the anchorman smiled and added a light side note. "But some veterans who did participate in the original invasion asked to be in the reenactment. They could not, but the city asks that they still attend. I personally, hope they do."

The next report, which had no accompanying videotape, said that Adolf Hitler's body may have been found in an unmarked grave that held thirty-two skeletons in Magdelburg, Germany. "There have been discussions regarding DNA tests of the skeletons, but no decisions have yet been made." The anchorman then added that tomorrow's weather would be coming up right after another set of commercials.

Joseph sat up to finish what was left of his warm vodka. He wished that Amanda was home so she could drink with him. He was stealing the stuff for her, risking his job. It was possible that he could find another job if he got caught, and there was always the outside chance that the Printer would pay him fairly if they met again. For the time being, it didn't matter. He could feel the alcohol soaking through his empty stomach. He flipped the channels to see if there was anything else about World War Two on television.

D-Day

Joseph wanted to see the beach. The D-Day reenactment was scheduled to start at noon.

"How fucking stupid," Amanda mumbled to herself.

Joseph asked what she had said.

"I said the thing at the beach is dumb. I can't think of a worse way to honor the people who died. They're making the war look like a Disneyworld attraction. It's gonna be a bunch of tourists and sadists watching. If I was a veteran, I wouldn't go to this. Why would they want to live through that again?"

"I don't know," Joseph said. He didn't even know what a sadist was.

"It's just a fireworks show," Amanda concluded.

"So you don't want to go?"

"No. You do?"

Joseph said that he was sort of interested in it.

"Maybe I'll go with. I'll sit on the hill and get a tan. You can do whatever you want."

"Okay." Joseph couldn't imagine that Amanda would leave him when they got to the lake. That would be different than leaving him alone all day in the apartment. She would not abandon him on a day when the weather was supposed to be so nice.

The streets were filled with people moving in long, disorganized trains, pouring out of the Wilson and Lawrence Avenue El stations. Walking in two carpenter ant lines, crowding the streets headed toward the lakeshore.

Cops were on every corner, leaning against pay phones or mailboxes, sweating through their uniforms. The heavy and constant rain of the previous month had ended and the ninety degree summer heat had begun a week before. The tourists were easy to spot. White T-shirts, colorful shorts, and usually a Cubs baseball cap. They were toting coolers and children and lawn chairs. They stared at the people along Broadway, the people who sat on the curbs and in the shade of the viaducts, the drunks and the beggars, the ones who were in the same spots where they had been every day before the war. Joseph heard people who had never been on the block, probably never been in the city, laughing and gasping at the garbage. They were weekend tourists who Joseph felt didn't deserve to be in the neighborhood unless they lived there. If the war wasn't going to be at the beach, they would have never gone to Wilson Avenue. One woman in a crisp sundress covered her nose and mouth with a handkerchief to protect herself as she stepped over a drift of spilled garbage. Joseph watched Amanda slip through the crowds like she was wading in a school of fish, letting them part and circle in the clear water at her knees.

A crucifix was held upright at Preacher Madison's corner. A voice was echoing under the viaduct and slipping between the buildings. It wasn't the Preacher Madison. The voice was younger and angrier. A large crowd of people had gathered and even more were slowing their walk so they could catch a glimpse of the corner preacher.

Joseph had never seen this one before. He must have been new to the church. He was younger, wearing a golf shirt and aviator sunglasses. Prowling the corner while he ranted on about society's permissive labels.

"In these times sin is not called sin.

"Modern times have created new definitions.

"Criminals are not called criminals. They are called victims of society. A whore is not a whore. She is a call-girl. She is an es-cort. Fornicators and adulterers are not called fornicators and adulterers. They are common-law wives and husbands. Gays and faggots are called people of alternative lifestyles instead of perverts. Faggotry is permeating society. They are in the military and they are in the government. There is some new law for them. Do not ask and do not tell. Even the government is supporting sin.

"Ask and tell. Ask and tell. That is called redemption. Ask the Lord and He will tell. These sins can be forgiven, but the Lord must be asked. He will tell."

A shirtless man stood at the back of the crowd. The ribs were visible under paper skin and his hips poked out above the waistline of his sagging pants. Blood marked a line from the crown of the man's skull to the middle of his back. He stood as if he didn't know that a stripe of dark red was drying between his shoulder blades. He was intent on listening to the young preacher's itemized list and applauding every point.

While bright and clean tourists filed into two buses parked along the curb and the drivers stood by the open doors, waving them in. "D-Day. D-Day. This is the D-Day bus."

"You wanna get on?" Joseph asked Amanda.

"Why not."

He pulled Amanda up the steps and found the last empty seats near the back.

The pavement ended under the Lake Shore Drive viaduct and the sky opened to a cloudless view of the park and the expressway. There was no more cement, only green grass and clusters of trees before the gray water.

Streams of people continued wandering in the direction of the lake.

The high ground, a man-made hill, could be seen in the middle of the park. A dirt path rode the hill's back. Picketers and protesters camped over the slope and white crosses had been staked into the grass to represent the tombs of the unknown soldiers. A bedsheet rigged between two posts announced, GAMES DO NOT HONOR THE DEAD.

WAR IS NOT FUN, said another post.

"I want to go up there," Amanda said, pointing up the hill to where the protesters were. Joseph followed Amanda and when he found that the hill offered no view except that of the crowds along the lake, he decided to keep going all the way to the beach. Amanda sat down in the grass. "Suit yourself. I'll stay here." She leaned back on her elbows and put her face up to the sun.

Joseph walked through the crowds packed along the rock ledge before the beach. It was a solid wall of people blocking his view. Over their heads he could see only the water out near the horizon. Joseph fought and squeezed for a position closer to the action. Past the sunbathers and the drunks and the little kids he shouldered rudely for a few inches of space. There was nothing but more people and the blue sky.

Loudspeakers were mounted on antenna towers along Montrose Beach. Joseph didn't know if the towers had been there previously or if they were built just for the occasion. A fence separated the crowd from the German tents. Helicopters supervising the day hovered and bobbed over the corners of the park.

Music started playing as the first two bombs went off in the sky; it was an old-time war movie theme with a marching beat that swelled into a triumphant roar. Clouds of colored smoke broke open and peeled apart in slow motion, blue, yellow, and orange. The boom echoed off in two directions and was followed by a sputter of fake machine gun fire.

Joseph couldn't see a thing. The music grew louder and he pushed himself sideways until he was out of the crowd and back on the grass. He decided that the war footage on the television was better.

Under the shade of a bent tree a family was having a barbecue. The father was wearing a green camouflage T-shirt and the youngest boy was dressed head to toe in the same pattern, including his socks, shoes, and hat.

Makeshift refreshment stands and vending carts selling ice cream and ears of corn were positioned along the beach. An old man in a wheelchair was rolling down the path before Joseph, a sign hanging from a coathanger at the back of his chair. PLEASE HELP. WW2 VET. I FOUGHT IN ITALIAN OFFENSIVE. A coffee can rattled from one handle of the chair and a small American flag made of stiff cloth hung parallel to the ground from the other.

The man stopped to catch his breath and Joseph emptied the change from his pocket into the coffee cup. "God bless you, boy," the man barked loudly as Joseph hurried to get away. He was embarrassed that he had given pennies to a war veteran.

From the wheelchair behind Joseph came another resounding "Thank you," that did not fit the image of the man's tiny body. The voice was young and healthy. A voice that was able to walk. Joseph didn't feel as if he had redeemed himself. He kept walking.

The machine gun fire died away behind Joseph. Occasionally a bomb exploded in the air and Joseph would turn to see the powdered cloud dissipating over the German tents. People were applauding and cheering.

A red and white shack with REFRESHMENTS written across the aluminum siding sat at the edge of the action. A line of people led up to a window in the front and another small crowd sat collectively in a weeded patch of grass. As Joseph got closer he recognized a barely amplified voice aimed at the lake.

The crowd was listening to Preacher Madison. Joseph didn't recognize any of the church helpers. No Brother Levon, no Brother Samuel. But among the audience were Sonny and McKnuckle.

They had all seen Joseph walk up. The Preacher saw him, and Sonny and McKnuckle saw him. Joseph felt the whole crowd watching him as if he had a sign hanging around his neck. Too late to turn back and too late to hide, he got in line and decided to buy a soda.

The portable amplifier shut off with a screech of feedback and Joseph felt the line shuffle forward. There were still people along the rock ledge, facing the lake and waiting for something more.

A few seconds passed before he felt a hand touch his shoulder.

"I'm glad to see you, son. Do you have a second to talk?"

"Yeah, I'm in line here." Nonchalance didn't cover anything. Joseph felt the Preacher's eyes peel away every layer.

The Preacher's heavy fingers wrapped around Joseph's arm and gently pulled him out of line and around to the side of the shack where there was an open door. A pock-marked face in a white paper hat came to the window, saw the Preacher, and then without a word brought back two cans of Coke. Joseph thanked the Preacher for the drink.

Preacher Madison led Joseph into the park, away from the beach.

"You know I have acquaintances with a lot of people," Preacher Madison began. "Sometimes it feels like I know everybody. People have been keeping me updated on you. It's because I worry about you. There is a lot out there to get mixed up in and I should have told you about this a long time ago. It feels like it has been a long time."

The orator's voice was gone now, it was a hushed and private tone. Joseph studied the man's face as if he had never seen it before. Saw the glassed were crooked and bent, the eyes behind them were yellow and hard. Pores like craters covered the knob of his nose. Joseph noticed all the faults that before hadn't seemed possible and felt this was his chance to defend himself. "I know what I'm doing." His voice came out weakly. It was a child's voice.

"Shut up," the Preacher whispered. "I know what you're doing. I know there is a girl waiting for you on the hill. You live with her in sin. I know that she is a drug user and she is killing herself. I gave you a chance and waited for you."

Joseph felt his legs buckle under him. He locked his knees in position only to keep himself from falling over. He stared at a single blade of grass and the ground swelling up toward him. It felt like the Preacher had punched him in the head.

"My parishioners have told me this, son. It is only because I worry about you. It is too easy to get swallowed up in this city. I know that you have stolen and hurt people. I know about that one man. I wish no harm to anyone, but if I did, it would be him. He is a sinner and a pervert. He destroys souls."

Joseph knew the Preacher was talking about the Mayor. It had to be Sonny and McKnuckle who told Preacher Madison. And in retaliation Joseph wanted to tell Preacher Madison about McKnuckle and Sonny, the toluene, and McKnuckle's women, but he knew that he would not be listened to. Joseph was a little boy in the eyes of the Preacher and his words were not worth anything. The Preacher's face faded away, Joseph no longer saw it.

"Do not try to justify your actions. I know that it is hard out there and I know that anything can be justified when the justifier gets away from the true God."

Joseph began to say something and the Preacher cut him off.

"I want you to come back to the church. Stop what you are doing. If you want to be out on your own, first come back to the church; we can help you. We will show you how to get a job and get along righteously in the world. You do not need to behave in this way, son. Come back to the church and follow in the Lord's ways. Many opportunities will be open for you. We have school, we have access to vocational training programs. You can start your life righteously. It would be foolish of you not to. Don't make the same mistakes that other have.

"If you do not come to the church, Joseph, I will have to call the police. I know that the word of a preacher is no good without evidence. I have that, too. There is a woman who just joined the church. It sounds like her husband knows you. He knows your girlfriend. The husband has his wife's children and they will fall into the same trap in which you have already placed one leg. Before this happens, the both of us can go to the police and ask for help."

"People are lying," Joseph told the Preacher. His voice didn't sound as confident as he wanted. And he hadn't placed his leg in any trap.

"Are they? Are all these people lying?"

"Yes." The word was said with the conviction of a child caught in a lie. Joseph thought that he was standing up for himself.

"Then what have you been doing all this time?"

The boy shook his head. There was nothing he could tell the Preacher. It sounded like the only thing Preacher Madison didn't know about was the bogus television Joseph recently bought.

"This is not a free life you are living. It is not a Christian life. I will wait for you to come back to the church. I expect you in my office tomorrow. Think it over tonight. If you don't appear, I will call the police. I have expected too much from you. I have given you too many chances. If you think this is freedom, you know nothing. You are accountable. Do you think that because you do not live like the rest of us, you are free? What can you do that I cannot? How many forces can you feel holding you down?"

Joseph shrugged his shoulders. The Preacher was lying. He couldn't call the police and he couldn't scare him into coming back. Joseph had Amanda. They could both leave town, buy a car somehow. Amanda could quit what she was doing and they could both get good jobs, save their money. Go somewhere else and start over with the money from the coins. Joseph had to find the Printer again. The Printer was right, there had to be more in the Mayor's apartment. There was no other way the albino could have lived so long on his own. Joseph was willing to risk going back to the Mayor's again.

Joseph turned away from the Preacher and began toward the hill. Preacher Madison said nothing else, but Joseph could feel the man's eyes like two pinpoints against the back of his neck.

The machine guns kept firing as he walked closer to the hill. Planes were flying over the beach, buzzing low. Some of the crowd was discouraged and leaving the scene. Joseph could not find the wheelchair veteran. Three drunks were talking to each other as they pissed against a cluster of stunted trees. Women sunbathed in bikini tops and cut-off shorts. Mounted police horses trotted between the campers' blankets. Some children had wandered out to the park and were entertaining themselves by swordfighting with broken tree branches.

Generally, the crowds seemed dissatisfied, but kept their places in the hopes of a big finale made of extravagant explosions and flying corpses. Anything short of a goring mutilation was barely worth the admission. That was what Joseph had been waiting for. But he wished that he had listened to Amanda.

McKnuckle, weaving drunk through the crowd, approached one lone police officer working crowd control on horseback and generously offered a sip of beer to the horse. The cop smiled to the obvious drunk and gruffly told him to keep moving. The warning went ignored, the beer cup was pressed to the horse's lip. McKnuckle coaxed the animal to take just a little taste. "C'mon, girl." Overspill foamed and poured to the ground. The cop began threatening to arrest McKnuckle if he didn't get away from his horse, but he refused to move the horse away from McKnuckle. An incoherent yelling match erupted and was quickly broken up by two more patrol cops who happened by. They calmed McKnuckle down and led him off, each holding onto an arm. They weren't going to arrest him, they just wanted to get him out of sight. They told him that they were on his side.

The screaming cop on horseback found an audience that immediately began booing when it seemed McKnuckle was about to be arrested. They were on the his side, too. They wanted to see the horse drink a beer. They wanted to see something.

"Come on," someone hidden in the crowd yelled, "let the fucking horse drink, man. It's a holiday." There was laughter and cheering. A few more people voiced their support for McKnuckle.

McKnuckle, as if he was responding to his audience, broke free and ran back to the horse. The two cops grabbed at the air where McKnuckle had been standing, then took off after him. The cop on horseback slipped his billy club out of his belt and pointed it at the sprinting drunk, giving him a last warning.

From the loudspeakers high over the beach came the first bars of the Marine Corps Hymn as McKnuckle jumped across the horse's neck. He clambered around desperately, grabbing at the reins before the billy club came down across the back of his neck.

The crowd gasped and yelled furiously and the horse bucked and tilted without losing the cop. The unconscious McKnuckle landed head-first in the dirt. Circling backwards, the horse whinnied and looked for a open space to run. The horse, with the cop furiously yanking the reins, kept backing up in tight and panicked circles.

One man broke from the crowd like he was trying to split the difference between the uniformed cops who were picking McKnuckle from the ground. Another man, as unexpected as the first, ran after and made a diving tackle for some unknown reason. Then the two rolled around, biting and cursing and pulling hair. A fat woman in a yellow sun dress dove on top of the pile and tried to separate the two. "Honey, stop it," she screamed as she stuck her fingers in the eye sockets of one man who might have been Honey.

As soon as McKnuckle was knocked from the horse, the crowd's disposition turned. Somehow it was understood that the police had something to do with the disappointing results of the Normandy celebration.

The cops fought to pull apart the three on the ground and the whole audience grew restless. Shoving matches, fighting for the best view of the wrestling match, began like little fires. People fell like dominos as they tried to watch the scuffle which hadn't subsided.

McKnuckle dusted himself off, stepped unnoticed to the edge of the crowd, and pitched an empty beer bottle at the two cops who finally had the wrestlers under control. The bottle sailed between them and broke open against the head of the woman in the sundress. She went down without making one noise.

The crowd screamed and then turned to see who had thrown the bottle. The fickle consensus decided upon McKnuckle because he was the only one who tried to run. He was knocked to the ground by the mob and his skinny body was swallowed under the twisting mass of arms and legs.

Joseph saw Sonny slip away unscathed.

Five or six more cops came running from the other side of the park. On top of the hill, even the protesters were intrigued. Two men were jumping up and down, screaming hoarsely at the enemy. While another had his girlfriend hoisted on his shoulders and waving one of the white crosses like a cheerleader's pompom.

The police horse somehow worked its way toward the rock ledge and the crowd perched there. Thick legs kicked out and the strong neck bullied through. The audience broke apart, pushing and shoving to give the horse room. Machine gun fire screamed over the drone of the World War Two airplanes circling the park. Colored smoke bombs popped open in the sky behind the brawling scene. Several soldiers on the beach slipped out of character and stopped what they were doing to watch the riot.

McKnuckle ran unnoticed from the crowd, choking and gagging, and disappeared behind the protesters' hill.

Amanda hadn't moved from her spot. Her eyes were closed to the sun. Her shirtsleeves were rolled up to her shoulders and the legs of her shorts were folded up on her thighs. The bottom of her shirt was tucked under the clasp of her bra to leave her pale stomach exposed. Joseph's shadow settled over her and she looked up to find what was blocking her sunlight.

"Did we win?" she asked Joseph.

"What?"

"The war."

It took him a second to figure out what she was talking about. Her eyes were shut again, she looked like she hadn't heard a thing that was going on along the beach. The other protesters were watching the scene.

"Yeah, they won."

"Not us?"

"We weren't on either side."

"Fucking right." Amanda stood up and brushed the grass off of her clothes. She turned to the water and saw the crowd breaking apart. From a distance the action between the cops and the crowd resembled dogs corralling a herd of sheep. "What the fuck happened?"

"I don't know," Joseph admitted and then noticed Sonny and McKnuckle sitting on the far slope of the hill. They looked up at Joseph. McKnuckle's shirt was torn open and his teeth were pink with blood. Sonny was clean and they were both smiling. Amanda thought they were smiling at her and she gave them the finger. It caused them to only laugh.

"Got a cigarette, boy?" Sonny asked Joseph.

Joseph said that he didn't and led Amanda back down the steep hill. The slope of the ground pulled them forward and when they hit level ground Joseph was running as hard as he could. He knew that Amanda did not keep up with him and did not want to. She was strolling along and Joseph kept flailing his legs until he was at the edge of the park, opposite the harbor and the expressway. The replica World War Two planes flew in a diamond formation high over his head, separated and doubled back over the buildings of the north side of Chicago.

He caught his breath and waited. Amanda was taking her time, kicking at the flowered weeds as she walked through the park.

Far down the path, Joseph saw Preacher Madison leading the dealer's wife toward Wilson Avenue. The woman held onto the Preacher's hand in the absence of her children.

The Next Time

A frantic low tapping came from the apartment hall late that night after Montrose Beach had been secured. The Printer was whispering, working himself close to hyperventilating behind the chain of the door.

"C'mon, kid. Open up. Chop chop."

The collar of his shirt was soaked in sweat and the man kept himself huddled inside his overcoat despite the ninety-degree June heat.

"The Mayor's gone for the night. I saw him, he'll be gone until the morning. He was going into the Hotel Chateau with some guy and they were both drunk as all hell. This is the perfect night to do it."

Joseph was tired. He hadn't expected the Printer so soon and thought of turning the offer down even though he couldn't afford to. The money was needed now if Joseph and Amanda were ever going to leave. Joseph was certain that if he showed Amanda that he was prepared, she would go. With the money from the Mayor's coins they would easily be able to leave.

Joseph imagined himself and Amanda quietly telling each other the secrets they should have a long time ago. He was ready to tell her about the church and the Preacher and the Mayor. He had wanted to get everything off his chest and be sure that Amanda would accept it. As soon as it happened, Joseph felt he would be able to do anything. But for now it all had to wait. Joseph held onto Amanda and her slight promises because there was nothing else.

Sometimes the things he wanted from Amanda were so sharply defined that he was certain he could explain it all. It was a photograph he could see. That was only once in a rare moment. If he blinked, the unnamed emotions would drift away. Like grabbing a handful of water. He needed some kind of success to bolster his recent losing record. When the clarity of his desires faded, Joseph was left with the constant uncertainties that had grown inside him.

Preacher Madison said there were people watching everything he did. Now Joseph could hear them talking on the street. He had doubted it at first, but now he knew better. Every day it was more obvious than the day before. They were all waiting for him to fall. He imagined the Preacher's hand on his shoulder and knew that he had to go with the Printer.

"Kid? You there?"

"Tonight?" Joseph asked just to make sure.

"Yes. Must be. I already talked to my coin dealer."

"I want to go with you when you sell these coins."

"Don't get angry," the Printer scolded. "I thought we already went through all of this."

"Well, I want more than seventeen bucks."

"There was nothing I could do about that. It's up to you to grab the expensive coins. Be careful."

"Why don't you then come up with me and pick out the good ones?"

"If I was going to do that, then I wouldn't need you at all."

"Then do it yourself," Joseph harshly suggested.

"Let me finish. I need you because you're younger. If someone is in there, or if someone comes up, then you can run out of there faster than I could. I, myself, am an old man. That's why I'm asking for your help."

"You just want someone else to get blamed."

"No, no. If I thought you were to get caught, I wouldn't send you. What good would that do me? I need your help, otherwise I don't think I'd have the energy for any of this." The Printer's voice cracked and Joseph finally believed this was a heartfelt plea. He waited a second before he said anything, but he and the Printer both knew what answer was coming.

Joseph looked around the dimly-lit apartment. Amanda was sleeping on the bathroom floor, her heels stretching over the threshold. She hadn't moved in the past hour. The apartment was empty of food, empty of beer. The chirping of the television resembled a voice coming from a tin can.

"Okay," Joseph whispered to the Printer. "Give me a few minutes."

"I'll wait across the street for you," the Printer concluded brightly.

Before the Printer slipped away, Joseph asked, "Where were you the other day?"

"It was an emergency I had to tend to. Sorry about that, kid."

Under a chain of streetlights they walked together, their shadows floating ahead long and violet beneath their feet. Joseph watched his shadow swing beneath him like a pendulum as he passed under each of the pavement's spotlights. Away from brightly lit Broadway, the lamps glowed dim pink and green and Joseph and the Printer finally disappeared behind the corners of the blackened three-flats. Their shadows were barely visible on the quiet side street.

No lights shone from the inside and no sound came from the windows. A red notice was taped to the front door. It said that the electricity would be turned off if the compounding bills for the three-flat were not paid by the end of the month.

The whole building was empty. Every step Joseph made was amplified a hundred times. As if the whole building had been left for him. As if the Mayor wanted Joseph to walk in and take what was left. He would be waiting on the couch to tell Joseph that he knew he would come back. That was what Joseph saw in the dark even when he knew it to not be true.

His hand led him along the walls and up the stairs. Slipping the lock was again one smooth and swift motion.

The apartment was worse than before. Water covered the floor and thin puddles splashed lightly under Joseph's shoes. Chunks of plaster had fallen from the ceiling while water kept dripping constantly from the pipes. The couch in the kitchen was soaked. Joseph opened the closets to find that the rain had formed a stagnant pool beneath the door.

The boxes of coins were just as they had been left. Joseph packed everything he could carry.

On the street Joseph didn't even see the Printer sneak up on him.

They walked to the far end of the alley. Instead of checking the coins, the Printer hurriedly stuffed his pockets and patted himself down until there was not one coin clinking. Shaking himself like he had the chills, his overcoat stayed silent.

"I'll find you tomorrow," the Printer told Joseph.

"Let me come with this time." Joseph held himself firm as if he was ready to fight again.

"Joseph." It was the first time the Printer didn't call him a kid. The tone was soothing and confiding. "I'm not going to rip you off. I know you've done a lot of hard work and it will pay out this time. Trust me."

"I'll find you tomorrow," Joseph gave in again.

"Good. Right."

And they parted ways again where the light entered the alley.

Joseph's stomach was growling and under his chest was a contracted lump surrounded by hollow space. Confident that Bates was long gone, Joseph used his spare emergency key to let himself into the darkened liquor store.

He filled his jacket with two forty-ounce bottles of beer, several bags of peanuts, and a loaf of bread. Groping the shelves he was able to easily find what he wanted.

The Printer was standing on the sidewalk when Joseph let himself out again.

"I saw you in there as I was walking past," the Printer remarked casually. Joseph noticed that the Printer was still carrying the coins and the Printer saw Joseph's eyes studying him. "He wasn't there. My coin guy went home for the night. I'll have to get him tomorrow."

"Okay," Joseph gave in without a fight. "Don't say nothing about me being in here tonight?" He saw that the Printer noticed his jacket filled with beer and food. He didn't want to ask for any further trust. Joseph had been caught and for a moment he wondered if the Printer was somehow connected to the hotel or Preacher Madison.

Joseph had felt this conspiracy growing around him for quite some time.

"I won't say a thing," the Printer promised and shut his eyes tightly. "I understand." They walked together for a few blocks, both their coats filled with someone else's belongings, and the Printer began one of his monologues. "You know, we're almost in the same position. You are looking for a start in life and I am looking to finish my life. Money always seems to be the solution, doesn't it? It's a temporary solution, but it's the one we need. I know I won't live forever, but you know how it is. If you don't have money, you're nothing. How much you have- that's how people judge you. That's how it is. Not that I have other people judging me. That's the only criteria I have now for judging myself. Other people's criteria. That's the only measure. How comfortably I can retire.

"Do you know how Hillary Clinton got her money? How she invested one thousand dollars and made a thousand percent profit?"

Joseph didn't know anything about that. He didn't know what the Printer was talking about.

"You see, that's how these brokerage houses take care of their clients. If two people each invest a thousand dollars, one client is Hillary, the other is some unknown schmuck, most of the profits will go to the big shot, Hillary. See, there's two piles of money, stocks, whatever." The Printer indicated the two piles of imaginary stocks with his free hand. "The one that goes up, that will go to the big shot, no matter who it originally belonged to. That money gets invested, no matter whose, it gets invested in another winner. Now whatever goes up next, that also goes to the big shot. It doesn't matter who that money originally belonged to, the profits will go to the more important person. And the nobody pays the bill. He has to pay the brokerage house."

Joseph understood that.

"To make money you have to be somebody and to be somebody you have to have money," the Printer concluded, grinning at the simple logic. "We're doing the same thing. Smaller scale right now. But as I said, it's a temporary solution. What are you planning for your life? What is it you are going to do?"

"I don't know."

"You should really consider something."

"What?" Joseph wanted to know.

"I don't know, it's your life." The Printer shrugged and concluded the subject.

Joseph nodded. His own future was not connected to these things the Printer spoke of. Stocks and president's wives. Among the few people Joseph knew there was always a great distrust of anyone who held power. The easy lives of doctors and lawyers were sneered at as those of cheats and fakes. City workers whose jobs were handed down as political favors and included full benefits and union protection were seen as fortunate and weak. They had kissed someone's ass for a chance to push papers across a desk or stand in traffic and wave a orange flag at passing cars. Lives of the secure were corrupt through and through. Those who could gladly embrace wealth and comfort and privilege were only stealing from those whose lives were unequal. No other way it could have been achieved when normal people sometimes had to fight like animals to get a little bit ahead.

"Here's where I turn," the Printer said, motioning toward a side street. "I'll see you tomorrow."

A sharp hollowness came back to Joseph's stomach. He had a feeling that he would not see the Printer again.

Amanda wasn't in the apartment.

Joseph emptied his coat and laid the banquet of peanuts and bread out on the floor. Sitting down, he opened the first beer and started drinking. It was still fairly cold. The other one would be warm before he got to it. Even if he drank fast.

The coins and the money from the Printer drifted through Joseph's mind. Combinations of scenarios and plans and results played out until the boy was the loser in every one. It seemed that even the daydreams got away from him, went too far past him. Joseph kept losing in each one. He thought that maybe he deserved to get ripped off by the Printer. The Printer only wanted to end his life, to hoard enough money to live comfortably during his last years. Joseph was young and had his whole life in front of him. There were other things he could have supposedly done. He could have become a good worker at the liquor store. He could have stayed with his parents, stayed with the church. He wondered where the point was passed so that he could no longer turn back. Inside the church and out, Joseph couldn't think of a place where he didn't feel trapped. Except for the nights he was with Amanda, the nights before they took the room on Magnolia.

With Amanda, he wondered if there was one little act that would have shown her the blind commitment that had been made, the few words that could have convinced her. Maybe that was why things were working out as they did for him. Bad things happened only to bad people. Joseph let one of the Preacher's sermons roll through his head. Maybe Joseph was bad, worse than the Printer, and somehow worse than all the others. Maybe that was it.

But bad things happened to everyone, Joseph argued to himself, because we are all sinners. There is not one person without sinful acts. There was not one person who has not had impure and vicious thoughts. Other people must somehow be making up for their sins. They must be repenting somehow.

Absolution would come in some way other than through The People's Church of Chicago. Joseph couldn't think how. Hidden deep, the nagging voice which was always correct told him that he would pay. He recalled his long-ago dream where he was the only one at night without a set of wolf fangs.

After his mind ran through all the possibilities, he did not know how long he could wait for Amanda.

Joseph took off his shoes and peeled away his socks and threw them in the corner. They were soaked from the busted ceiling and flooded floor of the Mayor's apartment. Joseph ate the bread and peanuts and drank the beer. And crashed to sleep before Amanda came home.

Between Argyle and Grace

The wind blew wrappers and garbage in circles from one side of the street to the other. From the window of the liquor store Joseph could see people strolling along or gathering in the park across the street. And in the corner of the glass he watched a figure stumbling across the near sidewalk.

The Mayor appeared clearly inside the window's frame and leaned into the lamppost face-first. His arms wrapped around the post as if he were struggling against an undertow trying to drag him back into the street. His legs gave way drunkenly and he slowly slid down the pole until he was sitting on the pavement. His chin dropped to his chest.

His grip finally loosened and his back fell to the sidewalk, his arms limp at rubbery angles. The door to the barber shop was blocked by his pink head. The heels of his shoes hung over the curb and one arm was reaching unsuccessfully for the liquor store. Several pedestrians asked each other if the man was dead as they stepped over his body.

The Mayor's albino eyes rolled back in their sockets independent of each other. When a woman walked past, the Mayor reached blindly for her ankle with his left hand. She kicked it away and then his right hand feebly groped the cement.

Joseph watched from the picture window of the liquor store. The Mayor groaned loudly from the sidewalk and laid his arm across his pink face. Someone standing above him asked if he was breathing. The Mayor drifted in and out of consciousness. Like he was floating off the sidewalk and then crashing back down again.

Phil the Barber opened his door and cracked the Mayor squarely in the head. The Mayor didn't respond and Phil tried to wake him.

"Yoo-hoo. Hey there. Hey, you."

Phil tapped the door gently and repeatedly against the Mayor's temple. Phil grunted, looked up at the clouds, and went back inside to call the police. The Mayor was going to chase away business, lying there like that.

McKnuckle burst into the liquor store and demanded that the Mayor be taken care of.

"He is. Phil called someone," Joseph coldly said without bringing his eyes to McKnuckle's. "He called the cops."

McKnuckle looked around at the shelves of whiskey bottles and cans of food and racks of potato chips and realized there was no one else in the store. "Who's Phil?"

"The barber, next door." Joseph pointed to the adjoining wall.

"That his name? Never knew his name." McKnuckle stepped closer. "Hey, chief. Why don't you take care of the man? You know him. I seen you around with him. You two is tight." McKnuckle smiled and exposed his broken teeth.

"I can't. I'll lose my job."

"Yeah, right. But I know what you do for him. We all know the Mayor."

"Oh, yeah? What do you know?" Joseph slid both hands under the counter, knowing that there was nothing under there. No gun, no knife, or mace. Bates had taken them home for some reason.

McKnuckle looked at the counter and sniffed. He studied the rest of the store as if there was something missing. He asked if the boss was around. Joseph said he wasn't.

"Is he your old man?"

"No, just work here."

Stepping toward the counter, McKnuckle began to explain how he was low on money and how he hadn't eaten in at least two days and Joseph stopped him by pointing at the NO CREDIT sign over the cigarettes.

"Okay boy. Remember that. You remember that. We know you, we know the Mayor. The big man. Okay, cool." McKnuckle whipped the door open and stepped high over the Mayor's chest. He shook his head in mock shame and strutted away from the window, laughing.

A female cop whom Joseph had never seen before was the first to show up. She stood over the Mayor and tried to wake him by calling his name. With the toe of her patent leather shoe she tapped the Mayor's shoulder. She knew who the Mayor was. Phil the Barber went outside and stood next to the cop. She nodded hello and they both studied the Mayor.

"Oh, Jesus," Phil laughed, "Lookit that. He went in his pants."

"Yeah, looks like it," the cop said. She gave the Mayor a few more kicks with the tip of her shoe. The Mayor only groaned once. People kept walking past, asking if the pink man was dead.

"No, just drunk," Phil explained every time.

Static popped from the police radio while Phil kept checking the clouds that crossed over the buildings.

"It's gonna rain pretty soon," he said. "I'd bet money."

The cop agreed that it might.

Joseph went outside when he was finished stocking the shelves. The female cop checked him out and asked what he wanted. "Nothing. I work here." Joseph pointed to the door of the liquor store and silently read the name tag on her chest. Vallenti.

"How old are you?" she asked.

"Twenty-one."

Joseph saw Phil nod his head, telling the cop that it was okay. He didn't have to actually be twenty-one.

The cop glanced at Joseph a few more times, not the way cops usually looked at Joseph. He had the urge to talk to her. He wanted to confess everything.

A man in a stocking cap walked up to Joseph and asked what happened.

"Nothing, he's drunk," Phil answered.

"Is he okay?"

"No," Officer Vallenti said, "he's unconscious. How okay does he look to you?"

"I don't know. What was he drinking?"

"How the hell should I know?"

The stocking cap had no more questions and stepped around the body.

"He's gonna want to get inside before it rains," Phil announced, pointing to the Mayor.

Another cop climbed out of a squad car and quickly checked out everyone standing at the curb. It was Frank, the cop who knew Bobbi. The one who helped the Indian catch Joseph stealing Mad Dog. This was the first time Joseph had seen Frank in his uniform. Joseph wanted to get away from the gathering crowd. Someone else was going to recognize him because of the Mayor.

McKnuckle worked his way back down the street, bouncing like a fighter in training, shadowboxing the parking meters. And soon he joined the circle that had formed around the Mayor as if they were to keep him from going somewhere.

"What's up?" Frank the cop mockingly asked the Mayor. He twisted his neck to the side, putting his ear to his shoulder to face the unconscious man eye-to-eye. "Hey, Mayor. How long you been here, Mayor?"

"About twenty minutes," Phil answered.

"He pissed himself," Frank noticed. "Didn't you, Mayor?"

"Don't give him a hard time." McKnuckle spoke up. "That's harassment. You can't do that."

"Who put the nickel in you? And when did you get out? I thought I saw you at Town Hall last."

"Yeah, they said I stole a magazine, but then they let me go. The magazine offender's cell was all filled up."

"Good, why don't you get away from here, then?"

"Don't be giving my man here a hard time." McKnuckle waved a finger in the cop's face. "Don't be abusing the rights of the unconscious."

"If he's your pal," Frank asked, aiming his nightstick at the Mayor, "why don't you get him out of here? You take care of him if you're so worried."

"Okay, pick him up."

"I ain't picking him up."

"I'm not, either. I don't know what he's got." McKnuckle looked at Joseph and winked, threatening to hint at something. "I know what he does and I ain't gonna touch him. I just don't want anyone giving him a hard time."

"Don't worry, McKnuckle, he can't hear a thing. I know that you're a concerned citizen. Just go home, unless you want to take your friend with you."

"No, no." McKnuckle shook his head and backed away. He smiled and pointed lazily at Joseph. "Not me, man. That's the boy."

When McKnuckle was down the block, Frank noticed Joseph and asked what that was about.

"I don't know," Joseph said and studied his shoes.

"Ooh, look. The clouds are coming now." Phil peered over the roof of the hotel. "It's gonna be a bad one. Come down like hell any minute now," he said to no one at all.

Phil turned and explained to Joseph how the clouds predicted the rain. Different clouds meant different things. If the clouds were flat on the bottom and puffy at the top, then it wouldn't rain. If they were frayed ropes banded together, then there would be a lightning storm.

Frank called on his radio for a wagon to come and pick up the Mayor. Two had passed with the afternoon traffic, but they were heading somewhere else in a hurry.

Half an hour passed and no one left the sidewalk.

The Mayor's eyes opened and he rubbed his hand along the side of his leg. Then his sight blurred and all the figures faded into the dark. That was the last he would see or hear for the rest of the day.

The Mayor was still and his breathing became shallow.

"Well, he's out," Officer Vallenti observed. "Too bad he didn't make it to the alley. Could have just leaned him up against a dumpster."

"Not my dumpster," Phil protested. "Put him next to the Koreans' garbage."

"We're not putting him in the garbage," Frank judiciously decided. "We'll wait for the wagon to come. I'll call again from the car. Does anyone care if I eat my lunch?"

No one cared. Phil leaned in close to make sure the Mayor was still breathing.

"Is he?" Officer Vallenti asked.

"Oh, sure." Phil checked the sky again. "I'm gonna get out of the rain before it starts, though," he said as he ducked into the barber shop.

Joseph and Officer Vallenti were left standing watch over the Mayor. She took off her hat and wiped the sweat from her forehead.

"Busy day?" Joseph softly asked.

"Yeah, yeah. I just came from a call about a home disturbance where this guy, this guy in a wheelchair, he was swinging his prosthetic legs at me. Caught me right in the jaw."

Joseph didn't see any bruises or marks. The cop studied Joseph's face and then asked if he was from the neighborhood. She didn't recognize him. Joseph didn't want to say that he grew up with the Wilson Avenue Jesus people. But he did want tell Vallenti that he didn't really know the Mayor, but instead he shrugged his shoulders and mumbled, "Yeah." Officer Vallenti was about to ask another question when Frank came back with a cold piece of pizza wrapped in tin foil.

Officer Frank ate his lunch and watched both sides of the street for the meat wagon. "The first of the month, the guy must have blown most of his check," he announced.

Old John came staggering up the street, hidden among the pedestrians and curious onlookers, trying to sell an 8-track machine he believed was a VCR. He noticed the Mayor laid out between Joseph and the two cops and asked what happened.

"He got drunk."

John clicked his tongue in disgust. He had no sympathy for drunks who fell over in the street. He stood next to Joseph and proudly explained to everyone walking past that the man on the ground wasn't dead, he was only drunk. Old John stopped pedestrians just to tell them that the man was not dead. If they did not see the Mayor, John was deliberate in pointing him out. The guy was only drunk and John was glad to help. Everyone else was tired of explaining it.

Phil reappeared and Old John seemed to brighten a bit more when the police wagon pulled to the curb.

Old John began to imitate a sob because he could not longer hide his giggling. He found something inherently funny about other drunks with no control. In the pocket of his sports coat he had a bottle filled with his own mixture of Kahlua and Peach Schnapps and he was waiting for the cops to leave so he could start drinking.

Two more cops climbed out of the front of the wagon. They asked Frank and Officer Vallenti what they had.

"Pizza," Frank said, holding out his lunch.

"A drunk," Vallenti said. She pointed to the Mayor at her feet.

The two new cops took the Mayor by the arms and carried him into the back of the truck. His heels dragged against the street, his body was a wet rag. They lifted the Mayor over the bumper and threw him in the back like the motion was something they repeated a hundred times a day. They said nothing else to Frank or Officer Vallenti.

John stopped his crying once the Mayor was out of sight and attempted to sell his 8-track machine to the police. "Very popular things," he assured the officers.

Phil disappeared inside his store. McKnuckle stood on the corner like he was waiting for a bus.

Vallenti and Officer Frank started walking back to their squad car. Joseph listened to their radios crackling with static as he went back inside the liquor store.

Joseph turned on the television set behind the counter. Old John was the only one left on the sidewalk. He checked both sides of the street and slipped the liquor bottle out of his pocket. He held it up to the light and watched the cloudy liquor swirl around. John took a long drink and saluted Joseph through the window.

And the boy felt that was a signal from John, telling him that he had made one step in the right direction.

Little Thieves

Bates was waiting for Joseph behind the counter of the liquor store. He was quiet about the whole thing, talking slow and stretching it out. Bates had noticed the vodka, beer, food, and candy that was regularly missing. A few seconds passed before Joseph realized that he was getting fired. Passively, he let the scene play out the way Bates wanted it to.

"How careful were you watching people in here the other night?"

Joseph's answer was proper. He said he had been watching the customers very closely.

"Were you?"

"Yeah."

"For the past few weeks, every time you worked, I notice things been missing. You sure you watching close enough?"

Joseph repeated himself.

"Then, fuck you," Bates interrupted. "I know you're taking shit out of here. The same stuff is missing every time. What do you think I am?"

Joseph looked down at Bates' feet. He knew that he should have raised his eyes to the man's face, but he couldn't. As Bates' excitement increased, his diatribe on trust and responsibility grew louder. Not one word was heard by the boy. Joseph felt as if a burden had been lifted from his chest even though he knew that he should have been upset. He probably should have defended himself.

Joseph was told to get out of the store. "If you ever come in here again," Bates warned, "I'll break both your fucking legs." Bates took a breath and let it out like steam. "If you got anything of yours in the back room, I'll go with you to get it. But I want you out of here, now."

"I don't got anything in your storeroom," Joseph said.

Bates pointed to the door and Joseph left. The little bell tinkled after him.

It wasn't that Joseph didn't like his boss, he sort of liked the job. He liked Bates and his friends and their bullshit stories. This was going to change things between Joseph and Amanda. It would force a choice on someone's part.

He agreed that he definitely should have been fired, but worried that he deserved more than that. He wondered if this was the beginning of the retribution he owed. He remembered that the Printer had never returned with Joseph's share of the coins.

Amanda hadn't come home during the night or by the next morning. The place was big and empty when she was gone.

The only thought that relieved him was that his connections to the world were diminishing. He would be freed and Amanda would know everything, she would finally understand. She would see that everything would be fine. All she had to do was trust Joseph.

Joseph thought that this would probably be the right time to go back to Preacher Madison if he was so inclined. The Preacher would want him to go to their classes. He would be supervised by one of the elders until he graduated from their basement schoolroom. They would allow him to get a job and then live in his own apartment in the commune hotel. Not at first, but eventually, there would be a punishment for leaving the commune. With the church came its rules. Then came the words of God.

He thought of his parents and how they were always reminded to be thankful. They were always reminded of the shepherd that takes care of his sheep. The voice of God brought down to earth through Preacher Madison.

Joseph decided that he would not go back to Preacher Madison because he knew that then he would have to pay for his sins. If he never returned, he would be safe.

It was time to tell her. Joseph couldn't feel it like he thought he would. He imagined that every inch of his body would know the time was right. He and Amanda would have to leave. They would start out with nothing because they now had to. Joseph reasoned that he had nothing to keep him any longer. Underneath all the arguments was a thin voice trying to hold him back.

He went down the back stairs, jumping two at a time. When his foot touched the landing of the second floor, he stopped running. He walked slowly and deliberately, his heel touching, and then his toe. Then the next foot, heel and toe. Joseph's steps made no sound. He held his breath until his chest was about to explode. Only two floorboards creaked as he worked his way all the way around the second floor. At the door to the apartment Joseph could hear nothing inside. He didn't want to knock if Amanda wasn't in there.

His body felt cool now, just his heart beating beneath his ribs and the rasp of his breathing coming up above that. He thought of the VCR's, the guns, drugs and money that had to still be in the apartment. There was no noise inside the apartment.

He turned the knob slowly and lifted the handle up against the frame when a tumbler surprisingly caught. Then there was a gentle click and the knob continued turning. It was unlocked and Joseph pushed the door soundlessly.

The dealer was in his chair. Amanda was kneeling on the floor before him.

Joseph filled a plastic grocery bag with his clothes and the half loaf of bread that had been sitting on the floor. His stomach turned, the hollow spot under his chest slid up and deflated like a balloon and then was gone.

His mouth opened and a spasm shook from the back of his throat. He hung his face over the toilet and waited. Stuck his finger down his throat, forced himself to dry heave and found there was nothing in his stomach.

Joseph felt unimportant and small. Other people could not be controlled. They all moved around Joseph as if he was standing still in a river stream. It was like trying to stop the water's flow.

He knew he had been cheated, but was not sure how. He had been given a life he did not want. The perfect one the Preacher had always told him about had been taken away, given away, to someone else.

The television that Amanda had harped so loudly and constantly for he pushed out the window. It met the ground with a muted crack.

It was the dealer's wife who had gone to Preacher Madison and told all about Joseph. Even though Joseph had no idea what the woman knew, he didn't understand how she could have known everything the Preacher had repeated.

Joseph wondered if the wife had joined the church. Maybe she had gone to the church for a handout and a Sunday meal and had ended up staying. He wondered if she was glad to be rid of her children.

That night Joseph slept in the Racine Gardens. Yellow construction tractors rested at the side of the park and half of the grass was torn out in heavy chunks. Deep gouges were bitten from the ground. A ditch-digger with rusted teeth and a dump truck filled with gravel sat silent across the sidewalk. The park was being torn down.

He told himself that he was a coward. He had run away from the dealer's apartment. They probably had not even notice him.

Joseph lay down behind the cement wall of the flower bed. The city sky was still light and Joseph could see the dim stars high between the buildings. It was a rare night when the stars were visible and he watched for over an hour as the clouds moved in, darkening the sky and hiding the view piece by piece. He heard footsteps shuffling in the gravel and hoped impossibly that no one was there.

Old John made it over the low cement wall, one aching leg at a time, on the second try.

Joseph whispered out to the old drunk, his voice trying to reel the man in. John stopped moving when he heard his name and he searched in all directions for the source.

"John, it's me. Joseph."

John backed away until he realized who it was climbing out of the dirt. Then he smiled.

"You scared the hell out of me," Old John told Joseph. "What are you doing here? I been looking all over for you."

"I got nowhere to sleep tonight."

"Me too. The faggots kicked me out."

"I thought you said they left."

"They did."

"What happened?"

"They came back." John shook his head and then remembered. "Lookit what I got." He pulled a new bottle of whiskey from his bag. The seal was unbroken and John was already stinking drunk.

"Where'd you get that?"

"I found it." John's answer for everything.

The two of them sat silently, leaning with their backs against the cement ledge as they started drinking. The whiskey burned Joseph's throat. John took gulp after gulp, like he couldn't taste a thing, like he wanted to hurt himself.

Old John pointed to the big yellow machines behind his back and tried to growl like a lion. They reminded him of something.

The park was spinning around Joseph before an hour had passed. His stomach bubbled from the warm whiskey and he could no longer form words in his mouth. Joseph pointed at John and John pointed back. Drunk laughter fell between them and Old John was able to stop giggling before Joseph.

Joseph was laughing so hard tears were pouring down his face. He couldn't stop.

He crawled to the fence and began puking. It felt good. It felt like a cool breeze had circled his body as his system tried to clear itself. Joseph crawled back and found Old John was cringing at the sight.

The little man asked Joseph if he was feeling all right.

"Yeah, but I think I'm going to go to sleep."

"Okay," John said. "I'm awake. I'll stay up and keep watch out. I'll guard you."

Joseph thanked John and wished that he could tell the old man about Amanda. Everything he had done for her. He curled into a ball and doubted that Old John would even understand. Before fading away, Joseph remembered hearing John hum tunelessly between drinks from the neck of the bottle.

In his drunken sleep Joseph had a dream of a train of cars. All moved in a slow procession down Wilson Avenue, colored with carnations and crepe paper. Streamers dragged through puddles. Paper dragons with human legs danced along the curbs. Headlights blinked in yellow cadences. Joseph couldn't see inside any of the darkened windows. He wasn't certain, but it felt like he was riding the hood of one of the cars and there was an arm trying to pull him down beneath the wheels.

The morning sunlight burned his eyes. Humid air choked him and his head was pounding from somewhere deep inside. Joseph squinted to block out some of the sun as he slowly remembered why he was in the park.

It looked like a black thread leading to small dark circles on the ground next to Joseph. The thread trailed away across the park, it grew thicker and Joseph didn't know what it was. He opened his eyes further to see it was a deep red stain drying on the cement.

Drops of blood were spattered along the line. Joseph, still drunk, tried to stand and only made it to his knees. He crawled to find John face down in a patch of green grass. Blood smeared his jaw and soaked the collar of his coat.

Joseph shook John's leg. Whispered to the back of his wrinkled neck. There was no movement and no response. He rested the palm of his hand against the old man's back, waiting to feel the ribs expanding and collapsing with each breath. The clothes were damp and there was no breathing and Joseph jerked his hand away.

He didn't want to turn John's body over. Blood had dried along the sidewalk. Knee and palm prints had crawled through an opaque puddle.

Someone probably saw the old man with a bottle and figured that he had some money left over. His throat must have been cut all the way across.

John was the last person anyone should have killed and Joseph felt that somehow it was his fault.

Joseph didn't know why he had been left alone. He hadn't heard a thing during the night. He felt how soft his throat was, how easy the skin would part.

He wished that it had been him, too. That would have been easy. It would have been done with and there would be nothing left for him to think about.

Joseph went to the edge of the healthy grass and began throwing up what was left of last night's alcohol.

Then he walked unsteadily to a pay phone on Wilson Avenue and reported a murder to the woman's voice that answered the 911 emergency line. She sounded irritated and bored and Joseph wanted to scream at her. She said the police would arrive at the address as soon as they could. Joseph was told to not go anywhere.

He could smell vomit and alcohol sweat rising from his body.

On a park bench he waited for the police or an ambulance, unsure what would come first. John's body was left in the grass, right next to the sidewalk. Joseph felt that he should move John somewhere else, hide him from the street and make him look more respectable. Roll him over and fold his hands across his chest with flowers from someone's garden placed between his thumb and index finger.

People walking past could see him. The few who did, glanced and quickly turned away. They didn't know he was dead. The blood could barely be seen from the spot where Joseph sat. John looked like he was only sleeping. Up close there was a copper smell and it could be felt that there was no heat, no breathing. The face and flabby skin had turned a bluish white. The blood had drained off somewhere else inside the body.

A cop car came first. Two officers got out and shut the doors and Joseph watched their heavy belts tilt as they walked. It was a white cop and a larger, black cop. The black cop's stomach stretched his shirt at the bottom few buttons and hung over the edge of his pants. The white cop went to John and the black cop only glanced at the prone body as he approached Joseph.

"What happened to him?"

"I don't know. He was like that when I woke up."

The cop looked at Joseph's face and clothes. Checked him from head to toe.

"You sleeping in the park?"

"I did last night."

"Was he here?"

"John?"

"You know him?"

"Yeah, yeah. He was here, too. We were drinking."

"What were you drinking?"

"Strong stuff. I don't know. It was his." Joseph could see that the cop smelled the alcohol and vomit.

"You got some ID, kid?"

Joseph went through his pockets. He knew that he had no driver's license or state ID. Finally he brought out a faded bible card with his signature and handed it over. The worn paper was useless and the cop handed it back.

An ambulance had silently coasted up behind the police car. The bar lights were off. Two paramedics slowly walked through the grass.

"Joseph Askew? Don't go nowhere." The black cop repeated himself, told Joseph to stay right where he was. Joseph did and only turned to watch the paramedics as they leaned over John's body.

"Throat hemorrhage," one of them announced.

"Any ID?" another asked.

"No."

Joseph watched the paramedics roll John onto his back, then his stomach, then his back again as if they were looking for something.

The black cop began telling the white cop everything Joseph had said before. They had been drinking together last night and the boy woke up and found the old guy dead.

"What happened to him?" Joseph asked again.

"His throat hemorrhaged," the black cop answered.

"What's that mean?"

"It's an occupational hazard of drunks. The booze weakens the inside of the throat until finally something breaks. Then you drown in your own blood."

The black cop walked away and the white cop said to Joseph, "Why don't you get out of here. Go find something to do. You got something to do?"

"No," Joseph said.

"Well, stay out of trouble."

And that was that.

From the corner where traffic cruised past and the city college hung over his head, Joseph watched the paramedics roll John's body into a black bag. They clumsily forced his knees bent to get him inside and then closed the bag over his chest and face. All zipped up the bag was too long for John's body. Joseph watched the ambulance slowly roll away and the cop car went a minute later.

While He Was Gone

Amanda knew that the dealer was waiting in his chair. Such a big man could not rest quietly. It was like there had to be something moving inside him, like wild animals that burrow beneath the earth.

Against the door, right before her hand touched the wood, static jumped to her fingers and she was certain that he was in there. A little shock snapped the skin of her knuckles. The fat man's presence spread past his doorway. She drew her breath and knocked solidly.

She was welcomed in before she knocked a second time. The dealer knew who was outside.

Amanda saw that nothing had changed. The apartment was only darker. The same dirty clothes, rotten dishes, smelly kids, and recently purchased and destroyed furniture was all there. In the corner were stacks of new merchandise, TVs and VCRs and stereos along with one lone, unplugged fax machine. The dealer was in his chair, filling it to capacity as each strained breath taken confirmed that the man's own weight was slowly choking him to death. He smiled at Amanda and asked how she was doing.

She was early and the familiar sight of the room and the thought of the final results of the visit comforted her. They relaxed her body, lessened the slight tweaks of discomfort that were coming on. She knew she would have to endure a little before it got better. If she didn't think much about it, she would be able to handle it just fine.

There was always the chance that she would have to stay all day, wait in the back room with the two kids and baby-sit until the dealer was ready for her to spend the night. The dealer knew when he had to do business and when he was able to play a little. The difference was immense.

The children were on the floor, playing with plastic army soldiers. The kids scared Amanda sometimes. At first she had tried to talk to them, to make the situation a little better, but they had not once responded. They were completely deaf to her. Infrequently would they hear their father. The louder the man yelled and the more bloody his threats, the worse became their behavior. They would suddenly look up at his bellowing as if torn from something important and laugh at his helplessness.

"What," the dealer asked Amanda, "do you want?"

She cringed a little and decided on the minimum. Just enough to last the day and hope that the price hadn't gone up since the last visit. After a pause he named a price. Amanda shook her head and the dealer imitated her. He parted his knees wide and scratched at the fold of his stomach that hung over his crotch.

His face parted into two halves as he smiled. Amanda tried to erase any thoughts from her head as she stepped closer. In the corner of the apartment she could feel the two kids playing with a new toy. She could feel them in the background as she lowered herself to her knees.

"Bang bang," one of the kids shouted before running from the room.

The dealer's hand pressed down against the thin tendons of her neck. She believed that the man would choke or smother her on a whim.

"Bang bang." Again from the next room.

She bared her teeth as she felt the shudder in the man's body. It ended weakly and her neck was released. She turned to the floor and spat on the carpet. All she could taste was dirty salt in her cotton mouth.

From the other side of the apartment came a barely noticeable popping noise. The little girl appeared in the doorway with a confused look in her eyes. The dealer pulled his pants up over his waist. "What's wrong, honey?" he asked over the top of Amanda's head.

The girl said nothing and the dealer hoisted himself from his chair to see what the kids were doing. Amanda stayed where she was.

"Oh, motherfucking Jesus Christ." The dealer carefully backed out of the bedroom. Beneath his feet, the little girl was mumbling incoherently.

Inside the bedroom door Amanda saw the little boy, spread out on his back, a circle of dark soaking up from his shirt and spreading across his stomach. The boy smeared blood on his face as he scratched desperately at his cheeks.

The silver gun in the other child's hand could have been a toy. There was no guard covering the trigger and the hammer was as big as the barrel. It fit naturally in the little palm.

"My fucking two-shot."

The child fired another bullet into the wall, causing Amanda to jump, and then clicked the gun empty. Her brother was sobbing between gasps of air.

The dealer backhanded the child and knocked her against the wall. He pried the tiny gun from her loose grip and searched the room for some idea of what to do next.

"Shit." The dealer juggled the gun between his hands.

"I'll call 911," Amanda offered. Her knees wouldn't lift her from the carpet.

"Wait. Take him out to the hall first."

"You can't move him."

"I gotta move him. I can't have him right there. Help me with this and I owe you one."

"You move the kid and call the cops, then. Why don't you give me my shit first?"

Neither one spoke for a moment. They had to be taken care of before the child was attended to. After that, there would be no chance of finishing anything. The little girl was kneeling over her brother, scared to touch him. Her brother was scared to cry any louder than a whisper.

"It was only a two-shot derringer," the dealer tried to justify himself. "He can't be mortally hurt. Help me lift him to the hall and you don't owe me anything for a long time."

She said nothing until the dealer tried again.

"Come on, you know I'm good if I say so." He was getting impatient and Amanda, hating herself for feeling this way at such a moment, liked to see him a little scared. She had never seen his eyes so big.

"Okay," she agreed.

They eventually carried the child, barely bleeding, barely breathing, out into the hall and then called 911. No neighbors poked their heads out their doors to see what was going on. The little girl was calmed down and quieted and told to lie down. Her brother would be fine.

The police came before Amanda had a chance to leave the apartment. And even though the boy had been placed in the hall, the police entered anyway. A search was made and a general inventory was quickly taken after the boy was placed on a stretcher. Caught with her pockets full, Amanda wondered why there weren't any smaller stretchers. She thought the boy looked silly. Her mind went numb before her wrists were cuffed in a plastic cord. The little girl was taken away in another car.

After the ambulance departed, it took the police several hours to carry out everything from the dealer's apartment.

Amanda and the dealer were tucked down into the back of the same police car. She cried as the fat man repeated over and over through the cage that it was all an accident. He was innocent. "Am I supposed to know what my kids are doing twenty-four hours a day? And where's their mother? Why don't you fucking arrest her, too?"

To The Well

In the broad daylight Joseph returned to the Mayor's apartment. Alone in the vacant lot the three-flat reminded Joseph of a derelict lighthouse sitting alone on the shore.

Doors were left hanging wide open and there was no one left in the apartment building. Walking up the stairs, Joseph saw that the other apartments along with the Mayor's were empty, the doors left ajar. No one would be hurt.

It was either Frank or Officer Vallenti who said that detox lasted for thirty days. Or maybe sixty days.

The front closet had been completely torn apart. Someone had been there after Joseph. He heard the Printer's voice echo from the bare back wall, "Sorry kid. Closer to the end than you." He knew it.

Empty whiskey bottles, beer cans, and grayed clothing covered the bedroom floor, leaving a path from the edge of the bare mattress to the curtained doorway. A crumpled bedsheet was piled in the corner of the room, the plaid mattress laid on the painted wooden floor. Stains had dried over the red and orange check pattern.

Joseph grabbed the edge of the mattress with his fingertips and leaned it at a vertical angle against the wall. Under the far corner hid four white envelopes that the Printer didn't find.

Joseph could feel the heavy coins wrapped inside the paper.

He folded the envelopes over and stuffed them into his pockets. Then dropped the mattress to the ground.

Under the kitchen sink he found a half-empty bottle of Southern Comfort. Unscrewing the lid, Joseph sniffed at the alcohol as if that would tell him something. It was sweet and strong and the fumes made him shiver, an automatic response to the memory of his first hangover. Joseph tightened the cap and put the bottle on the table.

While in the apartment, he washed his face with soap and hot water. Poured handfuls of water over his neck, let it trickle down his spine and chest. There was no mirror over the sink and Joseph wanted to see what his face looked like. He expected he would see a change, but didn't know what kind.

Joseph worked out his plan as he dried his hands on a stiff towel. He wanted nothing to be left for the Mayor when he got out of detox. He wanted there to be no memory of the Mayor. Not for himself or anyone else.

The grease-stained oven was waiting in the corner of the kitchen. Joseph twisted the first knob on the stove's console until he heard the hiss of gas. A circle of pointed blue flames grew from the front burner of the stove. Joseph opened the oven door and set the dial at 325 degrees. Then he blew out the pilot light.

With the bottle and the coins he ran from the building, expecting the bricks and pipes and floorboards to rain over his shoulders.

The sun reflected off the tips of choppy waves, dotting the transparent gray with shards of opaque white. Joseph wiped the sweat out of his eyes with the tail of his t-shirt. Raising the Southern Comfort up into his sight, he squinted one eye and checked his level.

Almost a quarter of the bottle was left. Joseph laughed and estimated that he had drunk half of the whiskey so far.

Sailboats and small-engined fishing yachts were tied to the docks in front of Joseph. He was sitting on the cement bank of Montrose Harbor. The man-made hills and carefully placed trees of the park were behind him. The D-Day beach was off to the left, the skyline of Chicago curved to the right, and the water spread far to the horizon.

Joseph wondered what the distance was to the horizon. He wanted to know how many miles his sight stretched.

Past the bows of the nearer boats and across a wide lane of water was a floating dock built of metal walkways supported over large floatation devices. Little sailboats were tied down between its planks. Joseph watched the dock sway with the afternoon tide as the boats tilted and rocked against the rhythm of the water. Like ice cubes in a glass. Joseph couldn't figure out how people got out to those boats.

He watched the motion of the water until his stomach was moving with the waves. He turned over and crawled into the grass with the whiskey bottle held in the crook of his elbow, pinned against his chest.

Before he passed out, Joseph patted down his pockets to check for the envelopes of coins. They were still there.

The bottle was gone when Joseph opened his eyes. He searched the grass surrounding him as if maybe it had rolled away. Joseph felt his drunk head pounding from the whiskey. The sun was going down and the water was shifting out past the breakwalls.

Behind the skyline the sun was hidden and the water darkened around one floating red stripe. The small boats had been lashed down and covered with tarps. One car idling in a parking lot gave a bit of privacy to a couple, half-naked and impatient, huddled in the back seat. Joseph watched until he recognized the naked backs of two men grinding in syncopation. Everything had shifted around Joseph as he slept.

He went to the edge of the harbor and sat down. There were two boats before him, their sails empty. Joseph spit into the water and the reflection of his shoes shook and broke away.

The boy decided that he would have to move ahead, force the last of his penance. As if he was making an offering to some vague idea. It was not the God of Preacher Madison, not the one Joseph had known. All of Joseph's losses had been someone else's gains. He did not know who to give to, so he made sure that he took away from himself. He figured it was basically the same thing.

Joseph tore the first envelope open and dumped three heavy silver coins into his palm. The edges of the coins were squared off into eight flat edges. A picture of some woman was on one side and a picture of a building was on the other. No date had been stamped, but the coins were turning green with age.

Joseph let the coins slide one at a time out of his palm. They hit the water with a plunk and disappeared into the murk several inches from the surface.

He emptied the next envelope the same way. Joseph sat and watched the coins drop to the water beneath his feet until they were all gone. Then a breeze picked up the torn envelopes and tumbled the pieces into the water.

The Mayor's building was still standing that night. Joseph didn't know what could have gone wrong. Maybe someone turned off the gas. Maybe a breeze killed the other flame. He wanted to cry, not because the building had not exploded, but because he saw now that he resembled his father. Drunken and desperate. Joseph had failed. He considered himself cowardly in all matters. Every chance he had, he had done the wrong thing.

The penance made no difference.

Joseph saw his own bedroom with the soldiers across the bedspread and the broken light fixture hanging from the ceiling. He saw the kitchen in flames and his mother's blank face.

Women staggered with the power of God.

He saw his father handcuffed and pushed down into the back of a police car outside the hotel. Everyone in the church standing there nervously like pigeons, dragged out of their beds by the fire alarms. Joseph remembered the winter wind coming hard off of the lake. The snow falling wet and heavy, catching onto his eyelashes. He remembered the fresh gasoline in the winter air and the hint of shame that he now fully knew.

True Love

Joseph was looking for Amanda. He wondered if she knew he had seen her with the dealer. He wondered if it mattered at all to her. He didn't know what to do. If he walked into their room and she behaved as if nothing were any different than before, Joseph felt he would be sick. He would attack her.

His last sight of Amanda came back to Joseph while he was asleep. He felt it would never leave him. All along she was still buying, even after Joseph ran out of money. He wanted to find her, make her promise that it would never happen again; tell him he didn't see anything.

With his good pair of pants packed in a plastic bag along with the jacket he had once tattooed with scripture, Joseph went south down Broadway. He had checked the library and the liquor store and the coffee shop. He searched every face on the street for some glimpse of Amanda. He didn't see anyone who looked like her. All the faces were ugly and jeering, selfish and cruel. Joseph wanted to tell them all what the world would do to them just because it could.

At the three-way intersection of Montrose, Broadway, and Sheridan a triangular cobblestone island provided an island of shelter from the traffic. Rooted under the worn bricks, thin trees with plumes of green blocked out the sun. Four-foot high boulders flanked the park benches and one metal garbage can was overflowing from a holiday weekend of take-out food and liquor bottles.

Bobbi and her boyfriend were alone on the island. It was a rare moment when any couple could have a little privacy inside the lanes of traffic. There were days when ten men perched like birds on a telephone line spent the day along the benches and boulders. But now, Bobbi and Hank were alone on the island and Joseph felt that he shouldn't interrupt. Once, he knew, a man had to get his jaw wired shut because of Hank and Bobbi. Joseph had seen the man. The wires were covered by a white padding outside the jaw, screws were drilled through the skin and bone, holding the plastic and metal in place. The man had propositioned Bobbi and apparently Hank took great offense.

Shade from a tree draped over the park bench where Bobbi sat. She picked at her hair and checked at her double chin in her compact mirror.

Hank was lying on his back, shirtless, resting across the rock like a pale lizard. Both he and Bobbi had half-pint bottles in paper bags.

When she spotted Joseph, Bobbi waved two fingers, telling him to come over. Hank mumbled something that resembled a greeting even though he had never met the boy. Joseph and Hank went on acting as if they were casual acquaintances.

"Honey," Bobbi said to Hank, "wouldn't it be nice to have a bonfire? Like at the beach?"

There was no response, so Bobbi asked the same question again. Joseph and Hank could hear the alcohol in her throat. The words were slow and heavy.

"Why you want to do that?" Hank asked.

"It'd be romantic," Bobbi whispered and then spun. "Wouldn't it, Joseph?"

Joseph nodded. He couldn't really picture it and he didn't really want to.

"And where you gonna do that?" Hank demanded.

"Here. We could do it right here."

"It's the middle of the day," Hank scolded.

"You don't snap at me, mister." Bobbi stood up and weighed the alcohol that was left in her bottle. "Help me, will you?" she asked Joseph. No further instructions came as Bobbi preened herself and shook the wrinkles out of her sundress with her free hand. She was still holding the pint bottle.

The Sheridan lights turned green and two Union Station buses ran past, dragging along the stink of fried chicken from a storefront across the street. Someone in a passing car whistled at Bobbi, but Hank didn't bother to look up. He knew that Bobbi was interested in no other.

"Have you seen Amanda?" Joseph asked Bobbi.

"Who, baby?"

"This girl I was with. She used to live..." Joseph stopped himself. He noticed Bobbi's eyes were glassy and knew when she was sober she couldn't remember half of the people she met. Bobbi probably had never laid eyes on Amanda. "Never mind," Joseph said. He wished that he hadn't crossed the street. Hank and Bobbi would have forgotten about him if he had kept walking.

Bobbi pulled the metal garbage can to the center of the island, right between the benches. She studied the position strategically, then picked up a few loose pieces of garbage and dropped them on top of the pile. The pint bottle was emptied into the rusted trash can.

Hank caught the sight of the last drops falling from the neck. "Hey, you're wasting good shit."

Bobbi took a pack of matches from her little purse. A breeze pulled the flame away from the first match head. Hank jumped off his rock as the second match fell into the garbage. Dropping somewhere under the Sunday newspaper, the flame scurried and caught, then dug to the bottom of the can and then climbed back to the top. In a short minute the fire grew too big. Flames snapped to points high overhead and the wind pulled in all directions.

"Oooh." Bobbi clapped her hands.

Hank was screaming. "What the hell you doing? What the fuck? Huh?" He looked down both sides of each street at the intersection, searching for the police, a witness, or an early fire engine. Nothing yet. He grabbed at Bobbi's elbow and tried to pull her away.

Rising heat curled the bottom leaves of the tree branches. Sparks were carried up. One branch caught, then another. The flames moved like fingertips pulling at the leaves.

Hank was shoving Bobbi through the Broadway traffic. Joseph was next to the garbage can. The heat pressed at his face and chest as little breaths of air were pulled out of his mouth. Joseph could hear Bobbi howling as she tried to hold her ground at the center line of the street. Joseph noticed that the trees were on fire.

"Hank, Hank, stop. I want to see." She jerked her arm free and turned to face Hank, who was much smaller than her. "I want to see it."

Separated by the yellow line they turned to face each other, positioned for a stand-off. Traffic around them crawled for a view of the fire that had spread to each sickly tree of the intersection island.

Little kids just out of school for the day pointed and screamed and ran closer. Joseph skipped to the opposite side of the intersection to hide in a group of Catholic school girls dressed in white blouses and plaid skirts. A cone of orange was burning, hovering in a plateau over the trees while the air above swirled like oil in water. It looked almost biblical, Joseph thought and began to laugh. He was nearly giddy because there was a small catastrophe and he had nothing to do with it. One dark-skinned girl made the sign of the cross and genuflected at the curb. Then Joseph heard the sirens coming from Racine Avenue.

Bobbi and Hank also heard the sirens. Hank had a head start and sprinted ahead of Bobbi; she kicked off her pumps and overtook her boyfriend at the corner. Joseph watched the two of them disappear behind a tavern.

Joseph had to push and shove to get out of the crowd. One of the girls called him an asshole as he broke free. A cop car rounded the corner and the girls began pointing in Joseph's direction.

Between the Jewel supermarket and the Salvation Army Joseph dropped to his stomach and began crawling under a chain-link fence. Before he was completely through, a hand fought for his ankle. One good yank had him down on his face and with another he was sliding backward under the fence. His front teeth scraped dirt and gravel as the wire fence pinched the back of his neck. A muscular and callused hand bound both of his wrists once he was clear of the fence and there was a knee in the small of his back. He had stopped laughing before he reached the fence.

"Where you going?"

Joseph didn't answer. With his tongue he was pushing dirt out of his mouth. It didn't seem to work, he was only creating mud. He turned his head to one side and could see the front end of a squad car. One cop was kneeling over him, another was standing in the background, next to the front bumper of the squad.

"Why you running? What'd you do?"

"Nothing," Joseph said. "I didn't do that. It wasn't me."

"What wasn't?"

"That fire."

"Oh, so you know about it? That wasn't you, then why you running?"

"Cause those girls were pointing at me."

"You scared of those little girls?"

"No." Joseph didn't know what to say. He shouldn't have even mentioned the fire. He shouldn't have denied anything until he was accused of something. Most likely, he told himself, he should have crawled faster.

"Maybe you like to start fires," the cop suggested as he shifted his weight and dug a knee into Joseph's back. "How many fires you do?"

"None. I never started a fire in my life." Joseph felt his ribs creaking as the cop leaned forward with his weight. He saw little stars in the dirt beneath his face and wondered if the Mayor's apartment blew up yet.

Another voice that belonged to the other cop yelling from the car, suggested, "Come on. We can't mess with the kid. Let the Town Hall guys pick him up."

The cop kneeling on Joseph's back, answered, "We'll wait for them."

"The car's already full. Let's take these two in."

Joseph was pulled to a standing position. He sucked air desperately as the other cop came close. He was much older than the first cop, he looked tired and it was obvious that he didn't want to bother with the boy. He spun Joseph to face the car and the fire burning high in the background.

"Did you do that?" the older cop asked.

"No. I swear it wasn't me."

"Good enough," the senior partner announced. "Let's go."

Joseph's arms were released and they snapped around as if there were springs in his shoulders. Both cops told Joseph that they didn't want to see him again. Joseph said okay. "Yes, sir. I didn't do it."

Cops always said that they never wanted to see him again, Joseph thought, but they never did anything about it.

Joseph noticed two shadows behind the cage of the back seat as the car dipped down under the weight of the officers climbing into the front. One figure had Amanda's sunken cheekbones and bony shoulders. Joseph moved toward the car as it pulled away from the curb. He held one arm raised, trying for someone's attention. The familiar figure in the back turned to Joseph as he ran into traffic. His spirit rose for a moment and then crashed back down.

He saw that it wasn't her. The face looked wide and broken. Nothing like Amanda.

He had forgotten about the cops and his twisted arms and his sore back.

"What?" the older cop demanded.

"Nothing." Joseph mumbled and shook his head. He stepped back to the sidewalk as the squad car did a U-turn and swerved around a fire engine. Joseph figured Amanda had returned to Belmont Avenue and one of her old boyfriends. If they did run into each other, it would be an accident. Joseph vowed to not return to the Magnolia building. It seemed official now.

There was one lone fire truck blocking the Broadway traffic. Two firemen in black rubber coats brought a hose to a hydrant at the corner.

They worked quickly and then ran the length of the hose across the street. Water streamed through the trees and the intersection and soaked the children who giggled and screamed and pushed each other under the shower.

Flames broke away in pieces, hit the ground and died. Dead branches fell to the cobblestone. The street was stained dark gray and thin rivers ran in corkscrew patterns to the sewer grates. Some old men waiting outside the window of the currency exchange applauded the firefighters.

Joseph found his concrete bed in the Racine gardens remained untouched while the surrounding grass had been completely gouged out and earth moving tractors rested at the edge of the garden. Spattered with clumps of dirt and streaks of rust cutting into the yellow paint, the machines looked like they would never move again. Dying topsoil lay like rolls of carpets stacked in pyramids. Dirt was piled up along the street, spilling over the curb. Jackhammer holes and spray-painted notations scarred the sidewalk, marking them for the next day's work.

He folded the scripture jacket he had not touched in a long time and slipped it behind his neck for a pillow. One sleeve reached out past his ear and Joseph knew the words by heart. "A continuing whirlwind: it shall fall with pain upon the head of the wicked."

While the other sleeve told him, "And these signs shall follow them that believe: In my name shall they cast out devils; they shall speak with new tongues; They shall take up serpents; and if they drink any deadly thing, it shall not hurt them."

Joseph fell asleep listening to the sound of boys setting off packages of fireworks. In the dark, small bursts like gunfire faded away down the block.

A Small World

A handwritten sign was taped inside the glass door of the Saint Augustine Drop-Off Center for American Indians. Pronunciation of the tribe's official name was spelled out under the title of the shelter hanging on the door. CLOSED FOR THE FOURTH OF JULY WEEKEND, the handwritten note said, giving notice several weeks in advance.

From the Wilson Avenue El Joseph rode high above the street and watched the third story windows of the brick three-flats roll past. Every window, it seemed, was darkened and every apartment was vacated for the afternoon. Joseph imagined that all of these people were out at work, or at the beach, or at the ballpark, or doing something valuable and productive. Working in offices with magnificent and sweeping views of the entire city, driving taxis that circle the Loop and then hustle out to the airport and back, serving coffee, dry-cleaning clothes, tending to hospital patients, sailing boats. Getting married, getting divorced. Driving trucks, directing traffic, sitting in libraries, sitting in schools. Washing windows, waiting tables, waiting for buses. Waiting for the day to end.

So that at night they could all be back at their homes, with their families and neighbors, and every window would be warmly and safely lit until it was time for bed. They would sleep until the next day when it would all start again. And would start again the next day and go on just like that until years passed and the people died and new ones replaced the ones before them and nothing really would change.

Joseph tried to count the high-rise windows as the train roared past. He lost track immediately.

The riders swayed back and forth in their seats like there was some slow music that Joseph couldn't hear. He saw them all moving, connected by invisible wires running from shoulder to shoulder.

Joseph tightened the muscles in his back and braced his feet against the wall to resist the jerking motion of the train. Trying to ignore it. He held his body as if he were catatonic.

A shoulder brushed against Joseph as he stared at the window. A dark face appeared behind him in the glass, peering over his shoulder. The eyes of the reflection were looking at Joseph's reflection.

"Got a cigarette, man?"

It was Sonny standing in the aisle. His voice was melodious and kind.

"No, I don't have any. Sorry." Joseph didn't know if he was supposed to recognize Sonny because Sonny sounded like he didn't recognize Joseph. He was just asking a stranger for a cigarette. Several more stops went past before Sonny spoke again.

"So, how you doing, man?"

Again Joseph didn't know how he should answer the question. He braced himself for Sonny's threats but would not defend himself from them. "I'm okay."

"Yeah. Hey, I heard about the fat guy. I feel bad your woman got caught up in that."

Joseph took his eyes away from the window, lost his catatonic posture. He didn't know what happened to Amanda and wasn't sure if Sonny knew what he was talking about. Maybe he meant someone else, someone Joseph hadn't ever met. "In what?"

"You got a girlfriend, right?" Sonny wanted to clarify. "I seen you out with her."

"I did."

"Skinny girl? Built nice? She used to hang out with some kind of little Nazis, right?" Sonny's voice was reassuring and understanding, like a teacher's voice, like it had been when he and Joseph first met. When he had shown Joseph what the possession of the spirit looked like.

"Yeah."

"Well I know you ain't one of those Nazis. I can tell that you too smart for that." Sonny shook his head. The animosity of the toluene incident was suddenly long passed. "You know, it's like those guys don't see nothing except what they want. They sound impressive when they spouting off on this or that, some racist doctrine or speech they memorized, but when they just talking that's different. Just white trash. Stupid assholes. Don't take that wrong. Because I already said that I didn't think you were like that."

"Yeah, okay. But what happened to her?"

"Your girlfriend?"

"Yeah, yeah."

"Now, I know this other woman, this fat guy's wife. Do you know him? His name's Cicero, or Campbell, something like that. Well, I know his wife because I was sorta doing her on the side a while ago. She was cool. Well, I saw her again with your preacher. I feel sorta bad about this. You got sorta fucked over, and I don't think you did nothing. I just found out myself. There was nothing I could do," Sonny admitted as if he had been on Joseph's side all along. "But the big-ass dude's wife, she went to the Preacher and told him all of her problems. I guess she ended up joining the church."

Joseph interrupted, he knew that already. He wanted to know what happened to Amanda.

"Yeah, they called the cops. The Preacher and the wife. The cops, I heard they went in and busted the fat dude for dealing. The city, DCFS, all them, came and took the kids. Your girl was taken in, too. They're throwing some charges at her. Nothing much. If it's her first time, she'll probably get nothing. The fat dude probably, too. If they don't got huge records, they'll be suspended sentences. Be back out in a few days. I don't know much about the fat dude."

"You know when she'll be out?"

"I don't know. Probably, she didn't do nothing. But maybe they'll nail her. Fuck it, you know, if they put her away it'll be for a reason."

Sonny didn't know about the little girl shooting her brother. He didn't know that Amanda had been arrested because she was holding the gun that looked so much like a toy. The dealer had said that he saw the pistol go off in Amanda's hand and that he had never even seen the gun before. The dealer was worried his children would go to their mother if the police found out that the gun belonged to him.

It would be after Amanda's arraignment that the little girl would tell the story to a caseworker. And even later the girl would learn that her brother died only because her father and Amanda haggled over prices and deals while the boy lay on the bedroom floor.

"It's the little people who have to even work at it to get arrested," Sonny continued. "It's all so crowded, the judges are happy to throw you out. You gotta have a page-long record before you do time. Or you gotta do something real stupid. Like my cousin. He's got such a record, every time he shoplift something, all he gets is time served or a suspended sentence."

It was then that Joseph stopped listening. The monologue faded away until he wasn't sure if Sonny was still talking or not. It didn't matter. Joseph thought about going to the police station to get Amanda. Or at least to see her. Joseph had no money. She wouldn't want to see him. She had been looking for a place to sleep and Joseph just happened to come with the room. He didn't understand how it had passed by so quickly. Maybe he had never given Amanda a chance. They could have gotten old together like real people. They could have been alone in their cabin far past the suburbs.

Maybe, Joseph thought, he had never told her anything. Maybe he only spoke out loud when he was alone. He had caught himself doing that a few times. Talking to himself. Joseph was sure he told her. He remembered doing so. They were looking out the windows, watching the rain pour down the brick wall that blocked their view. Amanda had agreed with a quiet yes or a mumble to everything Joseph planned.

He remembered that it was raining. Joseph had liked it when they were locked in together because of the rain.

Joseph had told Amanda everything, she just wasn't listening.

He wondered if she was sitting in a jail cell. The fact that Sonny was the one bringing the news didn't bother Joseph. A short time earlier he would have noticed.

The train moved along on its tracks through the El stops of Wrigleyville and Lincoln Park. Girls in short skirts and tank tops were laughing and giggling as they came through the doors. Joseph saw their reflections in the window.

"I heard about your hotel," Sonny said.

"What hotel?"

"The one you lived in, boy. The Jesus Hotel."

"What about it?"

"Man, there was a fire. The place went. Didn't you see it on the news? It got gutted. It happened right before the ten o'clock news program, I know because they had the live TV trucks there and shit. On the news they wouldn't say the address, but I recognized it. The police and fire trucks got there just as the whole place got going good. No one was in the place except for the janitor and a security guard. The news said everyone was out. Like they were at some nighttime mass."

"When was this?"

"Last night. Don't you got a TV?" Sonny was quiet for a second as he watched Joseph's face. Then he asked, "Your folks still stay there? At the hotel?"

"No, they moved a long time ago. They live somewhere else."

"Oh yeah?" Sonny wasn't interested in hearing about Joseph's parents. Joseph wasn't going to tell him, anyway, because he didn't know, himself. "I bet it was on purpose, man. I bet someone could make some money on that place."

Nothing Sonny had to say would now upset Joseph. He had been numbed to any kind of news.

Sonny's hands twisted at the top of a paper bag that appeared out of nowhere. A small hiss and Sonny had the beer cap in his palm. He offered Joseph a drink.

With the comfortable weight of a forty-ounce beer between his hands Joseph bent forward and took a long sip, hoping no one was watching. Sonny took the bottle back and drank without caring if anyone saw or not. And the beer was passed back and forth until the train sank underground to the subway and the faces of Joseph and Sonny were hidden in shadow.

As if Sonny was greatly relieved of something he shook his head and smiled. Sharing alcohol had created a temporary bond. Joseph could feel it as Sonny spoke. "We just keep seeing each other. I saw you at the beach. You know that you saw me. No one saw my man, he got lucky. They could still be beating on him if they wanted." Sonny laughed and Joseph smiled hesitantly, not sure if he should yet trust Sonny even though he wanted to. So he only listened. Maybe all animosities had passed. Joseph, suddenly drained, needed to listen to someone's voice.

"I told McKnuckle to get lost," Sonny explained the events after the mock D-Day. "He was gonna get in trouble and I was going to end up in with him. I love him, but I don't need that. Told him to go downtown. That was where I got into the churching in the first place. There's this church, this weird-ass thing called Hymie Johnson or something like that out in Indiana. The church people drive to the city on weekends. These born-again, white bread, do-gooders they always want to help us poor niggers out of the mud. I ain't ever been in the mud, right? No matter how ugly my surroundings are, I ain't dirty. But they want to show us stupid assholes the way to the Lord. The two dudes who started it were Hymie and Johnson. They wrote a bunch of books of their own and their own school and all this other stuff. Now they sit back and collect the money. Got all the others, the lackeys and freaks, out there recruiting.

"Like when they wanna gather up some new sheep, they take these buses, all painted camouflage green like God's army and they drive a couple hours across the border, into Chicago and park by the Water

Tower and the Hancock. Right by Michigan Avenue with only four or five guys in each bus. They preach on the street and try to convert anyone who's sleeping in the park or just looks like they don't have a place to stay. I let them find me on Lower Wacker a few times and I went along. The crackers offer a straight shower and two hot meals. Show us how a little kindness is all we need. You know, the smiling faces and the positive slogans and signs up on the walls. Men hugging each other and blessing each other. Always trying to improve someone else.

"They take you out to the big green campus. It's all farmland and nothing else out there. Looks like a college out in the middle of nowhere. At first you could think it's a summer resort, but later you see it's like an armed camp. Money all over the place. They got security guards who drive around their property with big .357 Cobras and Glocks. Everything belongs to them. Far as you can see, it's theirs. If they wanted, they could do whatever they want. No one's gonna check. It's like it could be an Indiana Waco cult. The church is the law.

"I ran the scams, you know, but they weren't in on it with me. I did it to them and they fell for it. They wanted me to stay. Some pastor told me I was a true receiver of the Lord. This was a long time ago and I still never forgot. Got a little cash for that, so it's hard to forget. But out of all the dudes they picked up, only two I know of ever stayed longer than a day. They kept on and got a scholarship to the school and are both learning to preach. No shit. And I knew these guys, used to be cool. They used to hang. Now they follow all the church rules and dress like they gonna go golfing everyday. They got no smoking. No drinking, no cussing. And no sex unless you married and the head reverend gives you the okay on your nuptials." Sonny laughed at his own summary of the church.

"Anyway, all anyone I know does is go for the ride, get a shower, fill up on buffet food and get driven back. See, they won't usually let you spend the night unless you gonna join up. So no one joins up, they just make the trip when they're real hungry.

"That's why I sent my man out to Indiana. Boy was acting too stupid over here. I thought maybe a week would do him good. See him last that long. He didn't want to at first. He said he wasn't in no trouble here and said there were too many Klan out there. He says the church is a front for the Klan. Fuck him. I told him no Klan was gonna burn him. The

Klan is old news, a weak group. The real nigger-haters are the guys who are both politicians and preachers. But anyway, we bullshitted for a while and I think I got him to talk serious about it. He takes me more seriously than I sometimes think. He says he might stay and go to school. The more we talked about it, the more he actually sounded like he wanted to go. It might be good for him to sit in the peace and quiet for a while. We'll see. I think he might have been bullshitting me on that. But he went. I know, because I took him. Put his ass on the bus just to help make those white boys feel good about themselves."

Sonny laughed and took a drink and passed the bottle to Joseph. "I'm thinking of moving," Sonny confided and pointed his thumb in the direction of the far north side. "I don't like it up here no more. I got a sister in West Virginia. I might move down there. I think the Indiana boys got the right idea sometimes. Relocation sounds damn good."

The train kept at a slow metal pace and the beer was almost empty. Joseph saw an old woman walking through the car. She smiled and nodded to Joseph and then sat down across the aisle. An image of McKnuckle breaking a beer bottle over the fat woman's head flashed through Joseph.

A picture of the old woman, the ex-nun who handed out pamphlets up and down Broadway, came to Joseph. The woman across the aisle could have been the ex-nun's sister. Old John liked her. He said she was nice and quiet and would have never hurt anyone.

Sonny's disclosure and Joseph's numbness made Joseph believe that any topic was open for discussion.

"You remember the old lady with all the make-up? The ex-nun?" Joseph suddenly asked Sonny.

A puzzled look crossed Sonny's face and he said he didn't know any old ladies.

"Yeah, everyone saw her around," Joseph innocently pried. He wasn't accusing anyone. Sonny may have done some things wrong in his life, but Joseph could no longer see the ex-nun as Sonny's work. He only wanted to reminisce about the lady. Joseph didn't realize that he had stepped out of the conversation's bounds. "You remember? She got killed on the walkway to the beach."

The friendliness that had been in Sonny's voice fell away as the train rose above ground again and sunlight poured like water into the car. "I think you drunk, boy. Probably a good idea if you get off the ride now," Sonny warned. "We a little too far south for you. A white boy could get hurt here. Understand?"

The train was pulling into the 22nd Street station. Joseph saw that he was the only white face on the train except for the old woman across the aisle.

"Okay," Joseph said unsteadily. "Thanks for the beer."

"Yeah, right." Sonny didn't even turn to look at Joseph as he climbed out of the car.

On the 22nd Street platform Joseph waited for another train to take him back to the north side. He wondered what Amanda would look like now. He wondered if he should bother trying to find her. Sonny had practically told Joseph that there was nothing for him to return to.

The Hustlers

The train car was sharply divided right through the middle. One half full. One half empty. People were all facing front, facing the empty side of the car. Joseph sat down opposite the crowd and saw that they were all watching him instead of staring out the windows or studying their laps. Eyes focused on him, moved away momentarily, and then settled again. He wondered what had happened on his side of the car before he entered and he wondered if the passengers were waiting for the same to happen again. Joseph felt like he had accidentally stepped onto a stage and the crowd was impatiently waiting for some kind of performance.

A few men wandered to the center of the car. One carefully read a warning posted above the automatic doors while the other began leafing through a pile of discarded newspapers on a vacant bench. The train approached the first downtown stop. The gray cement platform slowed down and halted outside Joseph's window. A young couple dressed for their summer vacation sat down, their profiles protecting Joseph's view from the rest of the car.

The man who had been digging for something in the papers had now moved to the center of the train. He held one section of the newspaper like some serving tray offering three whiskey caps lined up side by side.

He moved the caps around, flashed a tiny red ball from beneath one cap and made an announcement. "Find the ball. Find it and win." Then positioned himself so that the couple sitting in front of Joseph could easily see the whiskey caps. The girl watched one shuffled turn and immediately began pointing. In a gawking southern voice she blurted out that the ball was under the middle cap. The hustler ignored her and let another man pick the same cap. Then gladly handed over twenty dollars for finding the ball. The girl protested, she knew the ball was there all along.

Joseph was relieved the spotlight he imagined had drifted away from him.

"Now, you woulda won twenty bucks if you had told me," the hustler suddenly reprimanded the girl.

The other man, the partner who already won his money, slipped away into the background.

"I did tell you," the girl pouted.

"Well, play again." The hustler lifted the middle cap and exposed the little red ball. He moved the caps in circles and half-circles using only two fingers. Two for each cap and two caps at a time. Little poetic movements, a small stage show held on the folded newspaper. The third cap was pushed back and forth with his thumb.

The caps stopped chasing each other and the girl knew where the ball was. She picked the right cap, but the hustler told her that she had to prove that she had twenty dollars before she won twenty. He refused to lift the cap until he saw twenty dollars.

It was so clear to see from the outside, Joseph thought.

"Show twenty to win twenty. I gotta see that you have twenty." The girl and her boyfriend hurriedly dug through their pockets. Each one found forty dollars and held the bills in the air. The hustler's eyes lit up and his partner moved closer with a section of the newspaper into the seats across from the tourists.

Joseph watched the whole thing. He wanted to tell the couple to stop. They were not going to win. They had lost as soon as eye contact was made. Joseph kept his eyes down when he wanted to scream. He did not want to be pulled into the game. There were more people involved, more than the two obvious ones before the tourists.

And they all tried again, this time for the money smoothly flattened out against the girl's knee. The red ball did not appear where the girl had last seen it.

Between two fingers the ball was swiftly picked beforehand and the cap was lifted to reveal nothing. The ball dropped again as a different cap was lifted. Joseph saw the move as if it were his own hand.

Twenty dollars was taken from the girl's loose fingers. Without any encouragement she asked to try again. She wanted her money back. The hustler held her off, suggested that they play one or two times just for fun. He wanted her to find the ball, he wanted to show her that he was not cheating. The girl was allowed to find the ball twice in a row. From the spectators came a third man who demanded to bet fifty dollars. The hustler's eyes opened in mock amazement before he went through the whole routine again, ignoring the girl for the time being. The ball was found and a folded bill was slipped to the new winner. No one saw the denomination. The girl and her boyfriend put forty dollars down on the next play. Joseph heard his own voice pleading in his head.

The hustler and his partner turned away for a second and Joseph roughly pressed his foot down on the boyfriend's toes, shut his eyes and barely shook his head. The boyfriend slowly decoded the message as the next round started. In whispers and squeezes he convinced the girl to stop betting and then the two of them tried to ignore the hustler and the partner standing directly over them. They sat there, suddenly deaf and dumb to the shell game. The money remained on the girl's knee.

The hustler kept the whiskey caps going, trying again for someone's attention. There were people laughing on the other side of the train car. The train slid along the tracks, rose above the street. Joseph saw the cloudy sky. He thought the hustler's partner might have noticed the hint Joseph had given to the boyfriend. He kept his eyes down at his shoes. When there were no more takers, the hustlers should have moved on to the next car, but they remained where they were.

The tourist couple stood up when the train pulled in at their station. Turning to Joseph, the boyfriend said, "Thanks, man," and stepped from between the doors and onto the platform. Leaving Joseph alone.

The hustler sat with his two partners, the quiet one and the other who had seemed to win fifty dollars. Joseph could feel their eyes tracing the folds of his clothing. He waited to see the movement, waited for them to come after him. They all stood up when the train reached the next stop.

The doors parted. Joseph's path was blocked by the hustler, the biggest of the three. From the corner of his eye Joseph saw one hand slip out from under a shirt. The two partners moved in behind Joseph, brushing against his shoulders.

"You wanna fuck me up? You think you real smart?" The hustler shoved Joseph with one hand. He saw the flash of a pink palm. An open slap buckled his knees and he stumbled backwards into the two partners. A fist caught Joseph in the temple and he felt his clothes twist up around his shoulders. Someone held onto Joseph and pulled him across the empty car as the train jerked and stopped farther down the platform.

Twice he swung wildly and then protectively drew his arms in. He clawed and scratched the air. And as he fell to the ground, a hand swept under his chin.

Something spread down Joseph's neck. He fell backwards out onto the platform as the doors parted and met again.

The El cars roared away with dirt and garbage floating after. The passing windows turned to a yellow and gray flickering.

A warm trickle rolled to the back of Joseph's neck. He wiped the palm of his hand against his throat, right below his Adam's apple. Warm blood covered his hand and his legs weakened at the sight. Nerves faded and shrank to threads. His legs floated away and he dropped to a sitting position in the middle of the platform. After the rush of adrenaline and the panic that had swirled around Joseph had gone, he felt nothing but an incredible peacefulness. He was surrounded by white noise. Hiss and compression in his ears.

Joseph wondered if he was dying, because he didn't feel anything. It almost felt good.

That was what he had heard. If you were dying, you felt no pain. Joseph didn't know if that was true. He wanted to see what he looked like covered in blood. Somehow he felt like he deserved it. Not because he interrupted the shell game, only because he felt his recent history demanded it. It would be a fitting ending, he thought. Joseph was willing to lie there and wait for it.

This would be his penance, the reparation which the little voice he never wanted to believe had known about all along. If he didn't pass away, he was certain he would be clean forever. Pressure forced a tiny click in his brain and Joseph was certain that judgment was about to be passed on him.

In the middle of the platform, holding his hand to his throat, he waited for some sign to tell him that this was the right thing.

He waited for an iron-rod sharpness to pass through his body. He imagined the line entering beneath his throat and running down the inside of his spine. It had to come at any second and he paused before each breath. Nothing came and Joseph still almost felt good. In the palm of his right hand was a small twitching beneath the skin. Some strand of a muscle he couldn't even see.

Blood soaked the collar of his T-shirt and he wondered how deep the cut was. Joseph looked around the platform for something he could use as a mirror. He pressed his palm to his neck and it came away smeared with blood, but much less than before. With one fingertip, Joseph felt around for the cut. A burning sting reached around to his spine and chest and told Joseph that he had found it. He ran his finger along the raw surface to estimate its length. He still was not sure. He pressed his throat again, timidly checking if his hand could slip inside the wound. He could not tell, he couldn't feel anything. He wiped his hands dry on his pants and then took his shirt off.

He wrapped his shirt tenderly around his throat and tied it in a knot at the side of his neck. His legs slid back into place beneath him and he took this as a sign to move on. He wasn't going to drop to his back. If he had fallen over, he would have stayed on the platform until someone came to drag his body away. He would have accepted that.

He was covered with days of grime and dirt. He stank of alcohol and sweat. Blood was smeared on his chest and throat. His scalp and back itched. He could discern every little movement and process taking place inside his body. He was aware of each muscle and bone as if a light was shining right through his tingling skin.

Joseph could only compare the sensation to that of waking after a long, deep sleep. He felt like a new person.

"Retribution will come," the Preacher Madison had told Joseph, "to those who do not seek it."

Another train heading in the opposite direction rushed past, an express that refused to slow. Joseph didn't die and he didn't know what this meant.

He stood up dizzily and started walking. Joseph felt the tears pouring down his face. He counted them rolling to the corners of his mouth.

Prodigal Son

All was makeshift, cheaply decorated and made holy at the last minute. The room had been a storage garage, four bare concrete walls, grease spots on the floor and little square windows hiding near the ceiling. Men were preparing for the service. Arranging chairs. Placing songbooks on each seat. A note had been posted at the doors of the Chapel of the People's Church of Chicago the day before. It was closed for renovations and services were now being held at the converted garage.

The rows of folding chairs were all slowly filled with worshippers chatting quietly among themselves. Preacher Madison was standing in his best suit at the podium. Behind him was a display of fake stained glass set on wheels. Before him was a blinking video camera. A satin blue cloth with a gold-stitched cross was draped over his podium. Two stage lights were aimed at the Preacher and because of them he could not see his congregation sitting in the dark garage.

The small crowd settled into a breathing silence as Preacher Madison began his sermon as he did all the others.

There were a few people Joseph recognized, but most he did not. He knew their faces, but not their names. None could see Joseph, bare-chested and spotted with blood, hiding behind the propped door in a back corner cluttered with junk that had been shoved out of the way. Joseph waited to hear the Preacher because he wanted to know what had happened with the fire. He wanted to proclaim that in some way it was his doing. He felt as if the fire he tried to set at the Mayor's had transferred itself to the hotel. A hint of guilt flashed but hadn't yet settled. Joseph had only felt the spark of it.

He knew the fire was not his and that particular guilt was not his. But all lines were growing blurry. He was guilty just because he had survived.

"Thank the Lord for we are all here again. Thank Him for his majesties that give us this day. And as you thank our Savior, let me thank you for giving me this opportunity. It has been hard with what has happened in recent days. The fire, it was a tragedy and a sin. The fire was only a test of our faith. And we have passed."

The words didn't bother Joseph. No one was hurt. He only wanted to hear the details of the fire. Joseph let his eyes drift into a stare as the voice droned. A spot on the wall focused his sight and the room elongated around him. He felt himself drifting upward, out of his skull. The other people in the room shrank as the new dimensions kept expanding. Joseph could see himself standing against the back wall, as if he were looking over his own shoulder. He was watching from far outside the group. He was daring them to catch him and take him back into the church. Joseph told himself that he no longer cared what happened, even though he refused to step from his hiding place.

Preacher Madison wiped sweat from his brow and tucked his handkerchief inside his coat. Joseph saw that he was not speaking to the audience, but to the camera before him. His stare did not waver from the lens as he described the significance of the fire that took the hotel.

It was the Devil's attempt at retribution. It was the Devil's tactic of conversion. "But people," he said, "the fire is also a sign. It is a good sign. It is not the fires of Hell. Not the fires of warning. Not the fires of temptation. Lucifer is also an unknowing messenger of the Lord. The fallen angel. The half angel. After fire there are ashes, and ashes cool to the touch and are rubbed to dirt. Dust. It is a sign to me that there is something returning to my life. I believe, and belief is the only separation between the holy and the evil. That is the only piece that separates Satan from the angels. Satan did not believe in his God. He thought that he was equal to his God."

Joseph began to drift from the sermon. He could see himself hiding in the corner and he tried to hold that perspective.

"The half angel is lamed by one wing. He moves in circles, pushed on by the one strong wing. The strong wing is the Lord guiding him. The Lord guides even the Devil when he can. It is the lamed side, the doubter, that keeps the Devil away from the Lord. The lamed wing does not fly right. The doubter can steer us all wrong.

"His time is long and weary. It is the split of an eye. Where he was not before, he is now. And thanks be to God. For he keeps us out of the Devil's hand when we allow Him and accept Him."

Preacher Madison humbly shut his eyes as his congregation applauded. The red light on the side of the video camera blinked three times and went dead and the Preacher's voice settled like an airplane slowing along a runway. Now he spoke directly to the rows of people in the folding chairs.

"Good morning," he chuckled. "Some of you may not know why we have the camera equipment here today. This afternoon service will be recorded and edited and sent out over several cable channels on the television. We will send the Lord into the house of any family that wishes to receive Him. Little by little we will be doing our part. Of course, it is only cable access, but it is a beginning."

The people politely applauded.

"For this venture to expand and grow, we will all have to share in the responsibility."

More cheered with an "Amen."

The Preacher waited, braced his voice and concluded. "We will begin taping in another minute." He took a drink of water, then turned to the man behind the camera and asked, "Is that correct?"

After a count of ten from the cameraman, the red light appeared as a pinpoint of bright blood on the side of the black camera. Joseph wanted to sit down. He felt dizzy again.

"What man of you, having a hundred sheep, if he lose one of them, doth not leave the ninety and nine in the wilderness, and go after that which is lost, until he find it?" Preacher Madison dramatically paused and looked over the people. Measuring each and every one.

"Every sheep in the flock is vital. All souls are equally important. To my great sadness I have lost some of my flock, some have strayed far. While others are close, still circling the pasture. Not yet decided if they belong in the company of the shepherd and the flock. And I say that they do belong. They do belong and I pray every night for their return. I have gone out past the fields and into the woods, searching for the lost sons. As much as I wish, they cannot be brought back by force. The lost must decide for themselves."

The Preacher's voice was pleading for the camera. There was no more fire and brimstone. Preacher Madison had changed himself again. Last chances lost to sinners were now given back in an appeal for a larger audience. Joseph shut his eyes and leaned against the wall, confident that none knew he was standing there.

A drop of sweat ran from Joseph's chin and crossed his throat. When it reached the tender cut, a sharp burn went down to his collarbones. He wasn't listening to the Preacher. To him, the Preacher was speaking of some abstract topic. Joseph didn't need to hear the words. He knew more than the Preacher Madison. He knew more than all the hotel and the church, more than the Preacher, more than his mother and father.

Joseph did not bother to recognize himself in the sermon. Preacher Madison could not see him hiding in the corner.

Joseph swayed for a moment, locked his knees straight and pressed his back against the wall. His point-of-view came crashing back down into his skull. The tips of his fingers dug into the grooves between the cement blocks as if they alone would hold him upright. He shut his eyes and saw white light. There was no relief when his eyes opened again. The light faded to three points that hovered in front of his face. He opened his mouth, wanting to ask for something.

"The lost can commit every sin under the sun and I will always pray that they return to me. They will always be accepted unto God. There is no point where they will be rejected and only after death may one pass the point of forgiveness."

The floor tilted away from Joseph and the wall pushed at his back. The Preacher's voice was slowly evolving into the voice that Joseph knew. Preacher Madison's composure dissolved as his righteousness grew.

"See the Lord. See the Lord," the Preacher's voice began to rise. "All must see the Lord. See the Lord because it is his field in which we stand. I am and always will be your shepherd."

Joseph began falling. The sounds of the room had turned to a buzzing that alternated between the hum of a light bulb and the rumble of a subway train. It was metal screaming. Joseph could hear every noise in the room. Every foot scuffing, every chair squeaking. The buzz of the fluorescent lights. His knees bent weakly and he awkwardly stepped forward to catch himself.

He held onto his throat like it would empty out if he didn't hold on. He didn't know if he was bleeding or not.

The roaring in his ears continued.

Joseph opened his eyes as he stumbled and saw that he had the full attention of the congregation. He had fallen out of his dark corner. The ground came to catch his knees and his chest smacked into the back of a chair, knocking it over with a prolonged clattering. Another chair toppled over Joseph as his back hit the floor. The buzzing and screaming flooded his ears. He knew people were coming closer. He saw the Preacher's face appear in the unfamiliar crowd over his head.

When he woke, he was scared to open his eyes. Beneath his back he felt a hard cushion covered with vinyl. Joseph kept his eyes shut as if he was still out cold and listened to the voices in the room.

"Is that Francis' boy?"

"Where was he? Was he in the church?"

"The poor boy looks horrible. Did someone call an ambulance?"

Some of the questions were answered and some were left hanging there. Joseph could tell that Preacher Madison was not in the room. Everyone sounded lost. They didn't know what to do.

A woman's voice announced that an ambulance was on its way. Another said the police were coming. Someone else ran out of the room to look for a first-aid kit and some ice. Hurried footsteps were crossing and running circles around Joseph's head. Soft shoes hit against the tiled floor and the echo was slight. He was in a small room. It was probably an office. He didn't know how long he had been asleep, but he still refused to open his eyes or twitch in the slightest. It was peaceful, lying like that.

Sausage-smelling breath was in Joseph's face. It was the voice of the same woman he had heard a minute earlier. "Son, we've been so worried about you. Preacher Madison was worried sick about you. He's done nothing but speak of you. You'll be okay. You tell the police what happened, James, and we'll get you to the hospital. Don't worry."

Joseph tried not to move. He didn't want the woman to know he was awake. He couldn't guess from her voice if she knew if he was awake or not. The only thing he wanted to do was tell the woman his name. She kept repeating the incorrect name. And she had been so worried about him.

A slow doubt crept through his mind. Maybe his name had been changed at some time, like Brother Samuel's name had been when he joined the church. Maybe his name was changed when he was born. Maybe the church changed his name without his parents even knowing. The woman's voice said that they had talked of him when he was gone. Maybe his name was James and someone didn't like it. He couldn't remember. It felt as if he had been gone for so long. They knew who he was, Joseph only wondered who had his name wrong. He knew that he hadn't been forgotten.

"Is he alive?" Someone new had walked into the room. Joseph didn't believe that the question was sincere. He wondered if they all knew that he was awake and just refused to open his eyes. There was no reason for this other than Joseph's wish to not see anyone. He wanted to disappear. He was not as strong as he had thought. He came to the church thinking that he would make one last appearance before Preacher Madison. And walk out proudly.

There was more whispering that Joseph couldn't understand. He heard a pair of hard-heeled shoes exit the room at a horse's trot, but there was someone else still standing there.

"Preacher Madison is coming," the new person confided in Joseph's ear and he laid completely still until the heavy footsteps of the Preacher crossed the room alone.

"Open your eyes, son."

Joseph did cautiously and saw Preacher Madison in a wooden chair sitting at the edge of the couch. His face was large and gray without his eyeglasses. Little red spots pressed at the bridge of his nose where his glasses usually sat. There was no one else in the room and there were stars focusing and defocusing in the air. Joseph rubbed his knuckles into his eyes until the little lights were gone. He and the Preacher were in a room somewhere off to the side of the new chapel.

The blood was sticky on his throat. No one had even cleaned him while he was unconscious. Joseph tried to sit up straight and the Preacher told him to lay back down.

"Son, how are you feeling?"

"I feel okay. I think I got dizzy." Joseph noticed that his voice was fine. He expected it to sound torn from the knife.

"Yes, you did get dizzy. You passed out in the middle of my sermon. We'll have to record it another time. Don't worry about that. I don't think your throat is cut very deep. You stopped bleeding. It's nothing to worry about. If it was, I think you would have bled to death by now. Thank the Lord you didn't."

"Okay."

"There's police coming. Is there anything I should know before they get here?"

"Like what?"

"Are you in trouble?"

"No."

"Who did this to you?"

"I don't know."

"You don't know?"

"No." Joseph waited a second before he asked, "Was my name ever different?"

"How do you mean?"

"Since I was little, was my name ever changed?"

"I don't think I understand you."

"Okay. It's nothing."

"If you are asking about your parents." The Preacher shut his eyes and rubbed at the bridge of his nose. "I'm sorry. I received a few letters that said everything was fine. But nothing after that. I think they've left the church. I know they've left their position unattended and without any notice. I wish that I could have done more, son."

"That wasn't what I meant. It's fine."

The Preacher patted Joseph's shoulder. "Just relax. I think you're delirious. Don't worry. I'm going to see if the ambulance is here yet. Do you want some water?"

"Sure," Joseph agreed. "Tell the police not to come."

"They're already on their way. Are you in trouble?"

"No." Joseph thought of Amanda. Imagined her already in jail. Saw the dealer sitting comfortably alone in another cell. He knew they would have given his name to the police. He hadn't done anything wrong, not like the rest of them; but he was tied to everyone. Joseph felt that he had to have been guilty of some crime, even if it was only by association.

There was no way he could have gotten to this point if he was not guilty of something.

"I didn't say anything to the police about you," Preacher Madison assured Joseph. "I called 911. You've been attacked. I was only threatening you before with the police. I wouldn't do that to you."

"I don't want to. I don't know who did it. How long was I asleep?"

"Only a couple minutes."

"Really?" Joseph was sure that it had been hours. The light was so different.

"Don't worry. You're safe here. Stay down and I'll get your water. Everything will be fine."

Joseph didn't believe a word the Preacher had said. There was no reason to trust anyone. He believed that he knew why he was alone. If he stayed, all his sins would be held up for the Preacher's examinations. His survival only confirmed his guilt, instead of washing it cleanly away. His heart sank with the thought.

Preacher Madison and all the others had disappeared. The hallway outside the room was empty and Joseph heard no one else walking the floors. Against the opposite wall was a burnt Exit sign. Under the sign was a metal door with an emergency bar across the center. Joseph wasn't sure where the hallway was in relation to the church garage. He didn't know where he was.

A lump of pain pulsed from Joseph's temple. He touched his fingers to the tender spot and wondered when that happened. He didn't remember getting hit in the head. The throbbing grew with every wobbly step. Water sloshing around his skull. Nausea hit Joseph and the wall swayed slightly before him. He kept his stomach down and moved forward. A little red sign on the handle said ALARM WILL SOUND.

There was no noise except for the squeak of metal on metal as Joseph shoved the bar and lurched through the doorway. He was standing in the alley. There was no one in sight.

Joseph began to walk north.

He never heard the people yelling for him after they found the little room empty. Some were calling for James and others were yelling for Joseph when he was finally discovered missing. Preacher Madison stood out on the sidewalk at the front entrance. When the paramedics arrived, they refused to drive around and search for Joseph despite Preacher Madison's assurances of probable success. "I'm sure we will find someone if we circle the neighborhood long enough," the driver told Preacher Madison. But they couldn't drive around aimlessly, they had a lot to do.

Two police officers reluctantly took a report and then drove off. They also told Preacher Madison that there wasn't much they could do for a crime without a victim.

Twenty Bucks

Joseph stopped walking when he reached the street he recognized as the border of Rogers Park. It was as far north as he had ever been.

His legs were sore and the muscles felt hard and thin. He believed that he had crossed a desert.

He found a storefront window, inside the glass was a liquor store completely emptied. The whole building was for sale. The whole building was Joseph's for the moment. It worked just fine as a mirror as he took the wrapped shirt away from his neck. He scrubbed dry blood away from his throat and stood before his reflection. A pale face and chest stared back at him. The cut slowly bled again. There was a dark quarter circle growing under Joseph's chin. It was a crooked grin opening wider and wider. It was Sonny's grin, it was the Preacher's grin.

A completely new face was appearing over Joseph's. He wiped the blood away and it came back with a slight sting that circled the front of his neck. When the knife went in, it did not hurt. Joseph couldn't remember what it felt like. The pain came after.

For Joseph, it always hurt worse long after the act.

He forgave Amanda and told himself that was the right thing to do. "The intent must come with the action to create sin," Joseph whispered to himself. Good is in both the intent and action, separate from each other. Results were not sins.

Words and meanings came flooding in bits and pieces back to Joseph. A babbling vocabulary of definitions. Joseph thought of how they could be strung together. He could argue that his salvation actually had come.

He could tell himself that no matter what happened, he would be safe. From now on. The argument withered and Joseph knew that nothing had changed. Sin was defined by the views of other people. And if Joseph was careful, there would be no other people.

At a rusted out water fountain Joseph washed the dirt and blood away from his face the best he could. He leaned his throat over the dribbling arc of water and watched the diluted blood slip down the drain. When he stood straight, the cold water trickled down his back and little black spots formed in the air before him. Joseph swatted at them like they were flies.

With his fingertips he pushed his eyelids down and the dark points turned to light. His thoughts raced ahead of him.

Joseph could feel the blood across his throat again. He looked down at his hands and they were still clean.

The hanging air was raw and humid from the morning rain. Joseph paced hurriedly up and down Jarvis. He knew who he was looking for. He imagined the girl would be in the same spot. He imagined she would have another bag of popcorn and her teeth would be stained a bright orange. Joseph chuckled at this. He checked bus stop benches and open doorways and porches and liquor stores. Buses flew past and Joseph craned his neck for a glimpse of the girl sitting in a window. He waited at the corner and watched people stepping from the automatic doors. Air brakes hissed and the bus pulled itself from the curb without dropping off the girl.

He sneaked into a dimly-lit arcade. Stumbled between the feet of children as he moved up and down the aisles. Everyone looked the same and Joseph wanted to yell out, but didn't know the name of the girl he was looking for. The little screens, which provided the only lights in the room, held the points-of-view from cars wheeling down mountain roads and jet fighters looping through empty blue air. There were monsters climbing buildings and cops shooting bad guys and tanks bursting into flames. Crowds gathered behind the players and cheered the action. Between the bloody flashing machines of kickboxers and automatic weapons and the sound of computerized screams and gunfire, Joseph panicked. He hurried from one corner of the room to the next. Felt like he was being tripped and shoved from all sides. But each time he spun around to find who was touching him, he found that all were deeply invested in the video games. He pushed his way to the door, hoping that the girl was not in the arcade. Joseph desperately crossed the same streets again until he found himself wandering through a park.

Sunlight cropped by trees and passing clouds, fell for only a moment across a park bench where a girl sat. The bench was in the middle of a path that crossed diagonally from one corner of the park to the opposite. The light was a circle that opened and closed. For one instant the scene was perfectly symmetrical. A square crossed and circled and in the center was the girl illuminated long enough for Joseph to find her. He walked toward her carefully, holding his neck as steady as he could. To keep the blood from spilling. He didn't want to scare her away. It may or may not have been the same girl. Joseph told himself that it was, even though he couldn't recognize her. She would have to do. She would be who he was looking for.

Pink skin shone through the patterned holes in the thighs of her jeans. Her bra crept out from under the shoulders of her tank top. She was eating a taffy apple, twisting her neck to one side and then the other instead of turning the apple. Joseph concluded that the girl was falling apart. She was bigger than he last remembered.

He waved to the girl and she only squinted her eyes as he approached. For some reason he was out of breath when he reached the center of the park. She looked at Joseph and asked what he wanted.

He pointed at her taffy apple. "Did you get that across the street? They're only a quarter." Joseph remembered seeing a taffy apple factory at the corner.

"No, that place ain't there anymore. Tore it down."

He turned and gazed at the piles of brick and metal beams, heaped in the corner lot. Only two concrete block walls were left standing. The girl said she had bought her taffy apple at the liquor store. She took a bite, chewed and swallowed, and then seemed surprised that Joseph was still standing in front of her. She asked for a cigarette. Joseph apologized and said that he didn't have any.

"Sure," the girl said. After discarding the apple, she sucked the taffy off of the wooden stick and twirled it into the grass. It was okay, she had her own cigarettes. She took two from her pack as if one was meant for Joseph. She stuck one behind her ear and placed the other between her lips and didn't notice Joseph's hand ready to accept either cigarette. The girl lit a match and brought it up to her mouth and Joseph could see the black marker across her knuckles and wrists.

"Do I know you?" she asked abruptly.

"Yeah. We met before. It was a while ago, a few months ago."

"I sorta meet a lotta people." She seemed very tired. As if talking to Joseph was a heavy chore. "I think I have a good idea how we could have met. I can't think of seeing you, though."

"Yeah," Joseph plowed past her reluctance. "I wanted to talk to you about that." He told himself that this was the same girl he had met before.

"Not today," she said. "I'm taking the day off. Too many cops lately."

"Not what I mean. You don't have to do this. I'm gonna straighten things out. I'm leaving town. I wanted to know if you wanted to go with. You can follow me."

Joseph had decided all by himself that he would take care of the girl. The plan had grown as he walked north. He knew there had been a reason for the direction he was heading.

The girl seemed so tired.

"What's your name?" he asked.

She stood up and brushed off the back of her tight pants. "I don't know you. I could go party with you some other time, but really, I can't leave, just pack up and go. Go where? There's nowhere to go. I don't know you. I got someone here. My boyfriend and my mother are both here. I don't want to go anywhere. I don't even know who the hell you are," the girl repeated, hoping to deter the bloody stranger. "But thanks for the offer." She smiled politely. "Come back if you want to party or something, you know."

"No. I don't want to party." Joseph thought she had misunderstood him.

The girl pointed to the bloody scarf around Joseph's neck.

"What happened to you?"

"Nothing," he told her.

"Sure."

Joseph didn't know what else to say. Somehow as he was walking from the storefront church, he had convinced himself that the girl would be ready to leave with him. Her bags would have been packed. She would jump up and hug him just for the offer. Then she would cry and admit that she didn't deserve to leave with him. She would fall to the ground with thanks after Joseph reassured her. Because it would be the only thing she ever wanted to do since the day she first saw Joseph. She would have given herself wholly to Joseph.

Instead, she was acting tough. She was playing like she didn't need any of that. Joseph knew it was just a pose. Just like Amanda.

Joseph hadn't moved away from the girl and she hadn't moved, either.

Blinking slowly, he saw the girl's face change. Something familiar had moved into the girl's eyes the same way the sun appeared to point her out to Joseph. For one moment Joseph saw his mother's eyes, quickly confirming that the girl wasn't going anywhere. The dread of moving from the spot where she sat crossed the girl's face and Joseph saw his mother. That had been her face every day.

Then the resemblance was gone. The girl was waiting for Joseph to leave.

Almost of its own accord, Joseph's arm flashed out. His hand clenched the girl's biceps. He could feel the soft skin and the tender muscles beneath his fingers. He felt his hand tense and squeeze down to the bone. "Hey. What the fuck?" The girl's eyes flashed awake. Her face twisted into something ugly.

Her arm yanked itself away from Joseph and her shin went up into his groin. Joseph didn't feel the bolt until she was out of his grasp.

He fell to the ground and rolled to his side. The ache grew like a balloon expanding inside his rib cage; it was impossible to feel where it began or ended. He pulled his knees up to his chest. Wet grass scratched at his cheek, poked at his aching throat. He could smell the freshly cut grass all around him, choking him, forcing him to take shallow breaths. He heard the cars passing along Clark Street and imagined the drivers undisturbed by the sight of what they thought was another drunk who fell in the park.

It made him smile. He felt that there was no one who would recognize him.

His head shaved. One eye swollen shut. Cuts and bruises running from his chin to his hairline.

Joseph saw himself with the slash across his throat. The grin smiling back at him. A division had been made inside him. A voice countered another and said that everything would be settled eventually.

He lay there and waited for the park to stop spinning. He waited to take a full, deep breath.

A stone path curved across the grass of another park that was a buffer between the dead end of Jarvis Avenue and Lake Michigan. The park was deserted and Joseph could hear the waves that popped up and pushed weakly against the metal and stone wall that kept the ground from eroding, sliding away into the water. The gray water stretched calmly out to the horizon, unmoving as a sheet of ice.

Under a park bench he slept until the sun was red and sitting heavily along the roofs of the buildings.

As the sun went down behind his back, the water came to life. Triangles of light swam like fish to the shore. Each wave picked them up and lifted them closer.

Joseph's legs felt like rubber, his clothes were soaked with sweat. He was hungry and there was a pounding ache between his temples.

A dark figure, a profile before the horizon, sat at the edge of a break wall that rode far out into the lake. His legs dangled off the rock ledge. Beneath a wide-brimmed hat the figure hung a fishing pole over the water. The man lifted his pole and reeled in some of the line. He checked his bait and cast his line again.

Joseph rose and walked closer and sat down on the rocks at the shore. He took off his shoes and dropped them into the sand. He shifted around and found a comfortable position, his back nestled between two rocks. He had all the time in the world. He remembered the last time he was at this park. The last time he was this far north. When fog slowly covered the water and reached into the park. He could only see what was immediately before him.

That was what he now wanted. Not to see the long span of the water heading to the horizon or the slow movement of the days. Not to know that guilt died in increments too slow to measure. To know where he was. He couldn't imagine filling in the days all by himself. The next day would be the same as the ones that had passed before. And the ones after that would go on just the same.

As Joseph stretched himself out, the fisherman turned back to the beach, hearing the mumble of a person talking to himself. He spotted Joseph then, but didn't acknowledge him.

Joseph could not see the man's face. Only the bent figure under the hat's brim. The fisherman solemnly went back to the water and the line before him. After some time the man lit a cigarette and flicked the ashes into the water. The sun kept going down and the buildings' shadows slowly crept toward the water. Joseph waited patiently and watched to see if the man was going to catch something.

God's Army

The chapel building stood windowless and perfectly square in the center of the fields that stretched to the trees lining the horizon. Behind the chapel and across a fresh black parking lot was the school. Farther back, sets of tennis courts and rows of level ranch houses built of blonde bricks were surrounded by uniform lawns. All official-looking buildings had been strung along a weaving two-lane that completed a full circle before leading out to the distant highway rippling slightly in the morning heat.

No other people were outside before the breakfast bell rang. McKnuckle exhaled and felt his lungs wheeze and sputter where weak spots had been burned over a period of years. There were holes in the fabric of his lungs. Air was coming down in thick gulps but went back out in weak streams.

He pressed his fingers to his gums where his front teeth recently had been. They had been lost at the beach on D-Day. McKnuckle touched his forefinger and pinkie to his closed eyelids and gently pressed to relieve the tension.

Under the shower, before the meal and the tour, he had leisurely scrubbed his body clean. He thought he saw his skin gleaming practically blue under the thick soap.

He shaved his jaw and scrubbed his head. Rash pimples would form later, but it felt good and clean for the moment. He smelled like perfume.

The clothes on his back were new. Given to him after the shower and before the meal. A striped knit sweater and pants made of a stiff material that would never wrinkle. A white man's clothes. He still had his own shoes over the pressed sweatsocks.

In a spacious and bright cafeteria he was fed chicken and hash browns, ham sandwiches and corn on the cob. For dessert there was cakes and Jell-O and Cokes in frosted glasses. He ate until he thought he would faint.

The bus that brought him out, across the Indiana border, was like a prison bus without the cages on the windows. And there was much more room. Only two other men chose to take the ride along with McKnuckle. No one else wanted to leave Michigan Avenue or Rush Street or the park on Delaware. The weather was nice. No one had much of a reason to leave except for McKnuckle who took Sonny's advice and thought it much better to get away from Chicago for a while. He thought that maybe he would consider this a vacation. He considered the possibility of staying for a longer period of time. Sonny had told him to do so.

McKnuckle wanted to show the place to his brother-in-law. He had tried to convince Sonny to come along, had told him that it would've been fun, but Sonny said that he was done with these people and he had seen it all before.

McKnuckle didn't mind if these people wanted to feed him and bathe him and show him around the church and all their other buildings, but he couldn't really listen to their talk. It seemed like no matter what they were telling him, it drifted away into nonsense.

The Properties, they had called all the church land. It seemed like they owned everything out here. McKnuckle wondered if that made sense.

Out past the fields the sun was just touching the tops of the trees, smearing orange in one stroke across the branches of each. A white truck with green lettering on the door motored past far off in the distance, pulling a wispy trail of dust behind.

Near the center of the church grounds McKnuckle heard nothing but a tight hum that seemed to touch his ears from all directions. A buzz of insects hiding in the grasses. A hum that was only heard when all else was quiet. Something that could be noticed only after it was covered. It came up from beneath the blades of grass and out from the trees at the horizon. McKnuckle compared it to the sound of women's voices or maybe a string of subway cars roaring past.

Recorded church bells began from a public address system on the church roof. McKnuckle pressed at his eyes again. The bells patterned themselves into the melody of a hymn and McKnuckle heard a group of people coming from the tall double doors of the chapel. They were singing along with the bells. None of them had the little church books he had seen before. The words were all memorized, sung with voices confident and flat and louder than the bells.

The monotone singing broke the almost silent hum he heard a moment earlier. The procession had buried it. McKnuckle tilted his head and listened carefully, trying to pick it up again. He couldn't. And he wondered if the others could hear the sound. The women's voices. Maybe they were accustomed to it and no longer noticed. Maybe the hum had always been there, present everywhere, and only he never heard it.

He thought that it could have been part of his headache. He wished that Sonny was alongside him. Sonny would know what it was.

A woman, fat and pale, broke away from the singing crowd and ran giddily toward McKnuckle. She hugged him tightly and roughly around the neck, pushing him to his heels. Almost knocking him to the ground. "Oh, I do hope you stay," she blurted out. "I hope you like it here. Did you sleep well?"

"I slept good. Better than home."

"This could be home, you know," the woman said. "You are always welcome."

"I know that, but I got family back home. Just my brother."

"Oh," the woman smiled, as if she were kidding a grade school boy who just received a Valentine's Day card. "You don't have a girlfriend? A guy like you?"

"Oh, no," McKnuckle corrected the woman. "I got a bunch of bitches back in Chicago. All waiting on me now, to be truthful." He smiled, showing the woman where his front teeth once had been.

She was the same woman who greeted McKnuckle when he climbed from the bus the day before. She had given him the whole tour of the place. Now he wanted to ask where the cafeteria was. He couldn't remember. She stomped away after hearing McKnuckle's answer, joining the ranks of singers before McKnuckle could even open his mouth.

He had lied to the woman who was concerned about his sleep, told her yesterday that he would sign a paper to stay for a week. There was some kind of deal McKnuckle remembered, but they told him to not worry about signing anything. They said they would do all the paperwork the next day. And they never came with the papers he was to sign and he was glad. He wondered if they knew he was lying.

Before he even got off the bus, McKnuckle knew he was going back to Chicago. He felt a flash of embarrassment. He considered his previous life and wished he could ask Sonny what had happened. Things had been much better, once.

McKnuckle watched the procession move toward the building that was their school. When they reached the door, the last verses were sung and the crowd applauded itself.

"Damn," he said to himself, laughing at the sudden thought, "I'm the only one out here."

And the sun kept pressing against the branches of the trees until it was released and the other two men who arrived with McKnuckle appeared out of nowhere.

One had decided to stay. The other would return with McKnuckle. The one who was staying had been offered some kind of scholarship to learn the Bible. McKnuckle knew that yesterday, but he didn't really believe it. He witnessed the man sign a contract and receive several little booklets regarding the school and the church. McKnuckle was certain the man would leave, anyway. The converted man tried to convince McKnuckle and the other man to stay. The other man wished the convert good luck and McKnuckle smiled and waved a hand in his face, dismissing him.

A green bus pulled out of the cavernous garage and followed a circular driveway to the front of the chapel. The engine idled for a couple of minutes and the driver accidentally ground the gears before he applied the parking brake and shut the motor down.

The bus driver approached, tired of his routine, and told the two remaining men that there was no smoking, no drinking, no nothing on the return trip. The rules were the same as those in the church.

They climbed aboard after the engine turned over. McKnuckle and the other man silently stretched themselves out on the two back seats, their feet dangling over the aisle.

And before the bus reached the Indiana border, the hum of the engine had lulled the passengers to sleep.